CYBER STORM

CYBER STORM

MATTHEW MATHER

HARPERCOLLINS PUBLISHERS LTD

To Julie Knuckey-Mather,
for always keeping us safe
and, of course,
for her love

PROLOGUE

Pulling my goggles up, I stopped and blinked, looking out into the night with my own unaided eyes. The night was pitch black and soundless, and my mind suddenly felt disconnected. Staring into the void, I became a dot of existence floating by itself in the universe. At first the feeling was terrifying, my mind reeling, but it quickly became comforting. *Maybe this is what death is like. Alone, peaceful, floating, floating, no fear . . .*

Clipping the night-vision goggles back into place, I could see ghostly green flakes of snow falling gently around me.

My hunger pangs had been intense that morning, almost driving me outside during the day. Chuck had held me back, talked to me, calmed me down. It wasn't for me, I'd argued, it was for Luke, for Lauren, for Ellarose—anything that would allow me, like an addict, to get my fix.

I laughed. *I'm addicted to food.*

The falling snowflakes were hypnotic. Closing my eyes, I took a deep breath. *What is real? What is reality, anyway?* I felt like I was hallucinating, my mind never quite able to take a firm hold of anything before skidding off. *Get a grip, Mike. Luke is counting on you. Lauren is counting on you.*

Opening my eyes, I willed myself into the here and now and

tapped the phone in my pocket to bring up the augmented-reality display. A field of red dots spread out into the distance, and taking another deep breath, I carefully put one foot in front of the other, continuing on my way across Twenty-Fourth, pushing myself toward a cluster of dots on Sixth Avenue.

NOVEMBER 25
CHELSEA, NEW YORK CITY

"We live in amazing times!"

I studied the piece of charred flesh that I held up in front of me.

"Amazingly dangerous times," laughed Chuck, my next-door neighbor and best friend, taking a swig from his beer. "Nice work. That's probably still frozen on the inside."

Shaking my head, I put the burnt sausage down at the edge of the grill.

It was an unusually warm week for Thanksgiving, so I'd decided to throw a last-minute barbecue party on the rooftop terrace of our converted warehouse complex. Most of our neighbors were still here for the holiday, so my almost-two-year-old son, Luke, and I had spent the morning going door to door, inviting them all up for our grill-out.

"Don't insult my cooking, and don't get started on all that."

It was a spectacular start to an evening, with the setting sun still shining warmly. From our perch seven stories up, late-autumn views of red and gold trees stretched up and down the Hudson, backed by street noise and city skyline. New York still held a vibrancy that excited me, even after two years of living here. I looked around at our crowd of neighbors. We'd gathered a group of thirty people for our party, and I was secretly proud so many had come.

"So you don't think it's possible a solar flare could wreck the world?" said Chuck, raising his eyebrows.

His Southern twang made even disasters sound like song lyrics, and kicking back on a sun lounger in ripped jeans and a Ramones T-shirt, he looked like a rock star. His hazel eyes twinkled playfully from beneath a mop of unkempt blond hair, and two-day-old stubble completed the look.

"That's exactly what I don't want you to get started on."

"I'm just saying—"

"What you're saying always points to disaster." I rolled my eyes. "We've just lived through one of the most amazing transitions in human history." Poking the sausages on the grill, I generated a new round of searing flames.

Tony, one of our doormen, was standing next to me, still dressed in his work clothes and tie, but at least with his suit jacket off. Heavyset, with dark Italian features, he was as Brooklyn as the Dodgers of old, and his accent never let you forget it. Tony was the kind of guy who started growing on you immediately, always ready to help and never without a smile and a joke to go along with it. Luke loved him too. From the moment he could walk, every time we went downstairs, he'd rocket out of the elevator as soon as it pinged to ground level and run to the front desk to greet Tony with squeals of glee. The feeling was mutual.

Looking up from my sausages, I addressed Chuck directly. "Over a billion people have been born in the past decade—that's like a *new* New York City each month for the last ten years—the fastest population growth that has ever been, or ever will be."

I waved my tongs around in the air to make my point. "Sure, there've been a few wars here and there, but nothing major. I think that says something about the human race." I paused for effect. "We're maturing."

"Those billion new people are still mostly sucking baby formula," Chuck pointed out. "Wait fifteen years until they all want cars and washing machines. Then we'll see how mature we are."

"World poverty in real-dollar, per capita terms is half what it was forty years ago—"

"And yet one in six Americans goes hungry, and the majority are malnourished," interrupted Chuck.

"*And* for the first time in human history, as of just a year or two ago," I continued, "more humans live in cities than in the countryside."

"You say that like it's a good thing."

Tony shook his head, taking a swig of his beer and smiling. This was a sparring match he'd watched before.

"It *is* a good thing," I said. "Urban environments are much more energy-efficient than rural ones."

"Except 'urban' is not an environment," argued Chuck. "The *environment* is an environment. You talk as if cities were these self-supporting bubbles, but they're not. They're entirely dependent on the natural world around them."

I pointed my tongs at him. "That same world we're saving by living together in cities."

Returning my attention to the barbecue, I saw that the fat dripping off the sausages had ignited into flames again and was searing my chicken breasts.

"I'm just saying that when it all comes undone—"

"When a terrorist launches a nuke over the US? An electromagnetic pulse?" I asked as I rearranged my meats. "Or a weaponized superbug let loose in the wild?"

Chuck nodded. "Any of those."

"You know what you should be worried about?"

"What?"

I didn't need to give him anything new to fixate on, but I couldn't help it. "Cyberattack."

Looking over his shoulder, I could see my wife's parents had arrived. My stomach knotted. What I wouldn't have given to have a simple relationship with my in-laws, but then, that was a boat most people were rowing with me.

"Ever heard of something called Night Dragon?" I asked.

Chuck and Tony shrugged.

"A few years back they started finding foreign computer code embedded in power plant control systems all over the country," I explained. "They traced command and control back to office buildings in China. This stuff was specifically designed to knock out the US energy grid."

Chuck was unimpressed. "So? What happened?"

"Nothing happened, *yet*, but your attitude is the problem. It's everyone's attitude. If Chinese nationals were running around the country attaching packs of C-4 explosives to transmission towers, the public would be crying bloody murder and declaring war."

"Used to be that they dropped bombs to knock out factories, but now just click a mouse?"

"Exactly."

"See?" said Chuck, smiling. "There's a prepper in you after all."

I laughed. There was no way I was going to start stocking up for disasters. "Answer me this—who's in charge of the Internet, this thing that our lives depend on?"

"I don't know, the government?"

"The answer is that *nobody* is in charge of it. Everyone runs it, but nobody's in charge."

Chuck laughed. "Now that sounds like a recipe for disaster."

"You guys are freaking me out," said Tony, finally finding the space to add something. "Can't we talk about baseball for once?" The flames on the grill roared up again, and he recoiled in mock fear. "And maybe you'd better let me take over the grilling. You got more important stuff to do, no?"

"And we'd like to eat some food that's not burnt to a crisp," added Chuck with a smile.

"Yeah, sure." Without enthusiasm, I handed the tongs over to Tony.

Lauren was looking my way again. I was attempting to delay the inevitable. She laughed as she talked to someone, brushing back her long, auburn hair with a sweep of one hand.

With her high cheekbones and flashing green eyes, Lauren attracted attention whenever she entered a room. She had the refined, strong features of her family, a sharp nose and chin that accentuated her slim figure. Even after being with her for five years, just looking at her from across a patio could still take my breath away—I still couldn't believe that she'd chosen me.

Taking a deep breath, I straightened my shoulders. "I leave the grill in your care," I said to nobody in particular. They were already back to discussing Cybergeddon.

Putting my beer on the table next to the grill, I walked over to my wife. She was at the opposite corner of the large deck on top of our building, chatting with her parents and some of our other neighbors. I'd insisted on our hosting her mother and father for Thanksgiving this year, but was already regretting it. Her family was old-money Bostonian, dyed-in-the-tweed Brahmins, and while early on in our marriage I'd done my best to earn their approval, lately I'd given up and settled into a grudging understanding that I'd never be good enough. But it didn't mean I wasn't polite.

"Mr. Seymour," I called out, extending my hand, "thank you so much for coming."

Dressed in a boxy tweed jacket accented with a navy handkerchief, a blue shirt, and a brown paisley tie, Mr. Seymour looked up, giving me a tight-lipped smile. I felt self-conscious in my jeans and T-shirt. Covering the last paces, I gripped his outstretched hand and pumped it firmly.

I turned to my wife's mother. "Mrs. Seymour, as lovely as ever." She was sitting on the edge of a wooden bench beside her husband and daughter, dressed in a brown suit with a matching oversized hat and a thick strand of pearls around her neck. Clutching her purse in her lap, she leaned forward as if to get up.

"No, no, please, don't." I leaned down to peck her on the cheek. She smiled and sat back down. "Thank you for coming to spend Thanksgiving with us."

"So you'll think about it?" Mr. Seymour said loudly to Lauren. You could almost make out the layers of ancestry in his voice, thick with both privilege and responsibility, and today, perhaps a little condescension. He was making sure I could hear what he said.

"Yes, Dad," Lauren whispered, stealing a glance my way and looking down. "I will."

I didn't take the bait. "Have you been introduced to the

Borodins?" I motioned toward the elderly Russian couple at the table beside them. Aleksandr, the husband, was already asleep in a lounger, snoring quietly away beside his wife, Irena, who was busy knitting.

The Borodins lived right next door to us. Sometimes I'd spend hours listening to Irena's stories of the Second World War. They'd survived the siege of Leningrad, now St. Petersburg, and I found it fascinating how she could have lived through something so horrific yet be so positive and gentle with the world. She made amazing borscht too.

"Lauren introduced us. A pleasure," mumbled Mr. Seymour, smiling Irena's way. She looked up and smiled back, then returned to her half-knitted socks.

"So," I spread my arms. "Have you guys seen Luke yet?"

"No, he's downstairs with Ellarose and the sitter at Chuck and Susie's place," replied Lauren. "We haven't had a chance to go and see him yet."

Mrs. Seymour perked up. "But we've been invited to the Met—dress rehearsal tickets for the new *Aida* performance."

"Oh yeah?"

I glanced at Lauren and then turned toward Richard, another of our neighbors, who was definitely *not* on my favorites list. "Thanks, *Dick*."

Square-jawed and handsome, he'd been some kind of football star in his Yale days. His wife, Sarah, was a tiny thing, and she sat behind him like a hand-shy puppy. She pulled the cuffs of her sweater down to cover her bare arms when I glanced at her.

"I know the Seymours love the opera," explained Richard, like a Manhattan stockbroker describing an investment option.

Where the Seymours were Old Boston, Richard's family was Old New York. "We have the 'friends and family' seating at the Met. I only have four tickets, and Sarah didn't want to go"—his wife shrugged weakly behind him—"and I didn't mean to presume, but I didn't think it was your kind of thing, old boy. I thought I could take Lauren and the Seymours, a little Thanksgiving treat."

While Mr. Seymour's accent sounded genuine, Richard's faux-British-prep-school affectation grated on my ears.

"I guess."

What the hell is he up to?

Awkward pause.

"We need to get going if we're going to make it," added Richard, raising his eyebrows. "It's an early rehearsal."

"But we were just about to start serving." I pointed toward the checker-clothed tables set with bowls of potato salad and paper plates. Tony waved at us with the tongs.

"That's all right, we'll stop for something," said Mr. Seymour, again with that tight-lipped smile. "Richard was just telling us about a wonderful new bistro on the Upper East Side."

"It was just an idea," added Lauren uncomfortably. "We were talking and Richard mentioned it."

I took a deep breath, balling my hands into fists, but caught myself and sighed. My hands relaxed. Family was family, and I wanted Lauren to be happy. Maybe this would help. I rubbed one eye and exhaled. "That's a great idea." I looked at my wife with a genuine smile and felt her relax. "I'll take care of Luke, so don't hurry back. Enjoy yourselves."

"Are you sure?" asked Lauren.

An inch of gratitude propped our relationship back up.

"I'm sure. I'll just grab a few beers with the boys." On reflection, this was sounding like a better and better idea. "You best get going. Maybe we can meet for a nightcap?"

"It's settled, then?" said Mr. Seymour.

Within a few minutes they were gone and I was back with the guys, piling my plate with sausages and rooting around in the cooler for a beer.

I slumped down in a chair.

Chuck paused with a forkful of potato salad halfway into his mouth. "That's what you get for marrying a girl with a name like Lauren Seymour."

I laughed and cracked my beer open. "So, what's the word about this mess between China and India over those dams in the Himalayas?"

NOVEMBER 27

The family visit didn't go well.

Thanksgiving dinner started the disaster rolling, first because we'd ordered a precooked turkey from Chelsea Market—"Oh my, you don't cook your own turkey?"—then the awkward dinner seating around our kitchen countertop—"When are you buying a bigger apartment?"—with the finale of me not being able to watch the Steelers game—"That's fine, if Michael wants to watch football, we'll just make our way back to the hotel."

Richard had invited us down the hall for after-dinner drinks, to his palatial three-story apartment facing the Manhattan skyline, where we were served by Sarah—"Of course we cooked our own turkey. Didn't you?"

The conversation had quickly turned to connections between the old New York and Boston family lines: "Fascinating, isn't it? Richard, you must be almost a third cousin to our Lauren," quickly followed by, "Mike, do you know any of your own family history?"

I did, and it involved steel working and nightclubs, so I said I didn't.

Mr. Seymour finished off the evening by interrogating Lauren about her new job prospects, which were nonexistent. Richard offered suggestions about introductions he could make for her. They'd politely asked me how my business was going—I worked as a junior partner in a venture capital fund specializing in social media—followed by proclamations that the Internet was just too complicated to even talk about, and then: "Now, Richard, how is your family investment trust being managed?"

To be fair, Lauren did defend me, and everything remained civilized.

I spent most of the rest of the time chauffeuring them around to meet their friends at places like the Metropolitan Club, the Core Club, and of course the Harvard Club. The Seymours had the distinction of having had at least one family member of each generation attend Harvard since its foundation, and at the name-sake club they were treated like visiting royalty.

Richard even graciously invited us to the Yale Club for a drink on Friday night. I nearly throttled him. Mercifully, it was just a two-day visit, and we finally had the weekend to ourselves.

It was early Saturday morning, and I was sitting at our granite kitchen countertop, feeding Luke, him in his high chair and me balancing on a bar stool while I watched the morning news on CNN. I was cutting apples into little chunks and leaving them in front of him on a plate. He was merrily picking each piece up, shooting a toothy, gummy grin at me, and then either eating the fruit or squealing and throwing it on the floor for Gorbachev, the Borodins' rescue dog mongrel.

It was a game that didn't get old. "Gorby" seemed to spend as much time in our apartment as he did at home with Irena, sneaking over to scratch on our door anytime their front door opened. Watching Luke throw food down to him, it wasn't hard to understand why. I wanted a dog, but Lauren was against it. Too much hair, she said—even having Gorby over was testing her patience, as evidenced each time she asked me to help remove dog hair from a suit jacket or pair of pants.

Banging his fists on the tray, Luke squeaked, "Da!" his universal word for anything involving me, and then stretched out his small hand—*more apple, please.*

I shook my head, laughing, and began cutting up some more fruit.

Luke wasn't even two years old, but he was the size of a three-year-old, something he must've gotten from his dad, I thought with a smile. Wisps of golden blond hair floated about his chubby perma-glow cheeks. His face was always stuck in a mischievous grin, showing a mouthful of white button teeth, as if he was about to do something he knew he wasn't supposed to—which was almost always the case.

Lauren appeared from our bedroom, her eyes still half-closed. "I don't feel good," she mumbled, staggering into our small bathroom, the only other closed room in our less-than-thousand-square-foot apartment. I heard her coughing and then the sound of the shower turning on.

"Coffee's on," I muttered, thinking, *She didn't drink that much last night*, while I watched some enraged Chinese students in the city of Taiyuan burning American flags. I'd never heard of Taiyuan, so while I dropped more fruit chunks in front of Luke with one hand, I queried my tablet with the other.

Wikipedia: *Taiyuan is the capital and largest city of North China's Shanxi province. At the 2010 census, it had a total population of 4,201,591.*

Wow. That was bigger than Los Angeles, America's second-largest city, and Taiyuan was China's twentieth-largest. With a few more keystrokes I discovered that China had more than 160 cities with populations over a million, where the United States had exactly nine.

I looked up from my tablet at the news. The image on the TV had switched to an aerial view of a strange-looking aircraft carrier. An anchor on CNN described the scene, "*Here we see China's first, and so far only, aircraft carrier, the* Liaoning, *ringed by a pack of angry-looking Lanzhou-class destroyers as they face off with the* USS George Washington *just outside the Luzon Strait in the South China Sea.*"

"Sorry about my parents, honey," whispered Lauren as she snuck up behind me, mopping her hair with a towel and dressed in a white terry cloth bathrobe. "Remember, it was your idea."

Leaning down to cuddle Luke, she kissed him and he squeaked his pleasure at the attention, then she wrapped her arms around me and kissed my neck.

I nuzzled her back, enjoying the affection after a tense couple of days. "I know," I replied.

A US naval officer had appeared on CNN. "*Not five years ago Japan was telling us to get our boys out of Okinawa, but now they're begging for help again. Japs have a fleet of their own aircraft carriers coming down here, why on Earth—*"

"I love you, baby." Lauren had slipped one of her hands under my T-shirt and was stroking my chest.

"I love you too."

"Have you thought more about going to Hawaii for Christmas?"

"*—and Bangladesh will be hit hard if China diverts the Brahmaputra. They need friends now more than ever, but I never imagined the Seventh Fleet parking itself in Chittagong—*"

I pulled away from her. "You know I'm not comfortable having your family pay."

"So then let me pay."

"With money that comes from your father."

"Only because I'm not *working* because I *quit* my job to have Luke." It was a sore point.

She turned to grab a cup and filled it with coffee. Black. No sugar this morning. Leaning against the stove, she cupped her hands around the hot coffee, hunching inwards away from me.

"—*starting cyclic ops around the clock, constant launch and recovery missions from the three American aircraft carriers now stationed in*—"

"It's not just the money. I'm not comfortable spending Christmas there with your mother and father, and we did Thanksgiving with them."

She ignored me. "I'd just finished articling at Latham and passing the bar"—she was speaking more to herself than to me—"and now everyone is downsizing. I threw the opportunity away."

"You didn't throw it away, honey." I looked at Luke. "We're all suffering. This new downturn is hard on everyone."

In the silence between us, the CNN anchor started on a new topic. "*Reports today of US government Web sites being hacked and defaced. With Chinese and American naval forces squaring off, tensions are heightening. We go now to our correspondent at Fort Meade Cyber Command headquarters*—"

"What about going to Pittsburgh?" I proposed. "See my family?"

"—*the Chinese are claiming the defacement of US government Web sites is the work of private citizen hacktivists, and most of the activity seems to be originating from Russian sources*—"

"Seriously? You won't take a free trip to Hawaii and you want me to go to Pittsburgh?" A muscle tightened up in her neck. "Your brothers are both convicted criminals. I'm not sure I want to expose Luke to that kind of environment."

"Come on, they were teenagers when that happened. We talked about this."

She said nothing.

"Didn't one of your cousins get arrested last summer?" I said defensively.

"Arrested." She shook her head. "Not *convicted*. There is a difference."

I stared into her eyes. "Not all of us are so lucky as to have an uncle who's in Congress."

Luke was watching us.

"So," I asked, my voice rising, "what was it your father wanted you to think about?" I already knew it was some new offer to entice her back to Boston.

"What do you mean?"

"Really?"

She sighed and looked down into her coffee. "A partner-track position at Ropes and Gray."

"I didn't know you'd applied."

"I didn't—"

"I'm not moving to Boston, Lauren. I thought the whole idea of us coming here was for you to start your own life."

"It was."

"I thought we were trying for a brother or sister for Luke. Isn't that what you wanted?"

"More what you wanted."

I stared at her in disbelief, my vision of our future together starting to unravel with just those four words. But there had been more than a few uncomfortable words lately. My stomach knotted.

"I'm going to be thirty this year." She slapped her coffee cup down on the counter. "Opportunities like this don't come around often. It could be my last chance to have a career."

Silence while we glared at each other.

"I'm going to the interview."

"That's the discussion?" My heart began to race. "Why? What's going on?"

"I just told you why."

We studied each other in mutually accusatory silence. Luke started to fuss in his chair.

Lauren sighed, her shoulders sagging. "I don't know, okay? I feel lost. I don't want to talk about it right now."

I relaxed, and my pulse slowed.

Lauren looked at me, and then away. "And I'm going for brunch with Richard to talk about some ideas he had for me."

My cheeks flushed hot. "I think he beats Sarah."

Lauren gritted her teeth. "Why would you *say* something like that?"

"Did you see her arms at the barbecue? She was covering up. I saw bruises."

Shaking her head, she snorted, "You're being jealous. Don't be ridiculous."

"What should I be jealous of?"

Luke began to cry.

"I'm going to get dressed," she said dismissively, shaking her head. "Don't ask stupid questions. You know what I mean."

Ignoring me, she leaned down and kissed Luke, whispering

that she was sorry, she didn't mean to yell, and that she loved him. Once she'd calmed Luke down, she gave me an evil look and stalked off into the bedroom, closing the door heavily.

Sighing, I picked Luke up, eased his head onto my shoulder, and patted his back. "Why did she marry me, huh, Luke?"

After two or three sniffling sighs, his little body relaxed into me. "Come on. Let's take you over to see Ellarose and Auntie Susie."

DECEMBER 8

"How many of these are there?"

"Fifty. And that's just the water."

"You're kidding. I've only got half an hour before I need to be upstairs for the sitter."

Chuck shrugged. "I'll ring Susie. She can watch Luke."

"Wonderful." I was struggling down the stairs holding a four-gallon container of water in each hand. "So two hundred gallons of water you're paying five hundred dollars a month to store?"

Chuck owned a chain of Cajun fusion restaurants in Manhattan, and you'd have thought he could store stuff at one of them, but he said he needed to have it close. A card-carrying member of the Virginia Preppers couldn't be too careful, he liked to say. He had some decidedly non–New Yorker sensibilities.

His family was from just south of the Mason-Dixon Line. He was an only child, and his mother and father had died in a car accident just after he finished college, so when he met Susie, they'd decided on a new start and had come to New York. My own mother had passed away when I was in college, and I'd barely known my father. He left when I was a kid, so my brothers had pretty much raised me. Our similar family situations had bonded us when we met.

"That's about the size of it, and I'm lucky I got this extra locker." Chuck snickered, watching my efforts. "You need to hit the gym, my friend."

I trudged down the last few steps to the basement. Where the rest of our complex was beautifully decorated and maintained—manicured Japanese gardens next to the gym and spa, an indoor waterfall at the entrance, 24-7 security guards—the basement was decidedly utilitarian. The polished oak steps leading down from the back entrance gave way to a rough concrete floor and exposed overhead lighting. Nobody really went down there. Nobody, that was, except Chuck.

I laughed halfheartedly at his jab, not really listening. My mind was turning over and over, thinking about Lauren. When we'd met at Harvard, anything had seemed possible, but it felt like she was slipping away. Today she'd gone for the interview in Boston and was spending the evening with her family there. Luke had been at preschool this morning, but I hadn't been able to find a sitter for the afternoon, so I'd returned home from work. Lauren and I had had some heated exchanges over her going to Boston, but there was more to it than that. *There's something she's not telling me.*

At the end of the hallway, I stopped and elbowed open the door to Chuck's storage locker. With a grunt I lifted my two water jugs and stacked them on top of the pile he'd started.

"Pack 'em tight," said Chuck, waddling up behind me with his own load. He stacked his, and we turned to go back and get more.

"Did you see that stuff online today?" he asked. "WikiLeaks published Pentagon plans for bombing Beijing."

I shrugged, still thinking about Lauren. I remembered the first time I saw her walking between the red-brick campus buildings of

Harvard, laughing with her friends. I'd just gotten into the MBA program, which I was paying for with money I'd earned from selling my stake in a media start-up, and she'd just started the law program. We'd both been filled with dreams of making the world a better place.

"They're making a lot of noise about it in the media," continued Chuck, "but I don't think it's a big deal. Just role-playing exercises."

"Uh-huh." Soon after Lauren and I met, heated debates in Harvard Square beer halls had led to passionate nights. I was the first of my family to attend university, never mind Harvard, and I'd known she was from an old-money family, but at the time it hadn't seemed relevant. She'd wanted to escape from the confines of her family, and I'd wanted everything she represented.

We'd married quickly after graduation—eloped—and moved to New York. Her father hadn't been impressed. Almost as soon as we were married, Luke had been conceived—a happy accident, but one that had forever changed the new world we'd barely settled into.

"You haven't heard a word I've said, have you?"

I looked up. Chuck and I had come through the back entrance of our building and were standing on the sidewalk on Twenty-Fourth Street. It was raining, and the icy gray skies matched my mood. Just a week ago it had been warm, but the temperature had sharply dropped.

This section of Twenty-Fourth, less than two blocks from Chelsea Piers and the Hudson River, was more of a back alley. Parked cars lined both sides of the narrow street below windows covered in mesh grills. The sound of cars honking floated down from Ninth Avenue in the distance.

To one side of our building there was some kind of a taxi repair shop, and a small group of men had gathered outside under the grimy awning, smoking cigarettes and laughing. Chuck had had his delivery of water shipped to the garage.

Chuck gently clapped me on the back. "Are you okay?"

We wound our way through the taxi drivers and mechanics to his pallet, off to one side of the garage, and picked up some more containers of water.

"Sorry," I replied after a pause, grunting as I picked up my load. "Lauren and I—"

"Yeah, I heard from Susie. So she's off for that interview in Boston?"

I nodded. "We live in a million-dollar condo, but it's not good enough. When I was growing up in Pittsburgh, I couldn't even imagine living in a million-dollar home." Affording the condo was a stretch on my salary, but at the same time I didn't feel like I could afford anything less.

"Neither could she, and by that I mean *only* a million-dollar home." He laughed. "Hey, you knew what you were getting into."

"And she's always off with Richard when I'm working."

Chuck stopped and put down his water containers. "Cut that thought short. He's a creep, but Lauren's not like that." He swiped his badge past the security device on the back entrance. When it didn't work after two tries, he rummaged around in his pockets for a key. "Stupid thing doesn't work half the time," he muttered under his breath. Opening the door, he turned to me. "Just give her some time and space to figure it out. Turning thirty is a big deal for women."

I walked in ahead of him while he held the door open. "I guess you're right. Now what were you talking about?"

"The news today. Things are getting totally out of hand in China. Have you been watching? More burning flags outside embassies, ransacking American stores. FedEx said they had to stop operations in China, even delivery of vaccines for the bird flu outbreak, and now Anonymous is threatening to attack them in retaliation."

Anonymous was the citizen hacktivist group we'd been reading about more and more in the news.

Reaching the storage locker again, we stacked the water containers. "That why you're stocking up?" I asked.

"Just a coincidence, but I also read that cyberattacks on the Department of Defense have stepped up an order of magnitude." Chuck had been researching the cyberworld ever since I brought it up at the barbecue.

"DoD's getting attacked?" I asked, concerned. "Is it serious?"

"It gets attacked millions of times even on a good day, but now some reports are saying the attacks are getting more focused. Makes me nervous someone is planning something in meatspace."

"Meatspace?"

"The Internet is in cyberspace, but *we*"—he paused for effect—"are in meatspace, get it?"

Opening the back door, we walked back out into the rain.

"God help us, now you have something new to be paranoid about."

Chuck snorted. "Only yourself to blame."

We walked back to the garage and found our neighbor Rory talking to one of the men.

"Thirsty?" laughed Rory. He must have seen us lugging the containers. "What's all the water for?"

"Just like to be prepared," replied Chuck. He nodded at the

man Rory was talking to. "Mike, this is Stan. He runs the garage here."

I shook Stan's hand. "Nice to meet you."

"Not sure how much longer I'll be running this joint, the way things are going," said Stan.

"Used to be we had Bob Hope and Johnny Cash," sympathized Chuck. "Now we have no hope and no cash."

"Ain't that the truth," Stan laughed, and all the cabbies around the entrance laughed too.

"You need any help?" asked Rory.

"Naw, thanks, man." Chuck waved a hand at the dozen or so containers. "Not too much left."

We headed back in for another load.

DECEMBER 17

"Could you give me your credit card?"

"Why?"

"Because mine are all canceled," replied Lauren angrily.

She'd been the victim of identity theft just after Thanksgiving. Someone had started taking out loans in her name, creating hedge accounts with online trading systems. It was a total mess.

"I can give it to you," I said, "but forget trying to order anything."

We were having breakfast. I was spooning back oatmeal, Lauren was drinking coffee and surfing the Internet on her laptop, and Luke was back to the fruit-chunks-and-dog game.

Ellarose burbled away on her play mat on the floor in front of the TV. Where Luke was a bruiser, big for his age, Ellarose was petite, small for a six-month-old. She didn't have much hair yet, and what she did have seemed to always be sticking out at right angles, like a sand-colored bird's nest. Her little eyes were constantly watching, wide open, seeing what was going on with the world. We were looking after her for a few hours so Susie could go shopping.

I was staying home for the day. The week before Christmas was completely dead business-wise, and it was a good time to catch up on paperwork. The kitchen counter in front of me was filled with scraps of paper and notes I was trying to organize. Unconsciously, I picked up my smartphone, swiping it to check my social media feeds. Nothing new.

"What do you mean, forget trying to order anything?" Where I was winding down for the holidays, Lauren was still going full speed and was dressed up in a suit for interviews. "We still have more than a week before Christmas. I'll just get the one-day delivery. Amazon said this year—"

"It's not Amazon that's the problem."

Picking up the remote from the counter, I turned up the volume on CNN. *"FedEx and UPS have ground to a complete standstill today due to what they say is a virus in their logistics shipping software—"*

"That's just great." Lauren slapped her laptop cover down.

"—blaming the hacking group Anonymous after they declared their intention to punish shipping companies for halting shipment of flu vaccines into China. Representatives of Anonymous deny the attack, saying they only initiated denial-of-service—"

"So where are you going today?" I asked.

"—projecting hundreds of millions of dollars of lost revenue for this holiday season, driving the economy even further into recession—"

"Meeting some headhunters downtown. Starting some dialogues to see if any low-hanging fruit comes loose."

I forced an encouraging smile. "That's great, honey." How was it that I'd had to start to lie to her about how I felt?

She'd become withdrawn since coming back from Boston. I was trying to give her space to go through whatever she needed to go through, but it felt like I was losing her. I was behaving as if I didn't care, when every fiber inside me wanted to reach out to her and shake her and ask what the hell was happening.

She sighed, glancing toward the TV and then looking back at me. I met her gaze but then dropped my eyes, giving her that space. Lauren continued to look at me and then leaned down to give Luke a kiss, whispering something in his ear. She picked up her laptop and quickly made for the door. "I'll be back just after lunch," she called over her shoulder.

"See you then," I replied to an already closing door. *She didn't even give me a kiss.*

I handed the last pieces of apple to Luke. With a grin he grabbed the fruit, then squealed with glee as he threw it onto the floor for an appreciative Gorby. For good measure, one of the chunks flew sideways and landed on the report I was trying to read.

I smiled and wiped his face. "Done with breakfast? Want to play with Ellarose?"

Picking up a napkin, I cleaned his face and then lifted him up out of his high chair to deposit him on the ground. He stood unsteadily for a moment, holding onto the legs of my stool for balance, before rocketing off toward Ellarose in the tottering-on-the-edge-of-disaster run he'd been working on. Reaching out, he caught the front of the couch, stopping himself like a wobbly ice skater. He looked down at Ellarose and then up at me with a big smile.

Ellarose, for her part, hadn't yet mastered the art of turning onto her stomach. She was lying on her back on her play mat, looking up at Luke with wide eyes. Luke squeaked and plopped down onto his knees to crawl over to her, putting a hand onto her face.

"Careful, Luke, be gentle," I warned.

He looked into Ellarose's eyes and then sat up next to her, protectively, and looked at the TV.

"*The extent of the bird flu outbreak within China is still unclear, but the US State Department has now issued a travel advisory. Combined with a growing anti-China boycotting movement—*"

"Crazy world, huh?" I said to Luke, watching him watch the TV. Gorby walked over to curl up behind him.

I went back to reading a report on the potential market for augmented reality on the Internet. I'd just been sent a pair of new augmented-reality glasses by one of the big tech companies. It was a technology that fascinated me, and I wanted to get involved in a start-up, but Lauren said it was too risky.

After fifteen minutes of reading and doing my expenses, I realized Luke was awfully quiet and looked up to see he'd fallen asleep against Gorby. I yawned. A nap seemed like a great idea, so I deposited Ellarose in her playpen by the window. I picked up Luke, his head lolling around like a sack of potatoes, and lay down on the couch, cradling my son on my stomach as I drifted off to sleep.

CNN droned on in the background. "*At what point does cyberespionage become cyberattack? With more on this, we go to our correspondent . . .*"

———————————

A loud banging on the door woke me up. As my brain emerged from its fog, a gruff voice joined the banging. "I'll huff, and I'll puff, and I'll blooow your door down!"

Luke had drooled all over my T-shirt. My muscles were sluggish. *How long was I out?* I groaned, struggling to sit up, carefully holding Luke. "Yeah, yeah, just a sec," I called out.

Holding Luke in one arm, I ambled to the door and unlocked it.

Chuck burst through, clutching brown paper bags in both hands. "Anyone for lunch?" he announced enthusiastically, proceeding to the kitchen counter, where he began unpacking.

Luke watched Chuck with half-open eyes. I returned to the couch and laid him down, covering him with a blanket, and then returned to Chuck. By then he'd emptied everything out onto plates.

"Is it lunchtime already? I conked out." I rubbed my eyes and stretched. "What is that?"

"Foie gras and french fries, my friend." Chuck waved a baguette around in the air like a magic wand. "And some Creole shrimp in butter dipping sauce."

No wonder I was getting fat. "I can feel my arteries hardening already." Reaching around the counter, I slid open a drawer to pull out two forks and handed him one while I dug into the french fries with the other. "You don't need to be at the restaurant this time of year?"

"This is the busiest time of the year." Chuck picked a meaty chunk of foie gras from atop the french fries. "But I have stuff to do here."

"More supplies for your doomsday locker?"

He grinned and stuffed the fatty liver into his mouth.

I shook my head. "Do you *really* believe it's all going to come apart?"

Chuck wiped his greasy lips with the side of one hand. "You *really* believe it never will?"

"People are always saying the world is ending, but it never does. Society is too far advanced."

"Tell that to the Easter Islanders and Anasazi Indians."

"Those were isolated groups."

"What about the Romans, then? And you're telling me we're not isolated on this speck of blue called Earth?"

Picking up a shrimp, I began shelling it.

"I've been researching the cyberworld, at *your* suggestion," said Chuck, "and you're right."

I regretted saying anything.

"What's happening now," he whispered, "makes the Cold War look like an age of transparency and understanding."

"You're being dramatic."

"For all human history, the ability of one country to affect another was based on control of physical territory. Guess what broke that for the first time?"

"Cyber?" I popped the shrimp into my mouth, savoring the rich flavor of Cajun spices and butter. *Oh, that's good.*

"Nope. Space systems. Ever since Sputnik launched in 1957, outer space has been the military high ground."

"What does that have to do with cyber?"

"Because cyber is the second thing that broke it. It's replacing space as the *new* military high ground." Chuck stuffed a mouthful of greasy fries into his mouth. "And outer space is already a *part* of cyberspace."

"What does that mean?"

"Most space systems are Internet-based. To us, things in space look far away, but in cyberspace, there's no difference."

"So what's the difference?"

"While *space* requires a massive amount of money, all that you need to get into *cyber*space is a laptop."

Switching from the shrimp to the fries, I hunted for a chunk of foie gras. "So that has you worried?"

He shook his head. "What's got me worried are those logic bombs in the energy grid you talked about. The Chinese wanted us to find them, so we'd know they could do it. Otherwise, we'd never have spotted them."

"So you're saying the CIA, NSA, all those three-letter agencies you love to hate, none of them would have seen it?" I said skeptically.

He shook his head. "People have this image of cyberwar, and they think of video games and everything being squeaky clean, but it won't be like that."

"So what will it be like?"

"In 1982 the CIA rigged a logic bomb that blew up a Siberian pipeline—it created an explosion of three kilotons, as much as a small nuclear device. All they did was alter some code from a Canadian company that controlled it."

Three kilotons? Aren't nuclear devices in the megaton range? "That doesn't sound *too* bad."

"That was thirty years ago. The new cyberweapons of mass destruction they're building, nobody's ever tested them," continued Chuck, his smile long gone. "At least with nuclear weapons you know they're scary—Hiroshima, Bikini—but with cyber, nobody knows how much damage they'll cause if they let them loose, and they're merrily sticking them into each other's infrastructure like candy canes on a doomsday Christmas tree."

"You really think it's that bad?"

"Do you know that when they set off the atomic bomb for the first time, during the Manhattan Project, the physicists running the show had a bet going whether it would ignite the atmosphere?"

I shook my head.

"Their best guess was fifty-fifty that they'd destroy all life on the planet, but they went ahead anyway. Government planning hasn't changed, my friend, and nobody knows what these new toys might do if they unleash them."

"So there's nowhere to run anymore if things go wrong, is that what you're saying?" I countered. "If something drastic goes down, do you really want to struggle to survive, only to watch everyone die? I'd prefer a nice quick exit."

He pointed to Luke on the couch. "You wouldn't fight with everything you've got, till your last breath, to protect him?"

I looked at Luke. Chuck was right. I nodded, conceding the point.

"You have too much faith in things always moving forward," he declared. "Since humans began making stuff, we've lost more technologies than we've gained. Society goes backwards from time to time."

"I'm sure you have examples." There was no use in trying to slow him down when he was on a roll.

"On a dig in Pompeii, they found aqueduct technology better than what we're using today." Chuck dug into the pile of french fries. "And how they built the pyramids is still lost tech."

"Now we're talking ancient spacemen?"

"I'm being serious. When Admiral Zheng led his fleet out of Suzhou in China in 1405, he had ships the size of modern aircraft carriers and took nearly thirty thousand troops with him."

"Really?"

"Look it up. Zheng was probably in contact with our West Coast Indians four hundred years before Lewis and Clark brought Sacajawea on holiday there. I'd bet the Chinese were smoking reefers with the Oregon chiefs on ships bigger than modern battle cruisers a hundred years before Columbus 'discovered' America. Know how big Columbus's famous *Niña* was?"

I shrugged.

"Fifty feet, and he had maybe fifty guys with him."

"Didn't he have three boats?"

Chuck stabbed the fries with his fork. "Before we'd even managed to paddle out of Europe in little buckets, China was already sailing the globe with thirty thousand troops on fleets of aircraft-carrier-sized warships."

I stopped eating. "What's your point? I'm not following."

"Just that society goes backwards sometimes, and all this stuff with China—I get the feeling we're fooling ourselves."

"They're not the enemy?"

"Just the wrong perspective," he said. "We're squaring them up to *be* the enemy, but mostly because *we* need an enemy."

"So you're saying you're wrong about the cyberthreat?"

"No, but . . ." Chuck left his fork in the fries and picked up a shrimp with his fingers.

"But what?"

"Maybe we're blinding ourselves to the real enemy."

"What enemy is that, my conspiracy-loving friend?" I asked, rolling my eyes, expecting some rhetoric about the CIA or NSA.

Chuck finished shelling his shrimp and pointed it at me. "Fear. Fear is the real enemy." He looked up at the ceiling. "Fear and ignorance."

I laughed. "With all this stuff you're stockpiling, aren't *you* the one that's afraid?"

"Not afraid," he said deliberately, looking straight into my eyes. "Prepared."

DAY 1: DECEMBER 23
8:55 A.M.

"It's two days before Christmas. Isn't it time to take a break?"

Lauren frowned at me from across our kitchen counter. "I have to go to this meeting. Richard really went out on a limb to get this guy to talk to me."

We had the bedroom door shut, but the screech of Luke crying came through the baby monitor on the counter, cutting her short. She grabbed it and shut it off, just like she'd been shutting me off for the past month.

I threw my hands in the air. "Well, if Richard set it up, then of course, abandon your family for another day."

"Don't start." She clenched her jaw. "At least Richard's trying to help me."

Taking a deep breath, I mentally counted to ten. It *was* almost Christmas, and there was no sense in this argument escalating. Lauren stared at me.

I ran a hand through my hair and sighed. "I think Luke's coming down with something. We need to go food shopping for the holidays, and, like I said, I need to finish delivering those client gifts." My new administrative assistant had forgotten to deliver a dozen of the personalized gifts that we'd created for our clients.

She'd missed the ones in Manhattan because they weren't on the long-distance mailing list. When we discovered the error, she'd been in a rush to get off to her family for the holidays, and with FedEx and UPS down, I'd stupidly offered to deliver them myself.

Of course, now it was the last minute. Yesterday Luke and I had delivered half of them, running all around Little Italy and Chinatown to some of our smaller start-up partners, but I still had a few left for our bigger clients. Luke had enjoyed the outing—he was a social butterfly and would jabber to everyone we met.

"Is delivering a couple of engraved pen holders really going to make or break your business?"

"That's not the point."

She took a deep breath, and her shoulders relaxed. "I forgot. I'm sorry. But this is *really* important to me."

Obviously more important than we are, I thought, but I held my tongue and tried to strike the thought from my head. Negative thoughts had a way of festering.

Lauren looked at the ceiling. "Can't you get Susie—"

"They're out all day."

"Then what about the Borodins?"

She wasn't going to give in. A pause hung in the air while I inspected the tiny plastic Christmas tree we'd stuck on a side table next to the couch.

"Fine. I'll figure it out." I managed a smile. "Go on, get going."

"Thanks." She collected her coat and purse. "And if you do take Luke out, don't forget to bundle up—both of you. I'll just go and calm him down before I leave."

I nodded and returned to surfing through some new social media outlets. The Web was incredibly slow. It was taking forever for new pages to load.

Lauren went into our room, and I heard her talking to Luke. She picked him up and paced with him, and the crying stopped. Lauren appeared a moment later with her coat on and came around to my side of the counter to give me a little hug and peck on the cheek. I shrugged her off. She swatted at me playfully, and then she was off and out the door.

As soon as she left, I went to check on Luke in his crib. He was still whimpering, but had calmed down and was cuddled up with his blanket. Returning to my laptop, I tried doing some more research, but the slow Web connection made it next to impossible. I couldn't be bothered to check the router, so I gave up and decided to get on with my day.

Leaving our front door ajar so I could still hear Luke, I walked next door to the Borodins. Our apartment was at the end of a narrow carpeted hallway, lit along its length by recessed lighting. Susie and Chuck lived to the left coming out of our place, with the Borodins to our right. The next door down from Chuck's was Pam and Rory's place, directly across from another hallway that led off at a right angle to the elevators. The emergency exit was next to Rory's, with the stairwell leading down six floors from there. Five more apartments lined the rest of the hallway, ending in the downstairs entrance to Richard's three-story condo on the opposite side of the building from ours.

Irena opened the door at my first quiet knock. They were always home, and she must have been standing just beside the door, cooking as usual. The smell of roasting potatoes and meats and yeasty bread wafted out as the door slid open.

"Mih-kah-yal, *privyet*," greeted Irena, her warm smile creasing the deep wrinkles in her face.

At nearly ninety years of age, she was stooped and shuffled

when she walked, but always had a bright twinkle in her eye. As old as she was, I'd still think twice before messing with her—she'd been a part of the Red Army that had defeated the Nazis in the frozen wastelands of northern Russia. As she liked to tell me, "Troy fell, Rome fell, but Leningrad did not fall."

She was wearing a green-checked apron, slightly stained, and held a tea towel bunched up in one hand. With the other she motioned for me to enter. "Come, come."

I glanced at their door frame and the mezuzah affixed there, a tiny but beautifully carved, ornate mahogany box. At one time I thought these were like Jewish "good luck" charms, but I'd come to understand that they were more about keeping evil away.

I resisted entering. Going in there always ended with a plate of sausages and recriminations that I was too thin. That being said, I loved her food, and I enjoyed even more the simple pleasure of being doted on. It made me feel like a kid, protected and indulged, and no self-respecting Russian grandmother would have it any other way.

"Sorry, I'm in a bit of a hurry." Whatever she was cooking smelled amazing, and I realized that dropping off Luke would give me the perfect opportunity to come back later and be spoiled. "I don't mean to impose, but would you be able to watch Luke for a few hours?"

She shrugged. "Of course, Mi-kay-yal, you know you don't need to ask, *da*?"

"Thanks. I need to go out and make some deliveries." Glancing inside, I could see her husband, Aleksandr, asleep in his recliner in front of a Russian soap opera on the TV. Gorbachev was curled up asleep beside him.

Irena nodded. "You bring Luke?"

I nodded back.

"And you wrap yourself up. It is much below zero today."

I laughed. Two women had already told me to bundle up and I hadn't even been outside yet. *Maybe I am still a kid.* "We use Fahrenheit here, Irena—it's cold, but not below zero yet. Still about ten degrees, I think."

"Ack, you know what I mean." Flicking her chin to tell me to get going, she turned to get back to her cooking, leaving the door ajar.

Back in my apartment, I rummaged around in the front closet, looking for winter coats, gloves, and scarves. Then I remembered: the weather had been so warm that Lauren had only just gotten around to taking our coats to the dry cleaner yesterday, and they'd been unable to give us same-day service thanks to the Christmas rush. Sighing, I pulled a thin black jacket off a hanger, picked up my backpack with the gifts in it, and went into the bedroom to put a sweater on.

Luke was wide awake, and his cheeks were bright red.

"Not feeling too great, buddy?" I said, reaching down to pick him up. His forehead was hot, and the little guy was sweating. He'd also wet his diaper, so I changed him, switching him into some dungarees and thick socks with a cotton shirt, and then took him next door.

Even under the weather, Luke managed a toothy grin upon seeing Irena.

"Ah, *dorogoy!*" she gushed, taking the still-sleepy Luke from my arms. "He has fever, *nyet*?"

I brushed Luke's head, feeling the sweat in his matted-down hair. "Yeah, I think so."

She pulled Luke into her bosom. "No worry, I take care. You go."

"Thanks. I'll be back about lunchtime." I raised my eyebrows, and by the way she smiled back, I knew there would be a feast on my return.

She laughed and closed the door.

A child was such an amazing thing. I'd gone through life before we had Luke wondering what it was all about, trying to sort out my hopes and dreams and fears. Then, all of a sudden, there was a little version of me staring back at me, and everything became clear. The meaning of my life was to protect and raise this new life, to love him and teach him everything I knew.

"Forget something?"

"Huh?"

Pam was standing in the hallway, outside her door. She was a nurse, and was dressed in scrubs, on her way to work. We'd become quite good friends with her and her husband, Rory, but we hadn't quite developed the kind of bond and easy relationship we had with Susie and Chuck. The thing was, Pam and Rory were strict vegans, and somehow that created a gap. I felt a bit guilty when I ate meat around them, no matter how many times they made it clear it didn't bother them and it was a personal choice.

I liked Pam a lot. She was a very attractive blonde, and hard not to like. Where Lauren was what you might call a classic beauty, Pam was a more voluptuous sort.

"No, I was just dropping Luke off."

"I saw that," she laughed. "Deep thoughts, huh?"

"Not really." I shook my head and walked toward her. She worked for the Red Cross and was stationed at a blood bank just a few blocks away. "Still draining veins, even before Christmas?"

"It's the season to give, right? Are *you* finally going to come down?"

The elevator pinged our floor, its doors opening. I was trapped.

"Ah, you know," I hemmed and hawed, "I've got a lot to do."

"The holidays are when we need donors the most," she urged in a singsong voice.

I let her enter the elevator ahead of me. Now I felt doubly guilty. Before I could stop myself, I said, "You know what? I'll come down right now." *Hey, it's Christmas*, I thought. *What the heck.*

"Really?" Her face lit up. "I'll slide you right in."

My face flushed at the imagined innuendo. "That'd be great."

Silence while we waited for the elevator to drop to the ground floor.

"You're going to need more than that."

"Huh?"

She was looking at my thin jacket. "It's freezing out. Did you see the storm warnings? The coldest Christmas since 1930. So much for global warming."

"They should have called it global *warning*."

We both laughed.

She turned to me. "You're an Internet guy, right?"

I shrugged yes.

"Did you notice that it was almost impossible to get online this morning?"

That got my attention. "I did. Are you on Roadrunner too?" *It must be some type of carrier problem in the building.*

"No," she replied. "On CNN they're saying it's a virus or something."

The elevator stopped at the ground floor and opened.

"A virus?"

11:55 A.M.

Giving blood took longer than I thought it would. Pam moved me to first in line, but it was a quarter past ten by the time I finally exited the Red Cross, donut in hand, to catch a cab into Midtown.

I figured I would do a round of our four clients in the center of town, drop off the gifts—shaking hands if anyone was around—and then run back to do some grocery shopping. I'd swing by home, drop off the food and check on Luke while I grabbed a bite to eat with Irena, and then head down to the Financial District for the final two client gift drop-offs and maybe a holiday drink or two.

I was buoyed by the feel-good sensation of giving blood, or perhaps high from a lack of oxygen and red blood cells, and my trip into Midtown took on a cinematic aura. I gawked out the window of my cab, watching the holiday shoppers bustling by on the streets, caught up in the excitement of New York at Christmas. Everyone was bundled up in hats and scarves in the intense cold, shopping bags in hand.

My first stop was next to Rockefeller Center, and after dropping the gift off I spent ten minutes staring at the tree outside, even offering to take pictures for a few tourists, enjoying the buzz of the crowds.

My route continued up past the Plaza Hotel, along Central Park, then looped back downtown. I had been texting with Lauren about what we needed for food, but she had stopped answering my texts. Finishing my rounds in Midtown, I hopped in a taxi and had it drop me back in Chelsea at Whole Foods. After cruising up and down the aisles for half an hour, filling my shopping cart and getting into the Christmas spirit, I finally arrived at the checkout line.

It was huge.

I waited ten minutes, trying unsuccessfully to check e-mail on my phone a few times, before asking a frustrated-looking woman in front of me, "What's going on?"

"I don't know," she replied over her shoulder. "Seems like they're having some problems with the computers."

"Mind watching my stuff while I go and have a look?"

She nodded.

I left my cart and wandered up toward the cash registers. The crowd's agitation intensified as I moved forward, ending in a knot of angry shoppers.

"Why can't you just take cash?" one of them said.

"Sir, we can't let you take anything out of the store unless it's scanned," replied a frightened cashier, a teenage girl who was helplessly waving around a bar scanner.

I slipped in behind the registers to address the cashier directly. "What's happening?" I asked.

Turning to me, she said, "It's still not working, sir."

She was flustered and must have thought I was a manager.

"Explain to me exactly what happened, from the start."

"The scanning devices just stopped working. We've been waiting for technical support for an hour, but nothing." In a hushed voice she added, "My cousin on the Upper East Side texted me and said their store was out as well."

An angry customer, a large Hispanic man, grabbed my arm. "I just want to get out of here, bro. Can't you take cash?"

I held up my hands. "Not my call to make."

He looked straight at me. I expected to see anger, but he looked scared. "Screw this. I've been waiting an hour." He threw a few twenties onto the counter in front us. "Just keep the change, man."

Grabbing his shopping bags, he pushed his way through the crowd. People around him were watching, and a few of them began to wind forward to leave money at the counter too. Others just started leaving, taking whatever they were holding without paying.

"What's going on?" It wasn't like New Yorkers to start stealing.

"It's the news, sir, the Chinese," replied the cashier.

"What news?"

"That aircraft carrier thing," was all she could add, but by that point I was already pushing my way toward the door, suddenly and irrationally fearful for Luke.

2:45 P.M.

"Why didn't you tell me before?"

I was pacing in front of the huge flat-panel TV that dominated one wall of Chuck's apartment.

"Figured you'd think I was being paranoid," replied Chuck. Blurry images of a smoking aircraft carrier filled the screen behind me.

I'd returned to the Borodins' in a rush and knocked loudly on their door. While hurrying the few blocks up from Whole Foods, I'd searched the news on my smartphone. The device had taken forever to respond.

There had been an incident in the South China Sea. A Chinese warplane had crashed. The Chinese were claiming it was an attack by American forces, but the Americans were denying they had anything to do with it, saying it was an accident. The governor of Shanxi Province, in northern China, was all over the news claiming it was an act of war.

Luke was fine when I arrived, but his fever had gotten worse. He was sweating profusely, and Irena said he'd been crying most of the time I'd been gone. I'd left him at the Borodins', letting him rest, and gone over to Chuck's.

"You didn't think this was maybe important enough to share?" I asked incredulously.

"Not at the time, I didn't."

CNN was on in the background. "*Sources in the Pentagon deny any responsibility for the crashed Chinese warplane, saying that it was the result of the inexperience of Chinese forces in operating at-sea carrier operations—*"

"You haven't had any food deliveries to your restaurants in several days and you didn't think I might be interested?"

"*—Poison Trojan has now infected DNS servers worldwide. The Chinese are denying responsibility, but the bigger issue now is the Scramble virus that has infected logistics systems—*"

"I didn't think it was relevant," replied Chuck. "We have computer problems all the time."

The virus that had shut down FedEx and UPS had moved on to infect the software of almost every other commercial shipping company, and the world's supply chain was now starting to grind to a halt.

"I've been reading the hacker message boards," added Chuck. "They're saying that UPS and FedEx are proprietary systems, and that the speed of the virus means it must have hundreds of zero days in it."

"What's a zero day?" asked Susie, who was sitting on the couch next to Chuck. She was holding Ellarose, whose head bobbled up and down as she watched me pacing in circles. Susie was a real Southern belle, a brunette with delicate freckles and a slim figure, but her pretty brown eyes were now filled with concern.

"It's a new virus, right?" Chuck ventured.

I wasn't a security expert, but I was trained as an electrical engineer, and computer networks were my field of expertise. "Sort of," I tried to explain. "A zero day is a software vulnerability that isn't yet documented, and a zero day attack uses these to get into a system. It's an attack that has had zero days to be analyzed yet."

Any system had weaknesses. The ones that were known usually had patches or fixes, and the list of new software vulnerabilities expanded at the rate of hundreds per week for the thousands of commercial vendors in the world. With a typical Fortune 500 company using thousands of individual software programs, the list of vulnerabilities could hover in the tens of thousands at any given moment. It was an impossible game of catch-up against an adversary that only needed one hole to remain open among literally millions that an organization had to continually fix.

While everyone, private and government, struggled to keep up with the list of known vulnerabilities, against unknown vulnerabilities, or zero-days, the situation was even worse. There was nearly no defense, precisely because the attack vectors were, by definition, unknown.

Chuck and Susie stared at me blankly.

"It means an attack that we have no defense against."

Stuxnet, the virus believed to have taken down Iranian nuclear processing plants in 2010, had used about ten zero days to get inside the systems it attacked. It was one of the first of a new breed of sophisticated cyberweapons. They cost a lot of time and money to build, so someone wouldn't be unleashing these ones without some purpose in mind.

"What do you mean, an attack that we have no defense against?" asked Susie. "How many of these are there? Can't the government stop it?"

"The government mostly looks to the private sector to protect this stuff," I replied.

CNN had switched to a discussion between four commentators and analysts. *"The thing that has me worried, Roger, is that computer viruses, especially sophisticated ones like this, are usually designed to infiltrate networks to get information out. These don't seem to be doing that. They're just bringing the computer systems down."*

"What does that mean?" asked Susie, staring at the TV screen.

As if answering her question, the analyst looked straight into the camera. *"The only thing I can assume is that we're being purposely attacked, with the only goal of inflicting as much damage as possible."*

Susie brought one hand up to cover her mouth. Saying nothing, I sat down next to them and tried calling Lauren for the dozenth time.

Where is she?

5:30 P.M.

"I'm sorry."

Lauren was gripping Luke in her arms, her knuckles white. When we'd retrieved him from the Borodins', he was crying great wailing sobs. I'd tried feeding him, but he didn't want anything. His forehead was burning up.

"Sorry doesn't quite cut it," I complained. "Come on, give Luke back to me. I'll try feeding him again."

"I'm sorry, baby," whispered Lauren, speaking to Luke, not me. Her face was flushed scarlet from the cold outside, her hair a tangled mess.

"Why the hell didn't you answer my texts for four hours?"

We were back in our apartment, and it was dark outside. I'd spent the whole afternoon trying to get in touch with Lauren. At half past five she'd finally shown up at Chuck's door, asking questions about what was going on, asking where Luke was.

"I had my cell off. I forgot."

I avoided asking what she'd been doing. "And you didn't notice all this was going on?"

"No, Mike, I didn't. Not everyone's surgically attached to CNN. When I found out, I rushed straight home, but there were no taxis and the Two and Three lines weren't working, so I had to walk twenty blocks in the freezing cold. Have you ever tried running in high heels?"

I rolled my eyes. Everyone's nerves were on edge, and it wasn't any use fighting. Sighing, I relaxed my shoulders. "Why don't you try feeding him?" I said. "Maybe if Mommy tries he'll eat."

Luke had stopped crying and was sniffling. Picking up a wet wipe from a plastic container on our coffee table, I tried to clean his face. He fussed and shifted his head back and forth, leaning back out of my reach.

Lauren peered into his face and put a hand to his forehead. "He really is burning up."

I took another look at him. "It's just a little winter cold." He looked unhappy, but not that bad.

My cell phone pinged a text message. Lauren's phone chirped as well, and through the open doorway to our apartment I could hear Chuck's and Susie's phones too. Frowning, I pulled my phone from my pocket and swiped the code to open it, clicking open the new text message. It was from the NY-ALERT emergency notification service Chuck had encouraged us to subscribe to: *Health Advisory Warning: Widespread infection bird flu H5N1 New York Connecticut. Highly pathogenic. Advise public stay indoors, emergency closure Fairfield County & Manhattan Financial District & outlying areas.*

"What is it?"

Looking up in horror, I watched Lauren wiping mucus from Luke's face with her hand, wetly kissing his bare cheek. I remembered taking Luke out to meet my clients in the days before, my mind filling with images of him getting kisses from people in Chinatown, Little Italy, all over the place. And then there was that Chinese family down the hall—the wife's parents had just arrived from the mainland. *Did I expose him to something?*

"What?" asked Lauren, her voice rising as she saw my face.

"Honey, put Luke down for a second and go wash your hands."

The words from my mouth sounded strange, like they were being spoken by some alien being. My mind raced, my heart pounded in my chest. *It's just a false alarm, it's just a cold.* The irrational fear I'd felt running back from Whole Foods flooded my veins again.

"What do you mean, put Luke down?" demanded Lauren. "Mike! What are you talking about? What was in that message?"

Chuck appeared in our doorway, and Lauren looked up at him. I'd crossed over to Luke and Lauren, holding a blanket I'd grabbed from the couch. I was wrapping it around Luke, trying to take him from her.

"It's just a precaution," said Chuck, advancing slowly into the room with his hands held out in front of him. "I'm sure it's just a coincidence. We don't know what's happening."

"What don't you know is happening?"

Lauren looked up at me and, trusting but not understanding, released Luke.

"Report of a bird flu outbreak," I whispered.

"WHAT?"

"We haven't heard anything on the news—" Chuck started to say, and then we heard the TV announcer's voice floating in from their apartment next door. "*Breaking news—Connecticut-area hospitals have just reported an outbreak of bird flu virus—*"

Lauren shot up and reached for Luke. "Give him back to me!"

I didn't resist. She glared at me, and I shrank back.

"He's right, Lauren," said Chuck, continuing to approach her. "I'm sure it's nothing, but this isn't just about you or him. We're all at risk."

"Then stay away from us!" She turned to me, the veins in her neck flaring. "So that was your first reaction? To quarantine your infant son?"

"—*CDC in Atlanta cannot confirm or deny the outbreak, saying that they don't know where the warning originated but that local emergency workers—*"

"That's not what I was doing. I was worried about you." I waved the blanket around in the air. "I don't know, what's the proper reaction when a deadly virus is announced?"

Lauren was about to unload a return salvo when Susie appeared behind Chuck. She was cradling Ellarose in one arm. "Keep calm, y'all. This ain't no time for fighting with each other. I know it's been tough between you two lately, but that's gotta stop."

Susie walked into the middle of the room, keeping her free hand up high, palm outwards in a calming gesture.

"Susie, I think you should take Ellarose back into—" I started to say.

"No, no," she objected. "If it's done, it's done, and we're all in this together."

Ellarose saw Luke and squeaked. Luke, puffy and congested, looked over at her and attempted a grin in return.

"Let's not go making mountains out of molehills," continued Susie. "Luke's got a little cold is all. This is a strange day, so let's all calm down."

With her steady words, the tension began to evaporate.

"How about I just take Luke down to emergency to make sure," I said after a pause. "He is sick, and I don't mind going." I smiled at Lauren. "Just to be sure."

"Wait a minute, that could be about the worst thing to do,"

objected Chuck. "Hospitals are the worst place to be if there's really an outbreak."

"But what if he is infected?" I replied, my voice on edge. "I need to know, no matter what, get him taken care of."

Lauren glanced at me. "We'll go together."

"I'll go and get some masks from downstairs," said Chuck. "You should at least wear masks."

Susie gave him an evil look.

"I'm being practical. Bird flu is twice as deadly as bubonic plague."

"What's wrong with you?" said Susie, exasperated.

"No, it's a good idea," agreed Lauren, gripping Luke. "Get the masks."

7 : 0 0   P . M .

Chuck went downstairs to raid his storage locker while we moved back into their place to watch CNN. He came back up loaded down with hockey bags stuffed with equipment and supplies.

After setting it all down in the middle of the room, he fished around, pulling out bags of freeze-dried food and camping equipment before finding the medical masks. They looked like the ones you'd wear if you were spray-painting something. He handed them out and then went out to distribute some to the neighbors.

Chuck tried to get us to wear latex gloves, but Lauren refused, and so did I. The idea of holding our infant son in gloves, protecting ourselves like he was some kind of pariah, was too much to seriously consider. If he was sick from whatever they were talking about on the news, we were already infected, so there was no sense in it. Wearing the masks was more to protect other people.

But in the outside world, who knew? Luke probably just had a cold, and we might be walking into a mass of infected people in a hospital. It was impossible to say, but we had to be sure Luke was safe. I put some of the latex gloves into the pockets of my jeans.

Susie went down the hall to see if Pam, the nurse, was home yet. I was hoping she might take a look at Luke, or sneak us in the back entrance of a hospital somewhere, but no luck. She and Rory weren't home. We tried their phones, but the cell networks were completely jammed.

While Chuck talked about how to recognize the signs of infectious diseases, dispensing advice about not touching or wiping our faces, I combed through a White Pages looking for nearby clinics and hospitals, scribbling the information on a piece of paper. I was relieved to find the phone book, stuck in the bottom drawer of a kitchen cabinet. I hadn't seen one in years. My first impulse had been to search the map on my smartphone, but the screen remained stubbornly blank. It was getting no incoming data feed. My usual stream of messages, after a brief flood of concerned e-mails from friends, had stopped as well. I couldn't access the Internet at all. Neither my smartphone nor my laptop would load any Web pages, or at least not anything intelligible. When I tried Google, either nothing would load and an error message would pop onto the screen, or a random Web page would appear: an African tourism site or a college student's blog. So I scribbled on paper.

As we left the apartment, half of our neighbors were out in the hall, talking in quiet whispers with masks hanging around their necks. They edged away from us as we walked out, mostly away from Lauren, who held Luke. The Chinese family at the end of the hall wisely stayed inside. Richard had called down for his car service to drive us, and I wanted to thank him, but as I held my hand out, he shrank away and put his mask on, muttering that we'd better hurry.

Outside, Richard's black Escalade and driver were waiting for us. The driver, Marko, was already wearing a mask. It was the first time I'd met him, but Lauren seemed to know him.

First we tried the Presbyterian clinic just around the corner on

Twenty-Fourth. It was listed as open, but when we arrived, people were streaming out and telling us it was closed. We circled around to the Beth Israel clinic nearby, but there was a line stretching onto the street already. We didn't even stop.

Lauren cradled Luke in layers of blankets, humming lullabies to him. He'd given up crying and was just sniffling and squirming. He could sense something was wrong, that we were scared.

The warmest things we'd been able to find in our closet for Lauren were a leather jacket and scarf, and I was still wearing the thin jacket and sweater from earlier. It was warm inside the Escalade, but bitterly cold outside.

I found myself worrying that Marko would abandon us somewhere if it got too late. *He must have a family somewhere too.* It would be impossible to find a taxi, with all this going on, and Lauren had said that the subways weren't working either. I tried bringing this up with Marko, but he just said not to worry, that everything was fine, that we could trust him.

I still worried.

The streets of New York had transformed from holiday festive to cold and desolate. Long lines of people snaked out of convenience and grocery stores and outside bank machines, and there were long queues of cars waiting for gas at the stations. People hurried down the streets, loaded with bags and packages, nobody speaking, everyone staring at the ground. None of the packages looked like Christmas gifts. New Yorkers always had the feeling that their city was a target, and now it seemed, from the hunched shoulders and furtive glances I saw on the streets outside, that the monster was rearing its head again.

It was a collective wound that had never quite healed, affecting anyone who came here. When Lauren and I had moved into the condo in Chelsea, she'd been concerned that we were too close to the Financial District. I'd told her not to be silly. *Had I made a terrible mistake?*

We stopped at the emergency clinic at the Greater New York Hospital on Ninth between Fifteenth and Sixteenth. The place was swarming with people, and not just sick-looking people, but crazy-looking ones too. The woodwork of the city was opening up. I got out and tried to talk to the police and EMTs at the entrance, but they shook their heads and said it was like this all over the city. Lauren waited inside the car, her eyes following me as I walked around trying to find someone to talk to, anyone that might be able to help. One of the cops suggested St. Jude Children's up at Penn Plaza on Thirty-Fourth.

I jumped back in the car.

On the drive to St. Jude's, Luke started crying again, wailing now, his face red and apoplectic with each shrill scream. Lauren trembled and began crying as well. I put my arm around the two of them, insisting it would be okay. Finally reaching St. Jude, we saw there was no crowd of people outside the emergency room, so we jumped out and ran in, only to be confronted by a mass of people inside.

A triage nurse gave us a quick inspection, replacing our masks with ones she called N95s, and we were immediately cordoned off into a set of rooms that were crammed with other parents and children. I found a chair for Lauren in one corner, next to a leaking water fountain, beneath yellowing posters about the importance of the food pyramid for young children's health. We waited for what felt like hours. Finally, another nurse appeared and led us into an examination room, saying that seeing a doctor wouldn't be possible, but that she'd have a look.

After quickly examining Luke, she said it looked like a cold and that there had been no cases of bird flu in their hospital. She promised us that they had no idea what the news was talking about and gave us some Children's Tylenol, asking politely but firmly if we could go home. There was nothing else we could do.

I felt powerless.

True to his word, Marko was waiting outside when we came out. The cold was intense. Opening the car door for Lauren and Luke, I felt my hands become numb. The wind cut through my thin jacket, and long plumes of vapor spun into the air with each tired breath. A few tiny snowflakes had begun to fall. The idea of a white Christmas usually excited me, but now it felt ominous.

On the drive back, New York was as quiet as a morgue.

3:35 A.M.

"I am not leaving them here!" I heard Susie shouting through the doorway.

"That's not what I'm saying," Chuck replied in a quieter voice.

Hanging back, I hesitated but then knocked. Footsteps padded toward me and the door opened, spilling bright light into the hallway.

"Ah, hey," said Chuck awkwardly, rubbing the back of his neck with one hand. "I guess you heard all that?"

"Not really."

He smiled. "Uh-huh. You okay? You want a cup of tea? Chamomile or something?"

I shook my head and walked in. "No thanks."

Their place, a two-bedroom apartment only slightly larger than ours, was filled with boxes and bags. Susie was sitting on the couch, an oasis in the middle of the confusion piled around her, looking embarrassed. They weren't wearing their masks, so I took mine off.

"You get a new mask?" asked Chuck.

"They gave us N95s or something. I don't know what that means."

Chuck snorted. "N95, hah! The one I gave you was way better

than 95 percent. You shouldn't have let them take it. I'll get you some more."

"It's like he's preparing for World War Three," Susie laughed. "You sure you don't want a cup of something hot?"

"Not hot, but maybe something strong."

"Ah, yes," said Chuck, heading to the kitchen. He produced a bottle of Scotch and two tumblers from a cupboard. "Ice, no ice?"

"Neat is fine."

He poured a generous dose into both glasses.

"So how's Luke?" asked Susie. "What did the doctors say?"

"We didn't manage to see one. A nurse examined him and didn't say much except it didn't look like bird flu. He's got a fever of a hundred and three. Lauren's taken him to bed and lain down with him. They're sleeping for now."

"That's good news, right? Pam came back when you were out, said you can wake her up if you want. She has a degree in tropical medicine, I think."

I wasn't sure how tropical medicine might help in this situation, but I knew Chuck was trying to be comforting. It was reassuring that Pam was nearby. "It can wait till the morning."

"So what would you think of a little vacation in Virginia?" asked Chuck as he handed my drink over.

"Virginia?"

"Yeah, you know, our old family place in the hills near the Shenandoah? It's in the national park, only a few cabins on the whole mountain."

"Ahhh," I replied, the light dawning. "Time to bug out?"

He motioned toward the TV, still on but with the sound muted. The headline scrolling across CNN was about a bird flu outbreak being reported in California.

"Nobody knows what the hell is going on. Half the country thinks it's terrorists, the other half an attack by the Chinese, and another half thinks it's nothing at all."

"That's a lot of halves."

"Glad you have a sense of humor."

Taking a sip from his drink, he grabbed the remote from the kitchen counter and turned up the volume on CNN. "*Unconfirmed reports of bird flu have been springing up all over the country, with the latest in San Francisco and Los Angeles, where health officials have quarantined two major hospitals . . .*"

I sighed and took a big gulp of my drink. "I most absolutely do not find this funny."

"Emergency services all over the country are screwed, cell phone networks jammed," said Chuck. "It's a total mess out there."

"Don't need to tell me. You should see the hospitals. Has the CDC confirmed anything?"

"They confirmed the emergency notifications, but nobody's been able to get in to find out what's going on."

"It's taking that long? It's been ten hours already."

Chuck shook his head. "With the Internet down and this Scramble virus messing with logistics, nobody knows where anyone is or what they should be doing."

Rubbing my eyes, I took another sip and looked out the window. It was snowing in earnest now, and a steady stream of flakes flashed out of the darkness, spinning and swirling with the wind.

Chuck followed my eyes. "These storms coming, it's going to be worse than Christmas a few years back, like a frozen Sandy."

I hadn't been in New York for the big blizzard in 2010 that had dumped over two feet of snow the day after Christmas, but I'd heard about it: seven-foot-high drifts in Central Park, with waist-deep snow in the middle of the streets. There were snowstorms almost as bad every year now. I'd been here for Hurricane Sandy, though, and a frozen version of that frightened me. New York had become a magnet for perfect storms.

"You guys should just get going," I said, watching the snow. "We can't leave. Not with Luke sick like this. He needs to rest, and we need to be close to hospitals."

"We're not leaving you here," said Susie firmly, looking at Chuck. He shrugged and finished off his drink.

"Charles Mumford," she continued after a pause, "don't be ridiculous. All this is going to blow over. You're being dramatic."

"Dramatic?" shot back Chuck, almost throwing his glass at the TV as he pointed at it. "Have you been watching the same stuff I have? China declaring war, a biological attack spread across the country, communications down—"

"Don't exaggerate. They did not declare war. That was just some minister puffing his chest for the cameras," countered Susie. "Anyway, look at all this stuff." She motioned around the apartment. "By God, we could hole up in here and survive till *next* Christmas with all this."

Finishing my drink, I tried to calm the mood. "I don't want you guys to fight. I think this will blow over and by tomorrow morning things will calm down." I turned to Chuck. "If you want to get going, I totally understand. Do what's best for your family. I mean it." I looked him in the eye, smiling, trying to convey my seriousness. Sighing, I added, "I need to get some sleep."

Chuck scratched his head and put his glass down on the kitchen counter. "Me too. I'll see you later, buddy." He walked over and hugged me, taking my glass.

Susie got up and gave me a kiss on the cheek. "We'll see you in the morning," she whispered in my ear, hugging me tightly.

"Please go if he wants," I whispered back.

Closing the door behind me as I left, I quietly opened our apartment door. After locking the door, I crept into the bedroom, softly closing that door as well. My whole world was lying on the bed in front of me. In the ghostly glow from the LED display on our bedside alarm clock, I could just make out the lumps that were Lauren and Luke. The room smelled humid and lived-in, like a nest, and that thought brought a smile to my face. I stood still and watched them, feeling wonder and joy, their rhythmic breathing soothing my senses.

Luke coughed and took in two or three quick, deep breaths, as if he couldn't breathe properly, but then he sighed and quieted down.

Silently, I stripped down and slid under the covers. Luke was in the middle of the bed, so I curled up around him, with Lauren on the other side. Leaning over, I brushed a lock of hair away from Lauren's forehead and kissed her. She mumbled and I kissed her again, and then, with a deep breath, I pulled one of the pillows under my head and closed my eyes.

Everything is going to be fine.

DAY 2: CHRISTMAS EVE, DECEMBER 24
7:05 A.M.

I awoke with a start.

My dreams were filled with confused images of angry men in forests. I was flying, my grip on Luke slipping, and Lauren was gone, sliding down a stairwell, down into the earth, while I floated and floated. A scream pulled me out of the vision, layers of dreams snapping apart, until I sat bolt upright in bed, gasping.

Breathing hard, I looked around. It was pitch black. *Wait, not totally black.* A thin light hung like a gray halo around the outline of our bedroom curtains. Luke and Lauren were still beside me. Breathlessly, I leaned down to Luke. *He's still breathing, thank God.*

It was quiet. Lauren shifted slightly. Everything was fine. Shivering, I pulled the covers around me and put my head back down on the pillow. Slowly, my heart calmed its thumping, and a dead silence descended.

It's too dark. I checked the clock beside my head. It was off, blank. *We must be having a power failure.* I picked up my cell phone from the night stand: 7:05 a.m. It was early, and it was freezing.

Quietly, I slipped off the side of the bed, rummaging in the hamper for my bathrobe, and then felt around on the floor for my slippers. Wrapping the robe around me, I shivered and left the bedroom.

The main room of our apartment was equally dead. None of the familiar little lights, none of the glowing time displays on the appliances. The little Christmas tree on the side table was completely dark. Outside, snow swept by the windows in the muted half-light, the pressure of the wind against the glass the only thing audible, a dull thudding with each squall of flakes.

Walking to our entranceway, I tapped the digital thermostat on the wall. It was also blank. I crept back into the bedroom and quietly pulled an extra blanket from the closet and laid it across Luke and Lauren, and then pulled out a sweater for myself, feeling unprepared for whatever was happening.

I decided to go and see if Susie and Chuck were up. Pulling on some jeans and sneakers and the sweater, I tiptoed next door.

Out in the hallway, the emergency lighting was on, a harsh, white light that spread out from floodlights above the exit stairwell, casting long shadows behind me in the empty space. Standing in front of Chuck's place, I hesitated but then knocked, and then again after a pause.

No response at all. *Could they have left?* I had a hard time imagining that they'd just leave like that, but then again . . .

I knocked once again, firmly this time, demanding their attention, but there was still no answer. I tried the door handle, and it easily clicked around, the door silently sliding open in front of me. Inside, the curtains were drawn back, and in the dim light I could see the jumble of bags still on the floor. I looked in the bedrooms, checked in the bathroom, but no Chuck or Susie or Ellarose.

Maybe they left all this stuff for us?

Pulling the blanket off their bed, I wrapped it around myself and shuffled into the living room, collapsing onto their couch. Fear crept into the pit of my stomach. *What happened? Why is the power off? And why didn't Chuck wake me if something went wrong?*

I thought of trying to reach my brothers, to see if they were okay. They had an oil furnace in the old house, with enough oil to last the winter, so at least they'd be warm if anything went wrong over there. My brothers were resourceful. I shouldn't worry about them.

The wind drove hard against the windows, echoing in the lifeless room. *Lifeless.* That's how it felt without the comforting, low-level thrum of the machines, without their little lights blinking, motors whirring, unseen but ever present, surrounding me in an electronic cocoon.

But one light would still work. My cell phone still had power, at least for now. I felt its pull like a phantom limb. *Maybe I should go check it, see if I have any messages and remove the battery, save the charge, just in case.* Maybe the cell networks weren't as jammed up anymore. *Or maybe a landline? Do they have their own power?* I thought so, trying to remember if I'd used a landline during a previous power failure, but I couldn't think of anyone who still had one.

I needed to find out what was going on, but how? *A radio.* They'd still be broadcasting. I didn't have a battery-powered radio, but I was sure Chuck must have left one in one of these bags. *Thank God he left all this stuff.*

I glanced out the windows again. It looked brutal outside. Yesterday morning my biggest problem was figuring out how to deliver some Christmas gifts—how quickly the world had changed.

What if Luke is really sick? What if an epidemic is raging out in that snowstorm?

"Little help here?"

My head swiveled around to find Chuck in the doorway, sagging under a load of bags and backpacks. He was trying to wedge himself through.

Stuck in the doorway, Chuck frowned. "Hey, are you okay? Is Luke okay?"

I don't think I was ever so glad to see anyone in my life. I wiped my eyes with the back of one hand. "Everything's fine."

"If you say so." Again he tried to force his way through, and again he asked, "A little help here?"

Shaking my head to clear it, I jumped up to grab some bags. Susie, also carrying bags, appeared behind him with Ellarose strapped to her chest. Tony, our doorman, was behind her and carrying even more than Chuck. Everyone was sweating, and they haphazardly dropped their loads as they entered.

"Want me to do another trip?" asked Tony, breathing heavy, leaning over.

"Why don't you take a break with Susie and Ellarose?" Chuck sighed, wiping his forehead with one arm. "Maybe fire up some coffee on the butane burner? Me and Mike'll get the generator."

The generator? Now it was my turn to frown. "Sounds heavy."

"It is heavy," laughed Chuck. "Come on, chubby, time to get your workout."

Leaving the rest of them behind, Chuck and I walked to the emergency exit to go down the stairs. The elevators weren't working. It was the first time I'd ever been in the stairwell, and the sounds of our feet on the bare metal steps echoed off the cinder block walls.

"So what happened?" I asked as we descended the first set of stairs.

"Power went off about five and I've been running up and down since then, grabbing as much stuff as I can before everyone else wakes up."

"Before everyone wakes up?"

"Call me paranoid, but I'd prefer if as few people as possible know how much stuff we're going to have socked away in Fort Mumford."

His apartment was already a military base. I wondered where the perimeter was. "What I meant was, what *happened* with the power? Why's it so cold?"

"It's cold because the power's out, and this building is wired for control using the Internet. There's oil in the furnace, but all the controls are digital and the networks aren't working."

"Aha." I remembered that a big selling point of this new building was the array of fancy building controls that used the Internet, letting you control the temperature of each room in your house remotely from Hong Kong if you wanted. The problem was that the onsite controls were run off IP networks, and from what Chuck was saying, they were down. "Shouldn't the backup generator come on?"

"It should have, but it didn't fire up, and it wouldn't run the heating vents anyway. All the building staff are gone. There's already a foot of snow, and more coming fast. National Guard's been called out, and they're telling everyone to stay put. We've gotta do this ourselves."

"Why'd Tony stay?"

"He sent his mom down to Tampa for the holidays to see her sister, remember?"

I nodded. "So, again, *what happened* with the power?"

Chuck stopped on the third landing, halfway down. "I was

scanning the news channels at about four forty-five when they started reporting power outages in Connecticut, and then, blammo, just after five, the lights went out."

"Is it the snowstorm?" The alternatives were frightening.

"Maybe."

"Did they say anything else about the bird flu?"

"Just a muddled mess," he replied with a shrug. "Nobody knows what's going on." He jogged down a few more steps. "Borders are shut down, international travel halted," he continued, detailing a worldwide crisis like items on a breakfast menu. "CDC can't confirm or deny anything, but hospitals everywhere are flooded with people reporting symptoms. They're saying it's some kind of coordinated biological attack, but I don't buy it."

"Why?"

Chuck's conspiracy-bent mind was always looking behind the news to seek out the "real" story, but for once I was eager to hear his theories. We arrived on the ground floor and exited to the lobby to take the basement stairs down. We stopped in the white marble foyer beside the Japanese garden, now starkly illuminated by the emergency lighting.

"Do you know that nearly 90 percent of the emergency notification systems in America are all supplied by the same company?"

"So?"

"Hack that one company and, wham, instant access to nationwide chaos."

"Why would someone do that?"

"Chaos, terror. But I have another theory." He opened the door to the basement. "Invasion." He walked down ahead of me.

I hurried after him. "Invasion?"

Chuck swung open the door to the first storage locker and began checking box tags with a flashlight. "Think about it. Disrupt government services, cut off supply lines and transportation, eliminate communications, and then confine civilians indoors before decimating the industrial base, in this case by cutting off power. It's the same cyberattack profile that the Russians used when they rolled into Georgia in 2008, more or less."

"That doesn't make any sense."

He found the box he was looking for and dragged it out. "I mean Georgia in Asia, not the Georgia with Atlanta."

"I got that."

He opened the box and looked back at me. "Come on, son, grab an end."

Leaning down, I picked up one end of the generator in the box, grunting to bear its weight as he lifted the other end, and we began shuffle-walking it toward the stairs. For the next few minutes we struggled up. It wasn't *that* heavy, but it was awkward, and it felt like we were carrying a body. I needed a break by the time we got to the third landing.

"Stop," I panted, putting the generator down and groaning while I stretched my back. "How much does this thing weigh?"

"The box said a hundred and twenty. It's a beauty, runs on gas, diesel, pretty much anything that'll explode."

"Vodka?"

"That we drink," he laughed.

Taking a deep breath, I wiped the sweat streaming down my temples. "Nobody has ever invaded America. You can't be serious."

Chuck laughed. "The Canadians did. They even burned the White House down."

"That was a long time ago, and it was more of a stunt than an invasion."

"History tends to repeat itself." He motioned down at the generator. "Come on, boy."

I took a deep breath, stretching my back again, and then leaned over to pick up the generator. "So your big idea is that we're being invaded by the Canadians?"

"Would explain the snow, *eh*?" he laughed. "Maybe not literally the same thing, but it's an idea."

"It is an idea." I rolled my eyes. *Blame Canada.*

I grunted and groaned my way up another two flights before begging off for another break. Chuck was sweating but looked comfortable, and he'd been doing this for hours already. I couldn't even hear him breathing but realized it would be hard to hear anything above my own labored wheezing and pounding heart. I decided my New Year's resolution would be to get a new gym membership, and more than that, to actually go.

Just then the door beside us, on the fifth-floor landing, swung open and banged hard into Chuck. In the open doorway I found myself staring directly into someone's headlamp.

"Oh, wow, sorry!" whoever it was exclaimed.

Chuck yelped at the impact, dancing backwards and shaking one hand. The man stepped into the stairwell, peering around the door.

"Sorry about that, I didn't think—"

"No worries," said Chuck, regaining his composure, but still massaging the hand the door had hit.

We all eyeballed one another for a second.

"Do you guys know what happened to the power?"

"We know as much as you," I replied. "I'm Mike, and this is Chuck."

"Yeah, I recognize you guys. I seen you going in and out sometimes."

I didn't recognize him, but there were a lot of people in the building.

"I'm Paul," he said, and then after a pause added, "from 514."

He stretched out his hand, and I began to extend mine, but Chuck pushed me back.

"Sorry," said Chuck, squinting into the light of Paul's headlamp. "Can't be too careful, that bird flu warning and all. Hey, could you turn that off?"

"Sure." Paul turned off his headlamp and looked down at the generator. "What's that?"

Chuck hesitated. "It's a generator."

"Like, from the building or something?"

"No, it's ours."

"You got any stuff we could borrow?"

"Sorry. We just got this," lied Chuck. "Left over from a job site I was working on."

"Oh yeah?"

Chuck stared at him. The pause became uncomfortable. "Yeah. And if you don't mind, we need to get going."

Paul shrugged. "Okay, just looking for a little neighborly help. This is some weird shit going on. Have you seen the snow outside? You can barely see the cars anymore."

Another second or two of uncomfortable silence.

"Well, good luck," said Chuck, motioning for me to pick up my end again. He picked his up with only one hand this time. "I'm sure the power will be up soon and we're just wasting our time."

We started up the stairs, and Paul went down, opening the door on the fourth floor and disappearing.

As soon we reached our floor, Chuck dropped his end. "Did you see his pants?"

I shook my head. "Why?"

"Soaked from the knees down, and his sneakers were soaked as well. He must have been outside."

"So what? Maybe he went out to have a look."

"At seven in the morning? I've never seen that guy before. Tony must have left the front door to the building open. And why in the hell did he go straight onto the fourth floor like that?"

"Maybe it's just a neighbor you don't recognize," I countered, but the hair on my neck prickled. *An intruder.*

"You drag this the rest of the way to our place. I'm going downstairs to lock things up."

Chuck rushed off down the stairs, taking them two at a time, and I watched him vanish as the hollow echoes of his footsteps faded. Opening the door to our floor, I leaned down, grunted, and pulled on the generator.

10:05 A.M.

Despite everything, the rest of the morning took on a festive air.

As soon as Chuck returned from locking up downstairs, I went over to knock on Pam's door and asked her to have a look at Luke. Tony went down and double-checked the front door, leaving a note saying he could be found up at Chuck's place.

Chuck instituted a strict rule that only our gang, which included Tony, would be allowed into their apartment. He made an exception for Pam, and after some protest, for her husband, Rory. After he fired up a kerosene heater, the apartment quickly warmed, and we woke up Lauren and Luke and moved them into Chuck and Susie's spare room.

After performing a quick inspection, Pam declared that Luke definitely didn't look symptomatic of bird flu, at least from what she understood, and that his fever was breaking. He still had a temperature of 102, dangerous but manageable, and she promised to stay close and check in on him.

Pam had been up all night at the Red Cross blood bank. It had transformed into an emergency clinic, with volunteer doctors appearing almost as quickly as the flood of people claiming symptoms. One of the doctors there had worked at the CDC doing research on avian flu. Pam had had a long chat with him about what was going on, and he'd explained that the news didn't make any sense—incubation, transmission, symptoms, and so on. It looked like it really was a false, or fake, alarm.

Our run-in with the suspected intruder was quickly forgotten, and Chuck insisted on opening a bottle of champagne to pour mimosas for everyone. It was Christmas Eve, he proclaimed, and a white Christmas at that, he added, looking out the window at the driving blizzard beyond. We all managed to laugh.

As we huddled together in the room that morning, warm and safe and unpacking Chuck's equipment as if we were on an indoor camping trip, the sense of danger disappeared. My baby boy was sick with a fever, but it was such a relief that it was just a regular flu or cold, I felt almost overjoyed.

In the background we kept a radio turned on. The broadcaster detailed the road closures—I-95, I-89, the New Jersey Turnpike— and the running tally of homes without power, estimated at ten million and counting across the Northeast. The subway system was shut down. They said the power failure was some kind of electrical cascade in the network, same as had happened a few years ago, and the snowstorm was making it worse.

The voice of the radio announcer, this small connection to the outside world, lent the morning a feeling of familiarity, the same as any other disaster day that New Yorkers would rally from to begin the process of rebuilding. Reports coming in on the bird flu scare were bearing out our feelings—the CDC couldn't confirm any cases, and they hadn't been able to identify the source of the warning.

Buoyed by the alcohol in the mimosa, I went next door to check on the Borodins. I remembered that Irena's daughter and family, who lived in a building next door, had gone away for the holidays, so they were alone. The radio was reminding us to check on the elderly, but I had a feeling the Borodins were just fine.

I went anyway.

Knocking on their door, I heard Irena telling me to come in, and I entered to find them as usual. Irena was sitting in her rocking chair, knitting, and Aleksandr was sitting asleep in his lounger, in front of a blank TV, with Gorbachev at his side. The only difference was that they were bundled up under blankets. It was freezing in their place.

"Some tea?" offered Irena.

Watching her carefully finish another stitch, I wished for hands as nimble as hers when I was ninety. *I'd be happy just to get to ninety.* "Yes, please."

They'd set up what looked like an antique camp stove in their kitchen, and a pot of hot tea sat steaming on it. The Borodins were Jewish, but they had a large holiday tree, beautifully decorated, occupying nearly half of their living room. I'd been surprised last year when they'd asked me to help them get a tree, but I'd learned that this wasn't a Christmas tree, but a New Year tree. It was the nicest one on our floor, whatever it was called.

Irena went to her pantry door, opening it to get some sugar for the tea, and for the first time I noticed their pantry was stacked, floor to ceiling, with cans and bags of beans and rice. She noticed me looking.

"Old habits die hard," she said, smiling as she returned to pour the tea. "How is the little prince?"

"He's good. I mean, he's sick, but he'll be okay," I answered, wrapping my hands around the cup of tea. "Isn't it awfully cold in here? Do you want to come over to Chuck's?"

"Ah," she snorted, waving away my concern, "dis is not cold. I spent winters in shacks in Siberia after the war. Sorry for you, but I opened the windows for some fresh air."

Aleksandr let out a particularly loud snore. We laughed.

"Do you need anything?" I cocked my thumb toward Chuck's place. "Just come next door, anytime."

She shook her head. "Ah, no. We'll be fine. Stay quiet, not bother anyone." Taking a sip from her tea, she considered something and looked at me. "If *you* need anything, Mih-kah-yal, you remember, you come here, *da*? We will be watching."

I said I would, and we chatted for a bit. I was struck by how calm Irena was. The power failure struck a chord deep within me, making me feel as if I'd lost a sense, as if I was blind or deaf without the hum of the machines. Next door, surrounded by Chuck's gadgets and gizmos and the steady noise of the radio broadcaster, I felt almost normal again. At Irena's, though, it felt different; colder certainly, but also calmer and more secure. She was from a different generation. I guessed the machines weren't a part of them like they were for us.

Thanking her for the tea, I went back to check on Luke. A collection of neighbors had congregated in the hallway. Bundled up in winter jackets and scarves, they looked much less happy than I felt.

"Goddamn building administration!" growled Richard as I came out of the Borodins'. "Someone's going to lose their job for this. Do you have any heat?"

"No, but Chuck has some heating gadgets. You know how he is."

"Could I buy one from him?" Richard started toward me. "My place is bloody freezing."

Holding up my hand, I waved him back. "Sorry, but this bird

flu thing, we should keep our distance. I'll ask Chuck, but I don't think so."

Richard frowned but stopped.

I turned and opened the door to Chuck's, feeling warmth wash over my face, ready to have a laugh with him over my encounter with Richard, yet I found everyone sitting still, staring at the radio. "What?" I asked, closing the door behind me.

"Shhhhhh," said Lauren tensely.

"*The extent of the crash is still unknown, as is whether it was a derailment or a collision,*" said the radio.

"What happened?"

Chuck moved around the couch, pushing aside boxes and bags. He was favoring the hand the door had banged into, holding it up to his chest. The snow beat urgently against the windowpanes as the wind churned the air outside. I couldn't even see the next building, twenty feet away.

It was a complete whiteout.

"There's been a crash," murmured Chuck. "A train crash. Amtrak. Halfway between New York and Boston early this morning, but they didn't find it until now. At least, this is the first announcement."

"*—terrible loss of life, at least in the hundreds, if not from the crash itself then from freezing to death in the blizzard—*"

12:30 P.M.

"Why couldn't we have stuck this inside and vented it out?"

Even with heavy gloves, my hands were numb, and I was getting tired of leaning halfway out a window nearly a hundred feet above the ground. No matter how much I tried to shake it off, the driving snow piled up on my face and neck and melted uncomfortably into the nooks and crannies where clothing met skin.

"We don't have time to weld and pressure-test any joints," replied Chuck.

Mounting the generator outside their living-room window was proving to be harder than we'd thought. It didn't help that Chuck could barely use one hand. His injured hand had swollen up like an angry purple grapefruit.

Tony had gone to help some residents on the second floor, and Pam had returned to the Red Cross station. We had Lauren and Susie take the kids into the spare bedroom to play while we opened the windows. The apartment was freezing cold and awash with melting snow.

"A slow death by carbon monoxide poisoning *is* peaceful," added Chuck, "but not what I had in mind for Christmas."

"You almost done?" I groaned.

"Just connecting cables."

I could hear him fumbling around and swearing.

"Okay, you can let go."

With a relieved sigh, I released the plywood platform we had the generator sitting on and leaned back into the apartment, swiveling my window closed as I did. Beside me, Chuck gave me a grin, his injured hand resting carefully on the generator. He pulled on the starter chord with his good hand, and the generator stuttered and growled to life.

"Hope the goddamn thing doesn't freeze out there," said Chuck, closing up the window with the generator hanging outside it, but leaving a small gap for the power cords to get in.

The apartment had no balcony, and we didn't want to risk putting it on the fire escape in case someone got the idea to come up and steal it. So we'd balanced it outside a window on an improvised platform.

"I'm more worried about water getting into it," I mused. "Not sure it's weatherproofed for sitting under a foot of melting snow."

"We'll see, won't we?" Leaning against the window, he gingerly pulled off lengths of duct tape from a roll, handing them to me so I could seal up the gap. "With enough duct tape, you can fix anything," he laughed.

"Perfect. I'll give you a thousand rolls and send you down to Con Edison to get the power back on."

We both laughed at that.

The radio was giving continual updates about the train crash, the increasing severity of the storm, and the power failure. All of New England was paralyzed. It was another Frankenstorm— this one a powerful nor'easter colliding with a low-pressure system rising up from the southeast. They were predicting it would dump three to four feet in the New York area as it sat on the coast.

Fifteen million people and counting were without power, and many were without food, heat or access to emergency services.

The updates about the train accident were a mass of conflicting information. Some eyewitnesses said the military was onsite almost immediately but that news outlets didn't report the accident for several hours, leading to speculation that the military was trying to hide the accident for some reason, and no cause was reported.

As the scale of the storm became clear and rumors surrounding the train accident spread, the mood in the apartment shifted from cheerful to anxious.

Pulling off my hat and scarf, I unzipped the parka Chuck had lent me and shook off the crust of snow that had wedged down the back of my neck. Chuck walked to the kitchen counter, stepping around boxes and bags, to turn up the kerosene heater, and then began rummaging around for extension cords.

Just then there was a knock on the door and Pam appeared.

"Back so soon?" I asked.

Lauren and Susie heard the knock and came into the main room.

Pam looked around the room as if she was trapped. "I had to leave."

"What happened?" asked Lauren.

"Only one doctor and half the nurses showed up today. We did the best we could, but it turned from people worrying about bird flu to people asking for medications and demanding shelter, and then the emergency generator quit."

"My God," said Lauren, putting one hand to her mouth.

"We tried closing, but people refused to leave. The battery-powered emergency lights came on, but when we tried to force them out, people panicked and starting grabbing anything they could get their hands on—" Pam burst into tears, putting her face in her hands and trembling. "People aren't prepared because they assume that somebody else will always fix the problem, and they're usually right," she said tearfully. "But this time there's no help out there."

It was true. New Yorkers somehow felt invincible, no matter how dependent they were on their complex infrastructure for survival. In the small town outside Pittsburgh I'd come from, the power could go out any time from storms, or even a car hitting a pole, but in Manhattan a blackout for any length of time was almost incomprehensible. Typical emergency shopping lists for New Yorkers included things like wine, microwave popcorn and Häagen-Dazs, and their biggest issue during a disaster was often boredom.

"There's help in here, Pam," said Chuck. "Come on, sit down and have a cup of tea. We're about to start the show." He held up an extension cord and waggled it in the air.

Lauren put her arm around Pam, talking quietly and taking her to the kitchen to put some water on the propane burner. Chuck and I went back to connecting the extension cords to the generator. We were going to try to power up some lights and the TV to see what was happening on CNN.

"The gossip in the hallway is that it's more than just one train crash," Chuck whispered to me. "They're saying there was a plane crash at JFK, and more all over the country."

"Who said that?" I asked in a hushed voice, sitting on a box. "They didn't say anything on the radio." I sat silent for a moment. "Don't say anything to anyone."

Chuck looked at Lauren. "Did her family get out before the bird flu alert?"

Her mother and father were supposed to have left for Hawaii the day before.

"We didn't hear anything," I replied, realizing there was no way we could have heard anything.

"I hope GPS isn't knocked out in this mess," said Chuck. "There are over half a million people in the air at any time, and without GPS, the pilots flying over water would be reduced to dead reckoning."

I plugged in the last of the cables. "Let's just get CNN on. Should I do the honors?"

Chuck handed me the power bar we'd plugged the TV and lights into. He went to the couch and picked up the TV remote with his good hand.

"Everyone!" I announced. "We're ready to go. Can I get a countdown?"

Lauren came into the room. "Just plug it in, Mike. Quit fooling around."

I shrugged. "Okay, here we go."

When I plugged the power bar into the generator, several of the lights we'd set up around the room blinked to life, and the TV clicked on. At the same moment, all the other lights in the house came on, and appliances in the kitchen started beeping.

I looked at the plug in my hand in amazement. "How in the world?"

Chuck motioned behind me. I turned to see lights on in the building across from us, shining faintly through the snow squalls, and then my mind clicked. "The power came back on?"

Chuck nodded as he worked the controls on the remote. Everyone grabbed a cup of tea and crowded onto the couch. The TV screen glowed as Chuck found the right channel.

I steeled myself for the worst, expecting to see burning aircraft wreckage in a snowy landscape. The image flickered, blocky and pixilated, going blank and then returning before finally stabilizing. A fuzzy field of green appeared, unsteady as if filmed from a helicopter, and then what looked like a field of wrecked houses. *Destroyed houses.* The image zoomed out to reveal a scene of devastation in a green valley, with the sloping, rocky sides of a canyon rising up into mountaintops in the distance.

"What, is that like Montana or something?" I asked, trying to make sense of what we were seeing. The fuzzy text below the image seemed to say something about China. "Did the Chinese do this?"

"No," replied Chuck, "that *is* China."

The image flickered in and out again. We were getting sound in staccato bursts. I read what was on the screen: *Dam failure in China's Shanxi Province destroys town, hundreds feared dead.*

Then the sound became clear. "*—warning US forces to back down. Both sides are denying any responsibility. An emergency meeting of the UN Security Council has been convened, but China is refusing to attend, while the US has invoked Article Five of the NATO collective defense treaty.*"

"Are they declaring war?" said Chuck. He got up, walked to the TV, and banged on the cable box. The blocky image stabilized.

"*This is Professor Grant Latham from Annapolis, an expert in information warfare,*" said the CNN anchor. "*What can you tell us about what is happening, Professor?*"

"*This is textbook cyber-escalation,*" said Professor Latham. "*Power outages across China have been reported, and this dam accident appears to be one of several critical infrastructure failures, but we have no idea of the scope.*"

"*Cyber-escalation?*" asked the anchor.

"*An all-out attack on computer systems and networks.*"

The anchor considered this. "*Do you have any recommendations for how people could be preparing themselves, anything they could do?*"

Professor Latham took a deep breath and closed his eyes before opening them and looking straight at the camera.

"*Pray.*"

7:20 P.M.

"His fever has definitely broken," said Pam, looking at the readout from the baby thermometer.

She showed it to me—101—then passed it to Lauren, who leaned down into the crib to coo at Luke. His face was still mottled red, but he was fidgeting and crying less.

"And *that* is *definitely* broken," added Pam, examining Chuck's swollen left hand.

Chuck grimaced. "Not much we can do about it right now."

"I can wrap it up," suggested Pam.

"Maybe later. It's not so bad."

We'd invited Pam and Rory, along with Chuck and Susie, over to our place for dinner. With the power back on, the mood was upbeat but still nervous, and the snowstorm was getting worse. Nearly two feet of snow had fallen in the last twenty-four hours, with another storm, CNN had announced, coming close on its heels.

The weather outside, though, was taking second stage to the surreal drama playing out on the world's news networks. Images of the destroyed village in China and the storming of the US embassy in Taiyuan had been replaced by images of burning American flags in Tehran. A video denigrating Mohammed had appeared on an Iranian Web service and had quickly spread, sparking rioting in Pakistan and Bangladesh.

It seemed the world had turned against us.

The source of the video was unknown, and the Iranians were claiming it was the US government. The Iranian president was claiming that the East Coast storms, power failures, and bird flu outbreaks were the divine hand of God, striking down evil America.

The idea of the video coming from the US government was complete nonsense, and was of course denied, but it was just one thing in a long list that governments around the world were denying that day. Nobody was claiming responsibility for recent events, yet *somebody* had brought the world to a screeching halt. The Internet had slowed to a crawl worldwide, bringing business and communications down with it. Europe was nearly as affected as America—the chaos had triggered runs on banks and long food lines, as well as rioting in Spain and Portugal. The only relatively unaffected areas were the Halal Internet of Iran, China behind its Great Firewall, and North Korea, which was barely even connected to the Internet. America was the most connected, however, and was suffering the most from whatever was happening. Conspiracy theories flooded the airwaves.

In spite of all this, or perhaps because of it, Susie had insisted on preparing a proper holiday dinner. Tony was going to join us. I'd even offered to invite Richard and his wife, but Lauren was uncomfortable with the suggestion.

"Why all of a sudden don't you want to have Richard here?" I'd teased. Chuck had rolled his eyes at me, but I wasn't able to resist. "He's been your best friend lately."

"I don't think it's a good idea," she'd replied. By that point

Chuck was shaking his head at me, and Susie was eyeing me as well, so I let it go.

We were using our apartment for dinner since theirs was full of bags and bottles of water. We shared the tasks of preparing the food, taking breaks to watch CNN and drink beers. The image on TV was blocky and pixilated all day, with the sound coming in and out, but that wasn't just a local problem. CNN reported that cable carriers across the country were experiencing technical issues with bandwidth.

Images of tanks surrounding the CNN building appeared from time to time, apparently highlighting how critical CNN's continued operation was to the nation. I wondered where the tanks were on our city corners. *A few tanks would be nice about now.*

"It's snowmageddon out there," commented Rory. During the day, he'd struggled up to the *New York Times* building, where he worked as a journalist as a sideline to his novel-writing career.

CNN played in the background while we talked. "*The Pentagon made very clear years ago that if the United States was subject to a cyberattack that resulted in loss of life, the US military would respond with a kinetic attack.*"

I'd spent most of the day trying to help neighbors to get their heating working. The power was back on, but the Internet was clogged, and the entire building was run on IP networks. The hallways had warmed up, so a large part of the solution had simply been for all the tenants to leave their doors open.

"*—kinetic attack means with conventional weapons, bombs, and tanks—*"

Of course, the Borodins were fine and needed no help. When I'd dropped in, the Russian soap operas were once again playing on their TV while Aleksandr slept in front of them. I was going to bring them over a plate of food after dinner.

"They're only plowing the big avenues," continued Rory. "Snowbanks on the sides of Eighth are higher than me now. Port Authority and Penn Station are already overflowing with people."

"—*the president has now declared a national emergency, invoking the Stafford Act to bring the military in for domestic—*"

I'd only gone outside the front door to our building. Beyond the awning, the snow was nearly waist deep, and it was below zero and windy. Not the sort of weather I wanted to be outside in, and I was impressed that Rory had braved nearly twenty city blocks to get to work on such a day.

CNN continued in the background. "*Sixty million people are affected by this storm on the East Coast, and though the power has been restored in many places, several million people are still without power, with emergency services remaining at a total standstill.*"

I looked at the TV, and then back at Rory. "Are we at war? Are they bombing China yet?" I was barely joking.

Rory shrugged. "The main thing we're at war with right now is this storm. That Professor Latham on CNN earlier was just being dramatic for the cameras."

"Come on!" I pointed at the television. "You're telling me that all this is a coincidence? China was declaring war yesterday after they said we downed one of their planes. Now the power outages, the train crash—"

"He has a point," said Chuck. "Somebody is doing something."

"Yes," replied Rory, "somebody is doing something, but you can't go bombing everyone on the planet when the Internet shuts off."

"It has to be China," I said, shaking my head. "Why else would we have attacked them back?"

"You mean that destroyed village under the dam?" asked Rory. I nodded, and he rubbed the back of his neck, pursing his lips. "The US military hasn't admitted to the attack. And China didn't declare war. They're denying everything. That guy on TV was just the governor of Shanxi Province trying to get some airtime. He'd been shut out of their Politburo process—"

"Nobody is admitting to anything! This may be a virtual attack," I said, my voice rising as I rose to my feet and pointed out the window into the swirling snow, "but *real* people are dying out there!"

"Boys!" came a quiet hiss. It was Susie, glaring at us. "Quiet, please! The kids are sleeping."

"Sorry," I said sheepishly.

"Could you please switch that off?" she demanded. "I think we've all had enough for one day."

"But we might miss something—"

"Mike, if you don't turn it off, you're going to miss a really nice meal," said Lauren. "Come on, you guys set the table."

Picking up the remote, I looked at the TV.

"*—the question now is what constitutes use of force, but there has definitely been loss of life. Over a hundred confirmed dead on the Amtrak crash this morning, with dozens more still missing; eight suspected deaths from bird flu; and already twelve reported dead from the power outages and looting.*"

I clicked it off.

9:00 P.M.

Candles flickered in the dim light while we all held hands. In the silence, the wind howled through the darkness outside, rattling the window panes and demanding entry. I wondered what poor souls were stuck out there right now, what convoluted paths had led them to be struggling against the elements, alone and cold somewhere. Lauren's fingers squeezed mine, and I smiled at her, trying to put the thought of being stranded from my mind.

"Dear Lord, please watch over us and keep these people, our families, safe," said Susie. "We thank you for this food, and for your gift of life. We pray for everyone's safety, and that you will guide us to the light."

Silence again. We were sitting on bar stools arranged in a semicircle around our black granite kitchen counter. It was as close to a dining-room table as we had. I'd festively positioned our little Christmas tree at one end of the counter near the wall. It glowed in alternating reds and yellows and blues under the overhead lighting. Lauren had lit a few vanilla-scented candles, which flickered between us.

"Amen! Let's eat!" said Chuck with enthusiasm, and the busy noise of humans being human filled the room as we dug into dinner.

I hadn't felt very hungry, but when they'd started stacking the kitchen counter with turkey, stuffing, mashed sweet and grilled potatoes, and more, my stomach started growling. By the way everyone else was piling their plates, it wasn't just me.

"You get to church much these days?" asked Chuck with a smile, pulling off one of the turkey legs. He'd noticed my hesitation when Susie had asked everyone to hold hands to say grace.

He was teasing me. Church brought to mind memories of bored Sunday mornings when I was a kid, fidgeting with my brothers in the pews. While the minister would drone on about something I didn't understand, I'd pick at the edges of the threadbare cushions, my little legs swinging above scuffed linoleum floors.

"Maybe this is God's punishment for the sinners of New York," joked Chuck as he smothered his plate in gravy. "I'll bet there are some Amish in Pennsylvania right now who're getting the last laugh."

Only half listening to him, I nodded. To my right, Pam was asking Lauren if her family had made their flight to Hawaii. Lauren responded that she thought so, but shrugged, and Pam asked why we hadn't gone with them. Lauren hesitated and then lied, saying she hadn't wanted to. Lauren had practically begged me to go; I wondered if she was telling a white lie to stick up for me, or if she was just too embarrassed to tell the truth. If I'd let her family pay, we might have been a million miles away, watching the drama unfold from some sunny beach, and Chuck would probably have been safely tucked away in his hideaway. But we were stuck in New York, and it was my fault.

Hearing Luke gurgle on the baby monitor, my stomach lurched and I put down a forkful of turkey.

"Did you manage to get it working?"

I blinked. "What?"

"The Internet, did you manage to get on this afternoon?" asked Rory from across the counter.

It took me a moment to switch tracks. "Yes, um, well, no," I stuttered. "I did get on, but it was extremely slow."

Rory nodded. "The *New York Times* tech group says the Internet is totally infected from top to bottom. They're going to have to switch the whole thing off and restart nodes, one by one, all across the world, like clearing a city house by house."

I nodded, not really understanding.

"Hey, when was the last time you ate meat?" asked Chuck, pointing toward the mock chicken on Rory's plate. Susie had made some special dishes for them.

"More than a decade ago," answered Rory. "I don't think I could stomach it anymore."

"Meat *is* murder," laughed Chuck. "Tasty, tasty murder. You'd be surprised what you can stomach when you need to."

Rory smiled. "Maybe."

"So what are they saying up at the *Times*?" Lauren asked Rory.

"Hey!" Susie pouted. "I thought we weren't going to talk about that stuff."

"I just thought maybe they'd heard something that wasn't on the news, you know, airplanes . . ."

The table went quiet.

"Nothing about any air or other transport accidents," said Rory. "But then we're barely getting any information, and what we are getting is a contradictory mess."

"What do you mean?"

"Even after 9/11, it took weeks to figure out what was happening. These cyberattacks look like they're coming from Russia, the Middle East, China, Brazil, Europe, even from inside the US itself—"

"Enough!" demanded Susie, raising her fork. "Come on, now, can we please find something else to talk about?"

"I just—" Rory started to say, but Susie cut him off.

"The power is back on, something I forgot to thank God for," she said with a smile, "and all this will probably be over tomorrow and you can talk your heads off about it. But I'd like to have a nice, normal Christmas dinner, so, please."

"Isn't this a fantastic turkey?" said Chuck loudly, changing gears. "Come on, a toast to our beautiful wives!"

I raised my glass together with Chuck and Rory.

"To my beautiful wife," I said to Lauren. She met my eyes, but then shifted hers down. Reaching over, I tried to turn her chin toward me, but she shrugged away.

"What is it?" I whispered.

"It's nothing." She met my gaze. "Happy Christmas."

I drank deeply from the glass of wine I'd been holding up, but Lauren barely took a sip from hers.

"A Merry Christmas to you too, baby."

"Just for a minute?" I asked again.

Lauren sighed and picked up a bowl from the soapy kitchen sink water. She began thoughtfully scrubbing it. We'd sent everyone else home, offering to clean up since Susie had provided the whole dinner. We were enjoying a glass of wine by candlelight while we did the dishes.

I wanted to turn CNN on to see what was happening. I'd been itching to turn it back on all night.

"Okay, just for a minute, but I want to talk soon," she said, looking at me steadily. "We need to talk, Mike."

That sounded ominous, and I stopped wiping the pot I was drying. After piling my plate with food at dinner, I'd totally lost my appetite. Lauren had been quiet, avoiding my eyes, and while she could have just been worrying about her family . . .

"What do you want to talk about?" I asked, trying to sound casual. My scalp began tingling.

She took a deep breath. "Let's finish cleaning up first."

I stared at her, holding the pot in one hand and the washcloth in the other, but she returned her attention to the sink, scrubbing industriously. Shaking my head, I stacked the last few pots and pans, put the last glasses into the dishwasher, and then threw the dishcloth onto the counter. Wiping my hands on my jeans to dry them, I picked up the remote.

Lauren sighed loudly again.

Immediately, CNN sprang to life. "*This is only the fourth time the armed forces have been called to DEFCON 3.*"

"What in the world?" I sat down on our couch. Lauren put down the pot she was scrubbing. Images of an aircraft carrier filled the giant screen on our wall. It was one of ours this time.

"*The only other times our military have been at DEFCON 3 were the Cuban Missile Crisis in '62, when we were at the brink of nuclear war with Russia—*"

"What's happening?" asked Lauren.

"*—the Yom Kippur War of '73, when Syria and Egypt launched a surprise attack on Israel, nearly triggering another nuclear war—*"

"I don't know," I replied, shaking my head. Lauren came to sit next to me.

"—and of course, on 9/11, when we were attacked by unknown forces that turned out to be al Qaeda."

I started to get up from the couch to go over to Chuck's place, to see if he knew anything more, but Lauren reached out and stopped me. Without questioning her, I sat down and returned my attention to the TV.

"*The only information we are getting is that CENTCOM, one of the US military's internal command and control communication networks, has been compromised—*"

"Mike, could we turn this off for a minute?"

I frowned at the TV, trying to understand what was going on. Multiple secret networks had been taken over, from the NSA to forward-deployed military units. They didn't know the extent of the infection, or the purpose. Our military was readying for some kind of attack.

"Please, Mike, turn it off," repeated Lauren.

I turned to her, shaking my head. "Are you serious? You want to have a talk now? The world is about to explode and you want to talk?"

Tears welled in her eyes. "Then let the world burn, but I need to talk to you *right now*. I need to tell you something."

My heart raced. I knew what she was going to say, and I didn't want to hear it. I clenched my jaw and shook my head. "Can't it wait?" I asked.

"No." Tears were streaming down her face. "I . . ." she stammered, "I, um—"

"*We have just received an emergency alert from the Department of Homeland Security. Oh my God . . .*"

The CNN anchor was at a loss for words. Lauren and I turned toward the TV.

"... *the DHS is reporting multiple unknown and unidentified aerial targets over the continental United States, and is asking the public for any information—*"

And then everything went dark.

The background hum of the machines went silent, and I found myself staring into blackness where the CNN anchor had been a split second before. All I could hear was the banging of my own heart and the rush of blood in my eardrums. I waited breathlessly, half expecting the brilliant flash of a thermonuclear explosion to burn through my retinas. But all I heard was the quiet howl of the wind outside while my eyes adjusted to the dim light from the candles still burning on the kitchen counter.

Seconds ticked by.

"Let's get Luke and go next door, okay?" I said shakily. "Find out what's going on."

Lauren grabbed my arm. "Please," she begged, "I need to get this out."

"What?" My anger and fear were boiling over. "You need to come clean right now?"

"Yes—"

"I don't want to hear this," I spat back. "I don't want to hear about how you're sleeping with Richard, how you're sorry, how you never meant to hurt anyone."

She burst into tears.

"You pick *this* moment," I yelled, "this goddamn moment—"

"Don't be such an asshole, Mike," she sobbed. "Please stop being so angry."

"I'm an asshole? You're sleeping with someone, and I'm an asshole? I'm going to kill that son of a bitch."

"Please . . ."

I glared at her, and she stared back at me defiantly.

"WHAT?" I shouted, throwing my hands into the air. Luke began crying in the background.

In the wavering candlelight she put one trembling hand to her mouth and answered me: "I'm pregnant."

DAY 3: CHRISTMAS DAY, DECEMBER 25
9:35 A.M.

"You didn't ask if it was yours, did you?"

I stopped digging and exhaled.

"You did, didn't you?" laughed Chuck. "You *are* an asshole."

My head sagged, and I rubbed my face with one snow-encrusted glove.

"And I mean that in the best possible way, my friend."

"Thanks," I sighed, shaking my head, and leaned down to scoop out another shovelful of snow.

Chuck leaned through the doorway. "Don't beat yourself up too much. She'll forgive you. It's Christmas."

I grunted and threw myself into finishing the excavation. Pam had wrapped Chuck's injury, so he had a club for one hand, making him useless for digging. *Just my luck.*

"You gotta stop imagining things," added Chuck, "stop seeing things that aren't there. That girl adores you."

"Uh-huh," I mumbled, unconvinced.

It was still snowing, not as hard as yesterday, but still—it was the whitest of white Christmases that New York had ever seen. Everything outside was covered, and the cars parked along Twenty-Fourth Street were the barest of lumps under the thick carpet of snow. This silent and blanketed New York was eerie.

Right after the blackout, we hadn't seen the glow of mushroom clouds on the horizon, so we assumed the worst hadn't happened. A few of us had gone outside and battled our way over two blocks to the Chelsea Piers, straining to see into the snowy blackness above the Hudson. I'd expected to see or hear something, a fighter aircraft battling an unseen foe, but no. After a tense couple of hours, nothing had happened except that the snow had gotten deeper.

The moment the power had gone out, Chuck had fired up his generator. Our building's fiber-optic line from Verizon should have worked even in a blackout—assuming you could power up your own TV and cable box. When we'd tried CNN, the image and sound had been scrambled for a few hours, and then it went totally blank. It was the same on all channels. The radio stations were still broadcasting, however, and they were filled with conflicting stories. Some said that the unidentified aerial targets were enemy drones that had invaded US airspace; others said they were missiles and that whole cities had been destroyed.

Around midnight, the president had broadcast a short message saying that there'd been some kind of cyberattack. Its full extent was still being assessed, he said, and they still had no information about the unidentified aerial targets, except that they didn't have any reports of US cities being physically attacked. He said nothing about drones. Power had been restored to many areas by then; at least, that was what the announcement said. We were still without power, however.

"You sure we need to do this?" I asked. "The power came back on yesterday after just a few hours. It'll probably be back on by this afternoon."

Chuck had had the idea of siphoning gas out of cars on the street. We wouldn't take it all out of any one car, he reasoned, and they wouldn't be going anywhere for the foreseeable future anyway. We needed more fuel for the generator. Gasoline wasn't something he'd been allowed to store indoors, and we figured the gas stations would be closed.

"Better safe than sorry, my granddad always said," replied Chuck.

While we were inside, this plan had sounded clever; outside, it was a different story. Just opening the back door was an adventure, with all the snow piled against it. I was barely able to squeeze out, and I'd spent twenty minutes digging the snow away from the outside of the door enough to open it properly.

"Come on, then, let's go," I told Chuck as I scraped away the last of it. Opening the door, he scrambled into the snow outside, and we waddled through waist-deep drifts to the nearest car. Underneath all my layers of clothing I was sweating, prickly and uncomfortable, while my hands and face and feet were numb from cold.

"Remind me to add snowshoes to my shopping list for the next disaster," laughed Chuck.

After brushing away two feet of snow from the top of the first car, we found it had a locked gas cap, so we moved to the next one. With that one we had more luck. After five minutes of digging out a trench, we positioned the empty gas canister as low as we could and inserted a length of rubber tubing into the gas tank.

"I remember buying this medical tubing and wondering what I'd ever use it for," mused Chuck, kneeling in the snow. "Now I know."

I held the end of the tube up to him. "I did all the digging. I believe the sucking is your job." I'd never siphoned anything in my life.

"Great." He leaned down and put his lips around the tube. After every few inhalations, he'd stop to cough out the fumes, holding his thumb over the end of the tube. Finally, he hit pay dirt.

"Merry Christmas!" I teased as he doubled over, coughing and retching out a mouthful of gasoline.

He leaned down and inserted the end of the tube into the canister, releasing his thumb. The satisfying sound of running liquid echoed out from the container. It was working.

I was impressed. "Not bad."

Wiping spittle from the side of his mouth with his club hand, he grinned at me. "By the way, congrats on getting pregnant."

Sitting there in the snow, I had a sudden flashback of being a child, of the days my brothers and I would go out back of our small house in Pittsburgh to build snow forts after a storm. I was the youngest, and I remembered my mother coming out on the back stoop to check on us. She was really checking on me, making sure I hadn't been buried under the snow by my roughhousing brothers.

I had my own family to protect now. Perhaps alone I could tramp off into the wilderness with a backpack, survive, and figure out whatever came my way, but with children everything became dramatically different. Taking a deep breath, I looked up into the falling snow.

"Seriously, congratulations. I know it's what you wanted." Chuck leaned over and put a hand on my shoulder.

I looked down into the four-gallon canister wedged into the snow. It was about a third full. "But not what she wanted."

"What?"

How much do I want to share? But there was no sense in bottling it up. "She was going to get an abortion."

Chuck's hand dropped from my shoulder. Snowflakes settled around us. "An abortion?"

My cheeks flushed hot. "I don't know. That's what she told me. She was waiting till after the holidays."

"How pregnant is she?"

"Maybe ten weeks. She knew when we had the Thanksgiving party, when her family was here and her dad offered that position with the firm in Boston."

Chuck pursed his lips, not saying anything.

"You know Luke was an accident—a happy accident, but still an accident. Lauren's father was expecting her to be the first female senator for Massachusetts or something. She was under massive pressure, and I guess I wasn't listening."

"And having another baby now—"

"She wasn't going to tell anyone. She was going to Boston in the New Year."

"You agreed to go to Boston?"

"She was going to go by herself, get a separation if I wouldn't."

Chuck looked away from me as a tear ran down my face. It froze halfway.

"Sorry, man."

I straightened up and shook my head. "Anyway, all that's over, at least for now."

The container was almost full.

"She's going to be thirty next month," said Chuck. "Milestones can stir up a lot of confusion in people, about what's important."

"She obviously decided what was important." I ripped the tube out of the container, and gasoline sprayed up onto me and soaked my glove. I swore and began screwing the cap onto the container to seal it. It jammed, and I swore again.

Chuck leaned over and put his gloved hand on mine, stopping me. "Take it easy, Mike. Take it easy on yourself, and more important, take it easy on her. She didn't do anything. She just *thought* about doing something. I bet there are a lot of things you've thought of doing that people wouldn't be too impressed with."

"But to think about doing something like that . . ."

"She's confused, and she didn't do anything. She *needs* you now. Luke needs you now." He picked up the container with his good hand and stood up, sinking back into the snow and falling sideways. Looking at me, he added, "I need you now."

Shaking my head, I took the container from him. We started shuffling back to our building.

"Why do you think CNN didn't come back on last night?" asked Chuck.

"Local carrier networks are probably jammed," I speculated. "Or generators ran out of power."

"Or CNN was bombed," joked Chuck. "Not that I would be entirely against that."

"Big data centers usually keep a hundred hours of fuel for backup generators. Isn't that what Rory said?"

"I think he said the *New York Times* had that much." He looked around at the deep snow on the streets. "Won't be any refueling for a while."

Reaching our building, we saw that snow had already drifted up against the door. *We better come and clear this regularly if we want to be able to get out.* Tony was still at his post at the other end of the main floor. He waved to us.

Reassuringly, we heard the rumble of a big plow coming down

Ninth Avenue and saw it sweep by in the distance between the buildings. It was nearly the only evidence that the city was still operating.

When the power had gone out for the second time, the local radio stations had still been broadcasting, but this morning many of them were static. The radio stations still transmitting were now filled with wild speculation about what had happened, but they were just as much in the dark as we were. The only consistent information was that this second blackout had affected not just New England but the entire United States, and a hundred million people or more were without power. The best the radio announcers could do was report on local conditions. We had no idea what was happening in the world, or if the world even existed anymore.

It was as if New York had been disconnected from the rest of the planet and was floating alone, soundlessly, in a snowy gray cloud.

8:45 P.M.

The faces before me glowed dazzling bright green, and then the green spotlight swept down the hallway, flashing off door frames.

"Cool, huh?"

"Very cool." I took off the night-vision goggles. "Lights, please?"

With a click, the lights we'd jury-rigged in the hallway, connected to Chuck's generator, turned back on.

"I can't believe you have ten thousand dollars' worth of night-vision goggles and infrared flashlights." I looked at the military paraphernalia stacked around Chuck. "And you don't have a shortwave radio."

"I've got one, but it's in Virginia at the hideaway."

Same place he should be, he didn't add.

"Thanks again for staying," I said quietly.

"Yeah, thanks for staying," said Ryan, one of our neighbors from farther down the hall. He raised a steaming cup of buttered rum.

His partner, Rex, raised his glass as well. "A toast to our well-prepared friend Chuck!"

"Hear, hear!" came a half-hearted cheer from the rest of the people crowded in the hallway, nearly twenty of us packed together on chairs and couches pulled out from our apartments. We all raised our cups to drink.

Susie had decided to host a hot rum toddy party for Christmas, and all of our neighbors were bundled and cuddled up together, holding steaming-hot cups of alcohol in their hands.

The building was retaining heat but cooling quickly. We'd switched to using electric heaters in Chuck's apartment. The kerosene heater was more powerful but produced low levels of carbon monoxide, and Susie was worried about the kids. For this gathering, we'd pulled the kerosene heater out and placed it in the center of the hallway. People were warming themselves around it as if it were a campfire.

The hallway had become our communal living room, a place to gather together and chat. We'd wired up a radio that played news in the background, mostly listing off emergency shelter locations around the city and saying that the power would be back on soon and to stay indoors. Most of the roads and highways were impassable, in any case.

Everyone was sitting in more or less the same positions as where their apartments were located along the hallway. The Chinese family from down the hall near Richard had finally come out and were bunched up together on a couch with the wife's parents, who'd come for a visit before everything fell apart. It was a bad time to have chosen to visit America for the first time, and none of them spoke English very well.

Next to the Chinese family was a Japanese couple—Hiro was the husband's name; I hadn't caught the wife's—and across from them were Rex and Ryan. The Borodins were sitting to my right. Aleksandr was awake for once, but just barely as he sipped the hot rum drink, with Irena beside him. Chuck, Susie, Pam, and Rory were to my left, and little Ellarose was sitting up on Tony's lap.

The only one missing was Lauren. I wasn't sure what to say to her, and she hadn't wanted to talk. I'd tried holding her, asking her to come out, but she wanted to be alone. She was in Susie's room, sleeping.

Luke had no idea what was going on. To him, this was all a big game, a party, and he was running around, dressed up in his snowsuit, saying hello to everyone and showing off a red fire engine toy he'd gotten for Christmas. It lit up and made noises and should have been annoying, but it was somehow comforting. I wasn't sure how long the batteries would last.

Richard walked over from his end of the gathering to sit down on the arm of the leather chair I'd dragged out from my place. "So can we have it?"

He'd been badgering us all day about taking the kerosene heater.

"I've got some food I could trade."

Somehow he'd acquired a large load of canned food and groceries, probably by offering someone a small fortune.

"If it keeps getting colder, we're going to freeze to death if we all stay in our own places. I'll take in that Chinese family and the gay guys and Hiro and his wife. Sarah and I will organize a shelter at our end, and you guys do the same at your end. All I need is the kerosene heater and a few other things."

I was impressed that he was offering to create a shelter in his apartment. *Maybe I have this guy wrong.* "You need to talk to Chuck," I replied.

Richard looked over at Chuck, who I was sure could hear our conversation. He was adamant that we needed to keep everything we had for ourselves, but Susie was just as adamant that we needed to share.

"Charles Mumford," whispered Susie to Chuck, "we don't need that thing. You go on now."

Chuck sighed. "Fine, yes." He turned to Richard. "And I'll collect some other stuff for you guys. That's a good idea, doing a shelter for the floor."

"And can we get a cable for electricity?"

Chuck sighed deeper this time. We'd snaked an extension into Pam and Rory's next door to run a small electric heater and light. Their place was tiny, smaller than mine and Lauren's, so it was workable, but we'd opened a can of worms. Now everyone wanted a connection.

"The generator is only six thousand watts, and we're already running three heaters."

Susie kicked his foot.

"Ah, forget it. Sure. Only for lighting? At nights? And everyone does siphon duty?"

"You bet," agreed Richard. "Good man." Getting up to leave, he turned to me. "Is Lauren okay?"

"Yeah, she's good," I replied without enthusiasm.

Richard frowned, but then shrugged and returned to his wife, who was trying to talk to the Chinese family. Luke was over with them, and the grandfather was admiring his new fire engine. I smiled at them, and the grandfather smiled back. We'd decided the bird flu warning was a hoax.

Just then the stairwell door opened, giving everyone a start. A face appeared, grinning awkwardly. It was Paul, the suspected intruder from the day before. Chuck's eyes narrowed. He whispered to Tony, who looked up at Paul and then shrugged back at Chuck.

"Hey, guys," said Paul with a small wave. The light from his headlamp flashed in my eyes. "Wow. Cozy up here."

Squinting, I raised one hand. "Could you turn that off?"

"Sorry, forgot. You're the only ones with real lights."

"Paul, from 514, right?"

"Uh-huh."

Chuck leaned toward me and whispered, "Tony locked the front door hours ago, and he says this guy sort of looks familiar. I guess I was wrong."

Everyone was quiet, waiting on us. I smiled back at Paul. "Want a drink?"

"That'd be great."

Conversations resumed, and I introduced Paul around while Susie fetched him a hot toddy. Paul shook everyone's hand, exchanging enthusiastic Merry Christmases until he got to Irena and Aleksandr.

"Merry Christmas!" he said, extending his hand.

Irena looked up at him, pressing her lips together and frowning. "Happy holidays, yes," she replied, nodding, but neither she nor Aleksandr held out a hand.

Has he offended them by assuming they celebrate Christmas? It wasn't often I saw them being grumpy, but the stress was getting to everyone.

Paul dropped his hand, still smiling, and pointed to a spot next to them on their couch. Irena shrugged and shifted slightly. He squeezed himself in next to her, cupping the hot toddy Susie gave him. He blew on it and took a sip. "You guys look pretty organized. Any idea what's going on?"

I shook my head. "We know as much as anyone else."

"But everyone has an opinion," said Chuck, raising his drink, "so how about a straw poll?" He gestured to Paul. "You start."

"Easy, gotta be the Chinese. We've been squaring off for a fight with them for years." He looked toward the Asian corner. "No offense."

The Chinese family smiled back, perhaps not understanding, but Hiro shook his head. "We're Japanese."

Chuck laughed loudly. "Probably not you guys this time, but what's *your* vote?"

Hiro looked at his wife, gripping her hand. "China?"

"Amen to that, brother," agreed Paul, raising his drink. "I hope they're bombing those bastards back to the Stone Age right now."

This time he didn't bother apologizing.

"India and China are in the middle of that huge fight over dams in the Himalayas," pointed out Chuck. "How do we know the Indians didn't cause that dam failure?"

"It's possible the Indians were involved," said Rory, "but the Chinese wrecking America would be like burning down your own house to get rid of the tenants. They own half of it."

"Political leaders do stupid things all the time," I pointed out.

"Not the Chinese," observed Chuck. "They got that thousand-year planning."

"Don't be too impressed," said Rory. "Their politicians are as bad as ours. But my bet is the Iranians. Did you see their ayatollah on TV just before the blackout?"

Tony liked that suggestion. "If we've been spoiling for a fight with anyone, it's the Arabs. Had a chip on their shoulder ever since they took our embassy hostage in '79."

"We did overthrow their democratically elected government and install a dictator that terrorized them," pointed out Rory. "And they're not Arabs, they're Persian."

Tony looked confused. "I thought you thought they did this?"

"Maybe," Rory sighed. "It's hard to say."

"Russians," said Richard. "It's the Russians. Who else could have invaded our airspace?"

"Ah, yes," laughed Chuck. "A commie under every cover."

"Do you know they just restarted strategic bomber flights over the Arctic?" Richard said to Chuck. "Same flight patterns as during the Cold War?"

"I did not know that," admitted Chuck.

"Yeah, they did," confirmed Rory.

"The Russians ran out of money for a few years in the nineties," continued Richard, "but you can bet they don't like playing second fiddle to America and China. Probably taking us both down at the same time." A quiet pause. "I bet half of America is a smoking crater already. That's why no military has shown up. We're screwed."

"You don't need to scare everyone," said a tiny voice. "I think this is all just an accident of some kind."

It was Richard's wife, Sarah, and he turned to her angrily. "As if you know anything," he growled. "The aircraft carriers, that destroyed village in China, DEFCON 3, train crashes, over a hundred million without power. This is no accident."

Everyone stared at them, and she shrank away.

I turned to Irena and Aleksandr, trying to divert attention away from Sarah. "So do you think it was your countrymen who attacked us?"

"This," said Irena, waving her hands toward the ceiling and sniffing, "is not an attack. An attack is when someone has a gun pointed at your head. This is criminals, crawling in the dark."

"You think criminals could wipe out the entire United States and invade our airspace?"

Irena shrugged, unimpressed. "Many criminals. Criminals even in the government."

"Finally, we get to the conspiracy theories," I said, turning to Chuck. "So is all this just an inside job?"

"One way or the other, we probably *did* do this to ourselves."

"I thought you liked the Canadian theory."

"Snow as a strategic weapon does have Canada written all over it," agreed Chuck with a smile. "But I'd agree with Irena—the only way this makes sense is some criminal element."

"Anyone else with an opinion?" I asked. Nobody said anything, so I stood up to recap. "We have the Russians and an accident with one vote each, Iran and criminals with two votes." I held my fingers up in front of me to indicate the tally. "And the winner, China, with three votes!"

The door to Chuck's apartment opened, and Lauren appeared, looking terrified.

What happened?

I took a step toward her. "Are you okay? Is the baby okay?"

It was the first thing that came to mind.

"Baby?" I heard Susie saying. "What baby?"

Chuck shook his head, holding up a hand to quiet her.

Lauren held her cell phone out to me. "It's my parents."

"They're on the phone?"

"No, they left a message, and my cell must have picked it up before the networks went dead."

"Was there an accident?"

"No accident, but their flight to Hawaii was canceled at the last minute when the bird flu thing started. They were in Newark and called to see if we could get them."

A moment passed while I processed this. "They're still at Newark?"

"They're *trapped* at Newark."

DAY 4: DECEMBER 26
7:35 A.M.

"Wake up."

I opened my eyes to blackness.

"You awake?" asked Chuck, quietly but urgently.

"I am now," I groaned, propping myself up on my elbows.

Lauren was asleep beside me, holding Luke. It was still dark out. In the grayness I could just make out Chuck kneeling beside me. We'd slept in his spare bedroom.

"Is everything okay?"

"No, everything is *not* okay."

Fear sharpened my senses, and I swung out of bed, still fully clothed. "What happened?"

"Someone stole our stuff."

I pulled my sneakers on. "From in here?"

He shook his head. "Downstairs."

I took a deep breath, and my pulse began to slow. *At least someone didn't come in when we were sleeping.*

With a nod Chuck led me out into the living room. The low whine of the generator filtered its way back into my senses. Tony was asleep on the couch. Chuck nudged him awake.

"Everything okay?" said Tony, startled.

"No," replied Chuck, kneeling to pick up some jackets and a bag. He threw the jackets at us. "Put these on and change into some boots." He picked up his hunting rifle. "We're going outside."

"Goddamn it!"

Chuck was holding a broken lock and staring into his now mostly empty storage locker. All the lockers had been broken into, but where most of the others had been stuffed with bicycles and boxes of old clothing and books, Chuck's had still been half-full of emergency gear and food.

"I guess that stuff was too heavy," said Tony, pointing to the water containers.

We wore headlamps, so I was blinded when Tony turned my way. I looked away and inspected the locker again.

"I am so stupid," said Chuck, swearing under his breath.

We'd checked the lobby level, and the front entrance was locked and secure, but the back door was open. Chuck had been the one with the keys, probably the only person in the apartment block with them apart from Tony. We must have forgotten to lock it when we came in yesterday. I'd been so cold and exhausted that I hadn't thought of it.

"It's my fault too," I said. "At least we dragged a lot of it upstairs already."

"Mostly just the gadgets," sighed Chuck.

On the way down we'd stopped on the fifth floor to knock on the door of 514, the apartment Paul had said he was from. There'd been no answer. In a rage, Chuck had kicked the door in. The place was empty. Whoever lived there had gone away for the holidays. We'd searched through the kitchen drawers for old bills and found only the names of Nathan and Belinda Demarco. No Paul.

After that we'd gone and knocked on all the doors on the fifth floor. No one answered at most of them. At one apartment, the residents refused to open their door no matter how we tried to explain who we were. In another was a scared-looking young couple, dressed in full winter gear, hoping we were emergency workers or the police. They explained that most people on their floor had gone away for the holidays, or left when they heard of the coming snowstorm. They themselves were leaving for the emergency shelters that morning, to find transportation out of the city.

Most of the building was empty already. Our floor was the only one that was full of people, probably because of all the gear Chuck had. Nobody we talked to had ever heard of a Paul living there.

Chuck looked in a locker near his. "They must have used the Rutherfords' kids' sleds, and they took the snowshoes from Mike and Christine. At least they left some skis."

There were a dozen storage lockers, and he knew everyone that used them.

"We need to go soon if we're going to track them."

We'd seen tracks leading out the back door from the lobby, a trail where they'd dragged everything out across the pristine snow that was still falling. The trail would be gone soon.

"Track them?" I asked, amazed. "We're going to chase them into a blizzard and, assuming we find them struggling with our stuff, ask for it back?"

Chuck produced a handgun from a bag he had slung around one shoulder. "You bet your ass." He gave one to Tony and offered me one as well.

"Are you nuts?" I held up my hands, refusing to take it. "I don't even know how to use one of those."

I hadn't said anything about the hunting rifle, but Chuck producing handguns shocked me. While criminals might be able to obtain firearms easily in New York, it was almost impossible for a regular citizen to legally own a gun. I didn't bother asking if he had permits.

"Time to learn," growled Chuck. "Tony, you know how to use that?"

"Yes, sir. Served in Iraq."

I looked at him. "Really?"

It suddenly struck me how little I knew about Tony. He was always the jovial presence at the door, a solid set of shoulders ever ready to help, but I'd never gone much deeper. He was the only one of the building staff to stay, and I had a feeling he only stayed because we had, because Luke was here.

"Really."

"Mike, why don't you stay upstairs while Tony and I go outside?"

Taking a deep breath, I slowed my thoughts down. *I can't hide upstairs—I want to know what's going on out there.* Maybe I could find out what had happened at Newark, if they'd shipped people into the city, something to raise Lauren's spirits.

I felt like I had to do something. "You know what? I'd feel safer having Tony stay here, where the kids are."

"You sure, Mr. Mitchell? With Lauren pregnant and all?"

Everyone knew already.

"I'm sure." I knew he'd take care of them like his own family, and to be honest, if they needed physical protection, he was a better bet than me. "I doubt we're going to find the thieves anyway, and I want to visit one of the emergency shelters."

My tone left no room for discussion, so Tony shrugged.

We moved upstairs into the lobby, and Chuck and I put on the snow pants we'd brought down as Tony explained the firing mechanism on the handguns. He slipped a few cartridges into the pockets of the parka I was wearing. A sense of unreality set in.

"Ready to go?" asked Chuck, pulling on heavy mittens, wincing as he covered the broken hand.

I nodded and put my gloves on, noticing that they hadn't quite dried out from yesterday. And that they reeked of gas.

Tony opened the lock on the back door and threw his shoulder into it, shoving back the snow that had piled up again. Cold air and snow blasted into the lobby. Chuck glanced at me and disappeared through the opening. Taking a deep breath, I followed him out into the swirling gray.

9:45 A.M.

Struggling through the deep snow along Twenty-Fourth, we followed the tracks of the sleds until they met the steep edges of the snowbanks lining Ninth Avenue. Chuck was intent on finding the thieves and hurried me along, but I was hoping we wouldn't find them, scared of what might happen if we did.

My fears proved unfounded when we got to Ninth. The drag marks became hopelessly muddled with other foot traffic. Any hope of following farther evaporated into the swirling snow.

Chuck stood fuming, looking up and down the street.

Dark shadows materialized out of the white to trudge past us, walking along the ravine formed by the edge of the buildings where the snowbanks ended. I nodded to one of them but got no response.

I knocked my boots together and shivered. "Up to Penn Station?" I wanted to bring some news home to Lauren. I felt guilty.

Giving up, Chuck nodded, and we began climbing, hand over foot, up the steep slope of the snowbank edging Ninth Avenue. I followed him to the top, and we slid down the other side into barely ankle-deep snow.

In the distance, headlights gleamed through the sleet, and a low rumble vibrated up through my boots. *At least they're still plowing.* We headed uptown toward the oncoming lights.

"Are you so crazy about your stuff that you'd really risk our lives?" I asked Chuck, walking in step beside him.

"It's risking our lives *not* to be crazy about guarding our stuff."

"Come on. The power came back on in less than a day on Christmas Eve, and even after Sandy most of New York was back up in a few days. There hasn't been any flooding or wind, just this snow."

"People don't learn." Chuck looked down and shook his head. "Critical systems are all interlinked, and this isn't *just* a physical storm."

"So what, you think it'll take a week? Even most of Long Island—"

"Something is happening here that's never happened before." He stopped and looked at me.

"You're always being dramatic. The power will probably be back on in a few hours."

"Have you ever heard of the Aurora Test?" asked Chuck, walking on.

I shook my head.

"In 2007, Idaho National Labs conducted a cyberattack exercise with the Department of Energy. They sent a 21-line package of software code from a thousand miles away, embedded as a virus in an e-mail, into a DOE facility. It caused an electrical generator to self-destruct by rapidly recycling its circuit breakers."

"So get a new generator."

"You can't buy these at Walmart. They're a few stories high, weigh hundreds of tons, and take months to build."

"Didn't the DOE fix the problem once they knew about it?"

"Not really. Most of the generators are legacy equipment, built before the Internet existed, and they're nearly irreplaceable."

"If they were built before the Internet, shouldn't they be immune from it?"

"They used to be, but someone had the bright idea of saving money by rewiring them using Internet controls, just like our building. It saves money, but now everything can be attacked *via* the Internet." He sighed. "It gets worse."

The snowplow was approaching us, so we stepped to the side, climbing up onto the snowbank while it growled past. A small light above the driver's head illuminated the inside of his cabin through windows streaked with melting snow. He was hunched over, wearing a mask, and I glimpsed a picture pinned to his dash that I imagined to be of his family, a family he was away from.

The plow rumbled off into the distance.

"How does it get worse?"

"The US doesn't even make generators like that anymore."

"So who does?"

Chuck trudged on in silence for a moment, then said, "Guess."

I could see where this was going. "China?"

"Yep."

"So they can be wrecked remotely, and we might have no way of getting replacements?"

"They may have *already* wrecked them. Maybe no electrical grid for months or years. And it gets even worse."

Now I sighed.

Chuck kicked a chunk of ice. "It's more or less the same story for all critical systems—water, dams, nuclear reactors, transport and shipping, food, emergency and government services, even the military. Name something that isn't wired into the Internet and doesn't use Chinese parts."

"Wouldn't they say the same about us? I mean, if they attack us, wouldn't we just do the same to them? Mutually assured cyber-destruction?"

"Not the same. We're the most wired country on Earth. Everything here is accessible via the Internet, much more so than for anyone else, and way more than the countries we're picking fights with. We're totally vulnerable to cyberattack on a massive scale, but they're much less exposed."

"But then we would just bomb them, right?" I pointed out. "Who would risk that?"

"Not so simple. How do you figure out who attacked? Half the world has an ax to grind with us for one reason or another. We can't bomb everyone."

"Sort of been the plan up until now, no?"

Chuck laughed. "I do like the way you keep your sense of humor."

We reached Thirty-First Street and began to battle our way along the block to get to the back entrance of Penn Station. Hugging the concrete walls of the huge New York City Post Office building, we made our way first along the row of shipping bay doors, and then along the side of a low wall that formed the edge of a protective moat around the building. The shadowy top of the Empire State Building loomed over Madison Square Garden as we approached.

The guard shack halfway down the building was empty, but there were lights shining in many of the windows. Staring up at one of the windows as we passed, I asked, "What's that saying?" I was thinking of the motto of the postal service inscribed on the front of the building.

Chuck knew what I meant. "Neither snow nor rain nor heat nor . . . I dunno. We can go have a look if you want."

"Nah, but I think the mail may be late today. I don't remember cyberattack on that list."

Chuck laughed, and we kept walking.

Climbing on top of the snowbank at the edge of Eighth, we had our first glimpse of what emergency services had managed to accomplish so far. My heart sank. Hundreds of people were crowded outside the back entrances to Penn Station and Madison Square Garden, with masses more visible in the distance down Thirty-First.

"My God, so many already?"

"We're here, aren't we?" replied Chuck. "People are scared, want to know what's going on."

With a few steps we jumped down the snowbank, crossed Eighth, and climbed the other side to join the teeming crowd. As we picked our way through, we heard murmurs of war and bombings from the huddled groups surrounding us. National Guardsmen were manning the entrances, trying to bring some order to the chaos. A line snaked up Eighth under the protection of some scaffolding and hastily erected plastic sheets meant to stop the wind. Gray blankets bearing Red Cross symbols were being handed out to people waiting.

Crowding around the entrance was an angry mob, some yelling and crying, all wanting to get in. The Guardsmen held their ground and kept shaking their heads, pointing to the back of a line that was getting longer even as we watched. Chuck waited for a few moments on the periphery and then waded in, dragging me along behind him.

"Sorry, sir, back of the line," said a young Guardsman, holding up his hand to us and pointing toward Eighth.

"We don't want to go inside," said Chuck loudly. "Are we at war?"

"We are not at war, sir."

"So we're not bombing anyone?"

"Not as far as I know, sir."

"Would you tell me if we were?"

The Guardsman sighed and looked down the line of people. "All I know is that help is coming soon, the power should be back on soon, and you need to get inside and stay warm and safe." He looked into Chuck's eyes and added, "*Sir.*"

Chuck moved closer, and the Guardsman stiffened up, clutching his M16. "Mask, sir," he said, nodding up at a sign warning of bird flu.

"Sorry," mumbled Chuck, pulling out the masks he'd brought from his stash. He gave me one, and I put it on. "So is this bird flu thing real?"

"Yes, *sir.*"

"But you don't know much more than me, do you?"

The Guardsman's shoulders sagged. "Stay warm and safe, sir, and please back away."

"There's nobody I could speak to inside that knows anything more?"

He shook his head, and his expression softened. "You could wait in line, but it's a mess in there."

The kid looked like he'd had enough already.

"Thanks," said Chuck sympathetically. "I bet you wish you were with your family."

The Guardsman blinked and looked skyward. "That's the truth. I hope to God they're okay."

"How did they call you up?" asked Chuck. "Phones are down, no Internet—"

"I was on active duty. We didn't manage to reach many when the order came in. And coordinating is hell—some land-based radio but not much else."

"Should we come back tomorrow, see what the news is?"

"You can try, sir."

"Did you hear of any people being shipped in from Newark Airport?" I said.

A crowd of people pressed in against us, pushing us into him. "Back!" he yelled, his face hardening again as he shoved against us with his M16. He found my eyes and shook his head before yelling again, "Back, goddamn it!"

Chuck grabbed me from behind and pulled me away. "Come on, I think it's time we got out of here."

3:40 P.M.

"Which one?"

"The black one, five rows up."

I pointed up into the sky. "That one?"

It was getting dark and snowing harder, nearing blizzard conditions again. We'd braved nearly thirty blocks to get to Chuck's parking garage in the Meatpacking District. The city was mostly deserted at street level, except for the fancy Gansevoort Hotel we'd passed on Ninth. It was still lit up like a Christmas tree, and there was a huge crowd of people outside trying to get in. Several large doormen were shaking their heads. Everyone was yelling. We passed by and tried to ignore it.

"No, the one next to that one," said Chuck.

I squinted. "Ah, wow, now that is one nice truck. Too bad it's fifty feet off the ground."

We were in front of a vertical parking garage, right at the corner of Gansevoort and Tenth, at the entrance to the West Side Highway. The perfect location for making a quick getaway from New York, assuming your getaway car wasn't suspended in space five stories up.

Chuck growled and swore again. "I told those guys to bring my truck down to the first level."

The parking structure was a set of open platforms—each platform just big enough to hold a car—suspended between vertical metal beams that closely stacked the cars against the wall of the building behind it. Each set of vertical metal beams had hydraulically operated lifts that could raise and lower the platforms to let operators get the cars off, but of course the lift controls needed power to operate.

"Nobody's going to come now. Couldn't we hot-wire a different truck? Something on the road?"

The snow had completely covered all the cars at ground level.

"No way. We need my truck. Nothing else is going to get us out of here, not with all this snow and ice." He looked longingly up into the falling snow at his baby. "Land Rover Wolf '94 XD 110, under-armor, snorkel, heavy-duty winch, thirty-six-inch IROK Radial snow tires—"

"It is pretty," I agreed. "Pretty damn high up. Even if we got it down, do you think it could climb that snowbank?" I pointed toward the eight-foot-high pile of snow and ice lining Tenth Avenue. It was the only obstacle to getting onto the West Side Highway from the garage lot, but it was a formidable one.

He studied the pile. "One way or the other. But we can't just crash it down from up there. Not even the Wolf could survive a drop like that."

"We better get going." The temperature had dropped, and I was shivering hard. "Let's think about it. At least it hasn't been stolen."

Chuck took one last look at his truck and then turned around. We scrambled out of the parking lot and started back up Ninth. The crowd outside the Gansevoort had mostly dispersed in the coming darkness. As we passed, several of the people still outside watched us closely, clearly interested in the backpacks we were carrying. Chuck put his hand in the pocket of his parka, gripping his .38, and stared back at them, but nothing happened. Breathing a sigh of relief as we left them behind, we passed the Apple Store. All the windows were broken, and snow had swept inside.

"A funny time to decide you need a new iPad," I laughed. Then I noticed something else. "This snow's getting deep."

We were walking right up the middle of Ninth Avenue. All day we'd been walking up and down the big avenues, and the plows had been rumbling back and forth. The snow hadn't gotten more than ankle deep on the plowed streets. We were now up to our calves.

I squinted into the gathering darkness but couldn't see any headlights coming our way.

"If they've stopped plowing, city services must be totally screwed," observed Chuck. "This is going to get ugly."

"Maybe it's just a slowdown?"

"Maybe," replied Chuck without conviction.

We decided we better grab what we could from Chuck's restaurants before somebody else did, so we wound our way back uptown, stopping at the one nearest our place and packing our bags with as much high-calorie canned and preserved food as we could find.

When we got back outside, it was nearly pitch black. Slogging the rest of the way back up to Twenty-Fourth, I had visions of the keys not working, of being trapped outside. The cold was unbelievable. *We could die out here.* My steps quickened.

By the time we arrived at the back door of our building, I was frozen. As Chuck fumbled the key into the lock, the door opened from the inside, and Tony's face appeared, smiling at us goofily. "Boy, am I glad to see you guys!"

"Not as glad as we are to see you!"

Chuck and I had our headlamps on, but Tony had been sitting in the dark. We asked him why. So he wouldn't attract attention, he said, and we left it at that.

Tony stayed behind to lock up and clean the floor, telling us to get upstairs and that everyone was worried sick. In a jolly mood we began climbing the stairs, pulling open our layers of clothing and taking off our hats and gloves, enjoying the comparative warmth and the thought of a hot meal and coffee and a warm bed.

Reaching the sixth floor, we stopped, and taking a deep breath, I opened the door. I expected to hear Luke come running, and I jumped out to surprise him.

Instead, I was met by a mob of scared, unknown faces. A large homeless man was spread out on the couch outside my apartment door, and a mother and two young children cowered on the Borodins' couch. At least a dozen more people I didn't know were crowded into the hallway. A young man wrapped in one of Richard's expensive duvets got up and extended his hand toward me, but Chuck burst through the door and pointed his .38 right in the kid's face.

"What have you done with Susie and Lauren?"

The kid held his hands up and gestured at Chuck's apartment. "Everything's fine. They're in there."

Behind us, Tony came charging up the stairs. "Wait, wait, I forgot!"

Chuck was still pointing his gun at the kid's face as Tony appeared in the doorway behind us, huffing and puffing. He put a hand on Chuck's gun, lowering it. "I let these guys in."

"You did what?" yelled Chuck. "Tony, that is not your decision to make—"

"No, it was my decision," said Susie, coming out of their apartment. She bear-hugged Chuck.

Lauren appeared in the doorway, with Luke at her feet. She ran to embrace me. "I thought something had happened to you," she whispered in my ear between happy sobs.

"I'm fine, baby, I'm fine."

With a deep breath, she released me, and I leaned down to kiss Luke, who was hugging one of my legs.

"We okay?" asked the kid, his hands still in the air. He looked like he'd had a rough time of it.

"I guess so," Chuck replied, putting his gun away. "What's your name?"

"Damon," said the kid, reaching out to shake my hand. "Damon Indigo."

DAY 5: DECEMBER 27
9:00 A.M.

Sunlight streamed in through the window. It was morning, but I had no idea what time. My phone was out of power, and it'd been years since I'd worn a wristwatch.

Then it dawned on me—blue skies. I was staring out the window at blue skies.

Lauren was curled up under the covers, with Luke wedged between us. Leaning over, I kissed her cheek and tried to pull my arm out from under her head. She sleepily protested.

"Sorry, baby, I gotta get up," I whispered.

She pouted but let me go, and I swung out of bed, carefully tucking the covers back around the two of them. Shivering, I pulled on my stiff, cold jeans, put on a sweater, and quietly left Chuck's spare bedroom—our bedroom now.

The generator was still purring outside the window, but the small electric heaters running off it weren't keeping out the cold very well. Even so, I admired the clear blue skies outside again.

Grabbing a glass from Chuck's cupboard, I leaned over the sink to fill it with water. I turned the tap, but nothing happened. Frowning, I turned the tap off and then back on, and then tried the hot water. Nothing.

The front door creaked open, and the noise of a radio announcer spilled in. Chuck's head appeared, and he saw me playing with the taps. "No more water," he confirmed, dropping two four-gallon cans of it on the floor. "At least, not in the taps."

"Don't you ever sleep?"

He laughed. "Water was off at five when I got up. Not sure if the city pressure can't make it up six floors with the pumps off, if the pipes are frozen, or if the city mains are off, but one thing's for sure."

"What's that?"

"It's goddamn freezing outside—at least ten below and windy as hell. Blue skies bring cold weather. I liked the snow better."

"Can we fix the water?"

"Don't think so."

"Do you want me to get some water with you?"

"Don't think so."

I waited. I could see he had something unpleasant in store for me.

"I need you to get gas for the generator."

I groaned. "What about Richard, all those people out there?"

"I had Richard go last night, and it was hopeless. He's about as useful as tits on a bull for stuff like that. Take the kid."

"The kid?"

"Hey, Indy!" yelled Chuck, leaning back into the hallway. From the distance a "Yes?" echoed into the room. "Get some weather gear on. You and Mike are going on an adventure."

Chuck turned to leave but stopped and smirked at me. "And fill *two* four-gallon cans, can ya?"

"What kind of name is Indigo?"

I was crouching, trying to hide from the wind, and letting the kid do the work. He'd been quiet on the walk down, just staring into space. When I asked him to dig out the first car, he began shoveling without a word.

"Family's from Louisiana. Used to farm the stuff down there. They named us after it."

He didn't look African-American, but then he didn't look Caucasian either—dark, short-cut hair, and exotic, almost Asian features. The most eye-catching thing about him, unusual at least, was a gold chain that hung around his neck with a crystal pendant swinging from it.

"Poisonous, isn't it?" I asked, referring to indigo, trying to make conversation.

We were outside on Twenty-Fourth Street, on the opposite side of the street, a few buildings down from our place. Our group had already siphoned most of the cars close by.

The kid nodded and continued to dig. "Sure seems that way."

Looking up and down the street, I imagined the millions of people trapped in this wasteland with us. From here, the city looked abandoned, but I could sense the masses hiding in the gray monolithic buildings that hunched shoulder to shoulder into the distance—a frozen desert between concrete towers.

I heard a hissing sound and worried it was a gas leak until I realized it was the sound of fine particles of ice being driven by the wind across the surface of the snow.

"So how did you figure out to come and knock on our door?"

He pointed up to our windows on the sixth floor. "Not many

other lights on. I wouldn't have bothered, but Vicky and her family, they needed help."

He was referring to the mother and two young children still asleep on the couch in the hallway. They'd looked exhausted.

"She's not with you?"

He shook his head. "But they were on the train with me."

"What train?"

He stuck his shovel into the snow and leaned down to clear ice from the gas cap, banging it slightly and then opening it. "The Amtrak."

"You were on that? Were you hurt?"

"I wasn't . . ." He sagged visibly, closing his eyes. "Can we talk about something else?" He grabbed one of the four-gallon cans. He looked at me, the sky reflected in his clear blue eyes. "Doesn't your building have an emergency generator?"

I nodded. "Couldn't get it started. Why? Think you could?"

"It wouldn't run the heating system even if I could."

"So why'd you ask?"

Propping himself up on one knee, he pointed at our building. "Chuck said his generator runs off gas *or* diesel. Did you check how much diesel there was in the emergency generator tank in the building?"

The wind whistled past us.

"No," I laughed, "we did not."

Not five minutes later we were standing in the apartment basement, listening to the hollow tinkle of the second canister filling up. It was cold, but much warmer than outside. We didn't even need to siphon the fuel, because there was a release valve on the bottom of the tank.

"Two hundred gallons!" I said excitedly, reading off the side of the tank. "That'll run our little generator for weeks."

Damon smiled, closing the release valve and screwing the cover onto the plastic canister.

I wanted to know what had happened at the Amtrak crash, but he seemed fragile, so I needed to tread carefully.

"One thing I will insist on," I whispered, even though nobody else was there. "This is our little secret, okay?"

He frowned.

"I mean, don't tell anyone else about the generator tank. We'll make getting gas our job. While everyone thinks we're off outside sucking it out of cars in the snow and cold, we can sit down here and relax, have a chat. What do you think?"

He laughed. "Sure. But won't they notice we're coming back with diesel instead of gas?"

The kid was quick.

"Nobody but Chuck is likely to notice, and he's good for keeping secrets."

Damon nodded.

"Feel like having the first chat now?" I asked.

"Not so sure."

"Come on, talk to me."

3:45 P.M.

"Can I come up?"

I looked down at the carpet, avoiding her eyes.

"We're already more than we can really manage," Chuck answered for me.

The woman in apartment 315, Rebecca, looked frightened. Everyone else on her floor had already left. She was wearing a shiny, puffy black jacket with faux-fur trim. Wisps of blond hair escaped from the edges of the hoodie she had pulled up around her head, lending her pale complexion an ethereal halo in the light streaming in from behind her. At least she looked warm.

"You really shouldn't stay here by yourself," I said, imagining her there at night, in the dark and cold, alone.

She fidgeted with the door frame with one gloved hand.

I relented. "Why don't you come up for the afternoon, have a hot coffee, and we'll walk you up to Javits later?"

"Thank you so much!" She almost burst into tears. "What should I bring up?"

"Pack as much warm clothing as you can," replied Chuck, shaking his head, "and it needs to be a bag you can *carry*."

The city was down to four radio stations that were still broadcasting, and the one doing emergency coverage for Midtown had announced that the Javits Convention Center between Thirty-Fourth and Fortieth had been turned into the evacuation hub for the west side of Manhattan.

"Can we borrow some blankets, anything warm?" I asked.

She nodded. "I'll bring everything I have."

"And any food you don't need," I added.

She nodded again and disappeared into her place, closing her door and casting us into darkness. It was still light out, but without any exterior windows, the hallways were shadowy caverns, a hundred feet of corridor lit by just the two emergency lights, one above the elevators and the other above the stairwell.

We were going door by door, doing an inventory to get some "situational awareness," as Chuck put it. Most of the building's residents were gone. Our errand reminded me of a few weeks before, when we'd knocked on doors with invitations to the Thanksgiving barbecue—just a few weeks ago, but in a completely different world.

"Fifty-six people in the building," said Chuck as we opened the door to the stairwell and began to climb, "and about half of those are on our floor."

"How long do you think the gang on the second floor will last?"

Apartment 212 had a small generator rigged up. A group of nine people had banded together in a smaller version of what we had going upstairs, but they weren't as well equipped.

Chuck shrugged. "Don't know."

Our floor was turning into an emergency shelter as people from other floors kept coming up. Richard continued to impress me. He had managed to go out and find another kerosene heater and a load of fuel, as well as more food supplies. Money was still buying stuff out there, at least for now.

"So the water is off everywhere," I said. It wasn't a question. We'd heard on the radio that the water was off all over the city.

"In survival situations, the order of importance is warmth, then water, and then food," replied Chuck. "You can survive weeks or months without food, but only two days without water, and you'll freeze to death in just a few hours. We need to stay warm and find a gallon of water per day per person."

We tramped up the stairs, our footsteps echoing around us. The temperature in the stairwell was dropping to the same as outside, and thick plumes of vapor hung in front of us with each labored breath. With one arm in a sling to protect his bad hand, Chuck was using the other to grab the railing, pulling himself up a step at a time.

"There's five feet of snow out there. Surely we're not going to lack water."

"Explorers in the Arctic were just as thirsty as those in the Sahara," said Chuck. "You gotta melt snow first, and that takes energy. Eating it lowers your body temperature and gives you cramps, which could be deadly. Diarrhea and dehydration are the enemy just as much as the cold."

I trudged up a few more steps. *Never mind staying hydrated, how are we going to deal with keeping clean, bathrooms, sanitation?* I still felt guilty about Chuck staying here for us. "Do you think we should just leave? Take everyone to the evacuation center?"

Where most of the apartment building was empty, our entire floor was still there, along with the refugees, and only because we'd had the generator and heating. Maybe we were making a terrible mistake. We didn't have enough food to support the nearly thirty people in our hallway for very long. It struck me how I thought of the people who'd migrated to our floor as "refugees."

"Luke still isn't well enough to travel, and Ellarose is too small to handle much. I think the evacuation centers will be total disasters. If we leave, we'll lose what we have here, and if we get stuck out there . . . then we'd be in real trouble."

I listened to the methodical rhythm of our boots as we continued walking up. I must have climbed these stairs two dozen times in the last two days. *So this is what it takes to get me to exercise.* I smiled, despite everything.

On the sixth-floor landing, Chuck turned to me. "We're in this now, Mike, and we gotta make it work, no matter what. Are you with me?"

I took a deep breath. "I'm with you."

Chuck reached out, but before he could grab the handle, the door burst open, nearly knocking him down the stairs.

Tony's head appeared.

"Goddamn it!" swore Chuck. "Could you be more careful?"

"It's Presbyterian," said Tony breathlessly. "They're asking for volunteers on the radio."

We looked at him, not understanding.

"The hospital down the street. People are dying."

8:00 P.M.

"Just keep ventilating."

The hospital stairwell was nightmarish. Inert bodies lay abandoned on stretchers under emergency lighting in doorways, with tubes and bags of blood suspended in a shifting forest of metal poles and stands. Between the pools of dim light, people were shouting and jostling, flashlights and headlamps glimmering, all in a mad rush downward and out into the freezing cold.

I desperately tried to keep pace as we raced down the stairs, holding a blue plastic bulb between my fingers, balancing it over the mouth and nose of a tiny baby. Every five seconds I squeezed it, delivering a fresh breath of air. The baby was from neonatal care, five weeks premature and born just last night.

Where's the father? What happened to the mother?

A nurse cradled the baby in her arms, running down the stairs as fast as we could manage together. Reaching the ground floor, we rushed toward the main entrance.

"Where are you taking him?" I asked the nurse.

She was concentrating on the path ahead. "I don't know. They said Madison Square Garden had services."

We walked through the double doors at the main entrance and then waited behind a gurney two staff members were trying to navigate outside. The old man on the bed looked up at me, his arms twisted around himself, trying to say something. I stared at him, wondering what he wanted.

"I'll take that."

An NYPD officer was reaching over to take the ventilator from me. Thank God Presbyterian was almost on Sixth, one of the only main streets they'd kept plowing. Walking outside, I could see a few police cars and ambulances and civilian vehicles through an opening dug into the massive snowbank bordering Sixth Avenue.

The nurse and police officer continued on, and a wave of people flooded past me. Noticing the nurse was wearing nothing but short sleeves, I ran after them, taking off my parka and putting it around her shoulders, and then jogged back inside the lobby, shivering.

The only thing I'd been able to think of, staring at that newborn on the way down, was Lauren. It was as if that little baby in the nurse's arms was mine, my unborn child. I was near tears, my breathing shallow and quick.

"You okay, buddy?"

It was another police officer. I took a deep breath and nodded.

"We need people outside to walk patients up to Penn Station. Can you do that?"

I wasn't sure, but I nodded again anyway.

"Do you have a jacket?"

"I gave it to a nurse," I said, pointing out the door.

He waved at a container next to the exit doors. "Grab something from lost and found and get out there. They'll tell you what to do."

Minutes later I found myself wheeling a gurney up Sixth Avenue, dressed in a faded, cherry red overcoat with stained, frilly white cuffs and wearing gray wool mittens. I'd left the heavy gloves Chuck had given me stuffed in the pockets of the parka I'd given to the nurse.

The coat was several sizes too small for me, and made for a woman, so I'd had to force the zipper up past my stomach. I felt like a red sausage.

Where the world inside the hospital had been frenetic, outside it was a surreal calm. Nearly pitch black and silent, the street was lit only by the headlights from intermittent traffic that passed back and forth, ferrying the sick. An ambulance swept past me, flickering light across the ghostly procession ahead, a ragtag parade of equipment and people staggering through the snow.

For the first half block the cold was bearable, but by the time I got to the corner of Twenty-Fifth, two blocks later, it was biting. Walking into a steady headwind, I warmed my cheeks by pressing the scratchy wool mittens against them, then pulled one of them off to feel something lumpy on my cheek. *Is that frostbite?* My feet were numb.

Hard-packed snow and ice covered the street, and I had to concentrate to keep the wheels of the gurney from getting stuck in ruts, constantly reversing course and shoving forward as it got jammed. The woman on the gurney was wrapped up like a mummy in layers of thin blue-and-white blankets. She was aware, awake, and looking up at me with scared eyes. I talked to her, telling her not to worry.

A bag of liquid hung from a support on the side of the bed, swinging back and forth, its tube snaking down into her covers. I tried to steady it, cursing someone for not securing it, wondering what was in it. *Will it freeze? What happens if it falls? Will it tear the tube from her veins?*

The gurney jammed in the snow again, almost tipping over, and the woman let out a small cry. With all my strength I righted it, panting, and continued on.

Between the lights of the passing cars and ambulances, my world became a dark cocoon of ice and cold, my heart pounding and eyes straining to see in the dim light of my headlamp. It was just me and this woman, bound together on the edge of life and death.

The thin sliver of a crescent moon hung above me in the darkness like a scythe, and I couldn't ever remember seeing the moon in New York before.

Seven blocks became an eternity. *Did I miss the turnoff?* Struggling, I peered into the darkness. There were still people ahead of me, and then, two blocks ahead, I spotted the blue and white of an NYPD van. Gripping the cold metal of the gurney, I forced us forward. While my face and hands and feet were freezing, my arms and legs were burning.

"We got it from here, buddy."

Two NYPD officers came around to take the ends of the gurney.

I was soaked in sweat.

As she was wheeled away toward a gap in the snowbank on Thirty-First, the woman said thank you weakly, but I was too tired to reply. Doubled over and panting, I smiled at her. Straightening up, I walked down the street into the darkness, back toward the hospital.

2:25 A.M.

"I wish we could offer more," said Sergeant Williams.

I shook my head. "This is great, thank you so much." I cupped the bowl of soup in my hands, luxuriating in its heat. My fingers tingled painfully as the blood returned, but my feet were still numb. On the way inside, I'd checked my face in the bathroom. It was sore and red, but there was no frostbite, or at least nothing resembling what I thought frostbite would look like.

Moving down the cafeteria line, I picked up a hard bun and a pat of butter. There wasn't much left except for some crackers and a few bags of chips.

The second floor of the office tower adjoining Penn Station and Madison Square Garden had been converted into an NYPD barracks, and it was packed. After I'd struggled through a few more trips back and forth, Sergeant Williams had stopped me, seeing that I was about to collapse, and offered to bring me up to their mess. Nobody had batted an eye when I entered wearing my frilly red coat. They were too exhausted.

Scanning the crowd, I couldn't see anyone I knew. Chuck had stayed in our apartment. He wasn't much use with his broken hand. Richard had disappeared when we'd announced our intention to come and help. Tony, Damon, and I had walked over to the hospital, but I'd lost track of the others in the confusion.

Everyone had been wearing masks during the hospital evacuation, but in the cafeteria nobody was. Either they knew something the general population didn't, or they'd given up.

Sergeant Williams motioned to an open spot at the tables, and we wound our way through the crowd to sit down. Wedging myself between some NYPD officers, I put down my steaming bowl of soup to shake hands all around. Sergeant Williams sat across from me, pulling off his hat and scarf and tossing them atop the heap of outdoor clothing littering the table. I added mine to the pile. It smelled like a locker room.

"It's a goddamn mess out there," complained one of the officers, leaning down into his soup.

"What happened?" asked another.

"The Chinese is what happened," the first man growled back. "I hope they've friggin' leveled Beijing."

"Enough of that," said Sergeant Williams. "There's enough bad already going on out there without us adding to it. We don't know what happened yet, and I don't want to hear any more talk like that."

"Don't know what happened?" said the officer. "It's like we're fighting a goddamn war in our own city."

Sergeant Williams scowled at the officer. "For every person causing mischief, there's five more like Michael here"—he nodded at me—"who are risking their lives to help out."

The officer shook his head. "Mischief? I'll give you goddamn mischief. You can all go to hell. I've friggin' had it." He shot up, grabbing his bowl of soup, and stormed off to another corner of the mess hall. The officers around him looked away, but one by one they all got up and left as well.

"You'll have to forgive Officer Romales," said Sergeant Williams. "We lost some people today in a shoot-out on Fifth. Some idiots decided to start looting the fancy shops there, a whole mob."

Leaning down, I undid the laces on my boots and loosened them, curling my toes. They were burning with an intense ache.

"Take the boots off," suggested Sergeant Williams. "Warm in here, but the boots are insulated. If you keep your feet in 'em, you'll be keeping 'em cold." He sighed and looked around. "Bodies and blood everywhere after that firefight on Fifth, and nowhere to put 'em, no way to get there with paddy wagons or ambulances, so we had to leave them to freeze right on the street. A hell of a thing."

Kicking my boots off, I brought one foot up onto the opposite knee and began kneading my toes. "Sorry to hear that." I wasn't sure what was appropriate to say, and perhaps nothing was. I switched feet to work on the other toes.

"City morgues are full up anyway, and the hospitals are fast becoming meat lockers."

A searing pain shot through the foot I was massaging. I winced. "What happened at Presbyterian?"

Sergeant Williams shook his head. "A gasket blew on the generator fuel pump when they were switching it from one tank to another. Eighty big hospitals in the city, plus hundreds of clinics, are all gonna come crashing down soon. We're near three days without power—even without equipment failure, none of them have reserves to last past five days on generator, and there's little refueling in sight." He dunked his bread into the soup. "Worst is the water. Department of Environmental Protection shut down tunnels two and three out at Hillview Reservoir when a system malfunction said sewage had spilled over, but when they found it was just a glitch, they couldn't open the tunnels again. Pure genius. Control systems are screwed, or some such nonsense."

"Can't they do something?"

"Ninety percent of city water flows in from there. They're going to have to blow the tunnel controls, but even then, with no flowing water for a few days at these temperatures, the smaller pipes are probably frozen up already. Not long till people start hacking into the ice on the East River to drink that polluted slop. Eight million people on this island are going to die of thirst before they freeze to death."

I stopped eating my soup and put both feet back on the ground, despite the pain it sent shooting up my legs. "So where's the cavalry?"

"FEMA?" he laughed, but then stopped himself. "They're doing their damnedest, but there's no contingency for rescuing sixty million people. Networks are all down, and they can't even find their people or equipment. Boston is as bad as us, add a frozen storm surge when that nor'easter hit, and more of the same story in Hartford, Philly, Baltimore."

"Didn't the president order the military in?"

He sighed. "Even Washington is up this creek, son. We haven't heard anything from there for the last day, like they've dropped into a black hole. Starting with the bird flu scare, the entire country's been thrown into chaos. At least from what we hear, and that's damned little."

"Have you even seen the military?"

"They showed up, but they have their knickers in a twist over the unidentified targets, thinking we're in some kind of new drone war and cranked up on DEFCON 2 to protect a country that's disintegrating behind the fences. Idiots are getting set to launch a war on the other side of the world while we starve and freeze over here. And still nobody has any idea what the hell happened."

"But somebody's done something."

"Yeah, *somebody* has done something."

I looked around the crowded room. "I've got my family here. Should we get out, get to an evacuation center?"

"Evacuate to where? It's a frozen wasteland out there, and even if you had somewhere to go, how would you get there?" He took a deep breath and reached out to hold one of my hands. It was an intimate gesture I wasn't expecting. "Do you have somewhere safe? Somewhere warm?"

I nodded.

"Stay there then, get clean water, and keep your head down. We'll sort this out. Con Edison says they'll have power in a few days, and after that the rest will sort itself out." He let go of my hand, leaning back to rub his eyes. "One more thing."

I put my spoon down and waited.

"There's another storm coming, nearly as bad as the first."

"When?"

"Tomorrow."

I stared at him.

In barely a whisper he added, "God help us all."

The baby screamed and screamed in my arms. I tried to hold it, but it was slippery, still in its placental sack. I was alone in the woods, my hands filthy, covered in leaves, with dirt jammed under my fingernails. I scrubbed and scrubbed my hands, trying to clean them, trying to hold onto the baby, but it slid and slipped. *My God, don't let it fall. Someone, please help me.*

With a gasp, I sat bolt upright in bed. Outside was a flat, gray light. *Overcast.* No sound except the purring of the electric heater beside the bed. Lauren was sleeping with me, Luke cradled between us. He was awake, staring up at me and smiling.

"Hey, buddy," I said to him softly.

I was sweating, my heart still racing, with the vision of the baby slipping sideways in my consciousness. Leaning down, I kissed Luke on his chubby cheek, and he burbled and squeaked. He was hungry.

Lauren shifted, and her eyes opened. "Are you okay?" she asked, blinking and leaning up on one elbow.

She was wearing a gray cotton hoodie and bundled deep under layers of blankets. I leaned over, reaching under the covers, and she flinched ever so slightly as my cold fingers found her warm flesh. Gently, I slid my hand down to caress her belly. Maybe eleven weeks, but her tummy was still flat. She smiled and looked away.

"Last night . . ." I sighed. "It was horrible. I couldn't stop thinking about you."

"Because I'm horrible?"

The electric heater whirred. I slipped my hand around to the small of her back and pulled her toward me, kissing her cheek. She trembled.

"No, because you're amazing."

"I am horrible, Mike. I'm so sorry."

"It's me that needs to apologize. I wasn't listening to you, and I wrongly accused you."

Tears filled her eyes. "It's not your fault."

"That kid, Damon, he lost his fiancée in the Amtrak crash. He told me about it when we were out digging."

"My God."

"And it made me think, if I ever lost you—"

Luke squealed between us. I smiled at him, fighting back my own tears. "One second, buddy, I just need to talk to your mommy, okay?" I looked back at Lauren. "You are everything to me. I'm sorry I didn't listen. When this is done, if you want to go back to Boston, I'm there with you. I'll be a stay-at-home dad, you get that job, whatever you want. I just want us to be together, to be a family."

"I want that too. I'm so sorry."

The gulf between us disappeared, and she stretched up to kiss me. Luke squealed again.

"Okay, let's get you some breakfast," Lauren laughed, then kissed me again.

The main hallway had become a communal space, with couches serving as beds at each end and chairs arranged around two coffee tables in the middle. Someone had pulled out a bookcase, which served as a stand for some lamps, the radio, and a coffeemaker. The kerosene heater stood on one of the coffee tables, filling the space with warmth.

The homeless man had gone, but the young woman and her kids were still there, asleep in a nest of blankets on the couch in front of the Borodins'. Rebecca, the woman from 315, had spent the night upstairs. The Chinese family was staying in Richard's place, and Tony was spending his nights in the main room of Chuck's place, on the couch in front of our bedroom.

By the time I got up, the kid, Damon, had already jury-rigged a rope and pulley system in the stairwell, and had banded together a work team. The elevator hallway was stacked with containers of snow they were hauling up to melt for drinking water.

Rubbing the sleep from my eyes, I waved to Tony as he appeared through the stairwell door with two buckets of snow. I made for the steaming pot of coffee on the bookshelf.

Pam was filling up a cup, and she handed it to me. "Could I speak to you a second?" she whispered.

I mumbled, "Sure," as I took the cup, and she pulled me to one side. I drank a mouthful of coffee.

"You're going to need to be very careful with Lauren. Even moderate dehydration and malnutrition can induce miscarriage."

"Of course I'll be careful." I took another sip of my coffee.

"That baby is counting on you."

"I know that, Pam." Now I felt annoyed. I was doing everything I could. "And I appreciate your concern."

She looked me in the eyes. "You come to me if anything—"

"I will."

She nodded and returned to hauling snow.

Rory and Chuck were sitting on the couch near our door, playing with their phones.

"Cell phones working?" I asked hopefully as I refilled my cup, glad to switch topics.

"Not exactly," replied Chuck without looking up.

"*More hospital shutdowns are scheduled for today,*" said the radio announcer, "*and the NYPD is asking for volunteers—*"

"Not exactly? What does that mean?"

"The kid showed me how to use a point-to-point messaging app. I'm installing it on Rory's phone."

"A point-to-point messaging app?"

"It's called a mesh network."

"*—heavy snowfall and high winds are predicted, hampering efforts of the military—*"

Taking a sip from my coffee, I sat down next to them, leaning in to see what they were doing.

Chuck pulled a small memory chip from the back of Rory's phone, clipped the battery back in, and turned it on. "We've collected a bunch of useful stuff on this," he said, holding the memory card between his fingers. "The kid's messaging app is amazing. We can text message each other, directly phone to phone, as well as across a network of phones, as long as they're within a few hundred feet. Doesn't need the cell network. There's even a Wi-Fi version of it."

"This radio station will be shutting down at 4 p.m. today in advance of the heavy weather and due to lack of refueling for our antennae transmission station. For continuing emergency broadcasting, tune in to—"

"Can you add it to my phone?"

Chuck motioned toward a Tupperware container filled with cell phones on the shelf under the coffeemaker. Each one was labeled with masking tape. "Already did yours and charged it up, and we're going to put it on as many phones as we can. They need to be unlocked, and it doesn't work on all models, but it works on enough of them."

"Guess you heard about the new storm?"

He nodded. "Another foot or two of snow coming. We're going to head out soon to help evacuate Beth Israel and Veterans over to Bellevue." He looked me in the eye. "They need all the help they can get out there. Can you come?"

He was talking about several large hospitals over on the east side, next to Stuyvesant Town and Alphabet City.

I considered for a moment. "As long as Lauren's okay with me leaving."

The cell phone in Chuck's hand beeped to life. He began typing something.

"You sure you're up for going out?" I asked him.

"Yep. The kid is going to stay here and get all these phones done, talk to the neighbors."

He was gamely trying to use his broken hand to hold the cell phone while typing with the other. The bad hand was purple and swollen.

I shook my head and then thought of something. "Have you checked on Irena and Aleksandr?"

"Not recently. Why don't you check on them before you head out?" Chuck nodded toward their door. "Oh, and one more thing. Can you cross-country ski?"

3:30 P.M.

The snow began again as the day slipped toward darkness.

Evacuating Beth Israel Hospital and Veterans over to Bellevue was a much more orderly affair than the scene at Presbyterian the previous evening. It was an organized closure, or as organized as it could be under the conditions. Emergency resources and fuel were being concentrated in just a few of the largest medical centers. The hospitals knew when the generator was going to lose power and were making the transfer ahead of time. Only the critically ill were transferred to Bellevue, with the rest going to evacuation centers.

Chuck and I skied over, using the gear the thieves had left in the lockers. We weren't the first ones to get the idea. A network of cross-country ski tracks had appeared on the streets. New Yorkers were adapting fast, and we saw all kinds of improvised snow gear on our crosstown trek, and even people on bicycles going down Sixth.

Cars were buried, but a few adventurous souls had dug theirs out and ventured onto the street, for the most part only to get stuck again.

After the requests on the radio, hundreds of people had turned up at Beth Israel to help the NYPD and emergency services, turning First Avenue into a buzzing hive of activity. Where New York had felt almost deserted before, today's mission had inspired a sense of camaraderie and togetherness. The city wasn't beaten yet.

I'd checked in on the Borodins before leaving. It was as if nothing had happened. Irena and Aleksandr were sitting in their usual spots—Aleksandr asleep on the couch with Gorby next to him, Irena knitting another pair of socks. Irena had even offered me some sausages she'd cooked for breakfast, which of course I'd accepted along with a piping-hot cup of tea.

The Borodins didn't want to come and hang out with the rest of us. Irena explained that they would just keep to themselves, that they'd done this before.

At the hospital evacuation, I ran into Sergeant Williams again. He honked and waved to me from a police cruiser as I was going one way up First and he was going down the other way.

"Time to get going back?" asked Chuck as the first fat snowflakes began to fall.

We'd managed seven runs back and forth, and I was exhausted. "Definitely."

They were still plowing First Avenue, and we walked down it to the corner of Stuyvesant Town. Its towers hung in the sky above us. The bronze plaque at the entrance listed a hundred residential buildings in this one complex, fifty thousand people within its red brick walls.

I was intensely thirsty. The Red Cross had arrived to hand out blankets and supplies, but they were short on water. We got one bottle each, but even with the water we'd packed ourselves, it wasn't enough. It had warmed up to about fifteen degrees during the day—still cold, but warm enough that I was soaked in sweat, and I was cooling off fast as the sun started to set.

Picking up our skis from the security checkpoint inside the lobby of the VA Hospital, halfway between Beth Israel and Bellevue, we strapped them on and headed back to the west side. We had a trip of nearly two miles across Twenty-Third. The snowfall was getting heavier. For the millionth time, I resisted the urge to check my cell phone for e-mail.

The evacuation had been a rumor mill, and I'd been on the receiving end of a dozen different theories about what was going on.

"So what did you hear?" asked Chuck

"*Air Force One* is down, and the Russians and Chinese have teamed up to invade," I said. With a dusting of fresh snow, the ski tracks along the middle of the street were quick, and Chuck was setting a fast pace in front of me. "People want to know why nobody has heard any more from Washington, why no military."

"About the same as what I heard, but my favorite is aliens," yelled Chuck over his shoulder. "I got stuck with a gang from the Village who're about to start wearing tinfoil hats to stop them from reading our minds."

"About as effective as anything so far."

"Mostly people are wondering where in the hell emergency relief is. And frightened of the next storm."

We skied silently for a few seconds, looking up into the thickening snowfall.

"It's scaring the heck out of me, too," I said.

Ahead, Twenty-Third looked like a frozen canyon. A double

set of ski tracks, flanked by foot trails, disappeared into the distance straight down the center of the road. From the middle of the street, the snow angled up toward the edges, covering the parked cars and blowing into snowbanks against the buildings, sometimes covering first-floor awnings and scaffolding. Channels were dug into the snow at irregular intervals at doorways and entrances, burrows of the human animals struggling to survive this onslaught.

Passing the corner of Second Avenue, we heard the sound of breaking glass, and a mob of people materialized from the gloom. A few of them had broken through the window of a food market, and the rest were waiting while the leaders cleaned away the glass at the edges of the window.

Apart from the smashed front window of the Apple Store in Chelsea, I hadn't seen any looting, but people had to be running out of food and water. While some had taken advantage of the situation, most New Yorkers had been holding on. With no help in sight, though, it had taken four days for scared and hungry to trump the law. There was an inevitability to it under the circumstances, and seeing it happen uncorked horrors crowding the back of my mind—Irena's stories of Leningrad, when roving gangs had started attacking and eating people, and the police had been forced to start an anti-cannibalism unit to combat it.

Stopping outside, we watched from a distance.

Far from being a mad dash of pushing and shoving, this was an orderly, almost apologetic looting. Two men stopped to help an elderly lady step over the smashed glass of the window. Seeing us looking at them, one of them shrugged at us. "Waddaya gonna do?" he yelled through the falling snow. "I gotta feed my family. I'll come back and leave some money when this is done."

Chuck looked at me. "What do you think?"

"What? Should we try to stop them?"

He laughed, shaking his head. "Do you want to grab something?"

I looked into the swirling white distance, toward home and my family. "Yeah, we should grab everything we can."

We unclipped our skis, strapping our gear to his backpack and joining the line of people waiting to get into the shop. Chuck fished out our headlamps, and we climbed in through the window. Picking up plastic shopping bags, we made our way to the back where it was darker and there were fewer people.

"Anything high-calorie, but try not to take junk food," instructed Chuck.

Even with the headlamps, it was confusing, and I grabbed what I could. I wanted to get out of there. Within minutes we were stepping back out through the front window, loaded down with as much as we could carry. My fingers were already aching from holding the bags.

"This is not going to be fun," I complained. The wind had picked up, driving the snow into our faces. *Maybe we took too much.* "I'm not sure I can carry this much all the way across town."

"No sense in trying to ski with all this," replied Chuck. "We'll just have to walk, and maybe drop a bag or two if it gets to be too much."

That gave me an idea. I put down the bags and fished through my layers of clothing to retrieve my phone, pulling off one mitt with my teeth. I opened up a geocaching treasure hunt app we'd used last summer on a field trip with Luke's preschool. Blowing on my fingers to warm them, I tapped a few icons.

"We just need to walk straight down Twenty-Third," said

Chuck, frowning. "I can show you how to work the compass later, but we'd better get moving—"

Shaking my head, I looked up at him. "Drop your bags here and go back inside to get more. I've got an idea. You said GPS is still working, right?"

He nodded. "What's the idea?"

"Just trust me, and get back inside before the place is emptied."

He shrugged, dropped his bags, and headed back to the store.

I put away my phone and picked up his bags and mine. Backtracking to Second, away from the people at the shop, I trudged awkwardly into the knee-deep snow, hauling the bags with me. I stopped in front of a cell phone store that still had a visible sign, kicked a big hole in the snow, and then carefully looked around to make sure nobody was watching. Once I was sure, I deposited a few bags in the hole and buried them, then took a picture of the storefront using the treasure hunt app. I repeated this procedure a few times, in a few different locations, until I'd hidden all the bags.

Chuck was waiting for me, new bags in hand, when I returned. "Ready to explain?"

I grabbed the bags from him. "We bury them in the snow and tag their locations with this treasure hunt app I have. As long as we can add a local image to the GPS data, it should be accurate to within a few feet. We can dig them up later."

He laughed. "Cyber-squirrels, huh?"

"Something like that."

The wind gusted, nearly blowing us over.

"We'd better hurry."

By the time we made two more trips into the food market,

it was stripped clean, and as we continued on our way home, we came across shops being looted everywhere. This new snow-storm was striking a deep fear into people, awakening their sur-vival instinct. The law had been broken, but not order. Rules were designed to maintain a community, and in this moment, the community needed to break the rules to survive. It was self-administering its own emergency services.

We stopped everywhere we saw looting, grabbing anything useful or edible and burying it outside as we continued on our way.

The darkness and snow would have been terrifying if not for the map software Chuck had loaded onto our phones. It provided a comforting connection, a small glowing screen we could open up from time to time to see the small dot of where we were and, more importantly, where home was.

Close to ten at night, we arrived at our back door. I was exhausted and numb with cold. Tony and Damon were waiting for us, keeping the doorway clear of snow. Upstairs, Lauren was still awake, and worried of course, but I collapsed into bed with-out a word and passed out.

DAY 7: DECEMBER 29

"Graceful degradation is the problem."

I grabbed a bowl from the counter. "Like an aging porn star?"

Chuck frowned, trying to make the connection. "If you view technology as sex," he mused after a pause, "then yes, maybe. Needs to keep working even if it gets old."

"And a lot of people like technology *better* than sex."

"You first among them," he replied with a smile. He picked up a bowl and waved it at me. "I've noticed how you've been itching for your e-mail."

"Boys, boys, we have children here," said Susie, shaking her head but smiling, holding her hands over Ellarose's ears.

We were all together in Richard's place, the only space large enough to hold twenty-eight people at the same time. We'd added three more refugees from other floors, but Rex and Ryan had left for the emergency shelters, to try to find a way out. Richard had offered to provide lunch for everyone, so we were crowded together in the open-concept first floor of his place.

"How long do you think this power outage is going to last?" asked Sarah, filling my bowl with the stew she'd made. It was amazing the stuff Richard had managed to find.

"I'd give it another week. This new snowstorm will be over

by tomorrow, and the NYPD sergeant told me Con Edison had things sorted out, at least for Manhattan. Lights should be on for New Year's."

Chuck raised his eyebrows. I shrugged. Where he was a pessimist, I was an optimist, and there was no sense in scaring people with his theories.

"Sounds good to me," said Tony.

We were trying to rotate guard duty in the downstairs lobby, but he was taking more shifts than anyone else. I'd just texted him, using Damon's messaging app, to come up and grab a plate of food.

The wind howled and churned outside the windows. We were down to a handful of radio stations still transmitting, and by consensus we tuned into New York Public Radio to listen to a steady stream of emergency announcements. Many were requests for assistance, but none were close to us, and in any case, it was too dangerous to go outside.

"What I mean by graceful degradation," continued Chuck as Sarah filled his plate, "is that there's no longer a way to revert to previous technology if something fails."

"Example?"

"Like this logistics thing that screwed up shipping. Everything is 'just in time,' with a handful of central warehouses located in the middle of nowhere that stock almost nothing."

"So no local stock if the supply chain gets disrupted?"

"Exactly. The complex systems supporting cities are balanced on a knife's edge. Knock out one supporting leg—logistics, for instance—and poof," said Chuck, blowing on his hand, "the whole thing goes down. Supply chain attack is the big weakness."

"So back to horses and carts?" said Richard, sitting at the kitchen counter with Damon, Chuck, Rory, and me. The kids were sprawled on couches with Lauren and Susie.

Chuck laughed. "Where are the horses?"

"The countryside?"

"There are none anymore, not like there used to be. We're five times the population of when humans last used horses for transportation, with maybe one-fifth the horses. And back then, 80 percent of people lived in the countryside and had a shot at supporting themselves. Now that 80 percent live in cities."

"Horses?" I said. "You're seriously talking about horses?"

Richard shook his head and smiled. "I'll leave you boys to your fun. I gotta go to the bathroom." He got up to leave.

With no running water, we'd started using apartments we'd broken into on the fifth floor as a communal latrine to maintain some semblance of sanitation. We collected wastewater in buckets and used it to flush the toilets. Richard picked up a wash bucket by the door on his way out.

"I'll tell you what the problem is," said Damon. "No legal framework."

"You think lawyers could stop this snowstorm?" laughed Chuck.

"Not the snowstorm, but the cyberstorm, yeah, maybe."

It was the first time I'd heard the term "cyberstorm."

Everyone went quiet.

"New York isn't being beaten by snow. It's had big snowstorms before," continued Damon. "It's being beaten by cyber."

"And you think lawyers could stop that?"

Damon looked up at the ceiling and then back at Chuck. "Do you know what a botnet is?"

"A network of computers that have been infected to use in a cyberattack?"

"Right, except not just infected. People can voluntarily let their computers be used as part of a botnet."

"Why would they do that?" asked Chuck, frowning.

Rory waved his spoon in the air. "There are very good reasons why someone would want to join a botnet."

While Rory and Chuck could both be described as liberals, Chuck leaned a little more to the right. "You enjoying that rabbit food?" said Chuck with raised eyebrows. Rory was trying to stick to his vegan diet, eating a plate of carrots and beans. "This may be a good time to decide to switch to a higher-octane food source."

"Vegetarian is the best option for survival situations, and we're not down to Funyuns yet," replied Rory, smiling. "And getting back to botnets, denial-of-service attacks are a legitimate form of civil disobedience, like a cyber version of a sixties sit-in."

"You're that blogger for the *Times* who covered Anonymous, right?" said Damon.

Rory nodded.

"So you support what Anonymous did to the logistics companies, what got us into this mess?" demanded Chuck.

"I support their right to defend and express their point of view," replied Rory, "but I don't think they were the ones—"

"We'll see how much you support them," said Chuck angrily, "when we lock you onto the goddamn roof in this storm."

"Hey, play nice," I said, raising my hands.

"It's criminal is what it is," grunted Chuck.

"Actually, it's not," pointed out Damon. "And that's my point about legal framework."

"So it's legal to operate a botnet and use them to attack?"

"It's illegal to *operate* a botnet," explained Damon, "but it's perfectly legal to join one, as an individual. In denial-of-service attacks, each computer just pings the target a few times a second, and there's nothing wrong with instructing your computer to do that. But when you control hundreds of thousands of computers and direct them to do the same thing, that's when the problem starts."

"So it's illegal to run a botnet, but legal to join one? That doesn't make any sense."

Damon shrugged. "And what's illegal in one place is legal somewhere else. You can hire a botnet over the Web, paid through PayPal, to attack a competitor. How is the FBI going to arrest someone in Khuzestan? They have international laws for dealing with money laundering, drugs, terrorists, but few for cyber."

Chuck frowned at Damon. "We need to make sure that anyone who messes with this stuff knows they'll be tracked down. Scare the shit out of them."

"Fear as a weapon?" shrugged Rory. "Deterrence based on fear is a holdover from the Cold War. So that's your idea?"

"Worked pretty damn well for forty years."

"And look where it got us," said Rory, his voice getting louder. "A democracy based on fear is not a democracy. Fear of the commies, fear of the terrorists—it never ends! You know who else used fear to keep people in check? Stalin, Hitler—"

"That is such a load of left-wing horseshit. You want somebody to blame?" Chuck pointed at the Chinese family huddled together on the stairs in the corner of the room. Then he lowered his hand. "You know what? I am afraid," he continued. "I'm afraid of what the hell is going on out there. I *am* afraid."

The room went silent, the only sound the wind whistling outside.

"Y'all want something more concrete to be afraid of?"

We all turned to the entrance.

It was Paul, the intruder from a few days before, and he had a gun to Richard's head. A group of men appeared behind him. Stan, the owner of the garage, was with them, also holding a gun.

"Sorry," said Stan, looking toward Chuck and Rory. "But we got families too. Nobody needs to get hurt."

Paul shoved Richard into the room and pointed his gun directly at Tony. "We don't got any heroes in here, do we?"

———————————————————————

"I'm sorry."

The wind howled outside. It was getting dark.

"It's not your fault, Tony. I told you to come up, remember? And I sure as hell didn't want a gun fight in here with the kids."

He nodded, unconvinced.

They'd slipped into the building during the few minutes when he'd come upstairs and the lobby had been empty. Upon entering Richard's apartment, they'd immediately zeroed in on Tony and removed the .38 from his pocket. They must have been watching us for a long time.

"We could just rush them," whispered Chuck.

"Are you out of your mind?"

Lauren had Luke on her lap and was staring at me, willing me to stay still. The thought of being shot in front of my son was terrifying. We had to let them take what they wanted. Even if they took everything, we still had what we'd stashed outside. It was better to wait this out.

"Quiet over there!" shouted Paul.

He was sitting by the entrance with Stan, and they'd corralled all of us at the opposite end of the apartment. We could hear the rest of their gang dragging and pulling things in the hallway. *Our things.*

"We can't let them take everything," muttered Chuck under his breath. With every scrape and bump we heard, he tensed up, cursing and glaring at Paul.

"Chuck, do not do anything," I whispered. "Do you hear me?" Chuck nodded.

"I said QUIET!" yelled Paul, waving his gun at us.

Outside the door we heard a grunt, and something heavy hit the ground. It sounded like they were dragging the generator. And then it went quiet. Paul fidgeted with his gun, smiling.

The door opened a crack and Paul turned toward it. "You guys done?"

"*Nyet.*"

A long rifle barrel appeared through the crack in the door, nudging it open. Irena materialized, holding an antique double-barrel shotgun. She was still wearing her cooking apron, stained as usual, with a tea towel thrown over one shoulder. Stooped over the gun, she shuffled through the doorway, the barrel shaking as she tried to keep it centered.

Paul and Stan backed away from the door, separating.

"Drop it, grandma," Paul said slowly, pointing his pistol at her. "I don't want to have to put you down."

Aleksandr appeared in the darkness behind Irena. The lights were out in the hallway. He was holding the ax from the emergency fire locker, and it was dripping with blood.

Irena aimed her gun straight at Paul's chest. "You know how many times I have been shot?" she laughed. "Nazis and Stalin couldn't kill me. You maybe think a worm like you can?"

"Put that freakin' gun down, lady!" yelled Stan, waving his own gun at us. "I'll shoot one of them, I swear to God."

Grunting, Aleksandr winced and stepped in beside his wife. "You hurt one hair, I eat your liver for dinner while you watch. I killed bastards like you before your whore mother was born."

"I'm warning you, grandma, put it down!" screeched Paul, his voice wavering.

He was pointing his gun at Irena's head but staring at the blood dripping off Aleksandr's ax.

Irena laughed. "*Tupoy*. So stupid. You want kill, don't shoot head." Her eyes narrowed. "You aim chest, more painful, less chance." Smiling, she bared a mouthful of gold-capped teeth and began squeezing the trigger of her gun. "Say good-bye, *dolboyeb durak*—"

"Okay, okay, stop," whimpered Paul, holding his gun up.

Irena motioned for him to get rid of it with a flick of her chin, and he dropped it on the floor with a loud thud.

"What the hell are you doing?" screeched Stan. He spun his gun toward Irena. "You never said anything about these freakin' psychos."

"Don't point that at my wife," growled Aleksandr, taking two powerful strides toward Stan, raising the ax. Stan dropped his gun and backed away, raising his hands to protect himself.

"Okay, okay!" I yelled, standing up and running toward them. Reaching behind Irena, I shut the door. "Where are the rest of them?"

Irena said, "One at end hallway, dead I think. Others ran away."

"We gotta make sure they're not in here," said Chuck, collecting the two guns from the floor and reaching into Paul's jacket to remove the .38 he'd taken from Tony, then handing it to me. "You watch these guys while Tony, Richard, and I go and make sure they're gone."

Chuck looked down at Paul's legs and then smirked at him. "Looks like *grandma* made you wet your pants."

DAY 8: DECEMBER 30

Something smelled awful.

"Just keep moving."

We were walking our captives over to Penn Station, to deliver them to the NYPD barracks there. The snowstorm had raged through the night, and it was still snowing, but only barely. Tiny snowflakes fell gently from a hazy sky, the world of New York a wintry tomb in muted grays and whites.

Trash had begun to appear across the pristine snow, most in green and black bags, but also loose bits and pieces. Paper and plastic wrappers spiraled together with snow in the circling gusts of wind. I was sniffing at some trash bags at the edge of the street, trying to find the source of the foul smell, when I was nearly hit by a splatter of brown sludge.

I realized what it was: people were throwing their waste from windows—piss and shit and whatever else they needed to get rid of. The dusting of snow was hiding the sight, but not the smell. Today it was just below freezing, and for the first time I was glad it was cold.

Paul laughed as I recoiled from the excrement.

Who threw that? I craned my neck upward. The building before me disappeared into the white sky after twenty floors.

Nobody was visible in the immense wall of windows stretching into infinity.

"Keep laughing, asshole," said Chuck. "I have a feeling you're going to be living in your *own* filth soon."

I didn't say anything, just kept staring up at the windows. It wasn't often that I looked up when walking the streets, and the immensity of the world above was mesmerizing. *So many people. My God, so many people.*

"You okay, Mike?" asked Tony.

I took a deep breath and focused. "More or less."

After securing our floor, Chuck had led a group of us through the building, making sure the invaders were gone. Paul's gang had raided almost all of the apartments, taking what they could, and had removed a lot of the food and equipment from our floor. Irena and Aleksandr had managed to stop them from taking everything, and the generator was still there.

The man Aleksandr hit with the ax hadn't been dead. He was writhing and whimpering in a dark pool of blood when we'd gotten to him. Pam had managed to bandage the deep wound between his shoulder and neck, but he'd lost a lot of blood.

He was Paul's brother.

Richard and Chuck had grilled Paul and Stan for names and addresses. Aleksandr and Irena had stayed there with us, not saying anything, just staring while we questioned them. Paul was clearly terrified we'd leave them alone with the Borodins. He'd answered all our questions almost immediately. They hadn't broken into the building; he had stolen keys from the front locker a few days before.

"Do you want to walk up Ninth?" asked Chuck, stopping at the intersection.

I shook my head. "Definitely not. Let's cross to Seventh and go straight up. The entrance to the NYPD barracks is on that side, and I don't want to get stuck in any crowds outside Penn."

"You sure?"

"We are not going up Ninth."

Chuck shoved Paul ahead of him. Damon was with us too, helping Paul's injured brother walk.

Chuck and Tony and a few others had ventured off at daybreak to an address around the corner that Paul had named. I'd refused to go. It had turned into an armed standoff. Of course, the people manning the entrance had refused to let Chuck in while he was waving his gun around and screaming about stolen food.

Tony whispered to me that Chuck had threatened to march Paul and Stan in front of their building and execute them if they didn't give us our stuff back. But the people there just told Chuck to go away, saying that they didn't know anything, and that they had families and children inside.

That building was on Ninth, and there was no way I was going to walk past it on our way to Penn. Chuck was in a grim mood.

We made our way single-file along the packed-down trail in the middle of Twenty-Fourth and then started up Seventh toward Penn. All of the ground-floor windows were smashed, with junk and trash poking out from the snowbanks. A lot of people were out on the streets, bundled up, toting backpacks and carrying bags, on their way somewhere, anywhere. This stream of human traffic merged into a river of people going up Seventh. Seeing us coming with guns out and marching our prisoners, everyone gave us a wide berth, but nobody stopped to watch us or ask what was going on.

As we reached the corner of Thirty-First and Penn Station,

the flow of people spilled into a flood. Thousands of people were massed together, shouting and shoving. Someone was yelling into a megaphone, trying to direct the crowd. A banner hanging above the north entrance said *Emergency Food*. The line stretched around the block.

Tony and Chuck had Paul's and Stan's hands tied behind their backs, and they held onto the cords. Chuck leaned over to Paul. "I want you to run, asshole, so I can put a bullet in your head. Just try it."

Paul studied his feet.

"Follow me," I said, waving them into the crowd. I could see a group of NYPD officers at the main door of the office tower above Penn. Winding our way through, we managed to get to the first barricade.

"I need to speak to Sergeant Williams!" I yelled at the police officer there. Motioning to Paul and Stan, I added, "These men, they attacked us, armed robbery."

The officer put a hand on his gun as he watched Damon supporting Paul's bloody brother. "You're going to have to put those weapons down!"

"Please, can you find Sergeant Williams?" I asked again. "He's a friend. My name is Michael Mitchell."

The officer pulled his weapon out of its holster. "You need to—"

"He's a friend. Please just ask him."

The officer backed up a step and spoke into his walkie-talkie, looking at us from time to time. He nodded and then holstered his gun, waved to us, and opened the barricade. "Follow me!" he yelled above the noise. "You're lucky he's here. You're going to have to give me those weapons, though."

Chuck and Tony offered theirs up, and I handed him the .38 I had tucked into my coat. He led us up a set of stairs and through the main lobby to the cafeteria I'd been in before. We released Paul's brother into the care of one of their EMTs. Sergeant Williams was waiting for us. The officer whispered a few words to him and then stood back.

Sergeant Williams looked at us with tired eyes. "Had some trouble?"

I'd been expecting him to lead us somewhere formal, to station us at a desk to fill in paperwork, to take our prisoners into a concrete room with double-sided glass. He just motioned for us to sit down.

"These guys attacked us last night—"

"We attacked you? You butchered my brother, Vinny, with a friggin' ax!" yelled Paul. "Goddamn animals."

"Shut your hole," said Sergeant Williams. He turned to me. "Is that true?"

I nodded. "But they were holding us, our wives and kids, at gunpoint, stealing our stuff. We had no choice—"

Holding up a hand, Sergeant Williams interrupted me. "I believe you, son. I do, and we can hold them for a while, but I can't promise anything right now."

"What do you mean?" said Chuck. "Lock 'em up. We'll give you statements."

Sergeant Williams sighed. "I'll take your statements, but there's nowhere to put them. As of this morning, New York State Correctional is releasing all minimum-security prisoners. No food, no water, no staff, generators out, and can't open and close cells electronically. Had to let them all go. Nearly thirty prisons emptied. God help us if they release any of the bastards in Attica or Sing Sing."

"So, what, you're going to let these guys go?"

"We'll lock them upstairs for now, but we may have to let them go, depending on how long this lasts. Even if we do, though, it's not forgiven, just delayed." He scowled at Paul and Stan. "Either that, or we put a bullet in their heads in the basement."

Is he serious? I held my breath, waiting.

Sergeant Williams clapped his hand on the table and roared with laughter. "You should have seen your faces," he laughed at Paul and Stan. "Goddamn idiots." He looked back at us. "Army is here now, taking control of the emergency stations. Martial law is being declared later today. From this point on, any more of this, and it *will* be a bullet, get me?" he said, returning his gaze to Paul and Stan.

They both nodded, some color returning to their faces.

"Okay, Ramirez, get 'em out of here."

The officer who'd led us in grabbed Paul and Stan by the arms and pulled them up from the table, leading them out of the cafeteria. He left our guns behind on the table with Sergeant Williams.

"Sorry, boys, it's the best we can do for now. Is there anything else?" asked Sergeant Williams. "Is your family all right?"

"We're okay, yeah," I replied.

For the first time since entering, I looked around the cafeteria. Before it had been a bustling beehive of activity, busy and lived-in but clean, but in just a few days it had become filthy. It was almost empty.

Seeing my face, Sergeant Williams anticipated what I was thinking. "Lost most of my men. I mean, not dead—although we have had a few officers down—but mostly gone home. No sleep, no supplies. Thank God the military's arrived, but so far they don't have a tenth of the manpower they need."

"You're not going home to your family?"

He laughed. "The force is my family. Divorced, kids hate me and live anywhere but near me."

"Sorry," I mumbled.

"Here is as good as anywhere for me right now," he continued, slapping the table. "And I may need *your* help before all this is over."

"We do have one thing you may find useful," said Chuck.

"Really?" said Sergeant Williams. "You have something that will help us with this mess?"

Chuck pulled a small memory chip out of his pocket. "We do."

DAY 9: NEW YEAR'S EVE, DECEMBER 31

"Appetite for risk," said Chuck drunkenly. "That's the problem with America, why we're in this mess."

"Risk?" I said.

"Yes," came the slurred response, "or, I mean, our lack of appetite for it."

We were back in Richard's place for a New Year's Eve party, with nearly everyone in the entire building, over forty people. After the break-in and the drama yesterday, we had two people on a rotating watch in the lobby, each armed with a .38 and a cell phone that could broadcast alert messages to everyone in the building through Damon's mesh network.

Some light had finally appeared at the end of the tunnel. The two radio stations still transmitting, New York Public Radio and New York Public Services, were predicting that power would be returned to Lower Manhattan within the next day. The Army Corps of Engineers had arrived and were throwing their weight behind fixing whatever the problem was. Heavy military helicopters were skimming the city all day, and the noise and commotion gave a feeling of safety, a sense that the big boys were here.

We kept on hauling up snow for water, foraging outside, and trading with neighboring buildings for supplies, and inside did our best to clean up, decorate, and cook palatable food. Chuck wired the generator into the music system and TV at Richard's and was playing videos and music from Damon's phone. Streamers hung from the ceiling.

We'd invited the group from the second floor, nine people, up for the party. In the raid two days before, Paul's gang had stolen some of their supplies as well. They were celebrating Irena and Aleksandr as the heroes who had stopped them, a role the old couple weren't comfortable with but accepted with smiles and nods.

People stood around in groups chatting; some even danced. If you closed your eyes, it was almost as if everything was normal— almost. Nobody had showered in five days.

"Appetite for risk?" said Rory. "Yesterday you were saying we need more fear, and today you're saying we need more risk?"

"I'm agreeing with you," replied Chuck.

"You are?" said a bewildered Rory.

"I thought about it, and you're right. Fear isn't the answer. If we're afraid of everything, then we're afraid to do anything, and that means we're giving *up* our freedom. You were right!"

Over Chuck's shoulder I could see Susie and Lauren sitting on the carpet in the living room, holding up Luke and Ellarose together, helping them dance. Everyone looked happy.

Chuck grinned, picked up a bottle from the middle of the table and poured himself another drink. We were sitting around Richard's kitchen table, with an assortment of his finest Scotches in the middle.

"A few weeks ago at one of my restaurants," said Chuck, "guess who walked in?"

This is going to be one of those stories.

"Who?"

"Gene Kranz."

Everyone but Damon shrugged. "Head mission controller for Apollo?"

"Right! Back in Gene's day, they were strapping themselves to rocket sleds and lighting the fuse with a cigar. Do you know the average age of the mission controller during the Apollo program?"

Now we all shrugged, but he wasn't really asking.

"Twenty-seven!"

"Your point?"

"My point is that these days people barely trust a twenty-seven-year-old to cook their burger, never mind land on the moon. Everything needs to be vetted by a million committees, and we're afraid of practically everything. We're just not willing to accept risk anymore, and it's killing this country."

"Exactly," agreed Rory. "We're afraid of terrorists, so we let the government start to collect personal information about where we are and what we're doing, put up cameras everywhere."

"No risk," said Chuck, wagging one finger in the air, "equals no freedom."

"But if you're not doing anything wrong," I pointed out, "you have nothing to be afraid of. I don't mind giving up a little privacy for the sake of security."

"That's where you're wrong," countered Rory. "You have *everything* to be afraid of. Where's that information going?"

I shrugged. In the new media business ventures I was working on, we collected huge amounts of information about consumers online and sold it to businesses. I didn't see anything wrong with it.

"Do you know there are new laws that give the government the right to look at everything you do online, watch everywhere you go?"

I shook my head.

"Anytime there's even a hint of the government limiting the public's ability to buy guns, people go crazy about them taking away our freedom, but this new law that gives the government the right to spy into every aspect of your life, without your consent—barely a peep. A clear violation of the Third and Fourth Amendments, but nobody says a word." He took a deep breath.

"You know what freedom really is?" demanded Rory. "Freedom is civil liberty, and the foundation of civil liberty is privacy. No privacy means no civil liberty means no freedom. You know why they don't just fingerprint everyone?"

"Seems like a good idea to me," laughed Chuck.

"Because once they have your fingerprints," continued Rory, ignoring Chuck, "you instantly become a suspect in every crime. They'll run your fingerprints against everything they find at a crime. You go from being a free citizen to being a criminal suspect."

"And fingerprints are just one way of identifying you," added Damon. "Location, your face on a camera, things you buy—all your personal information creates a *digital* fingerprint."

Chuck wasn't convinced. "But who really cares if the government has a bunch of information about me? What are they going to use it for?"

"What are they going to use it for? That's *exactly* the question. And if they have it, then anyone can steal it," replied Rory. He pointed at me. "And the new media applications you work on are even worse."

I raised my hand. "Hey, come on now."

It was now obvious that Rory was even drunker than Chuck. His eyes were swimming as he glared at me. "If you're not paying for a product, you *are* the product. Isn't that right? Aren't you selling all the private information you collect on consumers to marketing companies?"

Chuck shook his head. "Where are you going with all this?"

"Where am I going?" said Rory, rising from his chair. He blinked and took another sip from his drink. "I'll tell you where I'm going. Our grandfathers stormed the beaches of Normandy to protect our freedom. And now, because we're afraid and not willing to accept personal risk, we're giving up those same freedoms that they fought and died for. We're giving away our freedom because we're scared."

He had a good point.

Damon nodded. "You can't protect freedom by giving it away."

"Exactly," said Rory, sitting back down.

Just then the music stopped and a voice came over the sound system, "*The sight is unbelievable. I don't even know how to describe it—*"

"Are you boys playing nice?" said Susie, holding Ellarose in her arms. Susie had snuck up behind Chuck during our animated discussion.

"We're just having a little chat," I replied.

Chuck looked up and wrapped an arm around Susie's waist, leaning in to kiss Ellarose.

"Come sit with us," said Susie to me and Chuck. "We have the countdown on the radio."

"*—thousands of people are standing in the snow, holding candles, lanterns, anything they can find—*"

Getting up, I frowned. "From where?"

She laughed. "Times Square, of course."

Picking up my drink, I crossed over to the couches and squeezed myself in beside Lauren, retrieving Luke and sitting him on my lap.

"*For the first time in over a hundred years, since Times Square was named Times Square,*" continued the announcer, "*it is dark on New Year's, but while the neon signs may be dim, the light is still burning brightly in the hearts of New Yorkers. People are appearing out of the darkness everywhere—*"

The room went quiet, spellbound. Outside, big snowflakes appeared out of the blackness, illuminated briefly by the light spilling from our sanctuary, and then fell away, disappearing again into the night.

"*—the official celebration had been canceled, and authorities had warned against a gathering, but people are still coming together. A makeshift structure has been erected in the middle of the snow, a projection screen and generators—*"

"Remember this moment," I whispered to Luke.

"*With one minute to midnight, the crowd has joined together in a spontaneous rendition of our national anthem. I'm going to try to position my microphone—*"

We could already hear it, beyond the noise and the static, the unmistakable sound of "The Star-Spangled Banner." Everyone was caught up in the emotion. It was our anthem, from another moment when this country was under siege, another time it was bent but not broken. The words stretched through time, connecting us with the past and the future at the same time.

And then the sounds of clapping and cheering. "*Ten . . . nine . . . eight . . .*"

"I love you, Luke," I said, squeezing and kissing him. Lauren kissed him too. "And I love you, Lauren." I kissed her, and she kissed me back.

"... *two* ... *one* ... *Happy New Year!*"

The room erupted with the sound of noisemakers and merry-making, everyone getting up to give hugs and kisses.

"Hey," someone shouted, "look over there!"

I was busy giving Ellarose a kiss when Chuck tapped me on the shoulder. People were crowding at the window at the far end of the apartment. Damon was waving us over.

"The lights are on!" he yelled, pointing out the window.

Where before there had been only dark, the falling snowflakes on the other side of the window were now lit from behind with a soft glow. Picking up Luke, I walked over.

It wasn't just a single lamp or streetlight; the entire street and the building facing us were illuminated. From this angle, between the buildings, we couldn't actually see lights, just their flickering reflection. But looking up, I saw that even the sky was lit up. The block next door must have power, just as promised.

"Come on!" yelled Chuck. "Let's go downstairs and have a look!"

"I'll stay here with the kids," said Lauren. "You go look."

I kissed her again. "No, come on, I want Luke to see this!"

In a mad rush fueled by the alcohol in our systems, everyone searched for something to put on. It wasn't that cold out, so I grabbed what I could find, taking care to bundle Luke up, and then clambered down the stairs with everyone else. In the lobby, the front door was jammed up with snow, so we squeezed, one by one, out the back door and onto Twenty-Fourth Street.

Luke was confused but smiling at all the action.

With my headlamp in one hand, I picked my way to the center

of Twenty-Fourth. The path there was packed down and rough, and in the semidarkness I took my time, watching my footsteps, holding onto Luke. Chuck and Tony were right ahead of me, with Damon following behind. The light was spilling onto Ninth Avenue ahead of us, and a crowd was already in the street, staring down toward Twenty-Third Street.

It began snowing harder, and the wind was picking up. Rounding the corner, I pushed past Chuck and into an open spot and looked up, expecting to see street lights, neon signs.

I was greeted by smoke and flames.

The high-rise on the corner of Twenty-Third and Ninth was on fire. Luke looked up, his small face reflecting the flames. Seeing the fire, he smiled and pointed, just as someone jumped through the smoke from a top-floor window, sailing silently through the air and hitting the snow below with a sickening thud.

The crowds backed away, and then two people ran to try to help the person who'd jumped. Lauren was behind us, and I looked back at her as she walked toward us, still in the darkness. She was smiling, not seeing what I was seeing, but when she saw my face she knew something was very wrong. I hopped back through the snow to her, grabbing Damon and asking, "Can you go upstairs with Lauren, take Luke back up?"

Looking up in horror, Lauren finally saw the flames. I turned her away and looked straight into her eyes. "Go back inside, baby. Please go back in with Luke." I handed him to her.

It wasn't just one building. Other buildings on the block had already caught fire. Black smoke was billowing up into the swirling white snow, an ominous cloud lit by the inferno that fed it. Thousands of people were huddled together in the streets, stretching off into the distance as far as the eye could see, mesmerized by the blaze. There were no sirens, no noise at all except the roar and crackle of the fire battling with the cold and snow.

New York was freezing and burning at the same time.

DAY 10: NEW YEAR'S DAY, JANUARY 1

"Try not to move." The man on the mattress groaned and looked up at me. His face was badly burned. "We're going to get help."

He closed his eyes, grimacing.

We'd turned the lobby of our building into a makeshift infirmary by dragging some mattresses down from the empty apartments and laying them on the floor. Pam was running the show with a doctor and some EMTs from neighboring buildings. The acrid stench of smoke and fire mixed with the smells of body odor and untreated wounds. We'd brought a kerosene heater down into the lobby, but we were running low on fuel so we'd started burning diesel in it. It didn't burn clean, which added the stink of soot and petroleum to the air.

We wedged the back door open to ventilate the area, and at least it had warmed up outside. It was above freezing for the first time in a week, and the snow had stopped. The sun was shining for the first time in days.

The fires outside were still burning, and I thanked God that our building wasn't attached to the neighboring ones.

A steady wind had blown all night, urging the flames from building to building. It wasn't just this one fire either. New York Public Radio announced that two other fires had started in

Manhattan during the New Year festivities—fires and candles didn't play well with alcohol. The authorities were now warning people not to start fires indoors and to be careful with candles and heaters.

Too little, too late, and besides, what are people supposed to do if they're cold and in the dark?

A torrent of people had run out of the burning buildings the night before. Many were suffering from smoke inhalation, and some were horribly injured, but most were unhurt. All of them, though, were terrified to be outside in the cold and dark, clutching whatever belongings they could carry, wondering where they would go.

A convoy of military Humvees had appeared from the blackness, crunching through the snow along Twenty-Third from the West Side Highway. There wasn't anything they could do about the fires. There was no water, no fire department, and no emergency services. They radioed in what information they could, loaded up the wounded, and within a half-hour were gone, replaced by a second convoy about an hour later.

A third convoy failed to appear.

By that time, a ragtag collection of local firefighters, doctors, nurses, and off-duty police officers had started trying to create order out of chaos. Not knowing what else to do, we began taking some of the wounded back to our building while trying to convince the residents of nearby buildings to do the same.

The newly homeless had made tearful pleas to be let into their neighbors' apartments. A few had found people willing to take them in, and we'd agreed to take two couples, but the requests became overwhelming. Standing back, we'd watched people begin their lonely walk up toward Javits and Penn, despondent, terrified, and many with children among them. A steady stream of new refugees had disappeared into the darkness and snow, begging bystanders for shelter, many with only their phones to use as flashlights to hold back the night.

A noise at the rear entrance snapped my attention back to the present. Damon appeared through the door with a young kid from one of the adjoining buildings. He waved at Pam and me to come over. He was holding what looked to be a huge bong.

"I went around and asked for painkillers and antibiotics," said Damon in a hushed voice to Pam. "Most of what I could come up with was Advil and aspirin." He held out his hand to reveal a few bottles. "Even this was difficult to get people to give up, but I have another idea."

"And that is?" asked Pam.

Damon hesitated. "We get them to smoke weed. It's a great painkiller." He motioned to the kid beside him, who must have been about sixteen. The kid smiled awkwardly and produced a huge bag of marijuana.

"These people are suffering from smoke inhalation, even burnt lungs," hissed Pam, wide-eyed and motioning around at twenty beds we had littered on the floor, "and you want me to get them to *smoke*?"

Damon's face fell.

"Wait!" said the kid. "We could make, like, brownies, or, no . . . tea! We could make some tea. Add a little alcohol to help dissolve the THC. That'd work."

Pam's face softened. "That's actually a great idea."

Someone on a bed cried out in pain.

"Can you get it done right away?" asked Pam.

The kid nodded, and Damon told him to go up to the sixth floor and ask Chuck for whatever he needed.

At that moment Damon's cell phone pinged. It had been pinging all day and night from people joining the mesh network he'd started.

After showing Sergeant Williams how to install the software, we'd asked him to get as many people as he could to start using it. The more people that were connected, the farther messages could travel. Damon had also gone out to neighboring buildings with memory chips and explained the procedure. Judging by all the incoming messages, Damon and Sergeant Williams had been busy. The meshnet had gone viral. Already hundreds of people had joined, with dozens more every hour. People were finding ways to charge their cell phones, whether with generators or solar cells or by digging out and starting cars. Someone posted a general broadcast message to everyone connected, explaining how to pull out a car battery and hot-wire it to charge phones.

"Could you broadcast a message asking people in our area for some more pot?" I asked Damon. He nodded and pulled out his phone.

"We can pick it up on the way back," I added.

We were going back up to Penn with the worst of the wounded. Two people in our lobby were in need of critical care, beyond what we could provide. Tony was rigging up backpacks with harnesses attached to makeshift sleds we could pull through the snow, and I walked over to the basement stairs to see how he was doing.

As I arrived, he was just coming up, pulling his cargo behind him. Luke had been "helping" him, really just running around and arranging piles of empty water containers, but he loved being near Tony. Tony had him under one arm as he came up the stairs.

"Emergency lights have given out," he said when he saw me. He put Luke down and Pam came over to take him upstairs. "We better start saving the charge on the headlamps. Batteries are scarce."

I reached down to help him haul the sleds up. We slid them into the lobby.

"You're the best skier," said Tony, picking up the harness-backpack he'd rigged together and demonstrating how to use it. "I think you and I should do the hauling and bring Damon along for backup."

Damon shrugged. "I'll try, man, but surfing is more my thing than skiing."

How does a kid from Louisiana, who goes to school in Boston, end up a surfer?

I sighed. When I put my jeans on this morning, I had to do up my belt one notch tighter than usual. On the bright side, it looked like I was losing some of that weight Lauren had been bugging me about. On the other hand, I was hungry—starving, in fact.

Starving. With a sinking feeling I realized I might get firsthand experience of what that really felt like.

Tony, Damon, and I put on our outerwear while some of the EMTs dragged the sleds over to the two badly burned people we were taking up to Penn. Despite muffled cries and whimpers from the injured, they began bundling them up against the cold and doing their best to secure them in the sleds.

Opening the back door, we scampered to the top of the snow piled outside. The sky was a flat gray, and the air felt warm. It was amazing how quickly the body adjusted to the cold. Just two weeks ago I would have been complaining about this temperature, shivering, but now, with it hovering a few degrees above freezing, it felt almost tropical.

Standing on the snow pile, our feet were even with the heads of the people inside the lobby. One person propped the door open, while the rest pushed the sleds carrying the patients up the steep incline of snow. It was awkward work, and each jolt of the sleds earned a cry of pain from their occupants.

Soon we had our skis on and were heading down the middle of Twenty-Fourth in single file, with Damon bringing up the rear on foot, hopping through the snow as best he could. The two-lane ski and foot trails had become well worn, with openings cut into the snowbanks lining the streets, so our pace was quick.

Rounding the corner of Ninth, we stopped to look down the street. The building on the corner of Ninth and Twenty-Third was now a burnt-out husk, but the fire still raged in buildings farther down the avenue and around the corner on Twenty-Second. Thick black smoke smudged the gray sky.

As we continued along Twenty-Fourth, the foot traffic became heavier, with people going in all directions, dragging and carrying what they could.

The trash I'd first noticed two days ago was now heaped along the edges of the street, and with the warmer weather each breath of wind brought the reek of human excrement seeping up through the melting snow. At the larger heaps near the intersections, rats competed with gangs of human scavengers, combing through the garbage, searching for food.

As if in a trance, I slid through this landscape of urban decay, watching people's faces, inspecting their bags, fascinated by what they'd decided to carry: a chair here, a bag of books there. Someone in the distance was carrying a golden birdcage.

Peering in through the smashed windowpanes of shops, I saw people huddled inside around oil barrels with fires, smoke pouring out of the windows, blackening the sides of buildings. Despite it all, it was quiet, just the soft shuffle of feet on snow and the hushed muttering of the displaced.

"Hold on a second!" Damon yelled.

Looking back over my left shoulder as I rounded the corner of Seventh Avenue to start the trek up to Penn, I saw Damon crouched at the side of the road next to a pile of garbage bags, using his phone to take a picture of someone sitting there.

What is he doing? This wasn't the time to start fooling around. I slowed my pace, not wanting to leave him behind. In a few seconds he was back on the trail with us, jogging to catch up and then running ahead of us and darting off into the snow at the side of the street again. Poking through some bags and not finding what he was looking for, he ran back to walk beside me.

"That guy back there was dead," he explained, out of breath. He fiddled with his phone, typing something, while he walked in step with me.

There are going to be a lot of dead people, and if they're dead, there's nothing we can do for them anymore. Unimpressed, I didn't say anything.

"We should be making a record of what happened. That could be somebody's loved one," continued Damon, finishing typing and putting his phone away. "I created a mesh address, connected to my laptop back at our place, for people to send pictures to and add text and explanations of where and when and what. When all this is over, maybe we can help piece things together, bring some resolution."

Taking a deep breath, I realized I had it wrong. There was something we could still do. *We can give their loved ones some closure.*

"That's a great idea. Could you send me the address?"

"Already did."

Something else caught his eye, and he ran off.

"Smart kid," said Tony from behind me.

Up ahead, the crowd around Penn Station was much larger than two days before. The snow was black and tramped down, covered in litter and waste, and thousands of people thronged the entranceways. Soldiers in fatigues had replaced the NYPD officers manning the barricades, their weapons visible, with a sandbagged command post hiding heavier weaponry just behind.

As we approached, a low murmur grew into a roar of voices, sirens, and instructions shouted over megaphones. We stopped and studied the crowd.

"No way we're getting in there," said Tony. "Maybe we should try Port Authority or head up to Grand Central or Javits?"

"They'll be just as bad." I had an idea and pulled out my phone. "I'll text Sergeant Williams. Maybe he can send someone out."

While I sent my message, Damon and Tony detached our harnesses, checking on our passengers and explaining what we were doing. Within a few seconds of my hitting the Send button, before I'd even put the phone away, it pinged an incoming message.

"He's sending someone to us," I said. The meshnet was a lifesaver.

Tony adjusted the blankets on one of the sleds and whispered that someone was coming.

"Did you get any messages about—" I began to ask Damon, but I was cut off by a shriek in the crowd just ahead of us.

"Give me the bag, bitch!" yelled a large man, pulling a backpack away from a small Asian woman.

The man's blond hair was clumped in dirty dreadlocks that swung around his head as he pulled and tugged. The woman clung to one strap of her bag, and he dragged her through the snow while pulling a handgun out of one pocket. The crowd dispersed around them.

"I'm warning you," he growled, pulling at the bag with one hand and pointing the gun with the other.

The woman looked up at him, screaming something in Korean or Chinese, but she let go and fell into the snow. "That's my bag," she wept in English, her head bowed. "It's all I have."

"Goddamn bitch, I should shoot you right now."

Beside me, Tony pulled out his .38, holding it hidden between us. Glancing at him, I shook my head and put a hand out, holding him back. With my other hand I brought my phone up, thumbing the camera on, and took a picture.

The man smirked at me. "You like that?"

I took another picture and clicked a few buttons. "No, I do not. I just took your picture and e-mailed it to the NYPD officer who's on his way out here."

His smile evaporated and was replaced by confusion. "There's no phones working."

"On that you're wrong, and what you're doing is wrong."

His confusion turned to anger. I wasn't much for confrontation, and had never been in a fight in my life, but right was right. "Just because we're going through a bad time, it's no excuse to start hurting people."

The man straightened up. He was a lot bigger than I'd thought. "You call this a *bad* time? Are you kidding me? This is the end of days, brother, and the Chinese—"

"What you're doing isn't going to help."

"It's going to help me," he laughed.

"People will know what you did. You committed a crime, and I've recorded it." I held my phone up. "This will be over one day, and you'll have to answer."

He laughed again. "With all this crap going on, you think someone will care that I stole a bag?"

"I do," said Tony, still keeping his weapon concealed. A small crowd had gathered around us.

"Does anyone else here care about this bitch?" yelled the man, looking around at the crowd. Most people stared dumbly, but many nodded, agreeing with Tony.

"It's not right," yelled someone from the back.

"Give the lady her bag back," said another person in the front.

The man shook his head. "Screw all of you."

He walked away from us, and Tony started to raise his weapon, but the man threw the bag back at the woman after grabbing a few things from it.

"Let him go," I said unsteadily, holding Tony back. I was shaking. "It's not worth it."

Tony grunted, not agreeing with me, but put his gun away just the same. The crowd began dispersing, with two people coming to help the woman up. Several people approached us.

"Is your phone really working?" asked a teenage girl.

"Sort of," I replied, motioning toward Damon. "You'll have to talk to him."

Within a few minutes, a large crowd had gathered around Damon. Most of them still had their phones, but they were uncharged. He started by explaining ways they could charge them, and then began taking the memory chips out of some of their phones to copy the mesh software onto them.

"That was a good idea, taking that guy's picture," said Tony.

We watched Damon tutoring the crowd on meshnets. He was like a cyber version of Johnny Appleseed.

"With no police, people think they can get away with anything," said Tony. "Taking pictures might make them think twice."

"Maybe," I sighed. "Better than nothing."

"*Much* better than nothing, and better than shooting each other."

In the mass of people near the Penn entrance barricade, I saw some commotion, and then Officer Ramirez's face appeared, bobbing through the crowd toward us with two other NYPD officers in tow. As he approached us, he was shaking his head. "We can't take any more."

I motioned toward the sleds. "These people are from the fire last night. They're going to die if they don't get help."

"A lot of goddamn people are dying," muttered Ramirez, kneeling down beside one of the sleds and pulling back the blankets. Seeing the extent of the burns, he winced and closed his eyes, standing back up.

"Okay, guys, grab these sleds," he said to the officers with him. Turning to me, he added, "We'll take these two, but after this, no more. It's as bad or worse inside there." He pointed toward Madison Square Garden. "Understand?"

I nodded. *That bad already?*

"One more thing," he said as he turned to leave. "That guy Paul you brought in? His brother died last night of his injuries, and we may have to let him go."

"Let him go?" I remembered Sergeant Williams' heads-up, but I still couldn't believe it.

Ramirez shrugged. "They released all the medium-security

prisoners today. We got nowhere to keep them all. We're keeping everyone we bring in for a day or two, taking statements, but we need to let them go until all this is over."

Rubbing my face, I looked skyward. *My God, if Paul's brother died, and they let him go . . .* "When?"

"Maybe tomorrow, maybe the next day," said Ramirez, before disappearing into the crowd.

I watched him go, and a sinking feeling settled into my hungry stomach.

"You okay?"

It was Damon. The crowd around us was gone. He had finished giving his meshnet lessons.

"Not really."

Tony had heard Ramirez too, and I could see him gripping the .38 in his pocket.

Damon watched us for a moment. "Just before that guy attacked the woman, you were asking me a question, if I had any messages from somewhere?"

I laughed. "Ah, yes."

"What was it you wanted to know?"

"Did anyone e-mail you saying they had some weed for us?"

"Yep, I had two texts."

"Good, because I could use a joint about now."

DAY 11: JANUARY 2

"Two days. Maybe three."

"Only two days?"

Chuck nodded.

"And Ellarose can't eat just anything," added Susie, cradling her baby in her arms. "We've barely gotten her off formula." She sighed and looked down. "Not that we had much choice."

I was going to mention breast-feeding, but it felt too awkward. Anyway, the calories would just be coming from Susie, and she was thin to begin with.

Lauren had noticed things missing yesterday when we were out and she'd gone downstairs to help Pam with the burn victims. We were in Chuck and Susie's place doing an inventory now, sitting on their couch in the middle of the main room. Luke was running around with Chuck's night-vision goggles on, squeaking and pointing at us.

"Careful with those, Luke," I said, taking them away.

He tried to grab them back, so I rummaged around in a bag next to the couch for something else. Picking up a cardboard tube, I gave it to him, and he stuck it in his mouth.

We had one of the cell phones turned on as a radio, using an app Damon had found. Yesterday Manhattan had been down to two official radio stations still transmitting, but today we'd discovered that dozens of local stations had popped up, "pirate" ham radio stations that were being operated by local citizens, each broadcasting over a radius of a few blocks.

"The entire country is in a shambles," ranted the pirate radio announcer we were tuned into, JikeMike, in the background.

Chuck looked at me, bemused. "You know you just gave your son a flare, right?"

"Come on, Mike, be more careful!" exclaimed Lauren, reaching past me to grab the flare from Luke.

He shrieked, but then he saw Tony in the hallway and ran off after him. Lauren shook her head at me.

"Sorry," I mumbled, still in shock. I hadn't really accepted that this could drag on; a part of me was convinced that the power would come on at any moment and end the survival game we were playing. "We only have two days of food left?"

Chuck silenced the phone on the coffee table. "About two days if we keep sharing our food with everyone on our floor," he said. "We got"—he looked at the ceiling, counting mentally—"thirty-eight people up here now, plus four on the ground floor in the infirmary. We can't keep sharing what we have. People have been stealing from us. This isn't going to be over in a day or two or three, no matter what they're saying."

The official government radio station was still broadcasting that the New York Power Authority would have power back up to Con Edison and Lower Manhattan in the next day, but nobody believed it anymore.

In the first real news we'd had of events outside of New York, we learned that a massive fire had razed South Boston, and Philly, Baltimore, and Hartford were nearly as decimated. New York was the only city without water, though, at least so far. No news about Washington, but some sketchy reports said that Europe was in a shambles as well, with the Internet still down.

Some kind of cyberattack on infrastructure had been confirmed as the root cause of the system failures, but nobody could say with any certainty where the attacks had come from. Command and control servers were located all over the world, most of them within the US itself, and they were being shut down one by one.

The US military was still jacked up on DEFCON 2, a condition that indicated a strong possibility of imminent attack, but attack from where and by whom was an open question. The military continued searching for the unknown entities that had breached US airspace just before the first string of major power failures. Pirate radio stations were buzzing with speculation that towns all over the Midwest had been invaded like a cyber–*Red Dawn*.

The news was interesting, but had become irrelevant to our immediate situation.

"Something isn't right," continued Chuck. "When Paul and those guys got in here that time, Paul said he stole keys from the front desk. But there were no keys missing—Tony went and checked. Somebody must have let them in."

"So what are we going to do?" I asked.

"We need to start digging in for the long haul. No more trying to save the world." Chuck held up his hand, fending off an objection from Susie. "We need to save ourselves."

"We can't just take everything for ourselves. We'd start a war in our own building."

"I'm not suggesting that. I think we should divide up what we have and explain to people that they're on their own from here on out. With that stuff we stashed outside, we should be okay."

"Assuming we can find it," I replied. It had seemed a clever idea at the time, but to hang our survival on it seemed incredibly risky.

"So let's go out and see if we can recover it. But we *cannot* share it or tell anyone else."

"This isn't right," said Susie, but with less conviction this time.

"This is going to get *ugly*," said Chuck. "It's already ugly, and so far we've been soft. We can't afford that anymore." He looked at me. "Get Damon to send out a message for a town hall meeting."

"When?"

"End of the day, when the sun goes down." Reaching down with one finger, he swiped the radio back on.

"*—I think we're not getting any news from Washington and Los Angeles because they've been wiped out by biological attack, a new form of that bird flu. I ain't leaving New York, no goddamn way, and if anyone comes to my door, I got my shotgun—*"

Damon had set up his control center at the end of our hallway, between the door to my place and Chuck and Susie's. Two cell phones were attached to the back of a laptop via USB cables.

"They're how I connect to our meshnet," he explained. "I've gone out into neighboring buildings, and we have people nearby maintaining cell phones active on the network at fixed locations." He pointed to a pad of paper with scribbled notes and diagrams. "Usually on the third floor of buildings on the corners of blocks, and every hundred yards or so. Sort of like our own cell towers. Those give us at least some fixed points in the network nearby, but the rest is completely dynamic."

I'd asked him to explain what he was doing, but it'd been a long time since my engineering classes.

"It's not a 'hub and spoke' network like you're used to, but point-to-point, and uses reactive instead of proactive routing."

It was beyond me. "How do people know how to use it?"

"It works as a transparent proxy at the bottom of the network stack," he explained, laughing as he saw my face. "It's totally transparent to the user. They just use their cell phone like normal, except they need to add a new mesh address for people in their contact list."

"How many people connected so far?"

"Hard to say exactly, but more than a thousand already."

Damon had created a "mesh 911" text address, routing it into the cell phones of Sergeant Williams' group. It was getting dozens of calls an hour.

"And people are sending you pictures?"

We were asking everyone on the meshnet to send images of people who were hurt or dead, and of crimes being committed, along with notes, details, anything they could think of. It was all being stored on the hard drive of Damon's laptop.

"Yeah," he replied, "dozens already. I'm excited it's working, but the pictures . . ." He hung his head.

"Maybe you should stop looking at them."

He sighed. "It's hard not to."

I put a hand on his shoulder.

Damon had been busy. He'd also created a mesh repository where people could share useful tips, survival techniques for cold weather, and cell phone apps like an emergency radio, flashlight, compass and map for NYC, burn treatments, and first aid. The first emergency survival tip was posted by Damon himself—how to distill marijuana into a liquid painkiller.

"You're doing a lot of good, Damon, saving lives. There's nothing more you can do."

"Maybe we could have avoided all this if we'd been able to see the future."

"We can't see the future, Damon."

He met my eyes, deadly serious. "One day, I'm going to change that."

I paused, not sure what to say, then decided to simply bring us back to the present. "Can you send a text out to everyone who's staying on our floor, ask them to be here for a meeting at sunset?"

"About what?"

I took a deep breath and looked down the hallway. Tony was playing with Luke, some kind of hide-and-seek game. "Just tell them to come. We need to talk."

"None of us thought it was going to last this long," explained Chuck. "We'll keep sharing the electricity and heating and tools, but you're going to have to take more responsibility for yourselves."

"And that means?" asked Rory.

I counted thirty-three people, all crammed together in the hallway. Despite our best efforts, it was getting dirty. There were stains on the piles of blankets and sheets covering the furniture. Nobody had showered in a week or more, and most of them hadn't changed clothes in the same length of time. The dank smell of sweat permeated the air. The latrine area on the fifth floor had become a mess already, and the reek seemed to come through the walls and floors. The carpet was soaked from our hauling up snow for melting in the small elevator hallway, and this dampness had seeped into the furniture and cushions. Mold was creeping along the baseboards.

"What we're trying to say is that you're going to have to start finding your own food," I said, inspecting the dirt caked under my fingernails. "We can't just keep sharing what we have."

What *Chuck* had was more accurate, and everyone understood the line that was being drawn in the sand. Those that Chuck and Susie were going to share with, and those they weren't.

"So every man for himself? Is that what you're saying?" asked Richard.

He'd taken in several fire refugees and was still housing the Chinese family. I'd started to develop a grudging respect for him.

"No, we still need to share duties for guarding the apartment, for water and cleaning, but for food we're going to need to begin rationing what we have here." I pointed to the food we'd piled on the coffee table. "We've divided up what we could share. Add this to what you have. You're going to need to start going to the emergency food lines."

Earlier this afternoon, Chuck and I had slipped out and used my treasure hunt app to try to recover some of the food supplies we'd hidden. It had worked. We'd dug up three bags on the first try.

"Each person gets one of these rations," said Chuck, pointing again to the pile on the table, "and then you're responsible for how slowly or quickly you decide to eat. After that, you need to make trips outside to find what you can."

Shaking his head, Richard made for the table and collected a pile of the packages.

Chuck watched him. "What are you doing?"

"We're ten people." Richard pointed back to the Chinese

family and refugees at his end of the hallway. "*We're* going to share what we have." He retreated to his place in a huff, and his group went with him.

Rory grabbed four packs of rations, looking at Chuck as he did. He and Pam had taken in a couple from downstairs. "I guess we know who our friends are now."

"I'm sorry," I said, "but we need to draw the line somewhere."

Rory looked at Damon, but turned silently and went back to his apartment, taking Pam and the other couple with him.

The nine people who remained were the young family Damon had brought with him and six people from the apartments downstairs. They just mumbled their thanks and took the packages.

Chuck, Damon, and I went inside Chuck's place to make dinner while Tony went back downstairs. "That went well," I said after a pause.

"I want to barricade our end of the hallway," said Chuck. "I don't want anyone except us coming over here anymore."

"Do you think that's a good idea?" asked Damon.

My phone pinged an incoming message, and I took it out of my pocket. *We had to release Paul and Stan,* read a message from Sergeant Williams. *We warned them not to come near you, but be on the lookout. There was nothing else I could do.*

"Yes," I replied to Damon, reading the message again before handing Chuck the phone. "I think a barricade would be a good idea."

Damon stared at me while Chuck read the message, a tendon in his neck flexing.

"And we need more guns," said Chuck from between clenched teeth.

DAY 12: JANUARY 3

We were crowded around the coffee table in Chuck's apartment, looking at Damon's laptop screen. Lauren was sitting beside me with Luke wedged between her knees. He was playing with a spatula. Ellarose had been crying in Susie's lap, but she went quiet and a tiny fart squeaked out. She began screaming again.

"I think that one's yours to clean up," Susie said to Chuck, handing over Ellarose. "I'll try to find some clean clothes and water."

Chuck sniffed Ellarose's backside but shrugged when he couldn't smell anything. While we'd managed the first few diaperless days by wrapping the babies in pinned-up toweling, our attempts to recycle the makeshift cloth diapers had become difficult.

Ellarose quieted down as Chuck rocked her, humming a lullaby, with a radio announcer speaking in a steady monotone in the background: "*If you are going out for emergency relief today in the Midtown area, the Red Cross is advising you to avoid Penn and Madison and head for one of the smaller relief stations.*"

We had a diaper bucket in one of the latrine apartments downstairs filled with bleach, but drying them meant hanging them near the kerosene heater. This wasn't popular.

"Using signal strength from the fixed-point cell phones I set up," explained Damon, "I can triangulate the position of anyone on the meshnet in our neighborhood."

"Have you found them?" I asked.

Damon wagged his head. "More or less, assuming they're connected, which I would assume." He pointed at seven pulsing dots on the map overlay he'd been working on all night. "The mesh addresses are sort of like phone numbers, and when people create them they usually attach their names. It's an open network, so anybody with a little technical skill can see everyone else right now. These mesh addresses I'm tracking, they all use names like 'Paul' or 'Stan' and have recently been in our neighborhood."

"Won't they be suspicious that we might be able to track them if they connect?"

Damon shrugged. "I doubt they know it was us who started the meshnet. People are just sharing it now—it's going viral by itself. Anyway, people tend to not think about that sort of thing."

"And they don't seem like the sharpest sticks in the shed," added Chuck. "Can you create some sort of alert if any of them comes closer than a block away?"

Damon looked up. "I could do that, send a text to everyone."

"Not everyone," said Chuck. "Just our gang. I don't trust anyone else."

"So you really think someone on our floor is in with Paul and his gang?" asked Lauren. "I can't imagine anyone—"

"Someone let him in," replied Chuck. "There were no missing keys, right, Tony?"

Tony nodded.

"And how did they know we'd all be in Richard's place at that party? Luck? I don't think so."

"Who do you think it is?"

"I don't know," said Chuck, shaking his head. "Those couples from downstairs, I don't know them, and Rory—"

"Rory?" Lauren exclaimed. "Are you serious?"

"He's friends with Stan, and he's into all that Anonymous stuff, hacking, criminals—"

"They're hardly criminals," I said.

Chuck shook his head. "Well, who do you think?"

"What about Richard?"

Lauren's nostrils flared. "What is wrong with you, Mike? Are you still jealous?"

"He's the one that brought us all together at his place," I replied.

"And generously fed everyone, if I remember."

Chuck put up one hand, holding Ellarose with the other. "Hey! We're just speculating. All I'm saying is that something isn't right, and we need to keep this tracking tool secret." He turned to Damon. "So can we track anyone, even people in our building?"

Lauren shook her head. "This is the same stupid behavior that got the world into this mess to begin with." She picked up Luke and left the apartment. Chuck scratched his head, waiting for the door to close behind Lauren, and then looked at Damon again.

Damon returned his gaze. "As long as they're in our neighborhood and on the network, yes, we can track them."

Ellarose's face turned bright red, and she began a new round of screaming. Chuck lifted her up and sniffed her again. "What's wrong?" he whispered to her, and then he turned to us. "Do you guys mind?"

He wanted to check her diaper.

"Course not," Damon and I muttered.

Chuck laid Ellarose on the coffee table beside the laptop. When he pulled back the diaper, I expected a brown streak, but instead saw an angry, bright red rash. It looked painful and infected, and Ellarose screamed. Chuck closed his eyes and then said, "Can you guys give me a few minutes? We need to talk about this some more, but I need to . . ." His voiced faltered.

"No problem," said Damon, picking up his laptop.

Diaper rashes in these unsanitary conditions were dangerous. Susie couldn't produce much milk under the stress, and Ellarose's stomach was having a tough time adjusting to the random food we scrounged. She was losing a lot of weight, but there wasn't much we could do. I could handle facing almost any pain or discomfort myself, but the children—

I looked at the closed door. "I'd better go talk to Lauren." And I wanted to see Luke.

DAY 13: JANUARY 4

"Put this over your nose and mouth," I offered, handing Chuck a bandana. I already had one around my face, and it wasn't for the cold. It stank outside.

The temperature had climbed into the high forties, and under bright, blue skies and sunshine the melting snow had turned the tracks down the middle of the streets into slushy brown rivers. We'd given up on the skis for this foraging trip, opting instead for thick rubber boots. The smell was as bad as in the latrines on our fifth floor.

"Lauren did have a point yesterday," I continued as I watched Chuck tie up the cloth. In bandana and sunglasses, he looked like a criminal.

I'd gotten an earful from Lauren the night before about setting up our own private spy agency. While we needed to keep track of Paul and Stan, she was adamant that we not use our tracking tool to spy on other people without their knowledge. Try as I might, I couldn't help feeling suspicious about her motives, wondering if she was trying to hide something from me.

She'd made me promise to bring the point up with Chuck.

"It's wrong to spy on our neighbors," I continued halfheartedly. "It's exactly what we were saying was the problem with the government."

"Don't you want to know where Paul and Stan are?"

We trudged a few more steps through the granular snow at the side of the slushy main path, sinking calf deep with each step. Every now and then my foot would sink even deeper and I'd have to carefully pull it out, usually ending up with a wedge of dirty snow packed into my boot. My feet were soaking wet.

"Of course, but that's not the same as spying on our neighbors."

"How's it different if we know one of them is working with the bad guys?"

"Because you *don't* know," I replied. "You're seeing conspiracies, taking away someone else's freedom to feed your paranoia."

"Paranoia, huh? Look who's talking. You're still thinking Lauren is doing something behind your back."

Sighing, I said nothing. We walked silently for a block.

The warm weather had brought a lot of people outside, some wandering aimlessly, but most scavenging. Through the broken windows of shops, we could see people picking through the empty shelves, searching for anything left behind. People were making an effort to pile trash bags together, and hills of them were growing at the intersections, glued together by windblown snow and debris.

I noticed that cables were strung from buried cars through the first-floor windows of a few apartments down the street. This was another one of Damon's ideas—to turn on cars and use them as generators. The idea had spread across the meshnet.

"You know, we need criminals," I said.

"We *need* criminals?"

"Society needs criminals. Without them, we'd be finished."

Chuck laughed. "Now this I have to hear."

"Any game theory simulation of society is more robust if you include a criminal element."

"Simulation, huh?"

"The criminals force society to improve. They weed out the weak, making us strengthen our institutions and networks."

"So they're the wolves and we're the lambs?"

"Sort of."

The nearest food stash marker on my treasure hunt app was at the corner of Eighth and Twenty-Second, and I pulled out my phone to check the map again. The wind had begun to pick up, and I shivered, motioning that we had to go down Eighth.

"Without a certain baseline amount of people who take advantage of others," I continued, "society just doesn't advance."

"Sounds like a bad deal for the ones getting taken advantage of."

"But a good deal for society as a whole. I'm not saying that we don't catch and punish criminals. I'm just saying that we need them."

We were nearing the spot where the bags were buried.

Chuck shook his head. "Nice theory, but wait till you meet one in a dark alley and tell me what you really think."

"Criminals help society *evolve*," I continued. "Slavery was legal back when Columbus got here, so you don't judge him, but he would be a criminal today. And Gandhi was a criminal when he broke the salt laws in India. They're both heroes now. Criminals help push the boundaries."

"So you're comparing Paul to Gandhi now?"

I snorted. "No, but there are criminals I admire."

"Who, Al Capone?" Chuck scoffed.

"Maybe those Anonymous hackers," I replied.

Chuck shook his head. "You can keep your criminals."

We'd reached the spot, and I took out my camera and brought up the picture I'd snapped of where we buried this load. I pulled my shovel from my backpack.

"This is it." Falling to my knees, I began digging. After a few quick shovelfuls of soft snow, I hit something. Pushing aside the snow with one gloved hand, I found the edge of a ragged plastic bag and pulled. Out popped a bag full of groceries.

Chuck laughed and took the bag from me. "Nice. I remember that one—steak and sausages. Jackpot!"

Digging through the snow with my hands, I found two other bags and pulled them out. I was about to tell Chuck that I thought the others were full of the same thing when I noticed a crowd had collected around us.

"How did you guys know that was there?" asked one of them. He looked like he hadn't eaten in a week. "I'll give you a million dollars for those bags. I'm a hedge fund manager. I swear I'll give you the money."

Chuck had his .38 in the pocket of his parka. As he swiveled around, I could see him gripping his gun, about to pull it out.

"Chuck, don't—" I started to say when something flashed out of the corner of my eye.

With a dull thud, a two-by-four cracked Chuck on the head, and he toppled forward, splaying face first on the ground like a rag doll. The bag he was holding spilled its contents, and the crowd pounced like hungry dogs, grabbing Chuck's backpack and dragging him away, leaving a dark red smear in the snow where his head had landed.

DAY 14: JANUARY 5

"He's lost a lot of blood."

"Will he be okay?" Susie's face was streaked with tears.

Chuck had been in and out of consciousness all day, and hardly aware of who we were when he did wake up. We'd laid him out on the bed in Chuck and Susie's bedroom after carrying him back to the building.

"I think so," replied Pam, feeling his pulse. "He has a strong, regular heartbeat, which is good. He needs sleep and lots of liquids . . ." She hesitated.

"What?" I asked.

"And he needs to eat as much as possible."

Nobody said anything for a moment.

"Thanks, Pam, we'll make sure he does," I finally replied.

Leaving Susie with Chuck, I walked Pam out of the apartment and past the barricade at our end of the hall.

The hallway had been empty all day. For the past three days, since we'd made it clear how dire the food situation was, everyone had been leaving in the morning to wait in line for food and water at one of the relief stations. The Red Cross was distributing one food pack per person per day, about a day's supply of calories, and after three days the other people on our floor—the hallway group, the ones with Rory, and the ones with Richard—had built up their supplies, surviving on starvation-level rations, where we'd nearly run out.

How quickly the tables had turned.

Susie was cooking up a rice mash for dinner, using almost the last of our food, and nobody on the rest of the floor was in a shar-

216

ing mood after Chuck had made it clear we weren't going to share with them.

We'd pinned our hopes on recovering the food we'd stashed outside, but we'd lost what we'd collected in the scuffle yesterday. Between taking care of the kids, nursing Chuck, Damon running the meshnet, and Tony handling security, nobody in our group had the five or six hours it took to get through the food lines or search for another one of our stashes.

The thing nobody had ever told me about hunger was just how much it hurt. I was making sure that Lauren and Luke got most of what I was allotted, and sometimes the hunger was just an ache, but often it was an intense pain that burned in my gut, making it impossible to concentrate. The worst was at night. My lack of food was translating into a lack of sleep.

Sighing, I slumped down on a chair next to Damon. He was almost surgically attached to the laptop he was using as the meshnet control center. It seemed all he needed to survive was a constant stream of coffee, but that was almost gone too.

"So people just whipped out their phones and started taking pictures?" he asked.

"It probably saved our lives," I replied, shaking my head. "You saved our lives."

When Chuck was hit on the head, I'd thrown my food into the crowd and jumped onto all fours to try to help him, grabbing one of his legs as the attackers pulled off his backpack. Fumbling in Chuck's pockets, I'd tried to get the gun out, but it had fallen into the snow. The guy who had hit Chuck with the two-by-four had wound up to whack me as well, and I'd cowered in the snow, holding my hands up to protect myself.

Just then, someone had yelled out "Stop!" and held up her

phone to take a picture. The man had towered above me, holding the club over his head, hesitating, and then someone else had taken a picture with her phone too. Under the public scrutiny, the attacker had retreated, dropping the two-by-four and scrambling to grab some of the food.

Fishing around in the snow, I'd found the gun buried under Chuck, stashed it in my pocket, and sent out a text message saying we needed help. Tony and Damon had arrived within minutes. By that time, the crowd had dispersed, and we'd carried Chuck back to the apartment like a sack of potatoes while he bled from his head wound.

"Social media as a lifesaving tool—wouldn't be the first time. By the way, I have pictures of the guy who attacked you and Chuck."

"Really?"

The meshnet was amazing, but up to that point it had been slow and patchily connected.

"Some hackers in the East Village figured out a way to upload the mesh software wirelessly, and it's gone viral now. Tens of thousands of people already."

The day before there hadn't been any uploads of our incident. I got up and studied the screen.

"Recognize him?"

The images were grainy but recognizable.

A large man in a red-and-black-checked jacket and wool hat menacing a pathetic-looking figure cringing in the snow. My head was turned away in the image, one hand held high to try to deflect the coming blow, but the other man's face was in full view.

Damon zoomed in.

"That's us." I hadn't gotten a good look at the time. *Where had*

I seen him before? "Hey! That's one of the guys from the garage downstairs."

I remembered seeing him lounging next to Chuck's pallet when we were unloading it. He'd been standing there when Rory was talking to Stan.

"You sure?"

I looked again, more carefully. *That's definitely the guy I saw that day.* "Absolutely."

Damon shook his head. "The bastards are hunting us down. I'll run a network map and see if I can filter this guy out, see if any of those nodes run into Stan's or Paul's."

"Is Rory back yet from the food lines?"

Damon typed away for a few seconds before answering. "Not yet, why?"

"No reason." I didn't want to fuel any more gossip.

Giving me a funny look, Damon shrugged and continued working.

"Can you add an alert text if any of those guys comes within a hundred yards of any of us?"

"Will be tricky to get in real time, with all the delays, but yes, more or less."

I shivered and scratched a sudden itch.

A cold draft was blowing through the hallway, even with the kerosene heater turned all the way up. The temperature had dropped again. I hadn't been outside, but with all the melting yesterday, the sharp drop below freezing had turned the streets into a skating rink, like a frozen obstacle course.

"So what else is going on?"

"I've hooked up with those hackers in the East Village, and they've already coded up a kind of mesh Twitter and set up other base stations like mine. People are creating neighborhood watches, barter exchanges, charging stations, crime reporting—communication is the key to civilization."

"Hackers, huh?"

Damon shook his head, still tapping on his keyboard, and then stopped to scratch his head and look at me. "I'm using the term 'hacker' in its original meaning of tinkering with code, of creating, not abusing. Hackers have gotten a bad rap. They didn't have anything to do with this."

"Those Anonymous guys admitted to attacking the logistics companies, and that was half of this mess."

Damon scratched his head again. "They didn't do this."

He seems awfully sure of himself. Shaking my head, I let it go. "It's freezing in here," I complained, itching again and shivering as another cold blast of air hit me.

"The window down the end of the hall is still open from when it was warm yesterday," answered Damon, coding away on his machine. "Why don't you close it?"

Nodding, I got up. I wondered just how deep Damon's involvement with Anonymous was.

DAY 15: JANUARY 6

A brilliant ceiling of stars hung above us.

"I didn't think New York had stars," said Damon, craning his head back to take them all in. "At least, not the kind in the sky."

I stared into the heavens. "The whole East Coast hasn't produced much in the way of pollution in the last two weeks, and the cold weather helps."

This was the first time I'd come up onto the roof since everything had started, and the dense star field that greeted us had been startling. The moonless night was a factor, but still, these were the stars I'd only ever met deep in the countryside.

It felt like the gods were peering down from their perches, gloating as they watched Gotham struggle below.

"You sure you want to do this tonight?" asked Damon.

I looked down at the blackness between the buildings. "This is the perfect night. Anyway, we don't have much choice, do we?"

Memories of Sunday school filtered into my mind. Tonight was the epiphany, the night when the Magi followed the stars to bring their treasures to the baby Jesus. We would be using our own magic to find treasure tonight, and I was hoping the stars, and the gods, would be kind.

"Are you a wise man, Damon?"

"Definitely clever, not sure about wise."

Shivering, I zipped my coat up tighter around my neck. Irena and Aleksandr had scraped the snow off the deck up here to melt for drinking water—it was easier to carry a bucket down a flight of stairs than up six. The temperature had plummeted; it was well below zero. A stiff wind began blowing, and we made for the wall at the end of the deck for some protection.

"I need a wise man tonight."

Damon laughed. "Then wise I am."

I studied the void of New York below. "No lights anywhere," I whispered to myself. From this angle, the only evidence that a city existed around us were the dark patches where the stars were blotted out by nearby buildings.

In a shifting pool of light from his headlamp, Damon settled on a bench against the wall and started working with my cell phone, attaching cables from it to my augmented-reality glasses. When the tech company had sent me the glasses before all this started, I'd thought I might get some amusement out of them; as it turned out, they might save our lives.

I sat on the railing next to Damon, gathering myself into a ball against the cold, and looked into the darkness, imagining the millions of people huddled out there. "You know what drove the twentieth century, laid the foundation for the world as we know it?" I ventured.

Damon fiddled with the phone. "Money?"

"Well, yeah, that, plus artificial light."

Without artificial light, humans were scared animals that scurried into their nests at sunset. Darkness brought out the monsters that existed in our primal collective imaginations, the creatures from under the bed, all of which disappeared with the flick of a switch and the warm glow of an incandescent bulb. Modern cities were filled with massive and awe-inspiring structures, but without artificial light, who would want to inhabit their dark interiors?

"Did you know that it was light that made Rockefeller into a titan?"

As an entrepreneur, I'd always had a fascination with how famous businessmen had started out.

"Wasn't it oil?"

Damon had the augmented-reality glasses on and was sweeping his head back and forth, muttering under his breath. Something wasn't working.

"Oil was the currency, but light was the product. It was America's desire for light that drove Rockefeller into, well, the spotlight."

Damon chuckled at my unintended joke.

"Before he began supplying kerosene to New York in the 1870s, when the sun went down America went dark. Kerosene was the first cheap, clean way to make artificial light. Before that, Rockefeller was just a down-and-out businessman sitting on a patch of soggy petroleum in Cleveland, not knowing what to do with it."

"I didn't know that," said Damon, not really listening.

"Yep, Cleveland was the Saudi Arabia of Wild West–era America, and by the early nineteen hundreds he was producing more kerosene than could be used for lighting alone, so guess what came next?"

"Rock Center?"

"Cars. Did you know that the first cars were electric? In 1910 there were more electric-powered cars on the streets of New York than gas-powered ones, and everyone back then assumed that electric cars were the future—they made a lot more sense than the crazy engines that ran on controlled explosions of volatile, toxic chemicals. But Rockefeller funded Ford to make sure that gas-powered cars, not electric, would be the way of the future, so he would have a place to sell his oil."

"I think I got it working," said Damon. He had the glasses on again and was swiveling his head back and forth.

"And, poof, there you have the mess of the twentieth century, the Middle East, all those wars, the world's reliance on oil, and a good chunk of global warming. Even maybe what's happening now. It all sprang out of the desire for light."

"That's because being in the dark sucks," said Damon, coming up to sit beside me and handing me the AR glasses. "Try them on."

Taking a deep breath, I put them on and turned off my head-lamp. Looking to the east, I saw tiny glowing dots of red in the darkness down at street level, spread out across the city.

"I loaded the map data from your treasure hunt app into the glasses," explained Damon. "They're connected now, wirelessly. So the spots where you buried those bags will appear as red dots through the AR glasses when you look through them."

"Yeah, I see them."

After what had happened with Chuck, we'd decided it was too dangerous to go out during the day to collect the food we'd stashed. Lauren had begged me not to, and I'd promised her I wouldn't. But we'd used up just about the last of our food. There had been riots at the emergency centers, and I didn't want anyone going there. Even so, we needed to eat, and Lauren and Susie were planning on going up to Penn and Javits with the kids the next day to wait in the food lines.

Unless I went out tonight to retrieve what we'd hidden.

We'd come up on the roof to confirm that the streets were as dark as we imagined, and to see if there were any lights out there. It was pitch black.

"You sure you don't want Tony or me to come with you?"

"We only have one set of night-vision goggles. Two people in the dark is a liability if one of them can't see. And I'm the only one available who actually buried the food, so I'm best equipped to figure out where it is." I paused. "Anyway, with martial law in place, we should only risk one of us going out."

Damon shrugged his okay. "So you won't need to look at your phone at all. Just walk toward the red dots."

In the pitch black of the streets, my phone would have lit up like a beacon, attracting unwanted attention.

"When you get near one of the spots, just tap the screen in your pocket and the AR glasses will cycle through the pictures you took when you buried the bags. If you pull the night-vision goggles over them, you should be able to overlay the images pretty well."

Taking my phone from him, I tapped, and a series of faint, layered images of pictures I'd taken when burying the packages appeared.

"What you were talking about is interesting, but that's the past," said Damon.

I played with my new toy, zooming in and cycling through the images.

"I'm more interested in the future, in being able to predict it."

"You're obsessed with the future, aren't you?"

Damon sighed. "If I'd been able to see just a little of it, I might have been able to save her."

I sometimes forgot what had happened to him. "I'm sorry, Damon. I didn't mean to be, well . . ."

"Don't be sorry. By the way, I have an idea of how we could get Chuck's car down from that vertical parking garage."

I was getting very cold already, and I realized I'd have to bundle up more if I was going to stay outside for a few hours on my scavenging trip. *I'd better get the .38 from Tony, just in case.* "Really? What's the idea? In short form."

In the light from my headlamp, Damon grinned. "Where there's a winch, there's a way."

I made my way slowly through the frozen landscape. It took me half an hour to walk the two blocks to the nearest buried bags. At least with the extreme cold, the streets didn't smell, and I wasn't worried about falling into a pile of wet human feces if I slipped.

The night-vision goggles used a combination of low-light imaging with near-infrared illumination, so even in the pitch black I could see well. With the infrared flashlight in my pocket, I could even light up the world in a brilliant, sparkling green if needed.

The red dot indicating the nearest bag location had grown in size as I'd approached, expanding until it was a red circle about twenty feet across—the GPS's approximate margin for error.

Damon was a clever kid.

Standing in the middle of the circle, I kicked aside a garbage bag and tapped the phone screen in my pocket. The image associated with this spot popped up on the AR glasses. It closely matched the storefront and light pole I was seeing through the night-vision goggles. When I backed up a few paces and stepped to the left, the images lined up. *Perfect.*

Dropping to my knees, I pulled off my backpack, taking the folding shovel out of it. With the butt of the shovel, I whacked the frozen surface a few times until it cracked, and then pulled big chunks of surface ice and snow away. I shoveled into the softer snow underneath, expanding the excavated area in a concentric spiral.

It was heavy work, and by the time my shovel hit the first bag, my back was killing me. I brushed away the snow with my gloved hands and pulled two bags out. In the ghostly light of the night-vision goggles, I looked inside one of them.

"Doritos," I snorted, shaking my head. "I love Doritos."

Reaching down, I pulled out the other bags and began stuffing them into my backpack while I looked to the next glowing red circle, about forty yards away. Above me, the steely pinpoints of the stars shone brightly between the buildings.

Itching and squirming, I tried to find a comfortable position. My dreams had been fitful, and I'd spent most of the night half in and half out of sleep. I'd lain down just before dawn. Exhausted, I scrunched up my pillow, trying yet another angle on the dirty sheets.

Someone or something was crying in my dream . . . then consciousness intruded and I realized it wasn't a dream.

Opening my eyes, I saw Lauren sitting on a chair next to the bed, wrapped up in the flower-patterned blanket she'd adopted. She had her legs crossed up under her and was leaning on Luke's crib, where he was sleeping soundly. She was pulling strands of her hair in front of her face and inspecting them, one by one, in the thin, early-morning light.

She was crying, rocking back and forth.

Taking a deep breath, I tried to wash the fog of sleep from my brain. "Baby, are you okay? Is Luke okay?"

Sweeping her hair back into place, she wiped the tears from her eyes and sniffled. "We're okay. I'm okay."

"You sure? Come on, come to bed and talk to me."

She looked down at the floor. I took another deep breath.

"Are you mad that I went out last night?"

She shook her head.

"I was going to tell you, but—"

"I knew you were planning on going out."

"So you're not upset about that?"

She shook her head again.

"Are you hurt, not feeling well?"

She shrugged.

"Lauren, what is it, talk to me—"

"I don't feel well, and my teeth hurt."

"Is it the pregnancy?"

Looking up at the ceiling, she nodded and began sobbing again. "And I have lice. They're everywhere."

All the itching of the past week took on a new dimension. My hand shot up to scratch the back of my head, and my entire body felt like it was crawling with foreign invaders.

"Luke's covered in them too," she said, crying. "My baby."

I got up and sat next to her on the chair, holding her and looking down at Luke. At least he looked peaceful. After a few deep breaths she quieted down and straightened up. "I know it's just lice," she sighed, "not the end of the world, and I'm just being a silly girl—"

"You're not being silly."

"I don't think I've ever even gone a day without having a shower before, not for as long as I can remember."

"Me either." I kissed her.

"And Luke and Ellarose have terrible rashes."

We both sat and watched Luke. I turned and looked into her eyes. "You know what today's project is?"

She sighed. "A new pulley system for bringing water up? I heard Damon talking about it yesterday—"

"No," I laughed, "today's project is a nice hot bath for my wife."

She bowed her head. "We have much more important things."

"Nothing is more important than you." I nuzzled her. She laughed.

"I'm serious. Give me an hour or two and I'll have a steaming-hot bath ready."

"Really?" She started crying again, but this time they were happy tears.

"Really. You can soak as long as you want, relax, and give Ellarose a proper cleaning, bring Luke in with his rubber ducky. When you're done, we'll use the water to wash clothes. It'll be great." I hugged her, and she squeezed me back, tears still running down her face.

"Why don't you relax?" I continued. "I'm going to talk to Damon and see how everyone is doing."

She lay down on the bed, curling into the blankets. I headed out, closing the door behind me.

In the main room, Tony was snoring on the couch, covered in a deep pile of blankets. He regularly took night watch duty and had been at the door when I'd returned just before dawn. The shades were drawn, keeping the room dark, and I didn't wake him.

Out in the hallway, nearly everyone was already gone, off to the relief stations for food and water. It was quiet.

Rory was reaching into one of the water barrels at the corner of the elevator hallway, refilling a water bottle. I nodded to him, and he stared at me but then nodded back and whispered good morning before he left to go down the exit stairwell. Two people were still asleep under a bundle of blankets at the other end of the hallway.

Damon was asleep behind the barricade of boxes that demarcated our area, so I crossed over and rapped on the Borodins' door to check on them. Within seconds, Irena opened the door. Aleksandr was asleep on his chair, and Irena was preparing a hot pot of tea. She told me they were fine, asked if I needed anything, and then asked how Lauren was feeling. I mentioned the lice, and she said she would prepare an ointment for Lauren and that it was easiest if the men shaved their heads.

It was interesting that nobody begged from the Borodins. They had a seemingly endless supply of tea and hard biscuits, but they made it clear that they wouldn't bother anyone, and even more clear that they didn't want anyone bothering them. Still, I would often catch Irena sneaking a biscuit to one of the children in the hallway.

After ten minutes and nearly as many biscuits, I filled my cup of tea and went back into the hallway. Damon was awake but looked dazed.

"You okay?" I asked.

"No," he grunted. "I've got a pounding headache, aching joints . . . I feel ill."

I took an involuntary step back. *Bird flu? Maybe we'd been wrong.*

Damon laughed. "I don't blame you. Go get the masks. Even if it's just a regular cold, this isn't the time to take chances." Looking up at me blearily, he scratched his head.

Should I mention the lice? "Want me to get you some water, maybe find some aspirin?"

He nodded and collapsed back onto the couch, still scratching.

"And some bacon and eggs?" I joked.

"Maybe tomorrow," he laughed from beneath his covers.

Back in Chuck's apartment, I crossed to where Tony was snoring and tapped him on the shoulder. "Damon isn't feeling well, and neither is Lauren," I whispered as Tony shook himself awake. "Keep the door to this place closed, and wear a mask if you go out."

Rubbing his eyes, he nodded. I retrieved some masks and aspirin from the bathroom, and a bottle of water from our stash, and then whispered the same warning to Susie, asleep with Chuck.

Damon was at his computer by the time I came back out, my mask already on. I poured water into a cup next to the laptop, and he took the aspirin from me, then put the mask on.

"The bad guys staying away?" I asked.

He pulled up some maps. "So far."

I paused, feeling sheepish about my next request. "Do you feel well enough to help me with something?"

He stretched and sighed. "Sure. What do you need?"

"A bath."

"Can I come in?"

"Uh-huh," came the muffled reply.

Opening the door to the bathroom, I smiled as I found my wife lounging under a mass of bubbles in a steaming tub.

Irena had given me an ointment and a fine-tooth comb, and instructed me on the best technique for brushing lice out of hair—starting at the roots, and working from front to back.

It had taken a lot longer than my promise of an hour or two to get the bath going. To start with, the barrels of meltwater in the elevator hallway had been empty. I'd been annoyed, and Damon had stayed quiet while I'd stormed downstairs and outside with him trailing behind, ready to fill more buckets and haul them up.

Once outside the back door, I understood why the barrels were empty. The snow was filthy and crusted with a thick layer of dirty ice. All of the snow near the front and back entrances had been dug out and hauled up, and trying to dig out new, clean snow was no easy task.

For today, I didn't need drinking water, just something to bathe in, so I started filling up buckets while Damon hauled them inside. In the fresh air, Damon began to feel better, but working with the masks on was hard.

Richard was standing guard in the lobby that morning, but I didn't feel comfortable telling him I was preparing a bath for Lauren. I just said we were refilling the water barrels and left it at that. He looked like he thought we were up to something, but he just watched us hauling them up.

I hadn't quite appreciated what would be involved. Chuck's bathtub was medium-size, but I discovered that filling it would take fifty gallons. Melting snow to water decreased its volume by a factor of ten, so filling the bathtub would take twelve barrel-loads of snow.

Damon heated the water in our old apartment, using one of the forty-gallon tin drums over an open oil flame contraption he'd been working on, with oil from the main furnace in the basement.

When all was said and done, it took us seven hours to haul up the snow, melt it, and heat the water, but seeing Lauren in the bubbles, a smile across her face, made it all worthwhile.

"I'll just be a minute more," she said as I entered the bathroom.

It was warm, and the mirrors were fogged with steam. The room was lit with candles.

What had started as an idea just for Lauren had morphed into a grand plan for our whole gang to have a good wash. We'd been washing our hands and faces, trying to do sponge baths, but in the eleven days since the water had stopped working, none of us had bathed properly.

"Take your time, baby." I waved the comb and ointment Irena had given me. "And I've got a special treat for you."

She smiled and slid forward in the tub to dunk her head and hair back into the water. As she did, her body broke the surface of the water, exposing her belly and a small but unmistakable bump. I remembered the baby development books from when we'd had Luke. *Fourteen weeks, about the size of an orange, arms and legs and eyes and teeth, a complete tiny person, and one that is completely dependent on me.*

Lauren pushed herself upright in the tub and wiped water out of her eyes, smiling up at me. I hadn't seen my wife naked in weeks, and seeing her now, warm and wet, I felt something stir inside of me.

"You going to give me that treat fully clothed?" she laughed, smiling seductively. She leaned over the side of the tub and clicked on her phone. The jazzy chords of a Barry White song began to play.

"No, ma'am." I undid my belt, which was three notches tighter than when all this began. I pulled off my sweater and then my socks and jeans, holding them up to my nose before putting them on the counter. *Wow, my clothes stink.* Standing half-naked in the steam of the bath, smelling the lavender bath soap, I caught a whiff of myself. *Actually, that's me that stinks.*

I locked the bathroom door, then pulled off the last of my clothes and slid in behind Lauren. The sensation of the hot water enveloping me was indescribable. I let out a low groan of pleasure just as Barry's deep baritone began telling us about all the love he couldn't get enough of.

"Nice, huh?" murmured Lauren, leaning back into me.

"Oh yeah."

I picked up the ointment and comb and began applying the cream to Lauren's wet hair, then combed her hair back, carefully watching for any little critters. Lauren held herself still while I worked. I'd never imagined that searching for lice could be sexy. An image of monkeys in a forest somewhere, cleaning nits from the fur of a loved one, popped into my mind, and I chuckled.

"Why are you laughing?"

"No reason. I just love you."

She sighed and pushed herself back into me. "Mike, I'm so proud of you." In one motion, she swiveled around in the tub and kissed me wetly. "I love you."

Reaching down, I gripped her buttocks and pulled her up onto me. I was aroused, and she smiled, biting my lip. Just then there was a loud rap on the door.

Seriously?

"What is it?" I groaned. Lauren nuzzled my neck. "Can you give us a minute? *Please?*"

"I really hate to bother you," said Damon, "but it's kind of urgent."

"And?"

Lauren licked my chest.

"They just announced that there's been an outbreak of cholera at Penn Station."

Cholera? That sounded bad, but . . . "What can I do about it? I'll be out in a few minutes."

"Uh-huh, but the real problem is that Richard is downstairs with a gun, refusing to let any of the twenty-odd people who've come back from Penn into the building. I think he's going to shoot someone."

Lauren shot upright in the tub. I closed my eyes and took a deep breath. *God hates me.*

"Okay," I replied in shaky voice, "I'll be right out." Getting out of the tub, I said to Lauren, "We'll finish this later?"

She nodded but turned Barry off and got up with me. "I'm coming with you."

For just a moment I allowed myself the pleasure of watching her naked, wet body climb out of the tub.

"Don't forget to put a mask on."

DAY 17: JANUARY 8

"How are you feeling?"

"Groggy," replied Chuck, "but good. You still think we need criminals in society?"

I laughed. "Not so much, maybe, no."

After three days of slipping in and out of consciousness, Chuck had come back to the land of the living. He was up and talkative, playing with Ellarose and Luke.

We'd purposely left him out of the loop while he was recovering, and I hoped whatever was making him "weak and achy" wasn't the same thing the rest of the people in our building were coming down with.

"So what did I miss?"

Susie was sitting behind him on the bed, holding Ellarose and rubbing Chuck's neck. Lauren was sitting beside her, and Luke, of course, was running around.

"The usual—plague, pestilence, an armed standoff, and the decay of Western civilization, but nothing I can't handle."

Last night had been a surreal juxtaposition, from a dream-scape of steam and candles and Barry White to a nightmare straight from a zombie apocalypse: a darkened lobby lit by head-lamps, screaming and cursing, guns being waved around while a ragged, dirty gang of humans pressed against the doors, banging, begging to get inside.

Thankfully, when I'd let them in, no brains had been eaten.

But Richard did have a point. If cholera had broken out at Penn Station, and they'd been there, then letting them back into the building was risking infection for all of us. On the other hand, forcing them to stay outside was tantamount to a death sentence.

In the end, I'd convinced Richard that we could quarantine the returnees—Vicky and her children among them—on the first floor for two days, which was safely longer than the incubation period for cholera. I'd looked it up on a phone app on infectious diseases Chuck had given me.

We'd gone back to using face masks and rubber gloves, brought down a kerosene heater, and sequestered the potentially sick in one of the larger first-floor offices off the main lobby. When I'd gone down to check on them this morning, everyone there was sick and aching, and so was everyone living in the hallway on the sixth floor. The symptoms weren't anything like cholera, though; they seemed more like a cold—or the flu.

I explained the situation to Chuck, and he shook his head. "Have you been ventilating properly? You've been mixing diesel with the kerosene to make it last longer, right?"

"I had to close the windows yesterday because of the cold," I admitted, realizing what I'd done. *How could I have been so stupid? The hunger made it difficult to think coherently.*

Chuck took a deep breath. "Carbon monoxide poisoning has symptoms a lot like the flu. We're not sick in here, because we're using the electric heaters, but everyone else is using the gas heaters."

I opened the bedroom door and yelled out, "Damon!"

Even ill, he was manning his computer control station, monitoring the hundreds of images that were arriving hourly from all over the city and routing emergency messages to Sergeant Williams.

Damon poked his head through the front door. I'd made it clear he wasn't allowed in here, so he peeked around the door frame, his eyes puffy and red.

"The sickness, it's probably carbon monoxide poisoning," I explained. "Open some windows and text everyone downstairs. And tell Tony."

Damon rubbed his eyes and nodded, then closed the door without a word. He was tired.

"They'll be better by tomorrow. No lasting damage," said Chuck. "But keeping the ones who were near Penn Station quarantined was a good idea."

I nodded, still feeling stupid.

Chuck scratched at the back of his neck while he swung his feet off the bed. "My God, cholera."

Susie rubbed his back as he leaned forward. "Are you sure you're feeling well enough, baby?"

"A little woozy, but not bad."

"That was a close call," I said. "The guy that attacked us—it was no random accident. It was one of Paul's guys."

Chuck sat back down. "What?"

"We have a picture of the attack—"

"You stopped to take a *picture*?"

It was easy to forget that, after being out of it for a few days, Chuck had only seen the first glimmers of the meshnet. Damon estimated that over a hundred thousand people were now connected.

"No, not me. Someone watching the attack took a picture. It's what people do now, how we're helping keep things under control."

Chuck took a second to absorb what I was saying. "Maybe you'd better back up and explain what's going on."

"How about some hot tea?" suggested Lauren. "And we can leave you guys to catch up."

"That'd be great."

Susie picked up Ellarose from the bed.

I explained to Chuck how neighborhood watches were evolving on the meshnet, the emergency service tools, and how we were keeping a record of everything that happened out there on centralized laptops like Damon's.

"Did you manage to go and get more food?"

Food was never far from anyone's mind, especially with the emergency centers quarantined. Hunger had a way of focusing the mind on every crumb.

"We have about three days of food left," I said. We'd become experts at rationing. "I went out at night, using the night-vision goggles and augmented-reality glasses to get around."

"You did what? I leave you guys alone for a few days—"

I smiled. "And something else."

"Eggs and bacon?"

I shook my head, still smiling. "I wish."

"So?"

"The kid figured out a way to get your truck down."

"Time to get out of here, huh?"

I nodded.

"So what's the idea?"

I started to explain Damon's plan, but before I could finish, we heard Damon yelling our names outside the apartment. I opened the bedroom door, and Damon's head appeared again in the main doorway.

"They're all dead."

"Who's dead?" I asked, horrified, imagining a flash cholera outbreak that had wiped out everyone in quarantine. "The first floor?"

Damon's head sagged. "The second floor. I just went to check on them, and they're all dead." He grimaced at me. "They had a kerosene heater, cranked all the way up, with all the windows shut."

I'd been down to visit those guys just the day before, and they'd been heating their place with an electric generator outside the window, just like us.

"Where'd they get the kerosene heater?"

"I don't know, but we have a bigger problem."

A bigger problem than nine dead people? The look in Damon's eyes made my stomach knot.

"Paul's on the move."

DAY 18: JANUARY 9

"They're coming."

My stomach growled. In a crazy part of my mind I hoped they were bringing food. *If we have to fight, at least there should be a food prize at the end of it.* A random, illogical thought—like realizing while driving that you could turn the wheel and slam into oncoming traffic. I usually couldn't explain why ideas like that came to mind. This time I knew why. Hunger was crowding out the fact that I was being hunted, that my family was being hunted.

I was steadily eating less and less, making a show to Lauren of eating, but stashing away crumbs and bits and pieces. When Luke and I played together, I'd produce my hidden treats for him. Anything was worth seeing a smile on his little face.

"Are you paying attention?" asked Chuck. "It looks like there are six of them."

I nodded, watching a collection of dots move across Damon's laptop screen, and then popped a glass bead from a decorative bowl on the kitchen counter into my mouth and began sucking on it.

A cold wind blew in from the open window in Chuck's bedroom. Susie, Lauren and the children had already gone out through the window onto the neighboring rooftop to hide in an abandoned apartment in the next building, and Damon was helping Irena and Aleksandr out. From there we could go down the back fire escape and re-enter our building at a lower level through exterior doors we'd left ajar.

We were going to trap Paul and his gang. The hunters were becoming the hunted.

Damon had hatched the plan, and it had been the tipping point in our decision to stay today rather than making for the truck. We wanted to try to get it down and escape, but since we didn't know when Paul and his gang might be coming, we'd decided to stay and fight.

Once we made the decision, we told everyone on the sixth floor, and the quarantined group on the first floor, that we were having a birthday party for Luke. It was a private party, we'd said, only our gang was invited, and we'd be off watch and not available.

If it had seemed odd, nobody had said anything, and we'd received only a few grudging stares from people who thought we were going to have a feast and weren't inviting them.

The party ruse had been Chuck's idea. I was sure it would come to nothing, but just before 5 p.m., right when we'd said that Luke's party was supposed to start, the gang of dots had coalesced on Damon's meshnet location map. It seemed somebody on our floor was talking with the people hunting us.

The dots began to move this way.

"They're going to leave at least one man at the entrance when they come in," said Tony. He was the only one among us with combat training, so he was leading the mission. "We'll get Irena and Aleksandr to handle that one. The four of us wait until the rest are up on this floor, then we come up behind them." He looked at Chuck and me. "You guys stay to the back, right?"

We had children and wives, he'd insisted, so he and Damon would bring up the front. Damon hadn't objected, but he was quiet the whole time we were planning this.

We were already dressed for outdoors, and Tony and Chuck made straight for the open window and climbed out onto the rooftop.

"What if they split up?" I asked.

Damon disappeared to put his laptop back at its station, then quickly returned, opening up his smartphone and handing me the AR glasses. "That's where you come in. You're used to using these to spot those buried packages—now the packages are the bad guys."

I put on the AR glasses and looked out the window. Out in the darkness, six small red dots were moving along Ninth Avenue toward us. The building across from us obscured Ninth, so the dots were superimposed to indicate where Paul and his gang were, as if I could see through the building.

"Dots on a screen are good, but with these you'll be able to see through walls."

"What if they don't all have smartphones on the mesh?"

Damon considered this. "We'll do a visual check from the roof."

I pulled myself out onto the rooftop, landing waist deep in snow, and then helped Damon out. It was dark out, but not yet night, and it was clear. We hid on the rooftop in the snow and looked down Twenty-Fourth, waiting for the men to appear.

As soon as they did, I gave the thumbs-up. Each of the augmented-reality dots corresponded with the position of one of the men who rounded the corner.

Watching them walk up our street, I realized I wasn't breathing, and I almost had to force myself to take a few quick, short inhales. For the first time in days I forgot I was hungry.

The group of men arrived at our building's back entrance, not a hundred feet away from where we were. I could see their faces. Paul produced keys from his pocket and leaned down to the lock.

"I pulled everybody off duty," whispered Tony. "There isn't anyone guarding the stairwell."

As soon as the men entered the building, we got up from our hiding spots and hurried down the fire escape. My breathing was heavy, my heart pounding. I could see the red dots through the wall of our building.

"One of them had a shotgun," whispered Tony. "Can you still see them? Where are they?"

"Still in the lobby."

Our plan was to cross over from this fire escape onto ours at the third floor. The dots began to move.

"No, wait, they're starting up now."

As Tony had predicted, one of the dots remained behind at the entrance. We'd reached the third floor by then. While the rest of the guys climbed over to our building's fire escape, I stopped to text the location of the guard to Aleksandr and Irena, who were hidden on the second floor.

When I joined the others, Tony asked, "Did they stop at quarantine on first?" We were all worried about Vicky and her kids.

I shook my head. As I watched, the red dots grew in size, appearing to crawl straight up the brick wall in front of me until the entire wall glowed red. "They're right in front of us." I whispered.

Everyone held their breath.

The pulsing red mass in front of me shifted and then moved upwards, separating again into individual spots above my head.

"They're not stopping at any of the other floors. Looks like they know exactly where they're going."

Chuck and Tony nodded, and on my signal we followed, shadowing their movement up the fire escape. The fifth floor was as high as we could go outside, so we waited there, outside the fire escape door that led directly into the stairwell, for the men to make their move.

"Tell us what you see," whispered Tony.

"It looks like they're outside the sixth-floor door, waiting."

"They're going to do this fast," said Tony, "probably send one or two of them toward Richard's place and the rest to Chuck's. As soon as they open that door, you need to tell us, and we'll go in."

The wind whistled as we waited. Chuck swept away some snow that had accumulated since we'd last cleaned this spot a few hours ago. I stared up at the wall, watching the red dots. Finally they moved, advancing through the door and dispersing into the hallway on the other side.

"Now!"

Chuck pulled open the door. Tony went in first, followed by Damon, with Chuck and me pulling up the rear.

"One of them went over to Richard's end," I whispered as we climbed the stairs to the sixth-floor landing. "It looks like the rest are waiting outside Chuck's."

Breathing heavily, we assembled behind the sixth-floor door. Everyone had their guns out, and I fumbled in my pocket for mine.

"The second they go into Chuck's place, you call it," said Tony. "Damon will go to Richard's end while the three of us surprise the four inside Chuck's. Everyone good?"

I nodded along with everyone else but kept my eyes on the red dots to my right. They were large and merged into one another.

Is that three or four people? Then I heard the attackers burst into Chuck's, yelling. I didn't need to say anything. Tony opened the door and slid into the hallway.

I held back, scared, but then forced myself out in time to hear Chuck yell, "You assholes looking for us? Drop the guns!"

I ran to Chuck's door, pulling off the AR glasses and holding my gun straight in front of me. Three men stood with their hands up, staring stupidly back at us. I recognized one of them as Chuck's attacker. One by one they dropped their weapons.

Tony rushed past me, going back to check on Damon. "All clear!" he yelled moments later.

"Do you have Paul?" yelled Chuck.

"No, but we've got Stan!"

Paul wasn't among the men in front of us either. *Did he slip past us down the stairs somehow?*

"Where's the sixth guy?" asked Damon, running up behind me. He gestured to the AR glasses in my hand.

I put them back on. Three red dots hovered in front of me as I looked at the three guys in our room, and swiveling around I could see Stan's dot at the other end of the hallway. Looking down to my left, I could see another dot coming up toward us, which must have been Irena and Aleksandr bringing up the one they'd captured downstairs. *That's five. Where's the sixth?*

"I only count five," I said after double-checking.

"Goddamn it!" yelled Chuck. "Tie them up. He's here somewhere."

We herded the four men we'd captured into my apartment, tying them up in our small bedroom. By that point Aleksandr and Irena had arrived, pushing ahead of them the man they'd ambushed downstairs.

"Where's Paul?" demanded Chuck, glaring at the men clustered on the floor.

Stan and three others just scowled back, but the man who had attacked Chuck wasn't so tough without a weapon in his hands. "He stayed out there," he responded, cowering. He seemed to know we recognized him. "Don't kill me, please."

"A little late to be begging," fumed Chuck. "Why did Paul hang back?"

"He said he was going to make sure nobody came up behind us. He hid in the doorway across the hall."

Chuck cursed, rubbing the back of his neck with his .38. "Why did you come back here?" he asked Stan.

Stan shrugged. "Paul said you still had a lot of stuff—food, equipment . . ."

"And you risked coming here again for that?"

Stan looked at his feet. "And the laptop. He said it had pictures of all of us on it." He looked up into Chuck's eyes. "Doing stuff, you know, to people—"

Damon thumped the wall. "Shit!" He looked into the hallway and his body sagged. "He took the laptop."

Tony and Chuck pushed past Damon, off to search the building for Paul, but I knew they wouldn't find him. I had a feeling he'd be staying off the meshnet as well.

"So what are we going to do with these guys?" I called out after Chuck.

"You leave that to me, Mih-kah-yal," answered Irena, poking Stan with the muzzle of her old rifle. "We have some experience with gulag."

"Nice to finally be on other side," added Aleksandr with a smile.

DAY 19: JANUARY 10

I moved the glass bead around in my mouth. *Who said that sucking on pebbles made you feel less hungry?* I spat it out.

The snow had come again, and this time I was thankful. Chuck and I were walking down to his truck, to see if Damon's idea would work. It was early morning as we made our way down Ninth Avenue, and a pristine carpet of white covered all the hurt and mess the city had become.

We hardly spoke, both of us lost in the rhythmic crunch and squeak of our footsteps on the new snow.

A tweet on the meshnet the night before had said that Americans threw away half the food they brought home—normally this would have struck me as wasteful, but now it was unimaginable. Trudging through the snow, I was thinking about all the edibles I used to toss after they had sat in our fridge for a few days, daydreaming about what I would do with them.

I felt embarrassed by our meager meals, feeling like I wasn't providing for my family, but Lauren always kissed me before we ate as if they were amazing feasts. A single Dorito had become a great prize, and at every opportunity I was squirreling away what I could save for her.

I have a few pounds to spare, I reasoned, *so why not?* But hunger was new to me, and unconsciously I would find myself eating something I was supposed to be saving, my stomach sabotaging my willpower when I wasn't paying attention.

"Look at that," said Chuck as we arrived at the corner of Fourteenth. He pointed at what used to be the Gansevoort Hotel.

We hadn't ventured toward downtown in two weeks, since the day after Christmas, when we'd last come to look at his truck. The city was barely recognizable. At the corner of Ninth and Fourteenth, right outside the Apple Store, was an urban park I'd often visited to enjoy a coffee and watch the hustle and bustle of people coming in and out of Chelsea. Now the tops of the park's small trees poked forlornly out of the snow at our feet, and snow-covered traffic lights swung at head height above mounds of frozen garbage.

The wedge-shaped building at the corner of Ninth and Hudson hung in space like the prow of a ship, snow and garbage piling up against it like water swelling up from the dark depths of an underground city. Jutting up from what looked like the center of the ship was the burnt-out husk of the Gansevoort. Its windows were smashed and dark smudges rose up the sides of the building, the blackened walls testament to a fire that had raged inside.

Hanging in front of the hotel was a billboard, still perfect and untouched. It was an ad for a premium vodka, featuring a smiling man in a tuxedo and a woman in a sleek black dress. They seemed like alien creatures, laughing as they surveyed the wreckage at their feet and enjoying a drink at our expense.

Something moved at the corner of my eye, and I turned to see someone looking down at us from the second floor of the Apple Store. Trash was piled against the floor-to-ceiling windows. As I watched, another person appeared.

I pulled on Chuck's arm. "We'd better get moving."

He nodded, and we continued.

We were traveling light, stripped down, with nothing that looked worth stealing—no backpacks, no packages. We wore ragged-looking clothing. In plain sight were our weapons, my .38 in a leather holster and Chuck's rifle slung over his back. The weapons spoke to people watching us. They said we didn't want to be disturbed. I felt like a Wild West gunslinger in a lawless, icy outpost.

The state of affairs in the hallway had taken an abrupt downward turn when the cholera outbreak had been reported at Penn three days ago and all the emergency shelters had been quarantined. Those daily trips for food and water had given the days a schedule, a pattern. They had given most of the people on our floor a reason to get up and get moving. Now they lay inert on the couches and chairs and beds, completely cut off from external contact.

But it wasn't just the absence of outside support. Up until a few days ago, we'd been coasting. People had been managing on what they could scrounge within the building: scraps of food, clean clothes, and clean bedding and blankets. But we were at the end of that supply—the clothes and bedding and blankets were stale and infested with lice, and every scrap of food in the building was gone.

More crucially, our system of gathering and melting snow for drinking water and cooking, which had worked well for the first week, and had been manageable for the second, was hopeless as we entered the third week. The barrels and water containers were dirty, and the snow outside filthy. We'd tried going over to the Hudson River, but the water at the edges of the piers was encrusted with ice.

We'd initially quarantined the people returning from Penn downstairs, but we'd given up after capturing Paul's gang. At that point, a half-dozen of us were holding thirty people at gun-point, and in any case, it had been impossible to guess if they were exhibiting signs of cholera. Almost everyone was ill in one way or another, most with diarrhea from drinking unclean water.

The latrines on the fifth floor were beyond disgusting, and people had migrated from bathroom to bathroom in each abandoned apartment, floor by floor, looking for one that was clean. Each residence had become as filthy as the next.

And we had nine dead people on the second floor. The only dead bodies I'd seen before had been laid out in funeral homes, carefully prepared to look like they were sleeping peacefully. But these people . . . nothing about them looked peaceful.

We'd opened the windows, turning a second-floor apartment, with them in it, into a cold storage area. I hoped scavengers wouldn't get in—human or otherwise.

Our plight was reflected in the rest of the city. Hope was evaporating into the cold winter air, even as the government radio stations kept insisting, day after day, that power and water would be restored soon, and to stay indoors, stay warm and safe. The refrain had become a joke: "Power on soon, stay warm, stay safe!" we'd say to each other as a greeting. The joke had worn thin.

"There she is," said Chuck, pointing up at his truck.

It was the first time I'd heard him excited in days.

An army convoy rumbled by, heading uptown on the West Side Highway. Where before their presence had been reassuring, now it made me angry. *What the hell are they doing? Why aren't they helping us?*

The meshnet was reporting rumors of emergency supply air-drops, but it was hard to believe anything anymore.

As the convoy disappeared, I looked up at Chuck's truck, still perched fifty feet in the air. Its position had turned into something of a blessing. The cars lower down had been scavenged for batteries, parts, anything useful, but his truck still looked intact.

"You think we could attach the winch cable to that?" He pointed to a billboard platform attached to the side of a nearby building.

"Not more than twenty feet, maybe less. Your winch is rated at twenty thousand pounds, right?"

"The half-inch cable has a twenty-five-thousand-pound breaking point, but it'll take a lot more for an instant. My baby's stripped down for improved mileage, but," mused Chuck, calculating in his head, "she must weigh seven thousand pounds with the skid plate."

"It's going to be close."

I was the only engineer among us. The best I could figure it, the energy of the vertical drop would be converted into a forward velocity as it swung, with maximum force at the bottom of the arc. It wouldn't start swinging until the truck was dragged off the platform, and we'd minimize the swinging by winching the truck up as it fell. By my calculations, even if we were careful, the truck would exert at least five times its weight in downward force at the bottom of its swing. This was much more than what the winch was rated for. And even if the winch didn't fail, there was another variable we were counting on; we needed the billboard platform not to come loose from the wall as this all happened.

"So Damon offered to ride this rodeo?" asked Chuck, shaking his head as we walked right underneath the billboard.

It was better if someone rode inside the truck to control the winch if we wanted this to work—and our lives depended on it working. Setting the winch in motion and letting it go without anyone inside risked jamming or breaking it. I still wouldn't have volunteered, but Damon was more certain of my calculations than I was.

"In exchange for us driving him to his parents' place near Manassas," I replied, nodding. "I figured that was pretty close to where we were going anyway."

Still looking up, Chuck began planning. "Tonight you go on another one of your food runs, and I'll start packing as much gear as we can carry."

I took out my smartphone. We still had meshnet connectivity, even down here. Damon was up and running on a new laptop, but the thousands of lost images were irreplaceable. I was texting Damon, telling him it looked like his plan would work, when an incoming message appeared from him.

"We're going to need a lot of water," continued Chuck, "and—"

"The president is going to be speaking to the nation tomorrow morning," I announced, reading the message on my phone. "It will be broadcast on all radio stations. They're going to tell us what's going on."

Chuck exhaled long and slow. "About time."

I put my phone away. "And if getting this truck down doesn't work, we're going to hot-wire something from the street, right? We need to get out of here."

"One way or another. But my baby is still our safest bet for getting to my place near the Shenandoah."

Overhead, a low droning sound began, and we backed away from the parking structure to get a better view of the sky. The noise grew in volume as a military transport growled into view, skimming the tops of the buildings. Its rear loading dock was down, and as we watched, a large pallet was pushed off the back. A parachute opened above it as it fell.

Chuck jumped through the snow toward Ninth Avenue. "They're air-dropping supplies!"

I followed on his heels. Rounding the corner, looking straight up the street, I was greeted by the surreal vision of a long line of crates descending on parachutes. The wind dragged the one closest to us into a building, smashing into windows. Dozens of other planes buzzed in the distance, all dropping loads over different parts of the city.

I watched, captivated. "Not sure if I'm happy or worried."

The crate nearest us crashed into the snow, and dozens of people appeared out of nowhere to converge on it.

"Come on," said Chuck, with a nod of his head, "let's see what we can grab." He pulled the rifle off his back and ran into the crowd, waving the gun in front of him.

Shaking my head, I followed.

"Did you know that we're the only animals with three species of lice?"

Scratching my head, I replied, "I did not know that," and then scratched my shoulder.

Damon was busy inspecting his sweater. "Yeah, I saw a Discovery Channel special on it a few weeks ago."

We had gathered everyone to listen to the president's message, scheduled for ten in the morning. The hallway was just warming up. We turned off the kerosene heater in the evenings. It was too dangerous to leave it on at night.

Twenty-seven people crowded together in the hallway, and Irena and Aleksandr guarded the five prisoners in their apartment. Thirty-four souls in our building that we knew about, all up on the sixth floor—plus the nine dead on the second.

The Borodins had volunteered to use their bedroom to hold Paul's gang. Lauren wanted us to hold them somewhere farther from the kids, but spreading ourselves out wasn't practical or safe anymore. We'd given up on guarding the entrance and stairwell and had started patrolling just our end of the barricaded hallway.

Irena told Lauren not to worry, that if the door to their bedroom moved, they'd just shoot, and that in a day or two the detainees would be too weak to put up much of a fight anyway.

"The head louse, the pubic louse, they're not so bad," continued Damon, "but the body louse"—peering closely at his sweater, he pinched at something and held it up for me to see—"now these are little bastards." He crushed the louse between his fingers.

The ham-radio-sphere was abuzz with speculation about what the president would be telling us—that we were at war, that we'd been invaded, that it was the Russians, foreign terrorists, the Chinese, domestic terrorists, the Iranians. Everyone had a theory.

Even more sinister were the meshnet reports that hundreds or even thousands lay dead inside Penn and Javits, and that cholera had spread to Grand Central Station. There were rumors of typhoid.

"I don't think I have any pubic lice yet," said Damon, looking down. "Guess it wouldn't be a big deal if I did. Haven't had much action lately." He laughed and looked up at me. I smiled and shook my head.

Richard was glaring at us. "Could you shut up about lice? I'm trying to listen."

If the physical environment was turning into a cesspit, the interpersonal environment was even worse. It was poisonous.

"That's just some stupid hack," shot back Damon. The president's message hadn't started yet, and we were listening to a commentator speculating about what he might say.

I tried to defuse the tension. "He was just messing around, trying to lighten things—"

"We've had enough of your messing around," growled Richard, "using us as bait, spying on us."

It had slipped out that we'd been using Damon's meshnet to

track everyone's movements, and that we'd planned the capture of Paul's gang without telling them what was happening. Richard and Rory were livid, but Chuck was just as angry.

"With good reason!" erupted Chuck. "One of you *is a spy* for them."

He wasn't holding back—he knew we would be gone by tomorrow morning. Just one more secret we were keeping from our floor mates.

"A spy? For *them*?" said Rory. "Who's *them*? Are you listening to yourself?"

Chuck pointed an accusing finger at Rory. "I don't want to hear a peep from you. You're the only one who's been near Paul's apartment, and those messages from here to there—"

"I already told you, I stopped and checked some garbage near that apartment. I didn't know we were under surveillance."

"You slimeball. All that Anonymous hacking stuff, and I *saw* you down there talking to Stan before all this started."

"You want to know who is buddies with Stan?" Rory pointed at Richard. "Talk to him."

"Don't drag me into this," said Richard, shaking his head.

"Why not?" I asked.

Richard laughed. "I bet you were using that system to track Lauren, weren't you?"

I couldn't help myself. "Shut up."

Lauren was sitting beside me. She pulled her hand away from mine and looked at the ceiling.

"What about your new friend?" continued Richard, pointing at Damon. "What do you know about him? Just accidentally landed here from nowhere, nobody knows who he is. If anyone is a—"

Chuck stood up. "This *kid* has saved your butt, saved a lot of lives. Without us, you'd all be out in the streets, maybe dying in Penn right now, or Paul would have stolen everything from you. A little gratitude?"

"Oh, we should be thankful to you? *I'm* the one taking care of people." He waved his hand back toward the group now inhabiting his apartment. "While you're barricading yourself in your palace. We know you have a secret food supply. And who made you the police? Why won't you give us any guns to protect ourselves?"

It had become a sore point. From the start, we'd kept hold of the guns, and after Chuck had begun to suspect our neighbors, he'd flat out refused to let anyone else have one.

On the couch in the middle of the hallway, Vicky's young children began to cry.

"I'll tell you why we're the police," said Chuck, smiling. "Because we've got the guns!"

Rory laughed. "So the sheepskin comes away. The ones with the guns make the rules. You're paranoid is what you are."

"I'll show you paranoid," growled Chuck.

"Could you men *please* stop this?" Susie gripped Chuck's arm, urging him to sit down. "There's enough fighting going on out there without us making it worse. This is our *home*, and like it or not, we're together, so I suggest you boys learn to make the best of it."

Ellarose began to scream. Susie gave Chuck an evil look and carried the baby into their apartment, cooing softly to her. Chuck sat back down, his shoulders slumping, the tension in the hallway easing.

In the silence, the radio crackled to life: "*In just a few moments, the president will be addressing the nation. Please, everyone, stand by. We will be starting in a moment.*"

The children on the couch sobbed, afraid and upset.

I eyed the Chinese family pressed in the corner behind Richard. They hadn't said a word to any of us, except Richard, in three weeks. They'd been thin to start with and had become gaunt. They stared back at me with the same vacant expression that many of the other refugees had started to display. I had assumed it was the circumstances they were afraid of, but now my perspective suddenly flipped. I'd always thought of our group as the providers, the protectors, but to them, we were the ones with the guns, the gadgets, the information—the power. This was our space, our place, and we hid things from them, were tracking and watching them. We'd become the ones they feared.

"*My fellow Americans,*" said the president's deep voice. Damon leaned over to turn up the volume on the radio as Susie and Ellarose came back out to join us.

"*It is with great sadness that I address you now, in perhaps this great nation's darkest hour. I know many of you now listening are scared, cold, hungry, in the dark, wondering what is happening, and I am sorry that it has taken this long for us to reach out to you.*"

The voice paused, and the lightbulb in the hallway flickered as the generator sputtered. Chuck jumped up to check on it.

"*Communications were almost completely wiped out in what we've come to describe as the 'event,' something we now understand to be a coordinated cyberattack on this country's infrastructure and the worldwide Internet.*"

"Tell us something we don't know," whispered Damon under his breath. The generator purred back to life, and light returned. Chuck stood next to Susie, resting his hand on her shoulder.

"*We still do not understand the extent of it, nor the extent of the breach of our territorial boundaries by unknown intruders. I speak to you now not from Washington, but from a secret location until we better understand our adversaries."*

This brought hushed murmurs from the room.

"While all of America, indeed the entire world, has been affected by this event, not all areas have been affected equally. Power failures were temporary west of the Mississippi, and have been mostly restored in the South, but New England and New York have been hit hard, with the situation made indescribably worse by a series of immense winter storms."

It was some comfort to hear that not all of America was in the same state as we were.

"Our nation's military was stepped up to DEFCON 2 during the event, the highest it has ever been in our history, but we have now backed down to DEFCON 4. Many of you may have wondered why our military has not been able to help by deploying more personnel locally. This is the reason: we have needed to keep our eyes turned to our attackers."

"I told you," whispered Chuck. "We're dying on the inside while they guard the goddamn fences."

"The one thing I can tell you, after weeks of investigation, is that it appears as if many, if not all, of the attacks originated with organizations associated with, or controlled by, the Chinese People's Liberation Army."

This brought a round of excited whispers. Everyone's eyes zeroed in on the Chinese family, but then we all looked away as we realized what we were doing.

"We now have four carrier battle groups positioned in the South China Sea, awaiting the results of a multinational standoff at the UN and NATO organizations. We will not back down, nor will we let our citizens suffer any longer. I have good news—I have enacted

special emergency powers to bring power and services back to New York City and the East Coast within the next few days, no matter what."

Cheers went up.

"But," said the president, pausing, "I regret to inform the citizens of New York that in the short term, the CDC has requested, and I have granted, a temporary quarantine of the island of Manhattan due to an uncontrolled series of outbreaks of waterborne diseases. This will last no more than a day or two, and I implore the citizens of New York to stay indoors, to stay warm and safe, and we will be with you shortly. God bless you all."

The radio went silent.

DAY 21: JANUARY 12

It was snowing again.

I had gone up on the roof in the morning with Tony to play with Luke and shovel new snow into a barrel for drinking water. Snowflakes swirled down soundlessly from the sky, smothering a city it seemed the outside world had cut off like a cancerous tumor.

Yet here we were.

After the president's message, we'd lain together in the hallway for the rest of the day, listening to the ham-radio-sphere explode. First came shock and denial, but after reports of the military checkpoints turning people back, this shifted to anger and bargaining. A good chunk of the best lawyers in America were trapped on Manhattan, and threats of lawsuits about violations of human rights and the Constitution flooded the meshnet and airwaves.

But what made for the most colorful listening were the conspiracy rants. If there was anything Americans were good at, it was conspiracy theories. The alien invasion theorists were my favorite—"*This has nothing to do with the Chinese or Iranians or anyone else on Earth; the government is hiding an alien invasion, pure and simple*"—but even they failed to lighten the mood.

Chuck declared he was going to storm the bridges, gun in hand, and would be damned if anyone would stop him. The futility of our situation began to dawn on us just as the first news of fighting and casualties on the George Washington Bridge came over the meshnet. By nightfall, the mood of New York had shifted from anger to depression and hopelessness. Where people had been resigned to waiting it out, when it was announced that they *couldn't* leave, that they were penned in like animals, suddenly everyone *needed* to leave. Pictures of people falling through the ice on the East River appeared on Damon's laptop, images of small boats getting stuck in the ice, of people drowning like rats.

The subway tunnels were useless. Without power, most of the tunnels in Lower Manhattan, and up past Chelsea, had flooded after a few days. With the cold temperatures, most of that was now frozen as well. Some people must have been attempting to hide down there, but we didn't hear anything about it, and we didn't go exploring to find out.

Morning had brought a listless agitation to the hallway. I'd slept out there, with Lauren and Luke curled up with me and Damon. Feeling abandoned by the outside world had made us all want to stay together.

We didn't even talk about our plans for retrieving the truck. It was useless.

Chuck sat dumbly, staring at the walls, while Damon was glued catatonically to the screen of his laptop. It was nearing mid-day, and I was fiddling with the station app on my smartphone, cycling through the ham radio operators.

"I don't believe a word of what the president said. I think there's something else going on they're not telling us about. That was just

a broadcast for New York, to keep us in line, to explain why they're keeping us in—"

I switched the station.

"—bring those assholes down to the East Village and show them what's going on. How can they leave us here? Why is nobody helping—"

I switched again.

"—believe it? If the rest of America is all right, do you think that the president would be hiding? We can cure cancer, for God's sake, why are they so afraid of some ancient—"

"Can you switch it to public radio?" asked Damon, sitting up. "Quick."

I changed stations and adjusted the volume. Rory turned up the volume on the main radio. Pam had been up all night, administering what care she could for our infections, upset stomachs, and colds, and was asleep beside Rory, but she stirred only slightly at the increased noise level.

"—the Iranian Ashiyane hacking group is now claiming responsibility for the Scramble virus that brought down logistics systems, with the Ashiyane group saying they initiated—"

"See, I told you it was the Arabs," said Tony, sitting up.

"They're not Arabs," said Rory.

"—retribution for the United States' attack on Iran with the Stuxnet and Flame cyberattacks of the years before—"

Susie perked up next to Chuck. Ellarose and Luke were asleep together in a small improvised crib in front of her.

"So it wasn't the Chinese?"

"—the initial attack was targeted at US government networks. It quickly spread to secondary systems—"

"Iranians are Persians, not Arabs," repeated Rory. "They pretty much invented science and mathematics. And the Ashiyane group they're talking about isn't the Iranian government."

"—*NATO is still considering a motion of collective defense, while the US government is on the brink of taking unilateral action*—"

"You seem to know a lot about these guys," said Chuck to Rory.

Rory shrugged. "I cover it for the *Times*. It's my job. The IRGC has a very sophisticated cyber unit."

"—*while global Internet traffic is at a crawl, Europe has begun to bounce back and land-based mobile radio has been restored in most of the East Coast*—"

"The IRG what?"

Rory turned down the volume on the radio. "Iran's military, the Islamic Revolutionary Guard Corps. It's like a mix of the Communist Party, the KGB, and the mafia. Imagine if Halliburton and the Gestapo got married—the IRGC would be their love child."

"Are they that good? Could they have done all this?" I asked.

Maybe it was some sort of ploy. A Middle Eastern group claiming responsibility for something beyond their scope, making noise, diverting us from where we should be focusing.

Rory laughed. "Commander Rafal, who runs the cyber division, is world-class. The thing you need to understand is that the US has no technical edge when it comes to cyber. Our military thinking is based on the idea of overwhelming technical and numerical superiority, but in the cyberworld, all that goes away."

"But we invented the Internet, didn't we?"

"Sure we did, but now it's global. You can spend ten billion dollars on a new piece of fancy military equipment, but all it takes is one bright kid with a laptop to disable it."

"So you're saying they could be the ones?"

"The Iranians changed the rules of the game by attacking civilian targets using cyberweapons—the Shamoon attack that wiped out fifty thousand computers at Saudi Aramco—so this wouldn't be out of line with their operations, especially as retaliation for the US cyberattacks."

"So you think this is justified?" said an incredulous Chuck.

"Of course not. I'm just saying it could make sense. But what you don't realize is how *important* it is that someone admitted to something. Maybe they can start to unravel this mess."

"So this is cyberwar," I said. "Dirty, smelly, diseased, quarantined . . ."

Rory nodded without saying anything. He looked incredibly thin and frail. He hadn't eaten much in weeks, insanely trying to maintain his vegan diet. I had a hard time imagining that he was the one who'd been talking to Paul, that he had some ulterior motive.

"Could you turn the radio back up?" demanded Richard from the other end of the corridor. "It's nice to hear your opinions, but I want to find out what's going on."

Rory adjusted the radio, and I wandered toward the middle of the hallway. Vicky had gone off with one of her kids, and the other, a boy no more than four years old, was sitting alone on the couch, playing with Luke's fire truck. I hadn't had a chance to speak with him yet.

"How are you doing?" I asked him.

He looked up at me defiantly. "Mom said not to speak to strangers."

"But we've been—" I started to say, then shook my head, smiling, and stretched my hand out. "I'm Mike."

The little guy examined my hand, considering it. The skin on his face was peeling, and his clothes looked two sizes too big, like he was a waif from the street. Dark bruises spread under his eyes from lack of sleep. He shook my hand. "I'm Ricky. Nice to meet you."

"Nice to meet you too," I laughed.

In the background, the radio droned. "*The US military is now considering the possibility of taking action on three fronts, something it was designed to do but never tested—*"

"My dad is a marine. He's out fighting," Ricky said matter-of-factly. "I'm going to be a marine one day."

"Is that right?"

He nodded and started playing with the fire truck again. The door to the stairwell opened, and his mother appeared, holding his sister in her arms. "Is everything okay?" she asked, seeing me hovering over Ricky.

"Everything is fine, Vicky. We're just having a chat."

She smiled. "As long as he's being a good boy."

"He's a strong boy," I said, ruffling Ricky's hair. "Just like his dad."

The smile on Vicky's face disappeared. "I hope not."

I said something wrong. We looked at each other in an awkward silence.

Just then I received a text from Sergeant Williams asking how we were doing. I said good-bye to Vicky and retreated to our end of the hallway, texting him back to ask if he had any ideas about how we could get off the island.

DAY 22: JANUARY 13

Pulling my goggles up, I stopped and blinked, looking out into the night with my own unaided eyes. The night was pitch black and soundless, and my mind suddenly felt disconnected. Staring into the void, I became a tiny dot of existence floating by itself in the universe. At first the feeling was terrifying, my mind reeling, but it quickly became comforting. *Maybe this is what death is like? Alone, peaceful, floating, floating, no fear . . .*

Clipping the night-vision goggles back into place, I could see ghostly green flakes of snow falling gently around me.

My hunger pangs had been intense this morning, almost driving me outside during the day. Chuck had held me back, talked to me, calmed me down. It wasn't for me, I'd argued, it was for Luke, for Lauren, for Ellarose—anything that would allow me, like an addict, to get my fix.

I laughed. *I'm addicted to food.*

The falling snowflakes were hypnotic. Closing my eyes, I took a deep breath. *What is real? What is reality, anyway?* I felt like I was hallucinating, my mind never quite able to take a firm hold of anything before skidding off. *Get a grip, Mike. Luke is counting on you. Lauren is counting on you.*

Opening my eyes, I willed myself into the here and now and

tapped the phone in my pocket to bring up the augmented-reality display. A field of red dots spread out into the distance, and taking another deep breath, I carefully put one foot in front of the other, continuing on my way across Twenty-Fourth, pushing myself toward a cluster of dots on Sixth Avenue.

On previous outings, in my haste to dig up the bags of food and get home, I hadn't thought to mark off the locations I'd visited. We'd tagged forty-six locations in total, and so far I'd tried fourteen of them on four trips. At four locations I hadn't been able to find anything. Maybe people had seen us hiding the bags at those spots and helped themselves, or maybe the food stashes had become exposed, or maybe I'd already visited these hiding places. My brain wasn't clear anymore. In any event, I guessed that at least a quarter of the remaining locations would be empty. Even so, that meant twenty or more locations should still yield something to eat. I was finding three or four bags per location, and each stash represented a day's worth of food for our group.

The numbers spun through my head. *Lauren needs two thousand calories, and the kids need nearly as much. But I need to eat more.*

I'd been light-headed all day, feverish. I wouldn't be helping anyone if I starved myself to death. I was allowing myself only a few hundred calories a day, but I'd read that Arctic explorers required up to six thousand calories a day in the cold.

And it *was* cold. The wind made things worse, and I felt like it might even pick me up and blow me around like a leaf.

Looking up, I squinted, trying to make out a street sign as I passed it. *Eighth Avenue.* The sign behind it mocked me— *Burger King.*

Imagine a nice, juicy burger, all the toppings, mayonnaise and ketchup. It was all I could do to keep myself from going through the open door and digging through the snow drifted halfway up to the ceiling inside. *Maybe somebody missed a burger in here? Maybe I could start up a propane grill?*

Pulling my mind away from burgers, I continued walking. We'd buried food at eight spots in the snowbanks on Sixth Avenue. It was a veritable gold mine, and that's where I was heading to hunt. My mind cycled through the numbers again. If I could recover it all, from all twenty-odd locations, we'd have twelve days or so until we'd be like them.

Like *them*.

Like the other people on our floor.

It'd been five days since the relief stations had closed, pinching off the only reliable food source for the other groups on our floor. It was my guess that it had been as many days since they'd had anything substantial to eat. Mostly they just slept.

In the morning, I'd gone to check on Vicky and her kids, pulling away the layers of blankets from the couch in the middle of the hall. The kids had blinked up at me in the dim light, their lips cracked and swollen, red and infected.

Dehydration was worse than starvation.

Damon and I had spent most of the day collecting as much snow as we could, dragging it up with the pulleys. Chuck had tried to help, but he hadn't recovered from the blow to his head, and his broken hand was swelling up again.

The hallway smelled of human excrement.

As brutal as conditions had become, there were still small acts of kindness. Susie went around offering water to everyone, sneaking out scraps of our food, doing what she could. I watched Damon bring over a blanket that he'd spent hours cleaning and give it to Vicky and her kids. He shared some food with them as well.

The whole day, the door to Richard's apartment hadn't opened even once. We'd knocked to make sure they were all right, but he'd told us to go away.

Arriving at Seventh Avenue, I looked up and down the street, but visibility was limited to about twenty feet in the falling snow. When I tapped the phone's screen, the heads-up display on my AR glasses switched to a top-down view of where I was.

I might as well head up Seventh and then circle down Sixth from Twenty-Third.

As I made my way to the intersection of the footpaths at the middle of the streets, my mind filled with images of the dead bodies we'd stacked in the apartment on the second floor.

During the day, the radio stations had rebroadcast the audio portion of a CNN news report, one that had aired on television networks in the outside world. It described conditions in New York as difficult but stable, and said that supplies were being delivered, that the outbreaks of disease were being contained. Nothing could have been further from our reality. The immense disconnect fueled speculation that the government was hiding something.

How can they not see what's happening in here?

I didn't care anymore. My life had been reduced to providing for Lauren and Luke, and after that, for Susie and Ellarose and Chuck. Our situation was bringing my priorities into sharp focus. I was shrugging off any artificialities, cleaning away all of the unimportant things I'd seen as essential before.

A strong feeling of déjà vu gripped me, but not from anything I'd experienced myself. I felt like I was living the stories Irena had shared with me about the siege of Leningrad seventy years before.

This cyberwar felt like it had nothing to do with the future but was a part of the past, as if we were burrowing backwards into humans' unending ability to inflict suffering upon one another.

If you wanted to see into the future, you just had to look to the past.

Reaching the corner of Sixth and Twenty-Third, I came upon the decimated remains of an air-dropped container. We'd gone out to get what we could when each airdrop was announced, but these events had turned into violent scavenging wars. Rory had been injured gathering some meager supplies, half of which were useless items like mosquito netting.

A large red circle glowed in front of me now. I clicked my phone for the image that would mark the exact location I was seeking, found the spot, and then dropped to my knees and began digging. After about ten minutes, I was rewarded. Potatoes. Cashews. Random items we'd grabbed off shelves in another world.

My mouth watered as I imagined eating some of the cashews—*Just a few, nobody will notice*—but I stuffed everything into my backpack and continued on to the next red circle, just down Sixth Avenue.

An hour later, I'd recovered all the bags from that location. I rested, treating myself to a few peanuts and the bottle of water Lauren had packed for me, then continued on.

The next red circle glowed under a scaffold at the edge of a burnt-out building. As I approached, a strong smell of scorched wood and plastic forced me to pull my bandana over my nose. Within a few minutes I found the prizes and pulled them out of the snow: bags and bags of chicken. *That's right—these are from when we raided the food market on Twenty-Third.*

My back was aching from bending over. The backpack was stuffed. It probably weighed fifty pounds. *Time to go home— chicken for breakfast.*

A voice came suddenly out of the darkness. "Who's there?"

Awkwardly, with my backpack half on, I wheeled around, fumbling for my gun. Ghostly faces appeared in the greenish light of my night-vision goggles—faces and outstretched hands. In my rush to start digging when I got to this spot, I hadn't looked around. I was in some sort of makeshift camp. The people who lived here must have fled from the burnt-out building.

"We can hear you digging. What did you find?"

I backed up until I was pinned against the plywood wall of the scaffolding.

"It's ours, whatever it is. *Give* it to us!" hissed another voice.

Dozens of green faces now circled me in the dark. They couldn't see me—it was pitch black—but they could hear me, sense me there. Their hands hunted through space, their feet shuffling forward in the snow, their eyes unseeing. I held the gun in my pocket. *Should I shoot one of them?*

I dropped my backpack and rummaged around in it. The nearest hands were only a few feet away from me.

"Back! I have a gun!"

That stopped them, but temporarily.

Grabbing a packet of cashews, I threw it at one of the closest figures. His face was emaciated, with eyes shrunken and hollowed, and he wore no gloves. His hands were black and bleeding in the phosphorescent light of my goggles. The package of nuts ricocheted off him, landing somewhere behind, and he turned and dove for them, colliding with two other people. I flung a few more packets behind them, and they all turned away from me.

I ran out of the enclosure, dragging the backpack behind me. In a few seconds I was back out on the open street, under cover of the falling snow. Taking a few gasping breaths to calm my thumping heart, I headed home.

As I'd fled, I'd glanced once over my shoulder to see them fighting like a pack of wild dogs over scraps. The tears came from nowhere. I was sobbing, trying my best to stay quiet as I trudged through the snow in the blackness—alone, but surrounded by millions.

DAY 23: JANUARY 14

"New York Power Authority says that power will be restored to many parts of Manhattan within the week," promised the radio announcer, adding, *"but then again, we've all heard that before, haven't we? Stay warm, stay safe—"*

"Would you like some more tea?" asked Lauren.

Pam nodded, and Lauren crossed over to her with the pot and filled her cup.

"Anyone else?"

Not more tea, but I'd sure like some biscuits. Sitting on one of the couches in the hallway, I daydreamed about cookies. *Chocolate-covered biscuits, like the ones my grandmother used to bring on the holidays, the graham cracker kind.*

"Yes, more tea, please," said the younger Chinese man at the end of the hall.

Lauren made her way down, stepping between legs and feet and blankets on her way. Her baby bump was noticeable even under her sweater, at least to me—*fifteen weeks.* I was down four notches on my belt, as skinny as I'd been in college. As my stomach disappeared, hers was growing.

A meshnet alert pinged my phone, announcing a med-swap meet-up on the corner of Sixth and Thirty-Fourth. *They better be defending it.* A lot of people out there wanted what was being bartered.

Noon tea was Susie's idea. Boiling the water meant we could sterilize it, and Lauren and Susie wanted to keep in contact with everyone at least once a day. The hallway had become like a convalescent home for hunger strikers, with rows of gaunt faces peering out from beneath stained blankets. The tea had bits floating in it, but it hydrated and warmed the body and, Susie hoped, the soul as well.

Chuck pointed out that getting warm bodies together in one room helped with heating. Each human body, he'd explained, gave off about as much heat as a hundred-watt lightbulb. So twenty-seven bodies equaled twenty-seven hundred watts of heat, half as much power as our generator produced.

We didn't talk about where all that energy came from. We used less energy if we moved as little as possible, but we used much more, he'd whispered to me, if it was cold.

After three weeks, even with us being as frugal as possible, all of Chuck's kerosene supplies were finished, and we were almost out of diesel. The two-hundred-gallon tank downstairs was nearly empty after three weeks of fueling two small generators as well as heaters and stoves, plus what scavengers had stolen.

We weren't running the electric generator much anymore. The hallway was lit with homemade lamps that ran on heating oil from the furnace in the basement. It was nearly the only thing we could use the oil for, since it was too viscous to run in the generator. Running the kerosene heaters on diesel alone created heat, but also unbearable fumes, so we had to keep windows open, which defeated the purpose.

"In a few minutes we'll be providing the latest updates on the cyberattack investigation, with—"

Susie turned down the volume on the radio. "I think we've all had enough of that."

"I haven't," said Lauren, putting down the teapot and sitting next to me.

We'd removed half of the barricade but still kept part of it in place—an upturned coffee table and some boxes demarcating which end of the hallway was closed off to other people. Lauren was doing her best to keep our end clean, bleaching blankets and clothing, which created a strong smell that was nearly eye-watering.

Lauren leaned forward to look at everyone. "Why didn't they just make the Internet more secure?"

It was a question circling the meshnet, asked with rising anger, and most of the blame was coming down on an inept government that should have protected us.

"I'll tell you why," croaked Rory from beneath his blankets. "You can try to lay blame, but the central reason the Internet isn't secure is because we don't *want* it to be secure."

This roused Chuck. "What do you mean *we*? I'm all for a secure Internet."

Rory sat up a little. "You might think you want a secure Internet, but you really don't, and that's part of what makes this possible. In the end, a *really* secure Internet isn't in the interest of the general public or software producers."

"Why wouldn't consumers want a secure Internet?"

"Because a truly secure Internet wouldn't serve a common interest in freedom."

"Seems like it would right now," said Tony. Luke was lying asleep on top of him on the couch next to Lauren and me.

"It does right now, but it comes down to what we were talking about before, about privacy being the cornerstone of freedom. More and more of our lives are moving into cyberspace, and we need to preserve what we have in the physical world as we move into the cyberworld. A perfectly secure Internet implies a trail of information somewhere, always tracking what you're doing."

I hadn't thought of it like that. A completely secure Internet would be the same as a world with cameras on every corner and in every home, recording our every movement, but it would be even more intrusive. A perfect record of *every* interaction we had would give someone the ability to peer into our very thoughts.

"I'd be willing to give up my online privacy to avoid this mess," snorted Tony. Luke stirred in the blankets on top of him, and Tony whispered to him, saying he was sorry.

"Wait, doesn't this contradict what you said before about needing to make the Internet *more* secure?" I asked.

"The problem is that we're trying to use the same technology—the Internet—for social networking *and* to run nuclear power plants. Those are two very different activities. We need to make it as secure as possible without giving some centralized power all the responsibility," replied Rory in a tired voice. "What we're talking about is a balancing act, an attempt to make it difficult to abuse the rights of individuals in the cyberworld of the future. Even this"—Rory waved his arms around in the candlelight—"whatever is happening now, it'll be fixed soon enough."

Rory barely looked strong enough to stand, and yet he spoke with such confidence.

"The bigger problem is that software companies don't want consumers to be secure," said Damon. He was bent over his laptop, his face illuminated in its soft glow. He kept it running in low-power mode, charging it overnight when we ran the generator.

"Are you saying tech companies actively want an insecure Internet?" I said.

"They want it to be secure from hackers," replied Damon, "but they don't want consumers to be secure from *them*. They hardwire back doors to update and modify software remotely— it's a fundamental security risk they purposely create. The Stuxnet cyberweapon exploited it."

"Of course they don't want consumers to be secure from them," laughed Rory. "They give us all that software for free specifically so that we *aren't* secure from them—so they can watch us, sell our information."

Damon looked at his computer screen. "If you don't pay for a product, then you *are* the product."

"How does someone tracking my online shopping affect security?" asked Susie, perplexed.

Damon shrugged. "It's all the little loopholes, all the hooks and ways to track your activity and get inside your computer that are put there by software companies—that's a lot of what hackers exploit."

"And you would know, wouldn't you?" grumbled Richard from the other end of the hall.

We ignored him.

The day before, it had come out that he was the one who'd given the group on the second floor the kerosene heater in exchange for their generator, which he'd put in his own bedroom. He was adamant that he'd told them to ventilate, but for someone who was perhaps responsible for the deaths of nine people, he wasn't apologetic.

"What about the government, then? Aren't they supposed to protect against this?" asked Lauren. "What's happening now isn't just a hacked bank account."

"Protect what, exactly?" asked Rory.

"Electricity and water, for starters."

"The government doesn't own that stuff anymore. Not their responsibility."

"Isn't it the military's job to protect us?"

"In theory, yes, a nation's military is supposed to protect its citizens and industry from other nations—establish a border and then protect it—but that doesn't work anymore. Borders are difficult to define in cyberspace." Rory took a deep breath. "Where the government and military *used* to be responsible for protecting a factory from attack by foreign national governments, now they're asking private industry to take over that responsibility in cyberspace." He shrugged. "But who's going to pay for it? And can a private company really protect itself from a hostile nation? Can we as private citizens act as our own armed forces? And what happens when corporations are as powerful as nations?"

Damon nodded. "We complain about the Chinese and Iranians, but we used advanced cyberweapons, like Stuxnet and Flame, on them first. Can we really be surprised that now they're using them against us?"

That sounded familiar, and it made me think of something. "'If you decide to use fire in battle, make sure that anything you need yourself isn't flammable.'"

"Sun Tzu?" asked Rory.

I nodded, thinking, *The more things change, the more they stay the same.*

"Well then," Rory laughed, "we should have been more careful, because we're about the most cyber-combustible country on the planet."

Nobody else thought it was funny.

"Do you have any food?"

The voice startled me, and I almost dropped the load of snow I was hauling. I recognized the voice. It was Sarah, Richard's wife, and I turned around, only to be startled again. The voice was Sarah's, but the face and body . . .

In the dim light of the stairwell, desperate eyes stared up at me from sunken sockets. Bent over, she pulled a ragged, stained blanket around her shoulders. I could see that her hair was littered with louse eggs. She glanced furtively behind her, and then turned to look at me, trying to smile from between cracked and swollen lips. Her teeth were yellow, caked with grime, and with a skeletal hand she touched an angry red lesion on the side of her face. Her skin looked so papery thin that I imagined it sloughing off as she rubbed at the sore.

"Please, Michael," she whispered.

"Uh, sure," I mumbled, horrified. I tied off my rope so the load of snow wouldn't fall. In my pocket I had a lump of cheese I'd been saving for Luke. I handed it to her, and she stuffed it into her mouth, nodding her thanks.

"SARAH!"

She cringed like a frightened animal. Richard appeared in the doorway, and she cowered away from him against the railing of the stairs.

"Come, Sarah, you aren't well," Richard said, reaching toward her and ignoring me.

She held up one bruised skin-and-bones arm to fend him off. "I don't want to."

Richard glared at her, then turned to smile at me. He was wearing a comfortable-looking fleece and North Face pants, and his pink, closely shaved skin radiated health.

"She's been sick," he explained with a shrug.

He moved forward and grabbed the blanket around her. She mewled as he leaned down and picked her up. He turned to me, his wife pinned in his arms. "Do you think you could drop some water at our end when you're done?"

I watched dumbfounded as he walked off.

"What was that about?" Chuck walked up the stairs, holding a four-gallon tank of diesel in his good hand.

"Sarah wanted food."

"Don't we all," laughed Chuck humorlessly. He waggled the container as he started up the last set of stairs. "Just a few more of these and that'll be it."

"She's not well," I said, still staring at the open doorway.

"None of us are well," replied Chuck, clunking up the stairs. "Have you seen what they're eating in the hallway?"

Some of the refugees had started catching rats in the downstairs lobby. Irena had showed them how, by leaving ground-up sleeping pills and other poisons in garbage piles—rats were too fast and aggressive to catch by hand. And if people were eating the rats, then they were eating the poisons in the rats as well. I'd found a large pile of well-cleaned rat carcasses in a corner of one of the latrine rooms.

I heard another door close—Richard's apartment.

"Have you been in their place lately?" I asked Chuck.

He stopped, putting the container down. "You sure as heck don't look good."

I *wasn't* feeling well, but then nobody was. The world began to spin, and I gripped the railing to steady myself.

"Whoa, you okay?"

Taking a deep breath, I nodded. "Just need to get this load of snow up and into the melt buckets, and then I'll go lie down."

Chuck studied me. "Why don't you go lie down right now and get some more to eat?"

That morning we'd pan-fried some of the chicken. Thinking about it made me salivate painfully. We'd tried to conceal what we were doing, cooking it up over a small butane stove in the corner of Chuck and Susie's bedroom, but I was sure the smell had permeated the walls. It was probably what had brought Sarah out of hiding.

"Seriously, why don't you go and get some more to eat? I'll finish this," offered Chuck.

He put down the container of fuel and looked over the railing at my bucket of snow. Damon and I were trying to bring up as much as we could. We needed more water.

When I'd come out of our apartment that morning, I'd almost gagged at the stench. If I thought I was used to it, that it couldn't get any worse, I was wrong. Two of the people sleeping in the hallway had defecated in their clothes, under the sheets, and were in terrible shape. Pam said it was from dehydration, and I hoped it was no more than that. She'd tried to clean them, but it was an impossible task. We'd commandeered anyone we could to help get more water.

A wave of nausea overcame the knotted hunger burning my stomach. Steeling myself, I waited for it to pass. "Are you still thinking of hunting Paul down?" I asked.

Chuck nodded. "But let Tony and me handle it. We owe it to everyone to get that laptop back."

He was talking a lot about the laptop, about how important it was to have all the records and documentation of events it contained. But we knew it was personal, that Chuck had an ax to grind.

With the collapse of government authority, responsibility for justice had reverted to the tribal groups we'd spontaneously created. Restraining hotheads in your clan required a strong, central force, but what if that force was the hothead?

About the only thing we had a lot of was time to think, and the thought of Paul out there was circling around and around in Chuck's head, one hunger replacing another. I was unable to muster the energy to argue with him anymore. We needed to focus on surviving, not dangerous goose chases, but I didn't say anything.

"I'm going to lie down for a bit." Smiling at Chuck, I turned to walk back to our place.

"And no," said Chuck, "I haven't been back there, in Richard's place. He says we have our end barricaded, so he won't let Susie or anyone in there."

I nodded without turning, taking a deep breath before going into the hallway. The radio was playing at low volume.

"—at least a dozen more people have been reported drowned as rescue workers try their best to save—"

What a joke—trying their best to save us.

The quarantine that was supposed to last for a day or two was now into its fourth, and people were trying to escape the city over the rivers. A wide layer of ice ringed the island of Manhattan, making it impossible to just step into boats, so people were walking out onto the slushy floes, pushing and dragging whatever floating contraptions they could. Many were falling through the ice or capsizing into the frozen waters.

Their desperation spoke to how impossible the situation had become.

With the big emergency centers closed, the homeless population on the streets had exploded. Some new centers had opened, but it was too little too late. More buildings had burned down, and with no heat, no water, and no food, the fighting over air-dropped supplies had become fierce.

We stayed off the streets entirely.

Tens of thousands dead. The official radio stations weren't saying anything, but those were the numbers floating around on meshnet tweets. A deadly epidemic was raging.

When I got back to Chuck's apartment, I found Lauren helping to prepare noon tea for everyone. She looked up at me, and her smile faded.

"My God, Mike, are you okay?"

I nodded. My legs were weak and nearly buckled underneath me. "I'm good. I'm just going to lie down for a minute."

My phone beeped in my pocket, and I pulled it out. It was a message from Sergeant Williams: "*I've found a way to get your family off the island, but I need to come over there.*"

I had trouble focusing on the screen, but I leaned against the door frame to respond, telling him to come.

A way out of here! Wanting to tell Lauren, I took a step forward. The next thing I knew, my face was hitting the ground. I heard Susie and Lauren yelling.

My world faded to black.

The baby was screaming in my arms again.

With dirty hands, I tried to clean it, wiping and wiping. I was wandering in a forest, stepping across a carpet of yellow leaves between the white stalks of birch trees. The baby was wet, I was wet, and it was cold.

Where is everyone?

I entered a village of thatched huts and mud alleys. Smoke was rising up from cooking fires, and children appeared, their faces caked with dirt—curious little animals. It was a long way to the next village.

Perhaps I should stop?

I needed to keep moving.

And then I was flying, bounding into the air and leaving the village behind. Below me the tops of the birch trees fluttered in the wind, their last few leaves hanging on fiercely to the upper branches.

The baby was gone, left behind in the village.

A city appeared before me, a stone castle ringed by stone houses, rising up out of the forests against a backdrop of snow-capped mountains. With two more vaulting steps I flew through the sky, landing on wet flagstones in an alleyway. A man pulling a horse and cart walked past me, oblivious, either not seeing me or not caring that I was there. His cart was full of dead bodies piled high like matchsticks, and the silent screams of the cursed rang out through the empty streets.

Everything in their lives depends on me, and yet they don't care.

Society had collapsed, another Dark Age begun.

Walking up the alley, I ascended a set of stone stairs at the side of the castle. Seagulls squawked in the distance as the sun began to set, and I could hear men in the forest, lumberjacks, hacking away at the trees. One after another the trees fell, the crash reverberating off the castle walls.

Reaching the top of the stairs, I opened a wooden door and entered. Now it was hot; I was burning up. A television was playing to an empty room. "*The latest round of climate talks have failed again, or at least failed to come up with any concrete results,*" said the TV news anchor. "*It looks like we will be blowing through the emission targets set twenty years ago, with scientists now predicting a global temperature rise of five to seven degrees by the end of the century. The Arctic is free of ice for the first time in a million years. Nobody knows what will happen—*"

Thwack!

I knew what would happen. We were a nation of freeloaders, 98 percent of us non-food-producers relying on the 2 percent who produced anything edible. The time had come for the 98 percent to pay their share, and it would be paid in blood.

Thwack!

I was back outside, among the lumberjacks. Where the forest had been, an endless landscape of stumps now lay before me, their shadows spreading across the land in the setting sun. Only one tree remained, and one of the men was hacking away at its trunk, laughing.

Thwack!

"Come in."

Thwack!

Opening my eyes, I saw Chuck walk through the door.

Our bedroom door.

Lauren was sitting above me, her eyes full of fear and concern. As I opened mine, she put a hand to her mouth, and tears ran down her face. In the back of my mind, I could still hear hacking, a metronome fading away.

"You sure gave us a scare there, buddy," said Chuck. He sat on the bed next to Lauren.

"Drink some water," Lauren whispered.

My mouth felt like it was filled with cotton balls, and I coughed. *I'm so weak.*

With a groan, I lifted myself up on one elbow. Holding my head, Lauren lifted a cup to my lips. Most of the water from the cup spilled around my face, but I managed to get some of it in my mouth, and I felt it unsticking my tongue and washing down my throat. Sitting up, I took the cup from her and drank deeply.

"See?" said Chuck. "I told you he was getting better."

"Do you want to eat something?" asked Lauren. "Do you think you can eat?"

I thought about that. *Could I eat? Did I want to eat?*

"Not sure," I croaked. I was naked under the sheets and soaked in sweat. Looking down, I barely recognized my own body. I was skinny. Bones were beginning to show. "But let's try."

"Could you get some of the rice with the chicken?" Lauren asked Chuck.

He nodded. "We'll get you fixed right up."

"Did you hear from—" I started to say, but coughed before I could get it all out.

Chuck stopped at the door. "From who?"

"Williams. Sergeant Williams."

He shook his head. "Why, should we have?"

I wanted to explain, but I was so weak.

"Shh," murmured Lauren. "Rest, baby. Just rest for now."

"He'll be coming here to get us off the island."

Closing my eyes, I heard Chuck saying, "I'll keep an eye out. You just rest."

And then the dreams began again, of leaping and flying above forests while the world died beneath my feet.

DAY 26: JANUARY 17

I heard screaming.

Am I dreaming? As I willed myself awake, our bedroom ceiling came into focus, and I blinked, listening to the silence. *What time is it?* It was dark. *It must have been a dream.*

"IT WAS HIM!"

Luke began crying in his crib next to me.

It wasn't a dream. Reflexively, I groped around the bed, feeling for Lauren, but she wasn't there.

"Just sit down, calm down," I heard someone saying out in the hallway.

That's Lauren.

More muffled voices and then clearly: "Give me the gun."

That's Chuck.

Sitting up, I felt dizzy and had to lie back down. Rolling over toward Luke, I cooed at him, telling him it was okay, but I didn't touch him. I wasn't sure what was wrong with me, but then neither was I sure that everything was okay. Marshaling all my strength, I slowly sat up and swung my feet over the side of the bed.

My smartphone was plugged in next to the bed. I picked it up. *8:13 p.m. No messages.*

The screaming had stopped, replaced by someone crying in

heaving sobs. Outside it was dark, but I could see tiny crystalline flakes sweeping by the windowpane in the faint lamplight. Our room was littered with boxes and piles of discarded clothing and sheets and blankets. I heard the purr of the generator in the background.

I leaned forward and found my jeans. They were filthy, but I put them on anyway, rummaging around to find the cleanest socks I could to layer on my feet. Grabbing a sweater, I stood up and steadied myself, testing my balance, then walked out into the main room, which was empty, and stuck my head out into the hallway.

Chuck, Susie, and Lauren were surrounding Sarah, who was on the couch outside our door. They looked up at me with surprise as I opened the door.

"What?" I wheezed. "You were expecting Luke? What happened?"

Chuck got up from where he was kneeling in front of Sarah. He was holding a large handgun. "Let's leave them alone for a minute," he said to me, pushing open the door I was leaning through. He looked back down at our wives.

Ellarose was cradled in Susie's arms. Her eyes looked sore and red, and were encrusted with pus, and her skin was wrinkled, flaking, paper-thin. She was quiet but looked scared, and she was tiny, shrunken.

"What's happening?" I repeated as he pulled me back through the door. "Is Ellarose okay?"

Chuck looked like he'd aged ten years in the past week. "Pam says she's okay, just losing a lot of weight. She won't eat."

"Where are Damon and Tony?"

"Over at Richard's—or what used to be Richard's."

"What do you mean?" I followed him over to the kitchen counter, where he filled a pot with water and clicked on the flame to a camp stove.

"Nearly out of butane," he muttered. He looked at me. "Sarah killed Richard."

"What?" My mind struggled to process this information. "How?"

"With this." He put the gun on the counter. It wasn't one of ours.

"She says he stole the laptop, not Paul, and he was the one helping them."

I sat down on one of the kitchen stools, still woozy. "So Richard's dead?"

Chuck nodded.

"And he was the one talking to Paul? Who helped organize the attacks on us?"

He nodded again. I'd never truly believed someone from our building had been helping Paul. It had seemed better that it remain a figment of Chuck's paranoia.

"Why?"

"Not clear yet, but seems like he was starving the people at his end, his wife included. Keeping everything for himself. Sarah said he'd been involved in some identity theft scheme with Stan and Paul, and that things got out of hand."

I sighed and leaned down on the counter, rubbing my eyes. I had a terrible headache.

"Good to see you up and about, buddy." Chuck adjusted the pot with his good hand. "You've been out for more than two days."

Coughing, I looked back up at him. "How have you been managing?"

"Damon has been sick too. Lauren and Susie have been taking

up the slack, and Tony went out and got more food last night. But the hallway is getting much worse, and the city . . ." He didn't finish, just watched the pot as it began to boil.

Getting much worse?

"Your buddy Williams showed up." He rubbed his eyes and pointed to a pile of yellow plastic items on the couch. "That's our ticket out."

Squinting, I looked more carefully. "Hazmat suits?"

"Yep." He dropped a tea bag into the pot and turned off the butane. "He says that if we can get the truck down, he'll put our names on the emergency worker list and drive with us out to the barricade on the George Washington Bridge. Everyone going in and out has hazmat suits on, so we wear these, we're on the list, we get out."

That makes sense, as long as he can get us on the list, but . . . "What about the kids?"

"We'll have to hide them."

"*Hide* them?"

He nodded. "Lauren's dead set against it. Thinks it's too risky. Can't blame her." He looked at the ceiling. "The radio says that power and water have been restored to some areas of Manhattan, but I'll be damned if any of our taps turn on."

I didn't trust the radio. "And the meshnet?"

"Meshnet's slowly dying out. People can't charge phones anymore. Some people say water is back on in the upper hundreds, but maybe it's propaganda. Maybe they want to keep us here."

"What do you think?"

"I think we should get out of here. Just a few hours of driving and we can be at my cabin in the mountains above the Shenandoah."

"I think so too."

"You're going to have to speak to Lauren."

Nodding, I dropped my head onto the counter.

He picked up the pot of tea and poured me a cup. I glanced at his broken hand. It looked terrible.

"You gave us a real scare." He patted me on the back with his good hand. "Why don't you go lie down again?"

Lifting my head from the counter, I asked, "Can you send Lauren to see me, when, well, you know."

The sobbing in the hallway became louder.

"We had to drive off two gangs of refugees yesterday at gunpoint," said Chuck, standing to take the tea to the women. "Talk to Lauren. We need to leave."

"I will."

"And get some more rest."

"I will."

"Damn glad to see you're feeling better."

"Makes two of us."

DAY 27: JANUARY 18

"What's wrong, sweetheart?"

Lauren was sitting in a fetal position on the chair next to the bed. It was morning, and the overcast skies outside filled the room with a flat, monotone light. I was feeling better today, but upon waking up, I'd found her crying. Luke was still asleep.

She didn't reply.

"Are you mad at me?"

The night before we'd had an argument. She refused to consider leaving the city, saying that the power would be on soon, the water was coming back, and that it was too dangerous out there. There was no way she was going to stuff Luke into a bag to hide him while we cleared the barricade on the George Washington Bridge.

She was scared, and so was I.

"What happened? Is it about Richard?"

Even if he'd been a creep, he'd been her friend. I couldn't know what she was feeling.

She shook her head again. Taking a deep breath, she swallowed. "I was taking them some water. Pam and Rory . . ." That was all she managed to get out before she began crying again.

"Is something wrong with them?"

She shook her head but shrugged her shoulders at the same time. Something had scared her. Like a battle-weary soldier, I found that the unknown didn't frighten me in the same way anymore, so I decided to go see if I could figure out what was distressing her.

Pulling on some clothes, I crept into the main room. Tony and Damon were sharing the couch, and both of them were asleep with the steady thrum of the generator in the background. Tony opened his eyes, but I whispered that everything was okay. I grabbed a headlamp and, after a second of hesitation, took Tony's gun. He opened his eyes again, and again I whispered not to worry.

We always kept a dim nightlight on in the hallway, and I kept my headlamp off as I picked my way through the inert bodies and blankets. The hallway smelled like an open sewer. Since we didn't run the kerosene heaters at night anymore, it was cold enough to see my breath.

As I passed the shelves in the middle of the hall, a shape under the radio reminded me of a box of donuts I'd often bring into my office for the gang. Despite the stink, I found myself thinking about chocolate-covered, crème-filled donuts and hot cups of steaming coffee.

At least I'm hungry again. That familiar pain was in my gut. *And I'm so thirsty.* The back of my throat was parched, and rolling my tongue across my lips, I could feel the blisters.

Reaching Rory's apartment, I clicked on my headlamp, took a deep breath, and went in, shoving the door hard to push back whatever garbage had accumulated behind it.

Inside, the room had a different smell, not as rancid as the hallway. It was still an odor of decay, but somehow also metallic. Memories of the days I'd spent as a teenager helping my uncle fix plumbing in the neighborhood came to mind, and I wondered if Rory and Pam had been trying to get water. The smell also reminded me of something else. I'd come across a foul mess in one of the latrine rooms downstairs, some of it even on the walls, and the stench there left the same tinny taste in the back of my throat.

Maybe they had an accident?

Their place was a studio. Two people, neighbors from the fourth floor, had been staying in the apartment and must have been under the lump of blankets I saw on the couch. Rory and Pam's bed was on a raised platform at the far end of the apartment. It was covered in blankets too, and their heads were poking out. They were filthy, their faces smeared black.

I nudged Rory awake. "You guys okay?"

He squinted into the glare of my headlamp. "Mike, is that you?"

"Yeah, are you guys okay?"

Looking closer, I saw that the smears on his face weren't black after all. He was covered in something reddish—

"Go away." He put his hand up over my headlamp, pushing me back.

His shirt was stained as well, and not just reddish, but blood red. I pulled the covers back. Rory was spooning Pam, and both of them were spattered in blood, their faces covered in it.

"Are you hurt? What happened?"

"Go away," he repeated, pulling the covers back over them. "Please."

I stepped on something that squelched underfoot. Looking down, I saw a thick plastic bag partially filled with black liquid. *Not black—red.* There were dozens of bags littering the floor around the bed. Where had I seen those bags before?

The Red Cross blood bank, where Pam worked.

They were drinking human blood.

Gagging, I backed away. The couch was littered with the same bags, and against the far wall I saw dozens more stacked, full and fat like bloody maggots.

Despite my disgust, a part of me was drawn to them. *Maybe not to drink, but we could cook it, make blood sausages. Blood has a lot of iron and protein, doesn't it?* Luke wouldn't know what it was, and Lauren needed iron. My stomach growled, but then I shivered. *I gave blood the day this whole mess started.* I imagined Pam drinking my blood, her face white, fangs out, her feline eyes watching me—

"We gotta leave," hissed someone behind me. "We gotta leave now."

I spun around, half expecting some creature of the night, but my headlamp instead found Chuck's face.

"They're drinking blood," I whispered.

"I know."

"You know?"

"Not an entirely bad idea, but I've been trying to keep it quiet and not freak people out. Blood keeps for forty days in the cold, and it's been cold out there."

How does he know things like that? The sense of unreality grew stronger, and I felt like my conscious mind was pulling away.

"Mike," said Chuck. "Snap out of it and listen to me. You've been out of action for a while, and things have gotten a *lot* worse."

A lot worse. The way he said it . . . "What aren't you telling me?"

"You need to convince Lauren to leave. *Now.*"

I kept staring at him. "What *else*?"

Chuck took a deep breath. "Those nine dead people on the second floor?"

"What about them?"

"There are only five now."

I didn't have to ask what had happened to them. Human bodies were the last source of calories left in New York. I leaned against the wall, the blood draining out of my face, my fingers tingling. Irena had mentioned it when we'd talked of the siege of Leningrad, of roving gangs that attacked and ate people.

"And Richard's missing," Chuck whispered, "or at least, parts of him are."

Parts of him. I shivered in horror. "Do you know who?"

He shook his head. "Who looks healthiest? Maybe people here, maybe people from outside. That'd be my guess." Exhaling, he added quietly, "Or my hope."

"Don't tell Lauren."

She probably already knows.

"Then get her to agree to leave."

The blood was returning to my face, my cheeks burning. I still wasn't feeling well.

Chuck looked me straight in the eye. "We leave first thing tomorrow morning."

"You sure you want to do this?"

Damon nodded.

From the top of the parking garage frame, it looked a lot farther down than it had from the ground. Chuck would have been better up top than me, but he still couldn't use one hand. It took me and Damon half an hour just to clean the snow and ice off the truck.

Tony was just getting back to ground level after climbing up to the billboard platform, dragging the winch cable along. He was the only one strong enough to pull it off—the eighty-foot cable weighed more than a hundred pounds.

We attached the cable close to the wall to minimize the cantilever force that would try to rip the billboard from the building. The wall was at ninety degrees to the parking platform, with the billboard sticking out from it, so we would be swinging into open space. Back on level ground, Tony gave me the thumbs-up, and I returned the gesture and nodded to Damon.

Putting the truck into neutral, Damon flipped the switch on the winch. The truck pitched forward.

"Slowly!" I yelled just as he put the brakes on, flipping the winch off. "Why don't you keep the parking brake on and let the winch do the work?"

"Good idea," replied Damon. He was wearing a motorcycle helmet we'd found in the garage. Together with a long scarf wrapped dashingly around his neck and thrown over his back, he looked comical. "I'll just inch it forward."

On paper, this had seemed risky but workable, but in practice—winching a three-and-a-half-ton truck off a metal gantry fifty feet in the air—it was ludicrous. After climbing up and getting a sense of the enormity of the task, I told Chuck it was insane and insisted that we go back.

But there was nothing to go back to, not anymore.

Damon flicked the winch switch on and then back off, looking at me to make sure we were good.

"Front tires have about another foot till they slide off!" I yelled.

He nodded, reaching to flick the switch again.

The past day had been busy. We'd hauled up enough water for us to wash and shave. Lauren had given everyone haircuts while Susie and Chuck had scavenged the apartments, looking for clean clothes. We had to look like well-groomed relief workers, not trapped natives, when we arrived at the military barricade, in case they decided to search us.

Tony went out at night to retrieve all the food supplies he could. He'd dropped them off here near the truck, burying them in snow. Carrying food through the streets would have increased our chances of getting attacked on the walk over. Carrying the last of the diesel was dangerous enough.

With a thud, the front tires of the truck fell off the front of the gantry. The truck skidded a few inches forward and then stopped. Damon looked back at me and smiled.

"You okay?" I asked, shaking my head. My heart was thumping.

Damon was amazingly calm. "Perfect," he replied.

He was smiling, but his hand on the winch switch was shaking. He flicked it on and off again, moving the truck forward a few more inches.

The walk over had been surreal. The last time any of us had ventured farther than Twenty-Fourth Street, just outside our back door, had been when Chuck and I had come down to check on the truck nearly a week and a half ago. Back then, New York had been a frozen wasteland, strewn with garbage and human waste, but it had since transformed into a war zone. The snow was trampled and blackened, covered in human filth. Burnt-out buildings framed the canyon of Ninth Avenue, looming above shattered windows and the wreckage of air-dropped supply containers. The weather had warmed above freezing, and dead bodies appeared out of the melting snow, piled together with garbage.

"Another foot and you'll be at the back tires!"

The truck slid forward a little more, coming to a stop with the back tires resting just inches from the edge of the metal platform, the front end of the truck suspended and swinging in the air. The Land Rover extended a few feet beyond the back tires, so even when they slid off, the back end of the truck should remain on the gantry, right until the last inch of the bumper slid off.

At least, that was the plan.

Growing packs of stray dogs and cats had joined the rats in the garbage piles in the streets. Chuck took a few potshots at the first ones we'd seen gnawing on human corpses, but we needed to save the ammo, and the shooting attracted attention. Anyway, the animals scattered when they saw people coming—maybe sensing they were in danger of being eaten themselves.

We were a ragtag gang. I was back to wearing the frilly woman's overcoat I'd picked up at the hospital. Up to that point, we'd gone out two at a time at most, but now we all needed coats, so we couldn't be fussy. We'd shuffled along, keeping our eyes down, weapons out.

It had been a long walk, and I still hadn't recovered. Climbing up onto the parking gantry had taken nearly everything I had, but adrenaline was coursing through my veins now.

Damon flipped the winch switch again. The back tires slid off the platform, and all three and a half tons of the truck landed on its back frame with a mighty crash that shook the entire parking structure. It slid forward a foot and came to a stop.

The truck was angled nose down at about thirty degrees, with Damon suspended in space at least eight feet from the edge of the parking structure in the driver's seat. The front of the truck was less than ten feet from the billboard platform.

"This is it!" I yelled to Damon. "Any last words?"

"Give me a second."

"Those are your last words?"

Damon grinned at me, and I grinned back.

Down on the ground, Lauren and Susie looked up. They looked so small. Luke looked even smaller. A crowd of about a dozen onlookers had gathered, and I could see more coming. Tony and Chuck were yelling, pointing their guns, telling them to keep back, that we didn't have any food.

"Time," said Damon, "is just an illusion." And with that, he flicked the switch on the winch.

What a strange kid.

One side of the bumper came free of the platform before the other, sending the truck spinning upside-down. With a lurch the other side came free, pitching the truck into a looping arc downwards, but also sideways toward the wall of the building holding the billboard platform. I hadn't considered that motion in my back-of-the-napkin calculations, and it probably saved the day, transferring a lot of the initial force back into the building. The sound of groaning metal filled the air, and the billboard platform bent under the strain as the truck swung in a great arc underneath it.

Bang! First one metal strut popped out of the wall supporting the platform, spraying bricks into the air, and then—*bang!*—a second one popped as the truck reached the zenith of its swing.

Damon had been winching the truck up toward the platform to minimize the swing force, but as it swung around back toward me, the nose of the truck nearly at the platform, he reversed course and began lowering the truck. It wasn't a moment too soon. The platform started to sag and come loose from the wall. The billboard slowly peeled off the wall as the truck, spinning like a top, descended toward the ground.

With a thud the truck landed on its rear bumper, spiraling into the snow. Luckily, as Damon lowered it the last few feet, it came down on its wheels, not its roof. The billboard platform came crashing down at the same time, the end attached to the winch cable smashing into the snow just a few feet from the truck but the other end remaining loosely attached to the building.

And then silence.

"That was *awesome!*" yelled Damon, his head appearing out the truck window, looking back up at me and shaking his fist.

The platform shuddered and groaned.

"Mike, get down here!" yelled Chuck. The ragged crowd of onlookers was growing. "We gotta get out of here!"

Exhaling, I realized I hadn't taken a breath during Damon's stunt. Regaining my senses, I walked along the metal platform to the ladder at the back of the gantry. By the time I'd climbed down,

Susie and Lauren were already strapped into the backseat with the kids, and Tony was throwing the last bags of food and containers of diesel into the trunk. Damon was on the roof of the truck, unhooking the winch cable.

I ran across the snow, slipping and sliding, arriving just as Damon was getting back in the truck. Chuck held the door open for me, and I jumped in. The winch whirred away, rolling its length of cable back onto the front of the truck.

Tony had driven Humvees in Iraq. Revving the truck, he looked around at all of us. "Good to go?"

"Good to go," replied Chuck.

I held my breath.

The onlookers were crowding around the truck, and Tony jolted it forward, dispersing the ones in front. Some people banged against the windows, begging us to stop, to take them with us, for any food.

As we drove out onto Gansevoort Street, the only obstacle to our freedom was the giant snowbank lining the edge of Tenth Avenue and blocking access to the West Side Highway. It was taller than a standing man but had been worn down in the middle by foot traffic. Tony pushed his foot down, accelerating.

"She'll make it," said Chuck, urging Tony onwards. "Everybody hang on!"

With a crunch, the truck hit the snowbank and began bouncing up, making it feel a bit like we were falling backwards. Then we were on the other side. Sliding down the embankment, we skidded to a stop in the northbound lane of the West Side Highway—on cleanly plowed pavement.

Tony put the truck into gear, turned it around and drove north toward the George Washington Bridge. We were meeting

Sergeant Williams at the southeast corner of the Javits Center. He was going to take us from there up to the military barricade.

"Let's get the hazmat suits on," I heard myself telling everyone.

Luke was beside me, strapped in between Lauren and me in the third row of seats. His little face looked scared. Looking down into his beautiful blue eyes, I undid his seat belt and sat him on my lap. "You want to play hide-and-seek?"

Relief workers weren't supposed to have children with them. Luke smiled up at me. *How can I stuff him into a bag?* My mind rebelled, but Lauren took him from me, kissing me, kissing him.

"You get your hazmat on. I'll take care of Luke."

I frowned at her.

"I made a crib for them, silly. Now get your suit on."

Unstrapping my seat belt, I wriggled into the yellow suit.

The George Washington Bridge loomed in the distance.

DAY 29: JANUARY 20

"Here, have some."

Irena handed me a steaming plate of meat. Starving, I took it from her. A cauldron was at full boil on her stove, and in a daze I followed her toward it as I gobbled down what was on my plate. Large bones were sticking out of the pot, the water boiling up around them. *Those bones are big, too big . . .*

"We need to survive, Mih-kah-yal," said Irena unapologetically, stirring the pot.

Someone was sitting in the larder behind her. *No, not sitting.* It was Stan, from Paul's gang, and he was cut in half. Only his torso above the waist remained, his eyes staring at me, unseeing and opaque.

A trail of blood streaked across the floor, pooling around Irena's feet.

"You need to wake up," said Irena, covered in blood, stirring the bones, "if you want to survive."

"Wake up."

Wake up.

"You're dreaming, honey," said Lauren. "Wake up."

Opening my eyes, I realized I was still in the backseat of the Land Rover, covered in blankets. It was dark. The sun was rising.

The interior light of the truck was on, and Susie was in the front seat, feeding Ellarose. The guys were outside, chatting, leaning on a concrete embankment.

I stretched my neck and groaned.

"Are you okay?" asked Lauren. "You were talking."

"I'm fine, just dreaming."

Dreaming about the Borodins.

Irena and Aleksandr seemed to have gone into some kind of hibernation mode, barely moving, surviving off their supply of hard biscuits and scraping snow for water from outside their windows. They sat in their living room with their gun and ax, watching the door to their bedroom, where the prisoners were.

When we told them we were leaving the city, Irena had pulled the mezuzah off their front door and given it to me, telling me to keep it with me, to hang on the doorway wherever we ended up. It was the first time I'd seen her argue with Aleksandr, and they spoke not in Russian, but an archaic-sounding language that must have been Hebrew. He was upset and didn't want her to take it down. I tried to refuse it, but Irena insisted.

It was in the pocket of my jeans.

"Where are we?"

My brain was still reassembling what had happened the previous day.

Crossing the military barricade on the George Washington Bridge had been tense, but in the end, almost anticlimactic. We'd met Sergeant Williams as planned. He'd slapped some NYPD stickers onto the sides of the truck, and we'd driven right up through the crowds to the checkpoint.

It hadn't gone entirely smoothly. We'd had to wait for an hour or so. Our names weren't on the master list, and our driver's licenses listed residences in New York, but after a little arguing and some calls back and forth to Javits, they'd let us through.

Lauren had fashioned a crib out of some packing crates, padding it with blankets, and we'd hidden Luke and Ellarose in it. We'd fed them well and timed it just right, and they'd slept through the whole thing.

"We're on the side of an overpass at the entrance to I-78," answered Lauren.

I'd been in a daze at the checkpoint yesterday, weak but doing my best to smile and look normal. Memories of the gray arches of the George Washington Bridge, like a cathedral spanning the Hudson River, floated into my mind, and then the feeling of relief after they let us through.

By the time we were on our way, it had been late afternoon. We'd followed the I-95, the only main highway that had been kept clear, down through New Jersey toward Newark Airport. The spire of the Empire State Building had stood in the distance, the Freedom Tower farther down, with New York cradled in between.

We're free, I remembered thinking, and then I must have fallen asleep.

"That's pretty much where I remember us getting to. What happened? I thought the idea was to get as far from New York as possible."

"When we turned off 95 onto the 78 overpass, the road got a lot worse, and the sun was setting. Instead of risking it in the dark, Chuck picked this spot to spend the night. You were out of it."

"How are Luke and Ellarose?"

"They're perfect."

Thank God.

I stretched. "I'm going to talk to the guys, okay?" Leaning forward and pulling back the blankets, I grabbed a bottle of water and kissed her.

"How are you feeling?" she asked, kissing me back.

"Good." I took a deep breath. "Really good." I gave her another kiss and opened the door, looking out toward the horizon.

The sun was rising over the Financial District. The Freedom Tower shone in the distance, beyond the frozen docks and cranes of the Port of New Jersey spread out below us. Looking to the left, I tried to make out the familiar buildings of the Chelsea Piers near our apartment, our prison for the past month.

We're free, but . . . "How do the roads look? Can we drive them?"

The guys turned around, deep into some discussion.

"Hey! Sleeping beauty!" joked Chuck. "Decided to join us, huh?"

"Yeah, yeah."

"You feeling good?"

I nodded. Maybe it was just the fresh air, but I was feeling better than I had in weeks.

"Unplowed in a while, but passable," replied Chuck, "at least for my baby. Get ready. We're leaving in five."

Leaving them to it, I stretched, walking around the truck, waking myself up. The snow was deep at the shoulders of the highway, but the middle was rutted with tire tracks. Other people had passed through, even when the plowing had stopped, and the snow was melting fast. Pulling my gaze from the sunrise above New York, I looked down the overpass at Interstate 78, past a container yard and toward New Jersey and Pennsylvania.

We were on our way.

Despite Lauren's objections, we'd stopped at Newark Airport. Chuck had insisted on at least looking for her mother and father. Lauren had repeated that she was sure they'd gotten out, but we tried anyway. Passing through one of the twenty abandoned, snow-covered tollbooths, we'd looped through the overpass, stopping at the main terminal. Damon and I had remained in the truck while Chuck and Tony had gone inside. From outside, the place looked abandoned. In under an hour they were back. Nobody had approached us while we waited, and they didn't find Lauren's folks. But Chuck and Tony were very quiet. We could only imagine what they'd found, and the ride back onto the highway was silent.

The highway was littered with abandoned construction vehicles—graders and rollers and trucks—all covered in a deep layer of snow. Houses and trees lined the road, and we passed a group of people chopping what looked like firewood. They waved, and we waved back.

Interstate 78 was a sunken highway here, and we passed beneath one overpass after another, every one of them hung with American flags—some new, some ragged—and banners proclaiming things like "We will not break" and "Stay strong." I imagined the cold and hungry people who had placed them there, spray-painting their messages on old sheets. They were messages for me, for us. *You are not alone*, they were saying. I silently thanked them, wishing them well wherever they were.

It was seventy miles along I-78 to Phillipsburg and the border of New Jersey and Pennsylvania, and then another seventy miles to where I-78 met I-81 going south to Virginia. From there it was a straight 160-mile drive to the Shenandoah mountains and Chuck's family cabin.

In normal conditions, the whole thing would have been a four-hour drive, but as we bounced along in the rutted tracks at the center of the highway, I figured it was going to take us more like ten. Even that assumed road conditions wouldn't get worse. But Chuck was determined that we get there in one day. No matter what, it was going to be dark when we stopped, so Chuck made sure Tony kept going as fast as possible.

It was a rough, violent drive, and I sat Luke on my lap, cradling him.

He was happy now. It seemed like some kind of adventure again, and I think he was as glad as we were to have gotten out of the rancid confines of our apartment. It seemed like a dream, in fact. The sun was out, and we had the windows down, enjoying the warm weather. Chuck was playing Pearl Jam.

The landscape opened up, the highway rising up out of the ground, revealing rolling hills and countryside. We passed smokestacks and water towers and cell phone towers that dotted the terrain—none of it functioning. I kept checking my cell phone, but there was no reception anywhere. Electrical towers rose the tallest of all, their wires strung across the highway and stretching off into the distance.

Small towns and villages started appearing, smoke rising up out of chimneys in the distance. We saw people walking in the streets.

At least they have a lot to burn. The forests seemed endless. *Is life normal out here?*

Then we passed a farm where butchered cows stood out

in red splashes against white fields. A group of people with machetes were hacking away at a carcass next to a grain silo, and one of them waved his giant knife at us while we drove by, urging us to stop.

We didn't, and we didn't wave back.

Damon fiddled with the radio as we drove, alternating between playing music and searching the airwaves for any working stations, but mostly we could only pull in the government channels from New York and the occasional ham radio operator. When he found these, we'd listen, sometimes to a community announcement, sometimes to a rant, but it became evident that there was no power, no communications out here either.

People were everywhere, though, walking along the side of the road, pulling loads on sleds, but we didn't encounter even one other vehicle. I dozed again, my mind dimly registering images—roadside McDonald's and Quiznos signs, a train wedged in the side of a hill, the red and yellow of an amusement park Ferris wheel.

The road conditions improved as we moved away from the coast. By the time we reached I-81 in the midafternoon, we were driving on pavement. I-81 hadn't been plowed in a while either, but there was much less snow. We stopped once to refill the gas tank with the diesel we'd brought in containers. We only had three hundred miles to go, less than the range of the truck with its full tank, but it was better safe than sorry.

We began to see motorists coming the other way as darkness fell, headlights appearing from the gloom and sweeping past us. The world almost seemed normal, except that the countryside was completely dark. A full moon rose up, casting ghostly shadows across the landscape.

Chuck announced that we were almost there as night fell, and he took an exit off the main highway. It was about a half-hour drive up the mountain, he said. He was excited, talking about all the supplies he'd hidden, the great meal we were going to have, and how cozy his cabin was. Damon said he was looking forward to using the shortwave radio, listening in on stations from around the world and finding out what was happening.

Lauren cuddled into me. We were holding Luke together under a blanket. An immense weight was lifting from my shoulders. *A hot meal, a clean bed.* Ahead, in the truck's headlights, I could see we were following a small dirt road covered in ice. There was snow in the forest, but only in patches.

As we pulled up to his cabin, Chuck was telling me about fishing in the Shenandoah, how this was going to be like a vacation. We jumped out and began grabbing our bags while Chuck ran up the front steps. It was a beautiful log cabin. In a flash, Chuck was inside, flashlight and headlamp on. We started piling things onto the porch.

"No!" shouted Chuck from inside.

We all froze, and Tony pulled out his .38. "You okay?"

"Goddamn it!"

"Chuck, are you okay?" repeated Tony.

I picked up Luke and Ellarose and backed away toward the truck, which was still running. Lauren and Susie followed, all of us watching the doorway. Chuck's face appeared, contorted and angry.

"What is it?" whispered Susie.

"It's all gone."

"What's gone?"

Chuck's head sagged. "All of it."

"We waited too long."

"That's not the right way to look at it."

It was mid-morning, and we were out back of the cabin, filling the wood-fired hot tub with logs.

Who else but Chuck would have a wood-fired hot tub? I laughed to myself.

The fresh mountain air was incredible, and it was warm, at least ten degrees above freezing. Through the birch and fir trees, the sun was shining down on us. Birds were singing.

"We're all here, we're mostly healthy," I continued. "So what if we're missing some supplies?"

There was fresh water, mountain snowmelt, bubbling down in a small creek right next to us, and we had a few days' worth of food. Chuck had shown me how to use an app for identifying edible plants in the woods, and we could fish and trap animals as well.

I had no idea how to trap, but there was an app for that too.

Chuck picked up another log with one hand, holding the injured one against his body. He threw the log into the woodstove at the side of the hot tub. The cabin was on fairly flat ground. We were grabbing wood from a pile under the back deck, standing in the leaves. "You're right." He laughed and shook his head. "Unbelievable, isn't it?"

Luke was at our feet. He'd found a stick and was running around, joyfully whacking leaves with it. With his ten-word vocabulary, he couldn't tell us how happy he was to be out of that hallway, but the smile on his face said it all. I smiled too as I watched him. He had dirt on his face, a shaved head, grubby, ragged clothes—squealing in the woods, he looked like a little wild animal. But at least he looked happy.

Whoever had raided Chuck's place hadn't taken quite *everything*. They'd blasted open his storage safe-room, but there were still spare clothes in the upstairs closets, and the bedrooms were intact. Most of the food and emergency equipment from the storage lockers was gone, along with the fuel from the generator and the propane canisters. But they'd left coffee.

After sleeping like a baby on fresh sheets, I'd gotten up early and spent the morning on the swinging loveseat on the porch, boiling a pot of coffee over an open flame in a fire pit. We were at over two thousand feet in elevation, and from the front porch, there was a beautiful view eastwards, down the mountain ridge toward Maryland. It had been more than a week since I'd had coffee, and drinking a cup of it, sitting in the swinging chair, breathing the mountain air under a blue sky—it was magic.

I remembered reading that some people thought the Renaissance had happened partly because of the introduction of coffee to Europe, thanks to the invigorating effect caffeine had on the psyche. I laughed. That morning I could believe it. It was almost enough to make me forget the horror we'd lived through, to stop wondering if the world was burning down around us.

As I sat with my mug, I'd noticed a smudge of black rising in the distance. Chuck told me it must be from the chimney of his neighbors, the Baylors.

"How long do you think Tony will be?" I asked Chuck.

We'd promised Damon that we'd drive him to his parents' home. Tony had volunteered to take him over to Manassas, where they lived, or as close as he could get to it safely. They'd left about two hours ago, after a round of tearful goodbyes and promises to keep in touch. If Damon had never come into our lives, everything would have turned out very differently, and probably much worse. In many ways, we owed him our lives, and his departure felt like losing a member of the family.

Chuck and I had debated whether one of us should go too, but I didn't want to leave Lauren and Luke, and Chuck felt the same about Susie and Ellarose. The truck's GPS was working, so finding the way back wouldn't be a problem for Tony.

"Should be anytime, depending on how far he got." Chuck raised his eyebrows. "*If* he comes back."

Chuck had half an idea that Tony might try to take off and drive down to Florida, where his own mother was.

Just then we heard the growl of an engine. Chuck reached for the shotgun propped up on the woodpile, but then relaxed. It was the sound of *our* truck. Tony was back.

I laughed. "*If* he comes back, huh?"

"You boys heating that up for me?" came a singsong voice as the deck door slid open.

It was Lauren. She laughed, self-consciously rubbing the stubble on her head.

When we arrived the night before, after calming Chuck down, we'd all stripped down and left our lice-infested clothes in a pile at the side of the front deck, dressing in whatever we could scrounge from the closets inside.

We all shaved our heads too, even the women.

"This is just for you, baby," I laughed, banging on the side of the hot tub. It was the first time in my life that I'd had a bare scalp, and I rubbed my sweaty, bald pate.

The hot tub had been covered and was still full of water when we'd arrived. That was a godsend because there was nothing coming from the city pipes that snaked up the side of the road, and filling it from the creek would have taken a day or two. We weren't heating the tub to lounge around in. Chuck had done an inventory in the cellar, and the chlorine tablets were still there, so we were super-dosing the water to try to clean our clothes, and ourselves.

Around the front, I could hear the truck crunching across the driveway, and then the engine switched off. A door opened and slammed shut.

"We're back here!" I yelled.

After a few seconds Tony appeared in the dappled sunlight at the side of the cabin. He looked comical. Tony was a few inches taller and quite a bit huskier than Chuck, so the clothes in the closets barely fit him. The jeans were two inches too short, and way too tight, and the jacket and T-shirt were much too small. With his freshly shaved head, he looked like an escaped convict on vacation.

He saw us smiling at him and laughed. "I feel like I've joined a cult—shaved heads, hiding in the mountains."

"Just don't drink the Kool-Aid," sniggered Chuck, nodding toward the hot tub. He leaned down and inspected the woodstove, now burning vigorously.

Luke saw Tony and ran over to be picked up.

"Everything good?" I asked.

Tony nodded. "Lot of people down there, and I didn't want trouble, so as soon as we got near his place on the main road, he just jumped out."

"You see anything?" asked Susie. "Talk to anyone?"

"Nobody's got any power, no cell signal. I didn't want to risk stopping to talk, not by myself."

There were no radio stations to tune in to up here and no meshnet or cell networks. Being here was better than being stuck in the death trap of New York, but we were pretty much cut off from any connection to the outside world.

We'd left the generator in the apartment—it was too heavy to carry—so the only way we could generate electricity was with the truck. Chuck had plugged all our phones into the cigarette charger, so they were all ready to go. We could use the phones to communicate with each other, as a mini-meshnet, and they were still useful as flashlights and for the survival guides we'd stored on them.

"So what's the plan?" asked Tony.

"Let's get cleaned up, do some washing, get an inventory of what we have—and relax," Chuck said. "Tomorrow we'll head over to our neighbors' place down the road, see how things have been here."

"Sounds good. One thing, though—I think the muffler is loose, probably from landing tail-first in the snow." Tony laughed. "That was pretty spectacular."

"I'll get the tools from the cellar and have a look," I said. I knew a thing or two about cars.

"Perfect," said Chuck, grinning. "Let's get to work, then."

We had never talked again about the missing bodies from the second floor, but now the memory flashed in my mind. I wanted to forget it, to pretend it hadn't happened. It all seemed like it was a million miles away now.

I made my way to the cellar, looking at the yellow carpet of leaves under the thin birch trees. Something didn't feel right, somehow. Taking a deep breath, I shook my head, putting it down to stress, and opened the rickety cellar doors.

"You're going to love these guys!"

Chuck was walking with me and Lauren down to the Baylors' place. Chuck's family had built their place before the area had been declared a national forest, and there were only a few cabins on the mountain.

We could see smoke from the Baylors' chimney curling up out of the woods again that morning, and after a full breakfast, and with all our old clothes washed and hanging out back, it was time to go down and say hello.

"They live here year-round, they're always here," continued Chuck. "Randy is retired military, maybe even CIA. If anyone knows what's going on, he will. They're so well equipped they probably barely even noticed that the power's been out."

It wasn't far, maybe a half-mile, so we decided to walk. Susie and Tony stayed behind to start diluting the now-super-chlorinated hot tub with creek water so the kids could have a swim. It was a beautiful day. The freezing cold of Christmas had given way to unseasonably warm weather, plus we were farther south.

The undergrowth at the sides of the dirt road winding down the mountain was abuzz with insects and life, its earthy dampness mixing with the smell of dirt baking beneath our feet. With the sun shining, I was sweating in my shirt and jeans. *I wish I had some sunscreen for the top of my head*, I laughed to myself. *It's never seen the sun before.*

Kicking some rocks down the road, Chuck was in high spirits. I felt like a new man, and Lauren and I were holding hands, swinging them as we walked down the path. As we rounded a corner, the Baylors' house appeared through the bare trees. We walked up their winding driveway, toward two cars parked out front, and then onto their front porch.

Chuck knocked on the door. "Randy!" he called out. "Cindy! It's me, Charles Mumford!"

There was no answer, but somebody was home. Country music was playing around the back of the house.

"Randy! It's me, Chuck!" he yelled louder.

I could smell something cooking.

"I'll check around back. Maybe they're in the yard, cutting wood or something. You guys stay here."

He jumped off the porch and disappeared. Lauren squeezed my hand. We wandered over to the other side of the porch, following the smell of whatever was cooking. Peering through the shuttered windows into the kitchen, I could see a large pot—*a cauldron*— with steam coming out of it. Bones were sticking out the top.

Pain shot up through my hand, and I looked down to see Lauren's white knuckles, her nails digging into me. Following her gaze to the dining room next to the kitchen, I saw a jumbled mess. I tried to figure out what I was looking at, angling for a better view through the shutters.

"Who the hell are you?" I heard Chuck say in a muted voice. Through the sliding glass doors at the back of the house, I could see him shielding his eyes to look at someone.

"I could ask you the same thing," I heard another voice reply somewhere on the back deck.

"Let's get out of here," urged Lauren.

"We need to wait for Chuck," I whispered back.

Her nails dug deeper into my hand.

I moved my head to get a clear view of the dining room. It looked like someone was lying on the ground—*covered in blood, hacked apart.* The smell of the boiling meat enveloped me, and I almost gagged.

"Get the hell out of here!" another voice, a new voice, yelled from the back.

Chuck had his gun out now, one of the .38s, and was pointing it at someone walking up the stairs to the back deck.

That person had a shotgun pointed at him.

"Where are the Baylors?" yelled Chuck, backing away, moving his gun back and forth from one person to the other. "What did you do with them?"

That sense of unreality gripped me again as terror settled into my gut.

"We told you to get *out* of here, boy!"

"I'm not leaving! You tell me what—"

With a sharp crack and a boom, Chuck's gun and the shotgun went off at nearly the same time. Chuck was shot at point-blank range, and even from a distance, we could see blood splatter as he was lifted into the air and fell spinning off the deck. Lauren cried out beside me, and we ducked down.

"Run," I whispered to Lauren, pushing her ahead of me. "RUN!"

Crouching down, we ran past the parked cars and down the driveway, and then straightened up, sprinting back up the road, our arms and legs pumping. My lungs burned. I felt like I was barely connected to what was happening.

I should have brought a gun. Why didn't I bring a gun? If I had, I'd probably be dead too.

Just run.

Behind me I could hear commotion, yelling. They must have seen us.

Run faster!

After what felt like an eternity, we reached the driveway of Chuck's cabin. Maroon 5 was playing on the truck's sound system, its windows down, and Adam Levine was singing "Moves Like Jagger." In the distance I could hear something else. An engine. They were coming after us.

I stopped at the truck to grab the other .38 from the glove box. "Go around back. They must be in the hot tub!"

We came flying around the corner to find Susie dancing on the deck with Luke, Tony kneeling down as he held up Ellarose's hands.

"Get down! We need to get out of here!" I screamed.

Tony looked at us in shock. "What happened?"

"Just get down! We need to get in the truck!"

Lauren was already reaching up to grab Luke.

"Where's Chuck?" asked Susie, her voice rising in fear. She took Ellarose from Tony, and they ran down the deck stairs toward us.

"Come on!" I yelled.

But it was too late. Over the crooning coming from the truck, I could hear a vehicle crunching into the gravel at the front of the house.

What should I do?

"Where's Chuck?" asked Susie again, pleading.

"He was shot. He's down at the other house," I replied, trying to think. "Tony, take the shotgun and take everyone into the cellar, I'm going to talk to them."

"Talk to *who*? What the hell happened?"

We could hear car doors slamming out front.

Susie was on the verge of tears. "Take Ellarose," she said breathlessly to Tony, handing the baby over. She kissed Ellarose, tears streaming down her face. "I need to find Chuck."

"What are you doing? He's dead, he's—"

But she ran off toward the other side of the cabin, away from us.

I pushed Tony and Lauren ahead of me, reaching down to open the cellar doors, urging them down, just as three people came walking around the corner, two of them holding shotguns. Leaving one of the cellar doors open, I stood my ground.

Maybe this is all just an accident. But those bones . . .

"What do you want?" I yelled, waving my gun. Without a word, one of them fired, and I felt a terrific concussion as the shot roared past me.

Terrified, I jumped down the stairs into the cellar, pulling the doors shut behind me and sliding a wooden beam through the handles in an attempt to keep them shut.

We need something to keep them out.

Next to the stairs was a metal rack stacked with wood. With shaking hands, I started dragging it over so it would block the doors if they were opened.

There must be a back way out of here.

But as I pulled, the rack fell over, crushing me.

Lauren shrieked.

"I'm okay," I groaned, trying to pull myself out.

"For God's sake, don't let them take the children!"

Lauren cradled Ellarose, crouching in one corner, as far from the cellar door as possible. It was dark in here and smelled of sawdust and oil and old tools. Luke was standing next to her, his face streaked with mud, mute with terror. I squirmed to get my jammed leg out from under the pile of logs.

"Don't worry, Mike, I'm not going to let anyone in here." Tony was up on the stairs, squinting into the sunlight streaming through cracks in the broken wood of the cellar door. "There are four of them."

"We killed your friend," came a whiny voice.

Lauren started to cry, clutching the children closer.

"We didn't wanna do that, mind you," the voice continued. "Now this is all messed up."

"Leave us alone!" I yelled. Tony took a step back down the stairs, pointing his rifle up at the cellar door.

"Send those kids and your lady out."

I strained again to pull myself from the fallen logs, in bone-cracking, skin-ripping agony. Lauren was shaking her head violently.

And then silence—just my heart pounding in my ears and the sound of shuffling through the leaves outside. I tried to steady myself, blocking out the pain, making sure the safety was off the .38. Tony glanced over, nodding, telling me he was ready.

With a terrific roar, one of the cellar doors shattered. Tony staggered back, dropping to one knee. Another shotgun blast, and he spun sideways but still managed to bring up his rifle and pull the trigger. Squeals of pain erupted outside, followed by another shotgun blast and then another through the cellar door.

Tony grunted and tried to get out of the way, collapsing in front of me. I grabbed his hand and pulled him toward me, but it was too late. His body convulsed. Looking into my eyes, he blinked back tears and then went still.

"Tony!" I grunted, trying to pull him toward me. His eyes stared back at me, unseeing. *My God, you can't be dead, Tony. Wake up! Come on . . .*

"Goddamn it, you blew Henry's ear right off!" said the voice from outside. "Either you send out your woman and those kids, or we'll burn the whole goddamn place down!"

Panicking, I tried to yank myself free again, shredding flesh, but I couldn't. Lauren was sobbing in fear, Luke watching me with wide eyes beside her.

"So what'll it be, boy?"

Clenching my jaw, I released Tony's hand and leaned down to the woodpile. *This can't be happening, this can't be happening—*

A gunshot boomed outside, thudding into the earth.

"What the hell?" screamed the whiny voice.

I could hear people running into the woods, confusion and yelling.

"There's someone in the house!"

More shooting, the sound of shattering glass. And then a sharp crack echoed through the trees, a different gun, farther away, and more shouting and gunfire. After a short silence, I heard a car's engine fire up and then the throaty rumble of our truck.

With a final excruciating effort, I pulled my leg free of the woodpile and jumped up, limping up the cellar stairs. The growl of the truck's engine grew louder, and through the cellar door I saw it roar past. It smashed into our deck, destroying it. The house shuddered above us, and then the noises began to fade.

I peered out and then threw the cellar doors open and poked my head out.

Susie was there, gun in hand, looking down the driveway. She glanced back at me. "It's okay. They're gone," she called out to someone ambling up toward the cabin.

He was holding a shotgun.

"He's got a gun!" I yelled at Susie, ducking my head back down. "Get out of there!"

Silence.

"It's me, you idiot," called out Chuck in a hoarse voice.

Relief washed over me, but I was already back down at Tony's side, ripping open his shirt. *Should I do mouth to mouth?* His body was a bloody mess. Lauren was still in the corner of the cellar, gripping the children and staring at me and then at Tony.

Does he have a pulse? Hands shaking, I held two fingers, sticky with blood, to his neck and leaned in to see if he was breathing. *No pulse. No breathing.*

"Get down here!" I yelled.

DAY 32: JANUARY 23

Lauren picked out a beautiful spot to bury Tony. It was in a clearing in the woods, to the north of the cabin, just beside a stand of dogwood trees. They were bare now, but soon, in the spring, Susie said, they would flower and bloom.

It would be a beautiful place to rest.

Beautiful, yes, but under a few inches of decomposed leaves the earth was thick with knotted roots and rocks. Digging as deep as we needed to had required hacking away at the roots and levering out the rocks. It was hard work, made harder still by what we were doing.

Tony had volunteered to stay at our building when he could have left for Brooklyn. I was sure he'd stayed for us, for Luke. If he hadn't, he'd be down in Florida, in the sunshine, with his mother. Instead, we were digging his grave.

There was nothing we'd been able to do for Tony. He'd been killed almost instantly. I'd tried to clean him up, but I'd resigned myself to covering him with a blanket. I'd sat and cried on the cellar steps, talking to Tony's motionless body, thanking him for trying to protect us. I couldn't bear the thought of leaving him alone down there, so I'd brought down a cot and slept with him.

The sun was out in a blue sky and birds chirped cheerfully

overhead as Susie and I pulled Tony's corpse through the leaves. He was heavy, well over two hundred pounds, so we dragged him in the blanket I'd wrapped him in. By the time we got to the clearing, a few hundred feet from the cabin, I was sweating, doubled over and panting from the effort. Susie and I did our best to lower him into the ground, but he slid in awkwardly, falling crumpled with his legs to one side.

"I'll fix him," volunteered Susie.

Gingerly, she climbed down into the hole, then set Tony in a comfortable position. I sat down in the leaves, staring up at the sky while I regained my breath.

"Is everything okay?" called Lauren in the distance.

Susie climbed back out of the grave, rubbing her dirtied hands on her jeans. She nodded at me.

"We're good!" I yelled back, thinking exactly the opposite.

Gathering myself, I stood up. Through the bare trees, I saw Lauren holding Ellarose, and Chuck slowly making his way toward us. Then I saw Luke, running around in his jerky hop-step motion. He'd been asking for Tony all morning. I didn't know what to say.

I pulled a grubby hand across the stubble on the top of my head and felt the sun's warmth on my face. My mind was still numb, not sure what to feel except scared.

But we were alive.

Night was falling, and a crescent moon was rising. I sat on the front porch, back in the swing chair, standing guard with the shotgun. A fire was roaring in the wood-burning stove in the living room.

At least we were warm.

Chuck had been wearing a bulletproof vest that Sergeant Williams had given him when he'd dropped off the hazmat suits. He wasn't sure why he'd put it on—just being careful, he said— but maybe it was why he'd been so bold, facing down those people, whoever they were, at the Baylors' house. Even in the vest, he'd been badly injured, with stray shotgun pellets left in his arm and shoulder.

The injury to my leg hadn't been too bad, just bruises and one deep gash where a nail had stuck me. Susie had bandaged it, and I hardly limped.

What the hell are we going to do now? We had no car, nearly no food—half of our supplies had been in the truck. Where this place had seemed magical just days ago, now it felt evil, threatening. I'd thought that maybe the madness was just in New York, that the rest of the world was still sane, but it seemed it was the same out here.

And then one of the stars moved. And blinked. Following the tiny light, I watched it descend while my brain tried to comprehend what it was seeing.

It's an airplane! It had to be. Spellbound, I watched as it settled into a glowing patch on the horizon, and then something clicked in my mind. Jumping off the swing, I ran to the front door, threw it open, and ran upstairs.

"Are they back?" yelled Chuck as I hammered up the stairs.

"No, no," I whispered urgently. Lauren and the kids were sleeping. "Everything is fine."

I opened the door to a bedroom to find Chuck lying down, covered in bloody cloths. Susie was leaning over him, tweezers in one hand and a bottle of rubbing alcohol in the other.

"What is it?" he asked.

"What can you see, right on the horizon, from here?"

Chuck looked at Susie and then back at me. "At night you can just see Washington—it's about sixty miles away. At least, you could see the lights of the city when they were on. Why?"

"Because I can see Washington."

DAY 33: JANUARY 24

"What happens if you don't come back?"

Lauren was pleading with me.

"I will come back—that's the whole point. I'll just be gone for one or two days."

Sitting on a fallen tree stump, she gripped Luke tightly in her arms. "Promise me that you won't talk to anyone."

"I promise. I'll make straight for the Capitol building, and if anyone stops me, I'll just show them this, right?" I held up her driver's license. She was a Seymour, the niece of Congressman Seymour, and her identification should be enough to bring the cavalry to help us. Her family must be beside themselves.

She still wasn't convinced.

"We can't just stay here and do nothing," I said. "Those bastards will be back after they get a chance to lick their wounds, and then what?"

"I don't know. We hide?"

"We can't hide here forever, Lauren."

Using some tarps, we'd constructed a makeshift camp up in the woods, far from the cabin. From there, we had a good view of the driveway and down the road. It was only a temporary solution.

We needed to take action, so I'd decided to walk into Washington. It was a desperate move, but then so were the alternatives.

Chuck had argued with me, telling me it was too risky. He thought we should wait, but that scared me more. We'd go through what little food we had in a few days, and then what? He wasn't going to be on his feet any time soon, so would I be fishing and trapping for us? And maybe he wouldn't get back on his feet at all. He needed serious medical attention, and so did Ellarose—she was wasting away.

Time had become our enemy, and I was tired of not knowing what was going on.

"One day, that's all. I will walk there in one day, and I won't take any chances, won't speak to anyone."

Lauren gripped Luke tighter. "You make sure you come back to us. You just make sure."

I left before dawn.

In my whole life, I couldn't remember ever walking more than a few miles at a time, maybe an afternoon hike here and there, but I was sure I could walk sixty miles—four miles an hour, fifteen hours, sixty miles.

I could walk sixty miles in one day.

One day.

In one day, I could find out what was happening to the world, why this had happened to us. Last we heard, the president had left Washington, but the lights there were on, and Lauren's uncle was a congressman. All I had to do was get to the Capitol building, explain who I was, who my wife's family was. Just one day and I would bring back help.

There was still a sliver of moon out when I left the cabin. I scrambled down the dirt road in the semidarkness with my head-lamp off. I passed the Baylors' house, my heart in my throat, but there were no lights on there, no movement. By the time I got to the main road, coming down off the mountain, daylight was spreading.

I set a brisk pace, despite a slight limp.

At ground level, the snow was gone. Hills and fields and forests spread out before me. Gradually, the dimness gave way to a burst of color as the sun appeared on the horizon ahead of me. Drops of dew clung to the grass bordering the road, and I felt energized, invigorated.

After all we'd been through, I just had to endure one more day.

There was no way for me to get lost. Down from the mountains and then due east, straight along I-66 until I hit the middle of Washington, until I saw the Washington Monument. Then right along the Mall and up to the Capitol building.

I had my cell phone, and the GPS worked, but without a data feed I didn't have the maps to go along with it, only the ones for New York that Chuck had loaded manually. Still, I'd brought it with me, just in case—maybe the cell networks were working somewhere.

I walked, and I walked, and I walked.

The sun rose in the sky, washing me with its heat. By midmorning I began to see car traffic along the road. I was following a side road that paralleled I-66, trying to stay out of view.

Keep your head down, don't attract attention, just keep walking.

Every now and then a car would hum in the distance, growing in size to flash past me on the main road. A part of me wanted to wave, to stop and talk, but a bigger part was afraid. Luke and Lauren were counting on me, and I'd promised I wouldn't.

I couldn't take any chances.

Walking, walking, walking—*How many miles have I walked already?*

I would fix my eyes on a hill, somewhere on the horizon, and then watch it. For what seemed forever, it would stay the same size, but then it would grow and I'd be walking past it, picking a new hill to watch. In one pocket I had Irena's mezuzah, and from time to time I would hold it, imagining some secret power protecting us.

My feet ached, and the cut on my leg burned.

By lunchtime, the sun was beating down on me and I was soaked in sweat. I had a small backpack on, filled mostly with bottles of water. The backpack made me so hot that I took it off from time to time to cool off the river of sweat flowing down my back.

After five weeks of freezing cold, I hadn't imagined it could get so hot. *I'll walk in my boxers. Why not?* Awkwardly, I took off my jeans and inspected my right calf. I poked at the edges of the wound. It was sore. Putting my sneakers back on, I examined my pale, skinny legs and soiled, mismatched socks.

My boxer shorts were loose on my hips. I'd lost so much weight that I'd cut yet another notch in my belt to keep my pants up—five notches in total. I must have lost six inches around my waist. I had to roll my boxers' waistband up to keep them from falling, but the cool air on my legs made it all worthwhile.

I had a little food, some peanuts, but I had money too, and credit cards. If the lights were on, then the city was alive, and I could buy something. I fantasized about my first purchase, perhaps a juicy hamburger, or maybe I'd stop for a steak. Then I thought of the meat boiling in the pot yesterday, and my stomach turned.

Who did this to us? Who turned us into animals? It couldn't just be an accident, not the way it had unfolded—the attack on logistics, the wiping out of the Internet, the bird flu warnings, and then an invasion of US airspace and power grid shutdowns. It couldn't be criminals—what would they gain? Terrorists? This was too coordinated, too well planned.

By the afternoon the pain in my legs was intense, and I funneled my pain into anger. *It has to be China.* The fighting in the South China Sea, all the news reports of their infiltration of our computer networks, *stealing* from us. As Washington grew closer, the question became more urgent, and the answer clearer.

I couldn't wait for the sun to go down, for the air to cool. The landscape changed from foothills to rolling hills, and the forests and fields to farmland and the outskirts of small towns. In the late afternoon I saw another person for the first time. I kept my head down as we passed on the road. Later, I stopped and put my jeans back on. By the time the sun set, there were several other people on the road with me, walking ahead of and behind me. Everyone kept their distance.

There was no power anywhere. Most of the houses I could see stayed dark, but some windows glimmered with faint lights I figured were candles. On the horizon, down I-66, the sky glowed, and the light was closer, much closer.

But still far away.

Should I keep struggling on? The pain had become nearly unbearable. My legs, my feet, my back—everything hurt. I gritted my teeth. *Can I walk through the night?*

I looked toward the horizon. It was too far. I needed rest. *I'll get there tomorrow.*

The crescent moon was back in the sky, casting dim shadows in the night. Up ahead, a dark mass blotted out the trees lining the road. Limping, I approached it, veering off the shoulder to have a look. It was an old barn or shed, its weather-beaten planks curled with time. There was no door. I pulled my headlamp out of my backpack and turned it on.

"Hello!" I called out.

The interior was littered with haphazardly discarded items—boards, old shoes, a rusting tricycle. An ancient Chevy truck sat hunched in one corner, no wheels and on blocks, covered in garbage.

"Hello!"

My voice echoed without answer. I was exhausted. Beyond exhausted. I picked my way to the back of the shed. In the light of my headlamp, I passed something that looked like an old sheet— *Maybe a curtain?*—and I picked it up. It was stiff with dirt, but I shook it out and cleaned it off as best I could.

I shivered, the damp sweat still sticking to my back, chilling me in the cool night air.

Reaching the Chevy, I climbed up and opened the door. A long bench seat greeted me inside, and I smiled, jumping in behind the wheel. Putting my backpack down as a pillow, I closed the door and lay down, pulling the curtain around me.

Something in my pocket dug into my side, and I realized it was the Borodins' mezuzah. I propped myself up on one elbow and wedged it into a rusted hole in the side of the truck door. *That counts as an entrance, doesn't it?*

As I lay my head down on the backpack, sleep came quickly.

DAY 35: JANUARY 26

The Washington Monument. I could just see its tip poking above the trees ahead as I emerged from an underpass. I'd awoken at dawn, stiff with cold and my throat parched. After downing the last of my water and finishing off the peanuts, I'd gotten back on the road to continue my trek. I almost forgot the mezuzah, but darted back to grab it just before I left the shed.

As I got closer to Washington, I began to see gas stations and convenience stores lining the highway. Most were abandoned, but I saw a line of empty cars parked outside one. Unable to contain either my curiosity or my hunger, I'd approached the building. Inside, the shelves were bare, and a man behind the counter informed me that there would be gas the next day.

He'd filled up my water bottles and, as I was leaving, offered me a sandwich, probably his lunch. I'd accepted and wolfed it down. He said that there was nothing for me in Washington, that I shouldn't go, and that it was safer to stay in the countryside.

I'd thanked him and continued on my way.

Pedestrian foot traffic was taking up one whole lane of the highway as we approached the city, and I was stumbling along with everyone else.

It was midday already. Office towers stretched into the gray sky to my right, abandoned cranes and construction equipment hovering between them. To my left was a line of skeleton trees, knotted with green vines. Signs for the Roosevelt Bridge pointed straight ahead, while signs for the Pentagon and Arlington pointed off to the right.

I was almost there.

What are they doing at the Pentagon? It was right there, barely a mile away from me. *Is there a plan? Are brave men and women being sent off to defend our homeland?*

I'd never done anything brave in my life, not in a physical sense anyway.

Is this brave? Walking sixty miles into the unknown? Fear had driven me to do it, but what had scared me the most was leaving Luke and Lauren, especially when she'd begged me not to go.

I walked with a growing crowd along the shoulder of the highway, a corridor hemmed in by high walls covered in creeping vines. We were a stream of refugees as we passed Fairfax and Oakton and Vienna on the way into the city. My love for Lauren and Luke was most of what kept me going that morning, what kept my legs moving through the pain, kept me putting each foot one in front of the other.

The other thing that drove me was my anger. Where before I'd just been trying to survive, as I approached Washington, and the prospect of this thing ending became real, my thoughts turned to retribution. *Someone will pay for this, for hurting my family.*

I followed the road onto the bridge over the Potomac. The tide was low, and seagulls wheeled in the distance. Ahead, the Washington Monument speared the sky. I followed the crowd along Constitution Avenue. Barricades kept us away from the Lincoln Memorial, funneling us toward some unknown destination.

We were being herded.

A light rain began. Low, heavy clouds had replaced the bright sun of the morning. Vehicles streamed back and forth on the road, half of them military. I resisted the urge to reach out and stop one of them.

But who would stop for me? I was just one of the ragged multitude, walking along in the rain, and anyway, my mission was nearly complete. *Just another two or three miles.*

Familiar, reassuring sights came into view—the White House, just visible through the trees, and the tops of the Smithsonian buildings farther down the street.

To my right, however, the National Mall, the open space of green that stretched from the Lincoln Memorial all the way to the Capitol, was completely obscured by a high fence topped with barbed wire. The fence was covered, but I could see through the gaps that there was a beehive of activity behind it.

What are they hiding?

Police were positioned at the intersections, keeping the traffic moving, but as I had promised Lauren, I didn't speak to anyone. As I neared the American Museum of Natural History on the Mall, I saw a stack of scaffolding stretching up one side. I wanted to see what was behind the fences, so I slid off to one side of the street and, making sure that nobody was watching me, wandered along the fence and under the scaffolding.

A blue sheet hung around the scaffold, so once I was under it I was hidden. I climbed up one level and then the next, ascending the side of the building. When I was several stories up, I climbed out onto the roof, lying flat as I reached the edge and looked out.

The National Mall was an immense city of khaki tents, military trucks, and aluminum structures. It stretched all the way to the Capitol building and, to my right, surrounded the Washington Monument and continued all the way into the distance, swallowing the Reflecting Pool and the Lincoln Memorial. *It must be the military mobilization.*

But something was wrong. The trucks didn't look like American military to me. As I tried to figure out what I was looking at, a helicopter took off from the middle of the military installation, rising up to haul a piece of equipment into the air. And then I looked at the soldiers behind the fence, not more than a hundred feet away. *That's not an American uniform.*

They were Chinese. I stared in disbelief, my body tingling. Rubbing my eyes, I took a deep breath and looked again. Everyone, as far as I could see, was Asian. Some were wearing khaki uniforms, some gray, and many wore camouflage, but they all had red lapel tags. And they all wore caps with one bright red star in the center.

I was looking at a Chinese army base, right in the center of Washington.

As I ducked back behind a ledge, my brain scrambled to assimilate what it had seen. The unidentified intruders in American airspace, the reason the president had left Washington, the reason we'd been left to rot in New York, the reason there was power only in Washington, all the lies and misinformation—it all made sense now. We'd been invaded.

Squirming, I pulled my phone from my pocket and took a few pictures.

There was no sense in going to the Capitol. There was no help there. If I was captured, I'd never get back to Lauren. I had to get out of there.

Adrenaline fueled my descent from the scaffolding, and I made my way back onto the street, back into the flow of refugees, trying not to attract attention. Nobody seemed to notice me, so I stopped walking and scanned the fences along the Mall. A police officer was standing a few feet from me, and I couldn't contain myself. "There's military in there?" I said, pointing to the fences, getting his attention. He nodded.

"*Chinese* military?"

"They're here," he replied, apparently resigned, "and they're not going anywhere."

His words hit me like a punch to the gut. I stared at him in disbelief, the Washington Monument rising up behind him in the falling rain.

"You just need to get used to it, pal," he added, seeing me staring. "Now keep moving."

Shaking my head, I continued to stare, wanting to do something, wanting to scream. *What are all these people doing?* Their heads were bowed as they walked. No one was talking. Beaten— like they'd given up.

Has America given up already? I started walking and then running. *It's not possible. How can it be possible?*

I had to get back to Lauren and Luke. That was all that mattered. In a daze I wandered through the rain, back to the Potomac, and then crossed it, leaving DC behind me. Instead of rejoining I-66, however, in my stupor I wandered onto the bridge a few hundred feet south of it and found myself at the entrance to Arlington National Cemetery.

I was at the edge of a large grass oval at the head of the walkway. It was covered by gaggles of Canada geese. They honked at me as I walked straight through them. The wide street was bordered by high, manicured bushes filled with tiny, red berries. *I wonder if I can eat them? They'd probably make me sick.*

Behind the bushes, bare tree branches stretched into the sky. I passed a memorial to the 101st Airborne, a bronze eagle flying above it, and I wondered where those men were now. Our flag was still flying at half-mast above the columned beige building in the middle of the cemetery, high on a hill at its center.

I need to keep moving, get some distance.

Reaching the edge of the cemetery, I stood in front of a circular fountain. It was empty, and nobody else was around. There were four arched entrances to the grounds, and I picked one to my left. I walked up a set of stairs and discovered that the inside of the arch was a glass-walled building. I could see an interior wall filled with pictures and paintings, a visual tribute to "The Greatest Generation," read a poster. Men like my grandfather, who'd fought on the beaches of Normandy, watched me as I walked up the stairs.

When I got to the top, row upon row of white marble headstones greeted me, on a lawn still perfectly manicured. Each grave marker was decorated with a fresh wreath and a red bow. It all looked so well tended. The headstones rose up the hill before me, scattered through the oak and eucalyptus trees. *Our heroes, laid out to see this abomination.*

I wandered between the gravestones, reading out names. Up the hill I walked, past the Kennedy brothers' graves and Arlington House. I stopped at the summit to look around. In the dreary rain, the Potomac stretched grayly into the distance, while Washington loomed behind.

I shook my head and began walking back down the other side. *What should I do?*

I realized how thirsty I was. It was raining harder now, and my tongue was sticking to the roof of my mouth. On the streets behind the cemetery, water was flowing in the drains, and I kneeled down with one of my empty bottles, trying to fill it. Someone approached me on the sidewalk but gave me a wide berth as he passed. *How I must look, groveling here like an animal, my clothes ragged and sodden, head shaved.* I wanted to scream at him, my anger boiling up and out.

Why is he walking so slowly? Where is he going? Couldn't he see the world had ended?

The adrenaline began to wear off as I made my way back to the highway, and the long journey ahead weighed upon me. I was weak and soaking wet. There was no way I could walk all the way back to Chuck's cabin. Cold and exhaustion gnawed at my bones and muscles as my anger ebbed. I wasn't just incapable of walking all the way back—I doubted I would even survive it.

Reaching the on-ramp to the highway, I decided to try to get a lift. I'd have to risk it. Head down, I limped along, holding my thumb out. I was shivering violently. *I need to get inside soon.*

Lost in my thoughts, I hardly noticed when a pickup truck slowed, then stopped right in front of me. A man stuck his head out the side window. "Need a lift?"

I tried my best to jog up to the truck's window, nodding. The temperature was dropping, and I was soaked.

"Where to?" asked one of the kids in the front. There were three of them, and country music was playing on the radio. *Good old boys.* I shrank back.

"Whoa, you okay, buddy?"

"Yuh-yeah," I stammered. "Exit eighteen, past Gainesville."

He turned to the others in the car, conferring with them. I stood in the rain and waited.

"You alone?" he asked, turning back to me and craning his neck out the window to look down the side of the highway.

I nodded.

He cocked a thumb toward the back of the pickup. "We can drop you there. Got no space up here, but there's room in the back. You'll be sitting in the bare box with a few other people, but at least it's covered. That work for you?"

I had no choice. Walking around back, I saw that someone had already pulled down the tailgate, so I jumped up and inside, closing it behind me as we accelerated away.

In the dim light, I could see the others crowded in the back: five people huddled together, sitting on soiled sheets and clothing. I pushed myself into one corner of the truck bed, away from everyone else. I sat quietly for a while, and I meant to stay quiet, but I couldn't. "How long have the Chinese been here? How long since they invaded Washington?"

Nobody said anything, but one of them threw me a blanket. I mumbled my thanks as I covered myself, still shivering.

Can I trust them? I didn't have much choice. Freezing cold and wet, I'd die out there on my own. This small box was as close to salvation as I had anymore. I had to get back to the mountains.

"How long have they been here?" I asked again, my teeth chattering.

Silence.

I was about to give up when a kid with blond hair and a baseball cap replied, "A few weeks."

"What happened?"

"Cyberstorm, that's what happened," said a kid with a Mohawk. He had about a dozen piercings, and that was just what I could see. "Where have you been?"

"New York."

A pause. "That was pretty intense up there, huh?"

I nodded—all the horror summed up in one gesture.

"Where's our military?" I asked. "How could they let us get *invaded*?"

"I'm glad they're here," replied Mohawk.

"You're *glad*?" I yelled. "What the hell is wrong with you?"

Blondie sat upright. "Hey, man, calm the hell down. We don't want any trouble, okay?"

Shaking my head, I pulled the blanket up around me. *These kids are the future?* No wonder all this had happened. Just weeks ago, America had seemed indestructible, but now . . .

Somehow, we had failed.

All that was important now was finding my family, keeping them safe. Sighing, I closed my eyes and turned away from the others, pressing my face against cold metal, listening to the rumble that pulled me deeper into the night.

The next thing I knew, someone was poking my shoulder.

"Heya, friend," said one of the cowboys from the front of the truck. The tailgate was down and he was standing on the side of the road.

We were at an exit. Were they kicking me out early?

"This is your stop."

Shaking my head, I realized I'd been asleep. Nobody else was in the back of the pickup anymore. The kids were gone. I was covered in blankets, and one was even folded under my head. They must have placed them around me when I was asleep. I felt bad for getting angry with them.

"Thanks," I mumbled, extricating myself from the blankets and grabbing my backpack. I jumped out. It had stopped raining but was getting dark again.

He saw me looking up at the sky. "It took us a bit longer than I thought. We had to drop those guys off—"

"Thanks," I said. "I really appreciate it."

He looked up the mountain. "You going up there?"

"No," I said, pointing toward the base of the hills. "Over there."

I was worried they would follow, or worse, go ahead of me.

He looked at me funny, and then shrugged and took a step toward me. I recoiled, thinking he was going to grab my backpack, but instead he hugged me.

"You take care, you hear?" the cowboy said.

I stood stiffly as he squeezed me tight.

"Okay then," he laughed, releasing me. "Be safe."

Mute, I watched him get back in the truck. They drove off.

I hadn't noticed it, but tears were welling in my eyes.

Putting my backpack on, I looked up the road rising into the mountain. It was getting dark, and I was going to have a hard time finding my way. There would be little moonlight tonight to help me. I began the walk home, my heart heavy, but glad I would be back with Lauren and Luke soon.

There was something else, something I'd been pushing to the back of my mind. It was Lauren's thirtieth birthday today. I'd wanted to bring her a gift of some kind, something that would promise freedom from all the pain and fear of the recent weeks, but I was coming back empty-handed. Worse than empty-handed. But at least I was coming back.

I hoped everything was okay up there.

Despite the pain, my pace picked up.

The glow on the horizon mocked me. It was nearly ten at night, and we were on the front porch of Chuck's cabin, staring at Washington twinkling in the distance. Just a few days before, it had shone like a beacon of salvation; now it had become a symbol of despair.

Susie stared out at the lights. "I can't believe it."

I held out my phone. "Look at the pictures."

She shook her head. "I've seen them. I mean, I can't believe this has really happened."

Luke was still up, and he was playing by the fire in the pit out front. He was poking a stick into the flames. "Luke," called out Lauren, starting to get out of her chair. "Don't—"

I grabbed her arm, urging her to stay seated. "He needs to learn for himself. Leave him. We might not always be here to protect him."

She looked like she wanted to disagree and push me off, but then stopped herself. She sat back down, still watching Luke but keeping quiet.

The night before, I'd gotten lost trying to find my way up the mountain in the dark, even with my headlamp. Everything looked the same, and in the end I'd lain down in the open, piling leaves around me for warmth, waiting for the sun to rise. It had rained again, but somehow I'd dropped off to sleep, and when I'd awoken, I was barely able to move, my arms and legs nearly paralyzed with cold.

When I'd stumbled into our makeshift camp in the early morning light, Susie had almost shot me. They were expecting a rescue convoy, helicopters and hot food, but all they got was me, half-frozen to death and delirious. I'd been dangerously hypothermic, exhausted, mumbling about the Chinese, spewing nonsense.

We'd gone back to the cabin and started up the woodstove, and they'd curled me up in front of it on a couch under some blankets. They let me sleep until the late afternoon. When I woke up, the first thing I did was tell Lauren how much I loved her, and then I played with Luke on the couch for a while, trying to imagine what his future would be like.

Everyone wanted to know what had happened, but I'd asked for a little time to myself, to process, to figure out how to explain that there was no help coming, that we were on our own.

That maybe we didn't live in the United States anymore.

In the end, I'd simply shown everyone the images on my phone. There were a lot of questions, but I didn't have answers.

"So they just let you go?" asked Chuck.

His injuries weren't healing very well, and being out in the woods for two days had made things that much worse. Susie hadn't been able to get all the buckshot out of his arm, and his bad hand looked painful too. His whole arm was in a sling.

"Yeah, they did."

"You saw our military, our police there? And nobody was doing anything?"

I thought back to my walk into Washington. Everything I'd

seen took on a new meaning once I'd seen the Chinese army base. I was replaying everything in my mind, trying to tease out the truth of things I'd seen but perhaps not understood.

"Our police were there, definitely Americans who were directing the stream of refugees. I saw some military on the road, but I think they were Chinese."

"Did you see any fighting?"

I shook my head. "Everyone looked beaten, like it was already over."

Luke was finished poking his stick into the fire and ran up the stairs into Lauren's lap.

"So no bombed-out buildings? It was all intact?"

I nodding, trying to remember all that I'd seen.

"How could they have just given up without a fight?" said Chuck. He was having a hard time accepting it. He believed me, but he couldn't fathom how it could be over so quickly. I still couldn't believe it either.

"It would be hard to fight back if the Chinese incapacitated the military's communications and weapons systems electronically." I'd thought about it. "We'd be reduced to cavemen trying to fight back against a modern army."

"So Washington just looked normal?" asked Lauren, cuddling Luke, trying to get her head around it. "Did you go to the Capitol?"

"No. Like I said, I was scared. I thought they were funneling us into a detention camp. I didn't think I would make it back."

"But there were people, Americans, just walking around. *Driving around?*" said Chuck.

I'd described the people I'd seen on the streets, some of them walking around as if nothing had happened, and told them about the cowboys who had driven me up here.

Susie sighed. "It's hard to imagine, but I guess life goes on."

"Life went on in occupied France during the Second World War," I said. "Paris gave up without a fight too. No bombs, no fighting, just free one day and then occupied the next. People still went out and bought baguettes, drank wine—"

"It must have all happened when we were in New York," said Lauren. "It *was* over a month that we were isolated. It explains the strange lack of information, the way things happened."

It did explain a lot.

There was no snow anymore, but it was still winter, and there weren't any bugs or crickets singing in the dark forests. The silence was deafening.

I sighed. "No matter what, it's better that we got out of New York. It looks like they're going to let it rot."

"Bastards!" yelled Chuck, standing up from his chair. He was waving his good fist at the bright smudge on the horizon. "I'm not going down without a fight."

"Calm down, baby," whispered Susie, standing to wrap her arms around him. "No fighting for now."

"We're barely surviving," I laughed. "How are we going to fight back?"

Chuck stared at the horizon. "People have done it before. The Underground, the Resistance."

Lauren glanced at Susie. "I think that's enough for today, don't you?"

Susie agreed. "I think we should get some sleep."

Chuck's head sagged, and he turned toward the door. "Tell me when you head to bed, Mike, and I'll come down and stand watch."

Lauren leaned down to kiss me.

"I'm sorry I missed your birthday yesterday," I said.

"You coming back safe was the greatest gift I've ever had."

"I wanted so much—"

"I know, Mike, but what's important is that we're together." She kissed Luke and stood up, cradling him in her arms. He was asleep.

I sat silently. Looking up at the door frame, I saw that some-one had stuck the Borodins' mezuzah on it. "Who did that?" I asked, pointing at it.

"I did," Lauren said.

"A little late, don't you think?"

"It's never too late, Mike."

I sighed and returned my gaze to the horizon. "I'm going to stay down here for a while," I said to her. "Is that okay?"

"Come to bed soon."

"I will."

I sat and stared at the glow of Washington in the distance, rolling through the images of the trip there and back in my head. I'd been gone just two days, but it seemed like years. An eternity had passed in my mind, and the world had changed.

I sat for an hour or so, anger simmering inside me. Finally, I got up, turning my back on Washington, and walked inside.

DAY 40: JANUARY 31

The weather had turned overcast and soggy again—miserable for going outside, but good for fishing.

"They must have had no choice," said Susie, still trying to understand what had happened.

We were descending to the Shenandoah River, down the mountain and into the valley to the west. A fine mist hung in the air.

I hope it doesn't start to rain. Anything that got wet stayed wet for days. Fog stretched into the distance between the trees. There were only two other cabins on this side of the mountain, and we stayed away from them on a wooded trail as we wound our way down.

"Maybe you're right," I replied. "Maybe this is what war looks like now. I wish I'd been better prepared."

Modern warfare—over before the first shot was fired. My mind couldn't help cycling back, remembering what I'd read about the cyberthreat, damning myself for not taking it seriously. I should have done so many things differently, protected Lauren and Luke better. It was my fault.

At the river, the track was muddy, and I looked for other footprints. None looked fresh.

"You can't prepare for everything," said Susie after some reflection. "And maybe this is better."

The skin on her face was waxy, paper-thin, and translucent even in the gray light. It was flaking off in chunks near her scalp. She caught me looking, and I shifted my gaze, spotting brownish oval pods hanging from a group of bushes just off the trail. "Hey, can we eat those?" I asked.

"Those are pawpaws," said Susie. "Surprised the squirrels didn't get them."

We walked over to the bush, and she pulled them off. "They're spoiled, though. These fruit in the fall." She put them in her pocket anyway.

"So what do you mean, 'maybe this is better'?" I asked as we collected more pawpaws.

"I meant that a cyberattack is better than being incinerated by a bomb."

I was quiet as we made our way back to the river. I wondered how the Borodins were doing, what had happened to the captives—if the Borodins had let them go, or if they'd starved to death.

Susie bent down and pulled on one of the fishing lines we'd set in the bushes. She shook her head, and we advanced to the next one. Tall, thin birch trees rose up out of the banks of the Shenandoah. Yellow leaves carpeted the forest floor. We passed a set of small rapids that gurgled and bubbled. We'd set several lines in the pool they flowed into. The survival guide on my phone said such pools were a good place to fish.

"Maybe we should just surrender," said Susie.

"To whom, exactly?"

"The Chinese?"

"You want to walk sixty miles to surrender?"

"There must be someone we can talk to."

"I don't think that's a good idea."

After what had happened on our first day here, we were afraid to go near any other cabins. We sometimes saw other people through the trees, but we kept our distance.

"There's always hope, Mike," said Susie, as if she was reading my mind.

Even if we did give ourselves up, where would we go? Would a Chinese prison camp be any better? I remembered the streams of refugees I'd walked next to through Washington. Where had they all been going? My mind filled with vague images of old war movies, concentration camps in steaming forests in Vietnam. It was safer to stay where we were. We had to hide, survive, and do what we could.

"They're going to leave eventually," she added, thinking what I was thinking. "They have to. There's no way the UN or NATO will allow them to stay."

I stepped out onto a rock in the pool at the bottom of the rapids and pulled on one of the lines. It felt heavy, like it was stuck, and then it began pulling back.

"Hey! We got one. It feels big!"

Catfish in the Shenandoah could get up to twenty or thirty pounds.

"See?" said Susie, smiling. "There's always hope."

I pulled the catfish out of the water, and it dangled in front of us, trapped by something it didn't understand. *I should have been better prepared. I shouldn't have let this happen to my family.* As the fish spun on the line, I looked into its eyes, and then grabbed it by the tail and smashed its head against a rock.

DAY 47: FEBRUARY 7

The forest came alive in the light of the full moon.

I crept silently through the trees. Tiny creatures scurried in the darkness, and an owl hooted, a haunting cry that echoed in the cool air. A carpet of stars hung above me, visible through the bare branches of the trees. The stars didn't seem distant; they felt close, as if I could climb to the top of the trees and touch them.

I'd become aware of the cycles of the moon. Asleep in our room, I could feel changes in air pressure and the winds that signaled a coming rain. Just weeks ago my senses had been numb, divorced from nature, but I was changing.

I was becoming an animal.

The violence we'd seen shouldn't have surprised me. Humans were violent. We were the apex predators, each one of us alive only because our ancestors had killed and eaten other animals, outcompeted everything else to survive. Each and every one of the creatures we'd descended from, stretching all the way back to the beginning of life on Earth, had survived by killing before being killed. We were the final product of a string of millions of killers.

Technology couldn't revert, but humans could, and they did so with startling ease and swiftness when the trappings of the modern world melted away. The tribal animal was always there, hidden just beneath our superficial lives of lattes and cell phones and cable TV.

I slept during the day now: in my dreams, I was trapped in the dingy, lice-infested hallway of our apartment building. Lauren would float before me in her bubble bath, clean and untouchable. And always, there was the baby, slippery and cold. During the days, I slept away my hunger, but with the setting sun and rising moon, my hunger and my anger returned.

The full moon had awoken me tonight. I felt it dragging me outside like an invisible hand, the hair on the nape of my neck standing up. It led me down to the Baylors' house with a knife in hand, ready to slash and kill.

But nobody was there.

I took the forest path down and around the mountain, toward a cabin I'd seen through the trees on our walks to the river. I'd been returning there, night after night, to watch, like a hunter stalking prey. The cabin glowed before me, and I crouched in the woods, waiting. I could see a lit candle in one of the windows, its flame flickering hypnotically. A man came into view, his face reflected in the candlelight. *Is he one of the ones from the Baylors'?* I couldn't tell. He looked out the window in my direction, and I held my breath. But he didn't see me, couldn't see me.

He was talking. Someone else was there.

I'd passed by a mirror in our room today and was stunned by what I saw. Someone else was looking back at me—sunken cheeks, a stubbly scalp, ribs sticking out, skin that hung in wrinkled sacks from my arms. I saw a prison camp inmate, and only my eyes were my own, staring back in shock.

The rising moon each night gave me strength, fueling a simmering anger.

Why should I give up? My grandfather had fought in the Second World War. Who knew what horrors he had to survive? My grandmother said he never talked about the war, and I was beginning to understand why.

The man in the window leaned forward and blew out the candle.

I gripped the knife in my hand. I'd never mentioned to anyone that the cowboy who'd driven me back here had hugged me when he'd said good-bye. He had been kind, but the sad look in his eyes made me angry now.

I didn't need pity.

Crouching in the dark, with my instincts urging me toward the cabin, I thought of that young cowboy again, of his tenderness with me.

Looking at the cabin, I imagined people sleeping inside and I began crying.

What am I going to do? Kill them? Maybe there were children inside, and even if there weren't, what had these people ever done to me? What was I thinking? My stomach spasmed with hunger. I backed away, stealing into the night.

I was an animal, but I was also human.

DAY 53: FEBRUARY 13

I just wanted to sleep.

"You sure?" asked Lauren. She wanted me to check the squirrel traps with her. "Luke is coming."

There was a time when I would have questioned the wisdom of taking our two-year-old son on a walk to find trapped rodents, but I just rolled over, turning away from her. Looking at her was difficult.

"Nah," I replied after a pause, kicking around the bed sheets. "I'm really tired."

I waited for her to leave.

"You've been sleeping for days. Are you sure? You know what day it is tomorrow?"

I had no idea, and I pulled the sheets around my head, trying to block out the sun shining in through the windows. "Please, I'm just tired, okay?"

For a long time she just stood there—I had the feeling she wanted to tell me what day it was tomorrow—but eventually I heard her footsteps retreating and the creak of the stairs as she went down. I squirmed, trying to find a comfortable position, but the lice were back, infesting everything. If I lay still enough, sleep would come and I'd stop noticing them.

I wanted to stop noticing everything.

I had always been a fixer, someone who solved problems. Tell me something that was bothering you, and I'd find a solution. But there was no fixing this, no way my mind could find a path through this maze. I imagined walking south, walking north, finding a bicycle, talking to someone on the road—but every option was fraught with danger and uncertainty.

So I slept.

The only thing I would get up for was food, but I'd grown tired of eating "forest greens," as Susie called them. We were eating weeds. Once every few days, there might be a catfish. We'd have to eat the whole thing in a day or two or it would spoil. Susie was trying to salt what we couldn't eat immediately, with mixed results.

Squirrel was better, but they weren't easy to catch. We'd trapped a few, but they were smart and had learned to stay away from our traps.

We weren't the only ones struggling for survival.

It didn't matter anyway. Anything I found to eat, I tried to save for Lauren. As my stomach continued to hollow, hers continued to bulge outwards. Her baby bump was plainly visible under her clothing now.

I tried to remember what day it was, what week. *What day is it tomorrow?* Why had she asked me that? We'd lost power in the last of our phones, and since no one had a watch, time was beginning to lose meaning.

Twenty-two weeks. She's twenty-two weeks pregnant. Just over halfway.

And then what? What do we do when she goes into labor?

She was right. We should have gotten an abortion. Now it was too late.

A new thought formed in my head. *Valentine's Day, that's what day it is tomorrow.*

Turning over, I closed my eyes tighter, balling myself up into a fetal position.

I slept.

DAY 59: FEBRUARY 19

The smell woke me up—an incredible, delicious smell.

It almost levitated me out of my bed. It was chilly, so I went to the dresser to see what there was to wear. I found rows of folded clothes, and I pulled out a sweater. It hung like a tent on my thin frame. I saw that our room was swept and tidy. The crumple of sheets on the bed was the only mess—that, and me.

What's that smell? Bacon?

Outside I heard the *thwack* of someone chopping wood, and I went to the window and pulled back the curtains. I could see my pregnant wife, her shirtsleeves rolled up and hair tied back with a kerchief, picking up a log and balancing it upright on a larger log beneath. The sun was shining in a blue sky. With the back of one hand, she wiped sweat from her forehead. In her other hand she was holding an ax. Planting her feet wide, she swung the ax around, and then—*thwack!*—the ax landed squarely in the log, splitting it apart.

My head felt clear for the first time in longer than I could remember, and I was so hungry. Through the open door to our bedroom I could hear something sizzle and pop. *Am I still dreaming?* It even sounded like bacon.

Slipping on my sneakers, I walked down the dim hallway.

Without thinking, I flipped the switch on the wall and then laughed at myself. The instinct to turn on lights and check my phone was still there.

At the bottom of the stairs was an open, wood-paneled space, with area rugs strewn on the floors and faded oil paintings of landscapes and old snowshoes on the walls. There was a stone fireplace against one wall, and Chuck was sitting cross-legged in front of it as coals glowed in the hearth. Hearing me, he turned around, holding a large iron skillet that had been sitting on the coals. He held it with his good hand, with the skillet's handle wrapped in a tea towel. His injured hand was still bundled in a sling.

"I thought that might wake you up," he said, smiling. "Come help me turn these over. I think I'm burning them."

"What is that?"

"Bacon."

I practically floated across the room. Chuck set the skillet down on the bare wood floor and held a fork up to me. "Well, not really bacon—it's not smoked and cured—but it's pig fat and skin. Try a piece?"

I squatted next to him, feeling the heat of the coals on my face. I hesitated. *I should keep this for Lauren, for the baby.*

"Go ahead," encouraged Chuck. "You need to eat, buddy."

I stabbed a strip of sizzling meat. I was dehydrated and winced in pain as I began salivating, but the taste exploded across my tongue.

"No need to cry," laughed Chuck.

Tears rolled down my face with the intensity of the experience.

"You can have some more. Have the whole pan. I was just frying this up to get some grease to fry the rest of the meat. And have some bread with it."

Reaching on top of the counter next to him, he produced a crust of burnt flatbread. I picked up another piece of bacon and stuffed it into my mouth with the bread.

"Where did you get bacon? The bread?"

"The bread is from cattail flour—I can show you how—and one of our traps by the river got a small pig. I heard there were feral hogs in these woods—the newspapers in Gainesville were complaining about them the last few years—but I sure ain't complaining today."

"A whole pig?"

He nodded. "A baby pig, anyway. Susie's in the cellar butchering it right now. I fried up these hunks of skin to get things going."

"*Susie's* butchering it?" She'd always struck me as squeamish.

Chuck laughed. "Who do you think has been taking care of things around here? I'm a cripple, and you," he said, pausing, "well, you've been taking a time-out. Our women have been out hunting and fishing, cutting up wood, keeping the place ship-shape and warm. Keeping us fed."

I hadn't thought about it.

"Grab some fiddleheads from over there," said Chuck, nodding toward a pile of greens on the couch. "We'll fry them in the bacon grease, soak it up, get some good stuff into you."

I took two handfuls and dropped them into the pan. They sizzled as he swung the skillet back onto the coals. Releasing the handle, he dropped the tea towel and looked down at the floor, scratching his head. "We know you go out at night sometimes," he said.

I'd almost forgotten.

"To be honest, I'm getting tired of sending my wife out to follow you. You have to stop, Mike."

"I'm sorry, I don't know—"

"No need to apologize," Chuck said. "I'm glad to see you're back, though. You've been dead to the world for two weeks."

I wasn't sure what to say. "Why didn't you come and get me up out of bed, tell me off?"

He stirred the fiddleheads. "We're all going through our own thing. We just figured you were going through yours. We couldn't *fix* you. You had to fix yourself."

"Did you see anything happen? Did you talk to anyone?" I asked.

Maybe things had changed since I'd been out of it.

"We've been watching Washington at night. No signs of fighting, no mass evacuations. I don't think anything has changed. And we haven't spoken to anyone."

"What's the plan, then?"

He stirred the greens, picking one out for me to taste. "We wait. There's got to be a Resistance or Underground or something. Maybe it's only the East Coast that's occupied."

"So we wait?"

Chuck looked at me. "We can do this, Mike. We're surviving. And Lauren is amazing." He nodded toward the door. "Why don't you go and say hello?"

Taking a deep breath, I stretched, feeling air fill my lungs.

"This isn't your fault, Mike. You can't fix it. Go and see your family. Go on out."

I looked toward the door, motes of dust spinning in the light streaming in from it. This was life, and it was time to get on with it.

"Yeah," I replied, getting up.

Through the window, Lauren saw me and smiled. The bulge of the baby was clearly visible. I waved, and she dropped the ax, running toward the door.

She was so beautiful.

DAY 63: FEBRUARY 23

"Can we eat this?" I asked Chuck.

I was inspecting a mushroom growing underneath a rotted log at the side of the river. I sniffed it and then poked its base, uncovering a mass of wriggling grubs in the earth.

"Not sure," he replied.

For some reason I remembered reading that the body had two brains. One in your head, the one we called the brain, and the other circling your gut, what they called the ENS, the enteric nervous system, our most ancient brain. In the same way that I'd become aware of the sky and the weather and the cycles of the moon, somehow I felt like I'd started listening to this ancient part of me, and right now it was sending a message up into my conscious mind: *Don't eat those mushrooms.* The grubs, on the other hand . . .

With a spoon I'd been carrying in my pocket, I began digging the insects out to store in a plastic bag.

We were down at the river, checking on the fishing lines and traps. Other animals came down from the hills to the water from time to time, so this was the best place to hunt and trap. The rifle was slung over my shoulder, just in case we saw a deer or pig, and, of course, for protection in case we encountered anyone unfriendly.

All of the other cabins in our area were empty now, even the one that I'd visited during my night prowls. We were alone, apart from the glow on the horizon that we watched each night, waiting for signs of activity or change as we attempted to eke out a marginal existence.

"What were the garbage bags on the deck for?" I asked. I'd noticed them this morning when we left. We were composting anything organic, and we didn't have any waste to speak of.

"That's one of your wife's projects. Tie clothes and sheets up inside garbage bags for two weeks and you kill all the lice, even the eggs. They all hatch and die."

I nodded as I surveyed the forest for anything that looked edible. There were lots of possibilities: berries, nuts, leaves, shoots. I'd always thought it was the human brain that had enabled us to conquer the planet, but really it was our stomachs, our ability to eat almost anything. The problem was that eating certain things could kill us. Or make us sick, but that was pretty much the same thing, given our circumstances.

"I might not mind being Chinese," I said.

I'd been thinking about it more and more. What difference would it really make? China had become more Western, with its money and wealth of material goods, and the United States had become more like the Chinese, spying on our citizens. Maybe we'd reached a middle point; maybe it wouldn't matter anymore who was in charge.

"Chinese-American, or American-Chinese, huh?" laughed Chuck. "That's what you're thinking?"

"We can't survive out here much longer," I replied.

The creek near the cabin had dried up as the last of the snow had melted, reducing it to a muddy path through the forest. To get fresh water we now had to walk to the river, over a thousand vertical feet down and several miles. Chuck had found some iodine to sanitize the water, but we'd run out, and now we had to boil it. It was difficult to boil as much as we needed on a daily basis, so we'd started drinking untreated water and suffered bouts of diarrhea. We were weakening and slowly starving to death.

After finding nothing in our fishing lines and traps, we filled up water bottles and then sat by the river near the short stretch of rapids. We had to rest a little before starting the long hike back up the mountain, empty-handed.

"How are you feeling?" asked Chuck after a long silence. The soft sound of the rapids was soothing.

"Good," I lied. I felt ill, but at least my head was back in the world.

"You hungry?"

"Not really," I lied again.

"Do you remember that day, just before this all started, when I showed up at your place with lunch?"

My mind rewound. Thinking about New York felt like remembering a movie about some fictional place I'd once imagined spending time in. The real world was here, this world of pain and hunger, of fear and doubt.

"When I was asleep on the couch with Luke?"

"Yeah."

"When you brought french fries with foie gras?"

"Exactly."

We sat silently, remembering the glistening chunks of pâté, reliving the taste.

"Oh, that's good," groaned Chuck, imagining the same thing as me, and we both laughed.

Clenching my jaw, I felt pain shoot through my mouth. I

rubbed at my face; my teeth were loose in their sockets, and my finger came away bloody.

"You know what?"

"What?"

"I think I have scurvy."

Chuck laughed. "Me too. I didn't want to say anything. When spring comes, we should be able to find some fruit."

"Always the man with a plan, huh?"

"Yeah."

We sat silently again.

"And I think I have worms," said Chuck with a sigh.

Again we sat in silence.

"I'm sorry you stayed for us, Chuck. You could have been here faster. All that preparation, I messed it all up for you."

"Don't say that. You're our family. We're together."

"You could have gotten away, farther west. I'm sure there's still an America out there."

A groan of pain interrupted me, and I looked at Chuck. He was holding his arm.

"Are you okay?" I asked. "What's wrong?"

He winced as he pulled his arm out of the sling. He'd been keeping it covered. I could see that his hand was swollen, and the tissue was black.

"It's infected. I think something from the buckshot got into my skin, infected my hand."

His hand had never healed from the injury back in the stairwell of our New York building. It was three times bigger than it should have been, with dark streaks tracking ominously up his arm beneath translucent skin.

"This started a few days ago, and it's getting real bad."

"Maybe we can find a honeybee hive in the woods."

I'd read in the survival app that honey was a strong antibiotic. Chuck didn't reply, and we sat in silence again, this time for longer. An eagle circled the treetops in the distance. White clouds studded the blue sky.

"You're going to need to amputate my hand, maybe my whole arm below the elbow."

I watched the eagle. "I can't do that, Chuck. My God, I have no idea—"

He grabbed me. "You have to, Mike. The infection is spreading. If it gets to my heart, it'll kill me." His cheeks were streaked with tears.

"How?"

"The hacksaw in the cellar. It'll get through the bone—"

"That rusty thing? It'll make the infection worse. It would kill you."

"I'm going to die anyway," he cried, laughing, turning his head away from me.

The eagle circled and circled in the distance.

"Take care of Ellarose for me, and Susie. Try to take care of them. You promise?"

"You're not going to die, Chuck."

"Promise me you'll take care of them."

The eagle was blurry now through my tears.

"I promise."

Taking a deep breath, he put his arm back in its sling. "Enough of that," he said, getting up. The river gurgled and splashed. "Let's get back."

Wiping my eyes, I got up, and we headed back up the trail.

The sun was going down.

DAY 64: FEBRUARY 24

I was outside with Susie when I heard the trucks.

Lauren had found some old seed packets, carrots and cucumber and tomato, hidden down in one corner of the cellar. The packets were ancient and yellowed, but the seeds might still be good. So we'd gone out and dug up a patch of ground in an area that would get the most light, and started planting them.

Chuck was inside, resting, and Lauren was making a fire to prepare some bark tea. Ellarose was lying in the grass on her back, staring up at the clouds in the sky and chewing on a twig Susie had given her. She looked like a hundred-year-old baby, shrunken and wrinkled, with red, peeling skin. She'd developed a fever and had been crying all night. Susie kept her close, always. It was heartbreaking.

We'd given Luke his own small trowel to use as a shovel, and he was industriously digging, smiling at me with every shovel-ful, when an alien growl floated up through the trees. A slight breeze ruffled the leaves, and I stopped what I was doing and listened hard.

"What is it?" asked Susie.

The wind died down, and there it was again—a low rumble, a *mechanical* rumble.

"Get the kids downstairs. Now!"

She heard the rumbling too, and she got up from her knees, grabbing Ellarose and then Luke. I ran to the house, jumping up onto the smashed back deck.

"Lauren, get down to the cellar!" I yelled as I entered through the back door. "Someone is coming! Get that fire out!"

She looked at me, shocked, and I grabbed a bottle of water from the counter and dumped it on the burning twigs in the fireplace.

"Who is it?" she asked. "What's happening?"

"I don't know," I yelled as I ran upstairs to get Chuck. "Just get downstairs with the kids and Susie."

Chuck was awake and already peering out the window. "Looks like army trucks," he said as I entered his room. "I could just see them for a moment on the ridge lower down. They'll be here in a minute."

I helped him down the stairs, grabbing the rifle as we passed onto the front porch. We couldn't see them, but we could hear them, and the sound was getting louder.

"Leave me here," said Chuck. "I'll talk to them, see what they want."

I shook my head. "No, let's get to the cellar. They can't know we're here. We'll hide, try to see who it is."

Chuck nodded and we made our way to the cellar. Susie had done a good job of rebuilding the doors from scrap plywood. Our wives stared up at us from the bottom of the stairs. Susie was holding a .38, and so was Lauren. We closed the doors behind us just as we heard trucks crunching on the gravel on the driveway. I mounted the stairs, trying to see what was happening outside through a crack.

"There are two trucks," I whispered. We could hear the sound of feet hitting gravel as the truck doors thudded shut. It sounded like a lot of people.

"Is it our guys?" whispered Chuck urgently.

"What do they want?" asked Susie, holding Ellarose in her arms, trying to keep her calm.

I angled my head to get a view through the tiny crack. The men in the driveway were wearing khaki-colored uniforms, but that was no help. Then I saw a face—an Asian face—as the man it belonged to looked my way. I ducked down.

"It's the Chinese," I hissed, backing down the stairs.

I picked up my rifle and kneeled on the hard earth floor. We could hear muffled voices and boots walking around in the house above our heads.

Chuck squinted in the dim light, listening. "Is that Chinese?"

We heard someone going up the stairs and then back down and out onto the porch.

"Maybe they're just having a look around?" said Lauren hopefully.

And then—

"Mike!" someone outside yelled.

Is he yelling my name? The voice seemed familiar. I frowned at Chuck and he shrugged back.

"Mike! Chuck! Are you guys here?" yelled the voice again.

I looked around the cellar at everyone. *Is that Damon?*

"We're down here," called out Susie.

"Shh," I said angrily, but it was too late. Footsteps thumped across the grass, and then one of the cellar doors opened. Leaning back, squinting into the light, I pointed my gun at the door, just as Damon's head appeared.

JUNE 29

The baby screamed and screamed in my arms, slippery and still wet. But I held onto her—and smiled.

"It's a girl," I said, tears coming. "It's a girl!"

Lauren was soaked in sweat, but I was nearly as drenched.

"She's so beautiful." I put her in Lauren's arms. "What do you want to call her?"

Lauren looked at the baby, laughing, crying. "Antonia."

I wiped away some tears. "Tony's a good name."

"Can we take her?" asked the nurse, leaning in to take Antonia from Lauren.

"She looks perfectly healthy," said the doctor. He walked over to the windows. "May I?"

I nodded and he pulled back the curtains, revealing a crowd of faces—Damon, Chuck, Sergeant Williams, Lauren's mother and father. We were at Presbyterian Hospital in New York, the same place we'd evacuated in what seemed like a different world just a few months ago. Susie was holding up Luke so he could see. I gave two thumbs-up, and they erupted into cheers.

"You okay?" I asked Lauren.

The nurse and doctor cleaned Antonia, giving her a physical before returning her to us. After everything we'd endured, we'd decided not to find out the sex of the baby beforehand. She was a gift we wanted to uncover one small piece at a time.

"Bring your friends in if you want," said the doctor. "Everything is perfect. It's a minor miracle after everything she went through."

I smiled at the doctor, and then down at Antonia, before signaling everyone to come in.

Chuck burst in first, holding a bottle of champagne in his artificial hand and four flutes in the other. They'd had to amputate his hand in the end, even after he'd been treated in the hospital, but he had money and good insurance. The robotic prosthetic they replaced his hand with was amazing. Even better than his old hand, Chuck liked to joke.

He popped the cork off as everyone came into the room to congratulate Lauren and meet Antonia. I walked toward him as he filled two flutes, the champagne overflowing and spilling onto the floor.

"Here's to never giving up," he laughed, handing me a glass. "And, of course, to Antonia."

Damon joined us, taking a glass from Chuck. "And here's to being wrong."

I laughed and shook my head. "To being wrong."

It was the first time we'd laughed about it, and it felt good. Drinking our toasts, we watched the rest of our friends gather around Lauren and Antonia.

I'd been wrong, but then the whole world had been wrong along with me.

It both had and hadn't been a Chinese army base in the middle of Washington, DC. The Chinese had been invited to set up a temporary camp in the middle of the city. It was only there for a few weeks, part of a massive international humanitarian relief effort to help the East Coast dig itself out from the "CyberStorm," as the media had started to call it.

The scale of the disaster wasn't apparent for the first two weeks, at least from outside New York. Worldwide communications had been disrupted and the patchy reporting that did get through indicated that power and water and emergency services would be quickly restored. In most parts of the country they were, except for the East Coast and particularly Manhattan.

In any disaster, there is always a delayed reaction, a gap the collective mind needs to comprehend something never seen before, and the events in New York were no different. The cyber disruptions alone would have been crippling for a short time, but add a crumbling New York infrastructure, where aging pipes, long corroded by seawater, burst when they froze during the water stoppage and cold temperatures, and then throw in the heavy snow and ice that had downed power and telephone lines and blocked roads—all combined, it created a deadly trap that killed tens of thousands.

"You okay, Mike?" asked Chuck.

I smiled. "You're not mad anymore?"

"I was never mad at *you*, more at the whole situation. I just needed a little time. We all did."

It had been four months since we'd been rescued, and it had been a hard four months. Ellarose had been hospitalized for malnutrition after losing nearly half of her body weight, and Chuck had been in the hospital for over a month as well. All of us had been sick.

I turned to Damon. "I still don't know how to thank you."

At Damon's family home, the power had been restored within a week and things had started to return to normal. He'd tried to track us down and had eventually gotten in touch with Lauren's family. Nobody had heard from us, so they'd searched for the location of Chuck's cabin, but the electronic land registries weren't back online yet and no one could find the address. Damon had an approximate idea of how to get there, so he had led a search party up into the mountains.

Damon looked at the floor. "It's me who should be thanking you. You saved my life too, letting me stay with you in your building."

From the cellar, I'd seen what I thought was a Chinese soldier, but in reality it was an Asian-American military man, of Japanese descent as it turned out. But my paranoid mind was only capable of seeing one thing.

It had been the same on my walk into Washington. I'd decided it was the Chinese who had attacked us, so my mind framed everything I saw to reinforce that prejudice. On the roof of the museum, I'd been looking at the Chinese Corps of Engineers. They were there because China was the only nation that had replacements for the twenty-ton electrical generators that had been wrecked, and the skilled manpower to install them.

If I'd bothered to look farther down the Mall while on that roof, I would have noticed Indian, Japanese, French, Russian, and German soldiers too. The entire international community had rallied to support the United States once the scale of the disaster had become known, especially when facts about *what* had happened began to emerge.

I put my champagne down on a side table. After a sleepless night, the alcohol was making my head swim. "I think I'm going to get a coffee. Anyone want one?"

"No, thanks," replied Chuck. "Do you want me to come?"

"Why don't both of you stay with Lauren. I'll be back in a minute."

Chuck and Damon nodded and joined the crowd around the bed while I stole away. Shutting the door behind me, I made for the vending machines. Today's edition of the *New York Times* was lying on a side table, its cover announcing, "UN Security Council Issues Cyber-Armistice and Forgiveness." I picked it up.

Ironically, it was the Iranians who had saved the day by being the first to admit to some part of the cyberattack. Of course, they probably hadn't *meant* to save us, but then it was hard to tell in this new world, where nothing was what it seemed.

As we'd heard on the radio what seemed a lifetime ago, at the start of the third week of the CyberStorm, the Ashiyane group had claimed that they'd released the Scramble virus to attack North American logistics systems in retaliation for the Stuxnet and Flame cyberweapons the United States had unleashed against Iran a few years earlier. To muddy the waters, they'd released it at the same time the Anonymous hacker network had started its denial-of-service attack against FedEx.

Forensic network investigators in China were able to unravel a chain of events that included a splinter group of their own People's Liberation Army unleashing a cyberattack on the US at the same time. Following the trail back to its origin, the investigators found that everything had started with a power failure in Connecticut, and they tracked this back to an attack by a Russian criminal group. The Russian gang had hacked into the backup systems of hedge fund firms in Connecticut, inserting a worm designed to modify backup financial records when the power at the firms' primary locations went out. It was this criminal group that had initiated the first power outages in Connecticut in an attempt to siphon money from the hedge funds.

The administrators at the hedge fund firms would have figured it out, probably faster than the criminals would have been able to extract funds, and the Russians knew this. So to up their chance of success, they'd done two things—initiated the attack on Christmas Eve, when few people would be working, and issued a false emergency alert about a bird flu outbreak.

The bird flu warning had been far more effective at creating havoc than they'd expected, and like the power outage, it had cascaded through the system. The Russian gang had been *too* successful, and had turned themselves from mere criminals into terrorists.

The CIA was hunting them down.

At the time, with Chinese and American aircraft carriers squaring off in the South China Sea, it was impossible to understand the power outages in Connecticut, bird flu epidemic, and logistics attack as anything but a coordinated attack by the Chinese in retaliation for US forces threatening their "protectorate."

When the Amtrak train had crashed, resulting in the loss of civilian life, US Cyber Command had initiated an attack on Chinese infrastructure in response. Even then, the Chinese Politburo had issued a strict warning against retaliatory action: they knew they hadn't attacked America first and were trying to figure out what was going on.

The rumors online were that the governor of Shanxi Province had instructed a splinter group of the People's Liberation Army to initiate a rebuttal attack on US infrastructure after the US attack on China. It looked like the official might also have sabotaged the dam in his region, wrecking a village in an effort to justify his actions.

It was understood that it had been this splinter group that had knocked out electrical generators and jammed up the water systems going into New York. Under normal conditions this would have caused major disruptions, but in combination with one of the most intense series of winter storms ever to hit the East Coast, the CyberStorm turned into a deadly disaster.

In the end, the CyberStorm was a swirling collision of simultaneous events in the cyber and physical domains. If it seemed a fantastic coincidence, it wasn't. Millions of cyberattacks a day occurred all over the Internet, like waves rolling across an ocean. By simple laws of probability, a series of cyberattack waves had coalesced, the same way giant rogue waves appeared occasionally in the ocean, seemingly coming from nowhere to wreak havoc.

With me in the waiting room were a number of reporters. They weren't here for me—they were following Damon. Damon had become famous as the founder of the meshnet, which had saved untold lives, helping maintain order when everything else had failed. Millions of distress calls and help messages had been logged on the meshnet, along with hundreds of thousands of images. People were now combing through this archive, searching for images of their loved ones, trying to figure out what had happened in the chaos. The authorities were using it as a resource to track down people who had committed crimes. The DamonNet, as they now called it, was still operating.

I grabbed some change from my pocket, popped it into the coffee machine, and selected a latte.

Reporters. They'd been half the problem, part of the reason it had taken so long for the scale of the emergency to be understood. With communications down and the storms pounding the city, reporters had no way to learn what was happening in Manhattan. CNN and other broadcasters had stationed themselves in Queens and the outer boroughs instead, reporting on conditions there. But nobody knew how desperate things were deep inside Manhattan. So the world heard reports that New York was experiencing difficulties, but the impression given was that Manhattan was sleeping underneath its blanket of snow. The extent of the catastrophe only became apparent when the island was quarantined "temporarily," and the world had watched in horror as people drowned and froze to death trying to escape across the Hudson and East Rivers.

I picked up my latte, blowing on it to cool it down.

It was part natural disaster and part man-made disaster, although even that distinction was debatable. Some climatologists were declaring that the storms were the result of climate change. In that case, the weather was man-made too, just like the CyberStorm that had collided with it.

And if everyone was to blame, was nobody to blame?

JULY 4

"Do you want to go see Uncle Damon?" I cooed at Antonia.

She stuck a few fingers in her mouth.

"I'll take that as a yes."

I laughed, wrapping her in the baby sling on my chest. She was so tiny, and this would be her first walk outside, the first time she would see New York. I wanted it to be special. We were going up to Central Park to see the Fourth of July festivities.

Our apartment was filled with moving boxes, and with Antonia stowed, I paused, taking a moment to say good-bye.

Power and water had been returned to our area within a few days of our leaving for Virginia. The water had actually been restored when we left, but the pipes into our building had burst. We should have stayed, but they'd been saying services would be back every day of the disaster. There was no way of knowing it would actually happen until it did.

Temperatures had started rising even before we'd left the city, and by the time we returned to New York in the first week of March, they'd had power and services for six weeks, all the snow was gone, and New York was scrubbed almost clean. The only reminders were the husks of burnt-out buildings that dotted the landscape, and a dark sense of loss that still hung in the air.

Most of the people in our building had managed to get away before the siege of New York began. They'd returned to what looked like a war zone, but now the garbage had been collected, doors and windows fixed, and fresh paint applied.

There was an almost manic urgency to push the episode into the past, to pretend it hadn't happened. Lauren's parents, while searching for us, had contracted someone to clean our apartment and the hallway. When we returned, everything looked like it had before the CyberStorm, as if it had all been a bad dream.

Everything was back the way it was—everything except Tony.

I sighed, taking one last look. The movers would be taking our stuff up to a new place on the Upper West Side. Closing the door behind me, I knocked on the Borodins' door. I'd tried to return their mezuzah, but Irena had insisted that I place it next to the doorway at our new place.

"Ah, Mih-kah-yal, Antonia," said Irena. Aleksandr had the TV on, but he wasn't asleep. He nodded at me, smiling, and I waved back. "You come in to eat?"

"Another time," I promised. "I just wanted to say good-bye, to thank you again."

They'd held Paul's gang until Sergeant Williams had taken custody of the captives. The prisoners had nearly starved, like everyone else, but in the end they'd made out no worse than the rest of us.

The Borodins seemed unaffected, as if they couldn't understand what all the fuss had been about, but then they'd lived through something even more horrific. In the siege of Leningrad, the city's population of three million had suffered through an event that lasted nine hundred days, whereas this one had lasted a mere thirty-six. Over six hundred thousand had died in Leningrad, while only seventy thousand had perished here.

Only seventy thousand. But it could have been so much worse.

"We will see you, yes? We will come up to see Antonia and Luke," said Irena, leaning forward on her tiptoes to kiss my cheek and giving Antonia a tiny peck on her pink head as well.

"Anytime," I replied.

We looked at each other for a moment, and then she returned to her cooking, leaving the door ajar. I continued down the hallway.

The hallway.

In my mind's eye, I could still see the couches and chairs lining it, crowded with people under blankets. The most powerful memory was the smell. The carpets had been torn out now, the wallpaper replaced, but I could still smell it. Even so, it had been our sanctuary, and a part of me remembered the days we'd spent huddled together, sharing our fears and crumbs of food, with a touch of fondness.

Pam and Rory had survived; in fact, everyone who was in the building when we left New York had been fine. We'd visited Pam and Rory, but we hadn't spoken about the blood. It wasn't necessary, somehow. In a strange way, they'd remained as true to their vegan sensibilities as they could have—the blood was donated willingly, and they hadn't harmed anyone.

The only person we didn't see was Sarah. She'd disappeared by the time we got back.

Sergeant Williams had made it his personal mission to catch up with Paul, whose case became a multiple homicide based on evidence from the meshnet. When he was captured, the full story had come out. Although Richard came from wealth, he'd been in debt, so he'd started an identity theft scheme with Stan and Paul, targeting out-of-town businessmen who used the garage's limo service. Nobody asked us where Richard was, and he became just another one of the thousands of missing people.

Richard had been responsible for Lauren's identity being stolen, which was also the reason he'd been keen to cozy up to her parents, to angle for their information. It had all spun out of control when the disaster had started. Paul had threatened Richard, saying he was going to tell people what he'd been doing if Richard wouldn't help him steal supplies. We suspected the deaths of the nine people on the second floor weren't as innocent as Richard had made them out to be, but we could only speculate.

Reaching the elevators, I pushed the down button, but then changed my mind and made for the stairwell. The familiar sound of footsteps on the metal stairs echoed in my ears as I descended. Down in the lobby, the Japanese gardens were back. But I went out the rear door.

Outside, I was greeted by a blast of warm air and the hum of New York. A jackhammer chattered in the distance, joined by a cacophony of honks and a helicopter flying overhead. Looking toward the Hudson, I saw a sailboat glide by.

Some semblance of normality had returned, but nothing would ever be the same again.

Walking along Twenty-Fourth, I crossed Ninth Avenue and looked downtown toward the Financial District. The Russian criminals had only been targeting hedge fund firms in Connecticut, but they'd brought down the entire system. Amazingly, once power was back on and the networks cleaned, most of the financial industry had been able to start right back up again.

The row of buildings that had burned down was already

demolished, with scaffolding going up for new ones. In just a few short months, the city had returned to almost normal, but there were still scars everywhere—demolished and damaged buildings, areas still off-limits.

The cost of the CyberStorm was estimated in the hundreds of billions of dollars, dwarfing any previous disaster in US history, and that didn't include the tens of billions of dollars of lost revenue and the costs of cleaning the networks and Internet. But the biggest cost was in human lives. At over seventy thousand and rising, it was a deadlier event than the Vietnam War.

The media, however, was already making comparisons to wars and other climate-based disasters, like the heat wave in Europe in 2003 that had killed seventy thousand people—in Paris, they'd had to open refrigerated warehouses to store the dead when morgues had overflowed. I remembered reading about it, a few lines of text I'd skimmed one morning with my coffee before getting on with my day. Now people all over the world were probably doing the same with the news about New York, just one item in the daily news cycle.

Reaching the corner of Eighth Avenue, I turned north and checked my phone. *Ten after two.* I was supposed to meet Damon and Lauren at the Columbus Circle entrance to Central Park at three o'clock. Enough time to enjoy a stroll.

Starting uptown, I walked a few blocks and soon passed Madison Square Garden. It was closed and would probably never reopen, but the area was crowded with people. The block was surrounded by an enormous memorial of flowers that piled out into the street, with photos and letters affixed to the exterior walls.

Damon and his followers had created a cyber version of the same thing, a memorial Web site where the hundreds of thousands of collected cell phone images from the CyberStorm had been organized. Loved ones were getting closure, even connecting with people who had taken the pictures to find out what had happened. Thousands more people were being brought to justice for their crimes, with witnesses contacted through their meshnet accounts.

In the physical world, rows of FEMA trucks still occupied the block around the makeshift memorial. FEMA had done its best to respond, but there was no contingency plan for rescuing sixty million people stranded under a frozen sheet of snow, without power or food and many without water. Compounding the problem was the loss of communications and computer networks— the rescue teams didn't know where anything was, how to get it, or how to contact people, and the roads had been jammed up with snow and impassible.

It had taken two weeks to recover enough information systems and communications capability to mount any significant response, and the efforts had started in Washington and Baltimore. It was only around the time we were leaving that attention had turned to New York.

Massive quantities of resources and manpower were devoted to New York once it became apparent what had happened, but there was no way to reach the city for the first few weeks. It wasn't just the cyberattacks—thousands of telephone lines, electrical lines, and cell towers had been brought down by the snow and ice.

The main water systems had only been down for a week, but in that time pipes had burst everywhere because of the extreme cold. When the water returned, only a trickle had made it to Lower Manhattan, and they'd had to turn it off to make repairs. In a city covered in several feet of snow and ice, with no communications or staff or power, this became an impossible task.

After the initial system failures, the president had immediately invoked the Stafford Act so the military could operate domestically, but for a few weeks we'd been on the brink of war with China and Iran, and the military had had its hands tied.

Add to that the radar signatures indicating a breach of US airspace on the first day of the attack. Most analysts thought it was some kind of automated drone attack, a new threat they were just beginning to understand. It was a month before it was confirmed that the radar reports were artifacts from a viral infection of the air force radar computer systems at McChord Field in Washington State.

Once an outline of what had happened had been sketched out, four weeks into the catastrophe, and Chinese and American cybersecurity teams had a chance to have some backroom discussions, a full-scale rescue had been initiated. This included the Chinese teams that had brought replacement parts and manpower to repair the East Coast electrical grid.

Passing Forty-Seventh Street, I spotted the red double-decker buses of the New York Sightseeing company lining the street. They were full of tourists, but not like before—these were "dark tourists," here to gawk at the rebuilding of our city, the same kind of people who found fascination in road accidents.

In the distance, toward Midtown, the neon signs of Times Square glowed even in the daylight, and above me a digital billboard scrolled a headline: *Senate Investigation Hearings Begin into Why Cyberthreat Not Taken More Seriously.*

I laughed quietly, shaking my head as I read it. *What are they going to discuss?* The government had, in fact, taken the cyberthreat seriously, but before the CyberStorm, the term "cyberwar" had more of a metaphorical quality, like "the war on obesity." Not anymore, now that the damage had been assessed, the costs tallied, and the horrors witnessed.

Was it just an unlikely series of events? Maybe, but once-in-a-lifetime events were happening in the world with unsettling regularity. Even with all the after-the-fact analyses, no one could quite figure out how it had all gone wrong at once.

Everything was interconnected, and big cities relied on intricate systems working perfectly, all the time. When they didn't, people began to die very quickly. The loss of a few supporting legs created problems too big to fix, ending in gridlock with no graceful degradation to previous technologies or systems.

A generation ago, to contain the terrifying danger of nuclear weapons, politicians and militaries had created rules of engagement based on deterrence. But there was no similar protocol for dealing with cyberattacks. What was the blast radius of a cyberweapon? How would you know who had deployed it? The vacuum of rules and international agreements had been as much to blame as circumstances in creating the CyberStorm.

People, of course, always found a way to survive. There was some talk in the media about cannibalism, and it had happened, but rather than demonizing it, the media had begun normalizing it, citing comparable historical incidents.

There had been an investigation into the cabins near us in Virginia. It turned out that the Baylors had been on vacation, and the people we'd encountered were interlopers. They had probably stolen gear and supplies from Chuck's cabin, but then, we'd stolen what we needed from our neighbors in New York. There was no evidence of cannibalism in the cabins, just some bones from pigs they must have caught, as we did. We'd jumped to conclusions tainted by our fears and the horrors we'd experienced.

I'd arrived at Columbus Circle, and I stood watching cars and trucks rumble around it. Up ahead, the trees of Central Park were like a green canyon between the high-rise buildings, and the monument in the middle of the intersection towered above us while fountains sprayed up around it. People were sitting on benches, enjoying the sun.

Life went on.

Waiting for the light to change, I looked up at the gray wall of the Museum of Art and Design to my right. A message was spray-painted in huge, looping letters across its curved front, stretching all the way from ground level to the roof. "Sometimes things break apart," read the message, "so that better things can come together." Below this was the attribution: "Marilyn Monroe."

I pointed up at the message. "See that, Antonia? Do you think better things are coming?" I certainly hoped so, for her sake, but a deep unease had settled into my soul.

As with many terrible things, some good might come of the catastrophe, it seemed. Sweeping changes to international law were being promised. At least, that was what they wrote in the papers. We'd see if any of it actually happened.

The separation between the cyber and physical worlds was disappearing. Cyberbullying was just bullying, and cyberwar was just war—the true age of cyber would begin when we stopped using it as a descriptor.

Walking into Columbus Circle, I saw Lauren standing next to Damon and waved. Lauren was holding a leash: our new rescue dog, Buddy. The shelters had overflowed with animals after the disaster, and it was one small way we could reduce the suffering.

"Look, there's Mommy!"

I couldn't believe I'd been so blind, so short-sighted as to believe she'd been unfaithful when all she'd been trying to do was better her life, and mine. The same delusional, single-track thinking had almost cost us our lives when I'd been unable to understand what I saw in Washington as anything other than a Chinese invasion.

"Hey, baby!" I called out. "Antonia and I had a great walk!"

Lauren ran up to us and kissed me. Damon followed, pushing Luke in a stroller.

It was a beautiful day, with perfect blue skies. American flags draped the entrance to Central Park. We were here to watch the Independence Day celebrations and see Damon receive the key to New York City from the mayor.

We walked into Central Park. At the edge of the crowd around the stage set for Damon's ceremony, we met up with Chuck and Susie.

"Go on, then," I urged Damon as we greeted each other. "Time to be famous."

He laughed. "'Time' is definitely the operative word."

Still a strange kid. I shook my head as he ran off toward the back of the stage. A crowd gathered, and I pulled Antonia out of the baby sling to hold her in my arms.

"Look," I said, lifting her up and pointing to the stage. Damon looked awkward in front of the crowd. "That's your Uncle Damon."

Antonia yawned and dribbled on me. I laughed, marveling at how something so tiny could be so beautiful.

A threshold had been crossed, and the world would never be the same again. Despite all the handshaking and smiling faces on TV, there were already rumblings of new conflicts, and I somehow doubted that the lessons we'd learned would be remembered for very long.

Looking around, one could imagine that none of it had ever happened. It reminded me of a trip I once took to Warsaw. When retreating from the city at the end of the war, the Nazis had leveled the entire urban center, destroying as many buildings as they could—Hitler was determined to wipe Warsaw off the map. Afterwards, however, its residents had rebuilt, brick by brick, effectively erasing Hitler the same way he had tried to erase them.

New York looked the same, but it wasn't, and never would be.

Standing in the sunshine with the people who'd been my family through this disaster, tears came to my eyes.

Antonia giggled in my arms. Seventy thousand people had died, but at least one life had been saved. If none of this had happened, Lauren might have gotten an abortion, and I would never have known about it. I would never have had Antonia in my life, never known that she had existed, and I would probably have lost Lauren as well.

Looking into Antonia's eyes, I realized my life had been saved too.

ACKNOWLEDGMENTS

I would like to thank the many people who lent me their time and insight, helping make this a realistic scenario of a full-scale cyber event, including: Richard Marshall, former Global Director of Cybersecurity, US Department of Homeland Security; Curtis Levinson, United States Cyber Defense Liaison to NATO; Major Alex Aquino, Head of Cyber Operations, US Air Force Western Air Defense Sector; and Erik Montcalm, Director of Security Technologies, SecureOps.

A big thank-you to HarperCollins Canada—especially Lorissa Sengara, Noelle Zitzer, and copy editor Sue Sumeraj—for their hard work in getting *CyberStorm* ready for the world, as well as to my early-edition editor, Gabe Robinson, and to Allan Tierney and Pamela Deering, who also helped in the editing process.

Thank you to all my beta readers (and sorry I don't have surnames for all of you): Adam, Adi, Alison Hodge, Amber, Amit, Ashvin, Barry Sax, Bill Mather, Bill Parker, Brian Lomax, Charles, Chrissie, Colby Zoeller, Craig Haseler, Daryl Clark, David King, Mrs. Dayfield, Ed Grbacz, Edwina, Erik Montcalm, Em, Harold Kelsey, Haydn Virtue, Hector, Jim Duchek, John Jarrett, Jon, Josh Brandoff, Joy Lu, Julie Parsons, Julie Schmidt, Junko, Justin, Kimmerie, Lance Barnett, Leonard, Leonardo, Lowell,

Luke, Marjolein, Matt, Max Zaoui, Michelle, Mike, Mircea, Mog, Naveen, Niels Pedersenn, Niki, Or Shoham, Peter, Philip Graves, Rob Linxweiller, Robin, Sam Romero, Samantha, Shabnam Penry, Sohna Ravindran, Stefano, Tara, Tim McGregorus, Tom Giebel, Warrick Burgess, William, and William McClusky.

And last but most definitely not least, of course, my bright and beautiful girlfriend, Julie Ruthven, for putting up with all the late nights and missed walks with the dogs.